W9-BXF-565

SUPPORTING *the* SKY

ALSO BY PATRICIA BROWNING GRIFFITH

The World Around Midnight

Tennessee Blue

The Future Is Not What It Used to Be

SUPPORTING

the

SKY

Patricia Browning Griffith

G. P. PUTNAM'S SONS / *New York*

This novel is a work of fiction. Any references to historical events; to real people, living or dead; or to real locales are intended only to give the fiction a sense of reality and authenticity. Names, characters, places, and incidents either are the product of the author's imagination or are used fictitiously, and their resemblance, if any, to real-life counterparts is coincidental.

Published by G. P. Putnam's Sons
200 Madison Avenue
New York, NY 10016
Published simultaneously in Canada

The text of this book is set in Weiss and Diotima.
Book design by Judith Stagnitto Abbate

Library of Congress Cataloging-in-Publication Data

Griffith, Patricia Browning.
Supporting the sky / Patricia Browning Griffith.
p. cm.
ISBN 0-399-14128-6
1. Mothers and daughters—Washington (D.C.)—Fiction.
2. Divorced women—Washington (D.C.)—Fiction. I. Title.
PS3557.R4894SB 1996 95-41608 CIP
813′.54—dc20

Printed in the United States of America
1 3 5 7 9 10 8 6 4 2
This book is printed on acid-free paper. ∞

I have been remiss in thanking the National Endowment for the Arts for a grant which enabled me to continue writing. I am forever grateful. Also to my late father, who, upon learning about the grant, said it was the best use of his tax money he'd heard of in years.

Thanks as well to my own Neighborhood Watch organization, especially Marvin Caplan, and our local orange-hat patrols, whose fortitude and good spirits inspired portions of this novel.

I also thank Faith Sale for her encouragement and her thoughtful and wise editing. And my love and gratitude to Bill and Flannery for living with me through another book.

For Molly and Sylvia,

Mary and Rita,

Barbara, Lin, and Virginia,

sisters and friends who've shared their stories and lives

I listen to the music of my heart but hear sirens instead . . .

MARGOT LOCKWOOD,
Left-Handed Happiness

I woke up this mornin' blues all round my bed,
Went to eat my breakfast, had the blues all in my bread . . .

HUDDIE LEDBETTER,
"Good Morning Blues"

SUPPORTING *the* SKY

A single mother living in Washington, D.C. tries to balance her roles as a public relations consultant, a volunteer for a neighborhood watch group, a single woman, and a parent of a sexually active sixteen-year-old daughter.

In the neighborhoods of the District of Columbia in the month of August, the air is filled with the cloying sweetness of confederate jasmine, a vine that grows wildly in the humidity of this partially refurbished swamp. Downtown, in the federal area of the city, well-tended, color-coordinated flower beds are marshaled like platoons at attention around the government buildings. There the air is filled with the smell of vendor hot dogs and the sounds of tourists, who seldom penetrate the narrow streets and broad alleys of the surrounding neighborhoods. But that particular hot morning in late summer I saw a bus of tourists when I went out to retrieve the newspapers off the steps of my old row house and see if there was any sign at all of my sixteen-year-old daughter, Shelly, lately of the partially bleached hair, paste-on fingernails, and nose ring, who'd failed to come home the night before from a trip to an amusement park in rural Virginia. I had spent the night waiting for a phone call or the slam of a car door followed by a key in the lock, all the while going through every possible catastrophe a parent might imagine. The mental images in Technicolor with sound had grown more vivid over the years. They seemed always hovering just outside my consciousness, like a committed stalker on the periphery of my vision. But rather than some sign of Shelly, that morning there was only the surprise of the tour bus, hulkingly oversized for our street and moving slowly like an invading tank. Inside, the tourists were hidden behind dark tinted windows, gazing no doubt at the native sighted there in front of her slightly tattered but gracious old Victorian townhouse, a vision of tousled disorder in a pink-flowered robe.

It had been so hot that summer of 1991 that my patio tomato plants produced only a few blossoms, which grew into tomatoes while the vines themselves shriveled around them as though dying in childbirth. Thirty days over ninety degrees, and as we headed toward September it was not looking much better. Before we could buy liquor on Sunday and had fancy nouvelle cuisine restaurants with cowboy decor, D.C. was considered a hardship post for foreign diplomats. Even now our area in political-speak is often referred to derogatorily as "inside the Beltway" and the local citizens' concerns are dismissed as skewed and unimportant, unlike the concerns of, say, Truth or Consequences, New Mexico. And while there may be actual proximity to the U.S. government, the fact is we live here like fleas on the federal dog, sometimes producing a momentary discomfort but more often ignored. When newspaper columnists denounce the city as middle-class and dull, they are, of course, talking about the minority white population, approximately a quarter of the males lawyers, who march along K Street in button-down shirts and suits beside women, who are often lawyers too, in panty hose and running shoes. If those columnists would look at the majority of the population, which is assorted hues of black and brown, they'd find more flamboyance and diversity, but the cameras are programmed mostly for pale images. Especially that one image, that large white Georgian mansion on Pennsylvania Avenue surrounded by a tall iron fence with stone buttresses around it and a hidden rose garden. If you've lived here long enough, you've heard older people tell about the days when they'd cut across the White House lawn on their way to town. Or when Eleanor Roosevelt tossed cheap throw pillows that said "Aloha" around the Green Room. What does it mean that today the place is a fortress? Has the world changed, or just us? Questions no doubt pondered in that house, as in so many houses over dinner, before newscasts, before and after meetings, and even on many beaches in the warmer months.

Night or day you can drive by the White House, two miles from my house, and see the newsman or newswoman caught in an intense circle of television light as if experiencing a heavenly visitation while addressing the small red light of a camera as he or she tries to report on the puzzling world around us, which so often seems on the brink of disaster.

Meanwhile, in deep background are the rest of us—queuing at bus stops and riding down steep escalators into the caverns of our neat Metrorail system, moving to and from our various tasks of cleaning buildings, patrolling the streets, teaching the children, lobbying, litigating, attempting to keep the peace. All of us laboring alongside the troubled ghosts of Washington past that, according to one of my neighbors, Mrs. Anita Nance, haunt the city. The ghost of Lincoln, we all know, resides in the White House, but there are others, according to Mrs. Nance, such as the noble ghost of Frederick Douglass, who haunts A Street Northeast, near the Capitol, and the ghost of Duke Ellington, who haunts our very own neighborhood. According to Mrs. Nance, Avon salesperson, oral historian, and charter member of our Neighborhood Watch group, often in the night when the wind is from the south one can hear, wafted from the bridge named for him, the mellow strains of an Ellington song such as "Satin Doll."

But despite our proximity to Duke Ellington's ghost, the local citizens are never seen to be in an enviable position. Indeed, a recent poet-in-residence at the Library of Congress who commuted three days a week from New York City, where for some reason he seemed to feel safer, signed his books in Washington with his name and the location, "Ground Zero."

For one thing, the War of Independence didn't do a thing for us along the Potomac. We would be perfectly justified in pouring tea into the Tidal Basin, but with the pollution of our waterways and the addition of foreign algae that expand and choke the natural wetlands, multiplying like magic, it is uncertain whether or not anyone would notice. "The Last Colony," the signs say as you enter our territory along Kenilworth Avenue. Which means that we inhabitants of this beautiful and sophisticated world capital where thousands come to demonstrate for their rights have no voting representation in Congress and so in these last years of the twentieth century are still subject to taxation without representation.

Later on that day of my long, hot vigil, trying to ward off panic while considering at what point I would phone the police, I lay on a chaise longue in my back patio, going perfunctorily through *The New York Times* and *The Washington Post.* Beside me, what Shelly called my boom box was tuned to a public radio fund-raiser playing old June Christy records between pitches. The program host had just played "Midnight Sun" and then offered, for a pledge of fifty dollars, a black coffee mug he claimed would protect a home from burglars. If somebody breaks into your house, he said, when they see that mug they'll leave. I realized immediately that this was a form of airwave extortion, generated by desperation in recession times, but I did adore that announcer, who each weekend regaled us with stories as well as music, and I had to appreciate the whimsy of the idea. Oh, if only the world were so simple, I thought, and wondered how many coffee mugs I'd have to buy before I saw my own dear daughter walk safely through that steel-reinforced door with so many locks it looked like a devotee of S&M.

Arlo, our formerly homeless, generic gray cat with a notched ear—Shelly had taken him in some years back—appeared at the top of my ten-foot patio fence. He leaned forward, surveying the landscape before leaping down and sidling up to me for petting. Then he settled in the shade of my chair, and scratched a flea before curling into a midday nap. Arlo was a free spirit, who days pretended allegiance to us, and nights, driven by passion, roamed in search of love and excitement. Much like my daughter.

Shelly had phoned the previous evening to say, in the sweet voice she uses when she's about to do something she knows I wish she wouldn't, that she was going to the amusement park and she'd be home around midnight.

"Who are you going with?" That seemed a reasonable question. She said she was going with some people she'd met. "Where?" I asked, since supposedly she'd spent the night with her girlfriend Miranda.

"In Georgetown," she said, mentioning an area of posh federal-style homes and tourist restaurants where teenagers cruised the streets and jammed the bars on weekends.

"Names?" I suggested.

"They're friends of Noel's," she replied, and announced she had to run, they were waiting on her.

Now that is a typical conversation with Shelly. And I had never heard of a "Noel." And when Shelly says she'll be home around midnight, what she means is the notion of coming home may occur to her about then. We have battled about this over the years, but as all nonfascist parents know, you have to choose your battles. Her reluctance to tear herself away from a party in Potomac or some go-go club in Southwest is a part of her life as a free spirit. And by free spirit I mean I've tried to trust her and let her become the unique person she could be, not realizing what I may be getting myself or her into. Let's face it, you'd have problems if you were bringing up baby nuns nowadays—let alone an exuberant sometimes blonde who matured early.

Where I grew up, in East Texas, in the era of "Make love, not war" (a principle I've tried to adhere to, along with "Save water, shower with a friend"), I may not have received a superior education in those public schools, but, I always thought, I'd at least grown up knowing all types of people. Yet what I have learned over the last seventeen years is that all types of people—meaning the public at large—have become considerably more varied than what I was faced with as a rather rambunctious teenager in East Texas, who started smoking at thirteen and fell madly in love all too easily. Those days wouldn't hold a candle to the intricacies, the variables, the possibilities of disaster available in this last decade of the twentieth century. It is crazy out there, it often seems, with a gun in every hand, and all the people I know are struggling, indeed battling, for decency, civilization, and survival for themselves and their children.

So here it was, the last week in August, hot and humid with the late-summer katydids, crickets, and cicadas shrill amid the impatiens and crepe myrtles tucked about the city's townhouses. It was supposed to hit the nineties again that day, and I was still trying to tan my legs enough so that I could, maybe one day of the year, as a symbol of freedom and my southwestern origins, go to work at my Santa Fe–style office of Harrison & Associates, Public Relations Consultants, without having to wear panty hose.

Lying there on my hot chaise, I could see the rear of my neighbors' second and third floors above their decks or patios, all of us lined up in our efficient row houses, going about our complicated lives in intimate proximity. That's what I loved about living in the city—the economy of that proximity. Where I grew up, the middle class thought they had to live with a couple of acres surrounding them, a moat of green Bermuda grass broken only by neatly coiffed flower beds and shrubs. Living here was like being at the beach, all the people conducting their sometimes messy lives on small rectangles of colorful towels or quilts, pretending to ignore the half-naked bodies around them. There was something sweet and respectfully humane to me about that. This is a racially and economically diverse neighborhood where we know one another's cars and cats. When it snows we push one another's cars out of snowbanks and shovel the older people's walks. When we see suspicious movement around one another's doors we phone 911, though sometimes the line is busy.

Next door, my neighbors Dan and Don, back from their early-morning AIDS walkathon, were ferrying drinks onto their deck. Shielded only by the privacy fence and the lacy leaves of a diseased elm tree, they were serving coffee and tequila sunrises to an assembling brunch group. I knew that when I turned off my radio they would turn on their tapes of pre-AIDS nostalgic rock from the sixties and seventies. Meanwhile, my neighbors on the other side, an older retired couple, were gone to church, and their Doberman was left to prowl and protect the premises. Directly behind me stood the stately home of Reverend Ezra Thompson, minister of the New Southern Rock Church of God, a man of towering principles and generous humor who exercised secretly by running circles in back of his townhouse.

Around noon the radio host started "Something Cool," my very favorite, with June Christy's soothing voice relieving somewhat the heat of the day. Suddenly I heard a sound inside the house, and my heart leaped—it might be Shelly! I strained toward the door, hoping. With my inner-city crime-stopper's caution, I had to consider the possibility of some unwelcome intruder. But the door to the patio was pushed open, and accompanied by something like an electrical charge before a storm, there appeared Shelly, sixteen, turbulent, and bordering on beautiful, pulling a young man after her. She's safe, I realized, clutching my bluebonnet T-shirt over my heart. Shelly, fine-boned and tall, built more like her father than me, with his broad sensuous mouth. Her wide brownish-green eyes seemed to gaze at the world with a calm detachment that gave her a challenging appeal. She had the tawny, compelling attraction of a lion cub that on second glance would cause you to hesitate, sensing the presence of something dangerous, maybe even fierce. But before I could feel full relief, before my stomach could calm the volcanic buildup of the past fifteen hours, the early stages of a whole new anxiety arose as I took in the figure of the young man behind her.

Now I do not consider myself a street-wise person, and if I prayed I would pray with all my heart to escape the racial prejudice rife in this country. But the minute my eyes settled on his red sweatsuit and gold chains, his immaculate white sneakers and the handsome bronze face commonly referred to as black, I knew I was looking at trouble. First of all, who in the world would wear a sweatsuit in this heat? I made a quick mental search for familiar signs of substance abuse, the contemporary litany of parenthood. As I stared into his pale brown eyes, I felt my disadvantage lying there below them, my bare white legs gleaming and smelling of the piña colada of Shelly's tanning lotion, my bare feet sticking up like a corpse's. I knew even before I saw the round love bite on Shelly's neck that he might as well have worn a signboard saying: "Brace yourself—more complications to come!" After all the depths of emotions I had experienced in the past hours, here was another looming threat, a minefield I had yet to traverse.

In a few brief seconds I read the easy carelessness of his body as they moved toward me holding hands. Across the street, a neighbor's dog, who hears sirens before humans do, began an extended howl. A second later he was joined by a siren down toward Sixteenth Street, where a squad car would have to weave its way through the streams of cars parked and double-parked at churches all along that broad boulevard. From the Tibetan meditation temple to the Buddhist temple on down to the Baptist church where Jimmy Carter once taught Sunday school, people assembling with dreams of salvation, what we all hope and search for in our various ways. And here I was, confronted with the red sweatsuit, symbol of an L.A. drug gang that had spread nationwide, I'd read in the paper, and within it the careless motion of a young man's body, a no-restraints looseness, a formidable sexuality in his easy-flowing movements that women are never too old to read. And with Shelly, caught in the hormonal tumult of sixteen, the possibilities took my breath away. Not the fear of sex for my precocious teenager, that crisis having been addressed more than a year before. It was a kid thing then, and this man before me was much more than a kid; rather, sex underlined, moving in big boots across a vast, hot, and complicated canvas. Then again, it rushed at me that I was being prejudiced, assigning him an attitude before I knew him at all. In the midst of my confusion, Shelly said,

"Moms, this is Dee." "Moms," an annoying term she pretends to use with affection to get on my good side.

"Hey." Dee smiled with a glow that could light Pittsburgh, and moved forward to shake my hand.

I paused, lost in the uncertain etiquette of disapproval. After all, it wasn't too many years ago that you didn't just sail into a girl's house holding her hand when she'd been out all night unaccounted for and smile as if you were offering a free trip to China. However, remembering from my churchgoing East Texas background that Jesus recommended consorting with the Pharisees, and deciding it wiser to stifle my anger and bide my time, I raised my hand in a compromise: I proffered a handshake but no smile, rather a wary study of his marvelously intriguing face. Dee met the admonishment of my unsmiling eyes and clasped my hand indifferently for only a second, indicating to me that my approval was of no great importance.

"I wish you'd phoned at some point," I told Shelly. "I've been crazy with worry."

She answered with a kind of wave of her head, her way of launching into a story. "I'm sorry, Moms," she began, looking not at me directly but down toward Arlo, who had roused himself and was rubbing against her legs. She bent to pet him, revealing the top of her buff stretch bra under her blue T-shirt. She straightened up and moved her hand to the back of her neck and lifted her long two-tone hair—the first four inches soft brown at the roots with natural golden highlights some women pay big bucks for, and the remaining flow of hair which settled below her shoulders bleached blond and less lively. She fanned her neck a moment as she talked and then let her hair fall, tossing her head gently and readjusting the five inches of silver bracelets she always wore up her left arm.

"We went to Kings Dominion and we had the best time!" Shelly glanced at Dee, made a brief reading of his reaction. "But on the way home the car broke down, so we had to get a tow truck, and we didn't have enough money and . . ."

I listened, desperately trying to find—in what I knew would be a long and fuzzy story—some specific time, place, or name.

". . . and by then it was after three and I didn't want to wake you up." Her eyes widened with innocence to demonstrate her consideration, met my own. *Call me no matter what time,* was the rule. And when she saw the familiar traces of anger and skepticism in my face, she turned away. The sirens grew louder behind her words and she looked at Dee, searching for his approval of this meager, vague report.

"When we got to Dee's cousin's house the phone was broken. . . ."

Ah, the number of broken phones in this area of the nation, and Shelly seemed bound to discover them all. It was just as she turned to look at Dee that I saw the round reddish love bite on her neck, tanned to perfection from her summer lifeguard job, where she reigned on a wooden throne. And then she smiled her lovely perfect-teeth smile, repaying me some of those hundreds of orthodontist dollars in the kind of slow beautiful smile I hoped to enjoy for the rest of my life.

Then, having fulfilled her duty and being satisfied with her performance, Shelly caught Dee's hand and started toward the door. As if I needed more reassurance of her presence, I called out, "Well, ain't it hot?" knowing the "ain't" would rile her, her mother's crude Texas ways. Sometimes I used it for effect. I had been known to stop a dinner party by saying "reckon." But it sailed past her.

"Listen, we're starving, is there something to eat?" She spun on her bright blue stretch sandals that matched her shorts and shirt, still hanging on to Dee's hand. He smiled at me with a touch of humor, as if he were being jerked around helplessly by this dear child. Just then "Something Cool" ended and I realized

I hadn't even heard it. I again watched the liquid, easy sexuality of this young man's movement. The door thudded behind him and I sat up at attention like a general both energized and horrified at having sighted the enemy over the hill. For half a minute I wished I were elsewhere, at a beach, any beach, even a Delaware beach rife with jellyfish in the afternoon, even a sweltering Texas beach where you find not diamonds but tar on the soles of your feet.

I turned off the radio, and the cordless phone I'd kept beside me those past hours rang. I rifled through the newspapers to find it beneath *Book World*.

"Rosemary, how ya doing?" It was Doreen, major organizer of our neighborhood orange-hat patrol, calling to report that the Alcohol Control Board hearing planned for the next week had been postponed. Our neighborhood was trying to rid itself of the Bluebird Bar & Grill, a haven for drug dealers, by opposing the renewal of its liquor license. Doreen lived behind me and down two houses. Had she been looking out her bedroom window through her daisy-print balloon curtains, we might have waved at each other. She asked if she could count on me for orange-hatting the next weekend, and I told her I'd patrol if I didn't have to maintain surveillance of my teenager.

"Oh, I know what you mean," Doreen, mother of three exemplary daughters, said with real feeling.

"Maybe you could get Dan and Don," I added.

I always suggested Dan and Don, though I suspected that some of the male orange-hats didn't welcome the prospect of patrolling neighborhood streets with an interracial gay couple.

"Well, see you later," Doreen said. "Have a good week."

Doreen is a nurse. When Shelly and I first moved in, she appeared at our door introducing herself and offering to help if I ever needed emergency medical assistance. I passed that on to my mother, who immediately felt better about our being in what she considered a godless, strife-torn city. Of course when Mama came to visit I drove her down Sixteenth, pointing out the churches and synagogues and temples, showing how it was the opposite of a godless city. And Mama felt some relief, despite the number of what she considered off-brand religions. Mama had never before seen a Buddhist temple. Indeed, you can live in East Texas your entire life and not see a Buddhist temple.

I stacked the newspapers. Beyond the dying elm Dan and Don started "Stairway to Heaven," and I moved toward the sliding glass door, readying myself for guard duty, wondering if I'd have to wait a whole year for the haunting sound of June Christy singing "Something Cool." At the door I paused, hoping for a miracle, that I might walk inside and find not this stranger in my kitchen, but Shelly's father, who would kindly take my hand and help me prepare for the next campaign.

We are, Shelly and I, what the Census Bureau a few miles away in Suitland, Maryland, calls a single-headed household. The Census Bureau itself, a collection of tawdry World War II structures surrounded by parking lots, is as unadorned as a list of numbers. Thus it is curious to me that it would use the imaginative term "single-headed household," which suggests a landscape of folk architecture with houses built like heads.

It is not that Shelly doesn't have a father—a kind, responsible man whom we both love in certain different and complicated ways: Tom Kenny, a lawyer, a funny, bright, loving good ole boy whom I married when we were young and madly in love with life and sex and our future together. That future, as perhaps most young futures do, seemed to hold nothing but progress, enlightenment, and success. It lasted exactly eight years of living together and three more living apart.

Tom was just out of the University of Texas law school when we married. He'd been working summers and part-time for a state senator, while I was working as a reporter for a newspaper in Fort Worth. Tom finished law school, we married, and shortly afterward, when the senator ran for national office, Tom followed the new congressman to Washington. Meanwhile I relocated to the Washington bureau of that same Texas newspaper. It was post-Watergate and the nation was still in shock. So, like the cavalry, we rode to the rescue—certain, as are so many young people who come to Washington, that our lives would be important, set as they were in the center of the intricate mechanism that is our government. We would learn how things worked, make intelligent, intellectual contributions. Like pioneers we set out to explore a new world, only moving east rather than west.

Now I look back sadly at those two young people, at the innocence, the passion, the hope. For we were products of the sixties who believed all problems were solvable. And in those first years in this beautiful city our lives seem to have moved in double time and in lock step under a bright warm sun with music in the background.

Then a cloud settled over the sun. The congressman made a mistake involving money and a television station license. A small thing, it appeared, at first, interceding for a constituent, not quite illegal, only influence-peddling. Imprudent perhaps. But there were adversaries, the former incumbent with a history of enemy lists and eager leaks, and suddenly it was there in the newspapers, and the embattled congressman and his staff were bombarded with that and a flurry of other charges.

There followed a game of musical chairs, because the rule was that someone had to be sacrificed. And when the music stopped, Tom seemed the obvious choice, the man standing between chairs, with enough stature to provide the necessary retribution.

Oh, the congressman was sorry. That was the year he was wearing white shoes, a white belt, and white pants with a sheen to them. But this was the way the game was played, and we should have realized that. In his words: "A public servant gets caught by the nuts, his staff is the one that hollers. That's what they're there for." "Public servant" had become a more complicated term.

The millions of people who have not been named miscreants on the front page of a major newspaper don't have much sense of what that means to your life, your waking hours, or of the sleepless nights, when suddenly it is the rest of the world that is gainfully employed, when even your child's playmates hint at criminal wrongdoing. All pleasures cease, even sex, which at first provides some solace. Your entire world is tainted.

After a few months of job hunting, household puttering, and nights drinking beer and listening to country-western music at the Tune Inn, Tom packed up and moved back to Texas with our two dogs. Shelly and I were to join him when her school was out.

We commuted for a few months, Shelly and I. Tom no longer flew to Washington. Indeed, he no longer flew. He retreated to an earlier, simpler life. He bought a pickup and rode around the countryside with the dogs. He rented an office and proceeded to make himself unavailable most of the time. He declined to practice adversarial law. He bought a hunting cabin too small for three people and too isolated to get in and out of in bad weather, and a lot of fishing and hunting gear. In retrospect, I think of him like Jesus going into the wilderness to reconsider his life, only Tom didn't come out. His real focus became the perhaps innocent natural world around him, while I was still focused elsewhere, covering the machinations of the Hill for that same Texas newspaper.

As he settled into another orbit we grew apart. At first I thought I could adjust to whatever I had to, that Shelly and I would good-naturedly return to Texas and make another life. But it wasn't the natural process I'd anticipated. After all, what would I do in East Texas? By then I'd come to love Washington, the museums, the beauty of the city, the excitement of seeing foreign flags flying along downtown streets when state visits were in progress, of hearing interesting and often controversial people of the world speak at the National Press Club. I knew the building on R Street where Russian spies supposedly lived, the house where Deep Throat was rumored to have resided. Furthermore, Tom and I had little to talk about anymore except a future he didn't seem to think was there. Looking back, I see it as a slow-spiraling nosedive ending in a painful explosion followed by a lingering fire.

Was I wrong not to pull away from life as he did? To stay involved with the world? Was I wrong not to spend my life studying the flora and fauna of the Sulphur River bottom with the highlight of deer hunting in the fall or maybe a tornado in spring? Was I wrong to keep my child in a city school with its opportunities and diverse cultures, trying to avoid the narrow cheerleading mentality of East Texas? I don't know. In all honesty.

Sometimes I have asked myself whether I would have done things differently if I had known what teendom would be like, if I had recognized the emotional toll of separation on all of us. Often as I have lain awake on those long, lonely nights of waiting for Shelly, I have asked myself whether it was a betrayal not to stick by Tom after the better had turned to worse. But hard questions like these were obscured as the relationship floundered, until there was enough blame and hurt to sink all possibilities of correction.

Once Mao Tse-tung declared women capable of supporting half the sky. I think of that sometimes when I feel overwhelmed. Even such a tyrant and visionary as Mao didn't intend a woman to support single-handedly the vast and turbulent universe that is the sky above her.

Yet like many others, I carry on, though wiser, sadder, and knowing the world is different from what I expected it to be. All the while living under the threat that my headstrong daughter might decide her life would be sunnier and less constrained amid the low hills and rolling highways of East Texas.

IN THE KITCHEN Dee was drinking a glass of milk, a wholesome performance that in my momentary paranoia I assumed was planned deliberately to throw me off guard. Shelly was searching the refrigerator.

"There is not one single thing in here but rabbit food!" she charged, with something of a lilt in her voice to soften the criticism.

I caught her exasperated smirk and felt the fury that had been smoldering for the past hours in my soul, just below the fearsome surface, ignite in an instant.

"Sorry I didn't have a banquet in wait." I tried to cover my anger with some humor and remembered that all the books said never to be sarcastic with your teenager. So already she had the advantage. Having bungled the first round, I simply turned away, marveling, as I often did, at her ability to transport me from one emotional corner to another in a dizzying second. Then I opened the refrigerator and cooled my face as I pointed out in a calm voice tuna salad, cheese, peaches. Peanut butter, I added, struggling to maintain my composure and thereby hoping for some information on this stranger downing his second glass of milk. My strategy was necessarily oblique, since I was enjoined from asking questions. "They think you're always quizzing them!" Shelly had charged me several times in the recent past regarding her many boyfriends. So I would try to be helpful and wait. Tuck in a question now and then sotto voce. Observe.

Like so many of the young, Shelly was basically an anarchist, believing in freedom above all—optional school, optional government, free transportation, legal drugs, optional parenting. That she had almost reached her final year of high school without self-destructing seemed a miracle, and so I spent my time trying to balance my responsibility for her safe conduct with her overriding demand for freedom and independence from that same overseer role. It was a tightrope I walked every day over my very own floors.

In the adjoining room the TV blared with a grade-B film noir about murder in a small town. Shelly never enters a room that has a TV set without turning it on, even if she's only passing through. Just like my mother, who adjusts the heat or air-conditioning whenever she passes a thermostat. I poured myself a glass of ice water and plopped some tuna salad on a lettuce leaf and watched Shelly make peanut butter and jelly sandwiches—one for herself, two for Dee—and pour him another glass of milk and one for herself. This hadn't happened in years. It was then I knew for certain this was a heavy influence.

They carried their food into the small room adjacent to the living room and sat together in the loveseat in front of the TV. Mentally I donned my armor of the primal mother protecting her young, and gathered up the papers and moved to the living room, where I could monitor with some dignity of distance. I opened the *Post* and reminded myself that she was, after all, home and safe. Another night past and my major objective achieved. That I had become nearly accustomed to vacillating between fury and fear, hope and despair, was now a fact of my life I appeared helpless to avoid or control. I listened to their brief conversations during the commercials. They were both Scorpios, Shelly had just discovered; she explained to Dee how that meant they were passionate, intense, and determined. Tell me about it, I thought to myself.

"Hell, I already knew that," Dee said.

"You didn't know that about me," Shelly answered.

"Sure I did," Dee teased her.

Shelly asked him to identify some sports figure in a commercial, and Dee impressively rattled off name, team, and relevant statistics.

"I don't like basketball, it looks smelly," she replied—a line she'd learned from me, inspired by the East Texas high school gym that always reeked of sweat, whether it was during a game or a student assembly or the senior prom.

Dee responded that anyone who didn't appreciate the artistry—he used that very word—of Michael Jordan or Magic Johnson ought to have her head looked into.

Shelly said she liked bowling; this was a joke.

"Bowling!" Dee exploded with disdain, and Shelly giggled.

The movie returned and they were silent. Their verbal communication was generally meager, as I had observed so many times of Shelly and her friends.

The next time I moved to the kitchen, Shelly and Dee were eating cookies and holding hands. Arlo was curled on Shelly's lap, sleeping peacefully, while she leaned against Dee's shoulder as he explained why he'd not ridden the roller coaster at Kings Dominion.

"When I was 'bout three years old, me and my mama was riding with a cousin down in Virginia in her Pontiac when the door comes open and I go out the door and Mama catches my shirt about one instant before my head hits the highway."

Shelly exclaimed sympathetically.

"I guess that's why I don't like heights. . . ."

"Oh, poor baby," Shelly said.

I rinsed my empty dishes and returned to collect their plates, reconciled once more to my role as witness to romance in progress.

"Thanks, Ms. Kenny," Dee said as I took his plate. And for an instant, seeing their bodies leaning together, I felt a flicker of envy as an observer of that quickening of the world called passion.

SUNDAYS, SHELLY AND I talk to Texas. Tom phones Shelly in the evening, since that's one of the few nights he can usually find her home. Their communications are private. If I'm in the room she flees as if it were a secret suitor. There is still, even after all these years, an element of surprise to his phone calls, and I confess I find it painful, their separate and private relationship apart from me.

On Sunday afternoons around five-thirty my mother calls from East Texas to talk for thirty minutes, until the rates rise. Since she has become mayor of her small town, she most often leads with some current affair-of-state concerning this awful little place that is dying daily because the interstate passed it by. I begged Mama not to run for mayor. She was the tenth person the city fathers had approached, and they were desperate by the time they made their pitch to her. She was respected, she'd been an English teacher for years and could use the subjunctive, and since the town had never had a woman mayor Mama thought it was her strike for feminism. So there she is, with everybody and his dog calling her day and night with complaints and problems, like a garbage can disappeared from somebody's alley, or a stray bull just trotted across the driveway, or the Happy Acres Nursing Center is without heat and threatening to sue the town's plumber. Meanwhile the citizens refuse to raise taxes and the city council has knock-down drag-outs in its weekly meetings. The city council is composed of two factions—one Baptist and one beer-drinking, or to be more specific, a group that regularly has fish fries. What they do is all go down to the river and get drunk around bonfires. We have recently learned that could be a process of male bonding. However, what we called it when I was growing up was frying fish and getting drunk.

The only thing the entire city council could agree on was supporting the National Rifle Association. But Mama told them she'd shoot herself before she'd support the NRA. That shows just how desperate they were for a mayor, because they'd sometimes have city council meetings, Mama says, when every one of them, Baptists and beer drinkers alike, wore those NRA shit-kicker caps so that it looked like a bunch of potbellied Boy Scouts.

But despite that allegiance they shared, the factionalism was stronger, and every few weeks one faction or the other would get mad and resign en masse from the city council. Mama would have to jump in her jumbo Oldsmobile and run them down in pastures or gas stations or insurance offices and tell them it was their Christian duty to come back. Or ask people on the other side if they wanted to leave running the town up to a bunch of Baptists. I told Mama that if the masses presently freeing themselves from the yoke of communism could see the goings-on in that little town as an example of democracy, they'd probably backslide to communism.

"Rosemary, you won't believe what's happened here," my mother said on this Sunday. Actually, I would believe anything that happened in her town.

"I've been invited to a mayors' meeting in Dallas."

"Well, that's nice."

She told me she'd asked Aunt Lucille to go with her, but

she wasn't sure it was safe for two sixty-something women to go to Dallas by themselves.

"Maybe you should ask Art Moser," I suggested. Art Moser was a nice-looking widower who'd always had the hots for Mama. He'd been smiling across the Methodist church at her ever since Daddy died.

I was joking, but Mama said, "I thought about him." To my surprise, she added, "But we'd have to spend the night and stay in a hotel. Do you think he'd get the wrong idea if I asked him to go with us?"

"Mama, it's according to what idea you have in mind. Surely he wouldn't expect that you'd invited him to ravish both you and Aunt Lucille."

"Rosemary, really!" Mama said with feeling. "You know what I mean!"

That's the way Mama talks where sex is concerned. Her conversation is so vague she could work for the federal government.

"Well, Mama, maybe you should just flat-out make it clear that you're interested in a romance."

"Rosemary, I'm not any such a thing!"

Mama asked how Shelly was doing. I told her she had company but she was right here watching TV if Mama would like to say hello. And before she could answer I called to Shelly, anything to distract her for a minute from the loveseat, where she sat holding Dee's hand in her lap, their feet, hers bare and tan, his in dead-white socks, entwined.

While Shelly talked to Mama I took a seat in the rocker near the TV. After a few idle niceties, I asked Dee where he lived. His white high-top sneakers stood heavy as concrete boots in front of the loveseat. He didn't look at me but kept his caramel-colored eyes on the television, so I could observe his clean-cut neatness, the openness of his face, not so common in young men of that age. But Dee was in no hurry to answer my question, and I realized I was doing what most white people must do: approaching him with suspicion, even fear. The pleasure of looking at him didn't erase that initial distrust, though I recalled stories of innocent young black men being harassed by police; women automatically crossing the street at the sight of them; a brilliant black athlete and scholar riding in an elevator with some whites who held a gun on him until the elevator reached their destination.

Dee said he lived in Southeast.

I nodded. If he lived in Southeast, that might mean Anacostia, the area known for drive-by shootings, where innocent people were hit through their kitchen windows, where children on bicycles were caught in crossfire. It was the saddest area of the city. Or it might mean out Pennsylvania Avenue Southeast, a nice middle-class neighborhood. So I didn't know any more than I had before. And what was I trying to find out anyway? If he lived in a castle, would it make me feel better that he was romancing my daughter? Was I suspicious just because he was black? Because he could be into drugs? Because he wore a red sweatsuit? There are so many built-in suspicions, nasty innuendoes that creep into our thinking and intrude on our consciousness. They explode into the light before we examine where they come from—which is exactly what was happening to me.

Then Shelly was back, holding the phone out to me.

"I still can't believe she's sixteen years old, and here she's nearly seventeen," Mama said. "Sweet sixteen and never been kissed." Mama was full of old sayings like that.

"If you read *Pollyanna* and believe in Santa Claus you might believe that, Mama." I knew she would never want anything closer to the actual truth than that.

It was nearly five and she had to go, Mama said.

"What are you doing tonight?" I asked her. She was having

a hard time choosing between two TV problem-of-the-month movies. As mayor, she felt she should keep up with any social problem that might befall her constituency.

"Mama," I told her, "if you'd just learn to program your VCR . . ."

"Oh, I know it," Mama answered. But she didn't want to fool with all that. Reading the small print gave her a headache.

"It's good to talk to you," I said.

"Oh, Rosemary, I saw Tom the other day." She is often afraid to mention him until the last moment; she has to build up her courage. Then it comes like a final salvo. After the sound of his name I could hear the familiar flatness enter my voice.

"Oh? How are the dogs?" I asked.

"Rosemary," Mama said, "he looked real good. And he said the dogs are okay." That's about all it was safe for us to talk about—the dogs.

"Yeah? Well, Mama, he always looks good, doesn't he?" That wasn't strictly true: he had gone through a period of drinking too much and got to looking puffy and sad.

"He said Beans had three more puppies."

"Really!"

I loved those dogs. Even after I couldn't live with Tom, I still loved those dogs. I loved them all. When I thought of them I could smell them, the dog smell when I'd hug them, and the comforting, peaceful feeling of hugging Tom.

"On that happy note, shall we adjourn, Mama?"

"I'm sorry, Rosemary. I thought you would want to know he's okay." Mama loves Tom too. She will never get over our divorce.

"I do, Mama. Thank you and good night. I appreciate your phoning."

I spent the remainder of the evening surveilling and planning the speech I would make to Shelly if I could ever find her alone. Typically, she would avoid me as long as possible, until, in my frustration, I would finally corner her and burst out with something like, "Think how I felt when you didn't come home last night! How could you be so inconsiderate?" I tried to come up with something fresh to say that would break through the passion of the moment, whether it was Dee or just the violent vitality and focus of her own will and desire. I knew that if enough time passed, my own self-righteous anger would slowly dissipate and I would tell myself to be happy that she was safe and forgo the unpleasantness of an angry confrontation.

Around seven I ordered pizza for three. Later, after my largely sleepless previous night, I kept dozing off, and, too bushed to maintain my vigil, I finally gave up. Shelly and Dee were sharing a bowl of ice cream with chocolate sauce in front of another movie. In a week she would go back to school, her last year in a public high school in northwest Washington, the one most acceptable—or maybe the only acceptable one—to middle-class whites in the District. It was there Shelly had encountered the broad range of our city's residents and learned, she believed, to be street-wise and tough. All summer long I'd been trying to persuade her to write the prescribed essays for her college applications and begin filling out the necessary forms while I figured out how to finance her higher education. Though Tom had been reliable with his child-support checks, I knew his casual law practice was not up to the costs of college. But at least she'd soon be safely in school during the day. Though I wasn't sure "safely" was quite the word.

"You're not going out, are you?" I asked her before I trudged upstairs, trying to sound casual rather than frantic.

Shelly said, "No," as if I were a maniac to suggest such a thing, when the fact is I could have awakened the next morning and she'd have been in the Yukon.

"Don't forget to bolt the door when Dee leaves," I said, sending several messages at once.

The phone rang around ten and Shelly picked up on the

second ring. I'd just settled into bed and begun to read the Sunday comics. I spent a moment staring at my phone beside the bed, knowing it was probably Tom, and wondering what would happen if I lifted the receiver. I had good reason to enlist Tom's influence in getting Shelly to complete her college essays, but we had established early on that only in dire emergencies did we work in concert. Day-by-day was too painful. So I reminded myself that being grown-up is very often just a matter of not doing what you want to do, and went back to what used to be called the funnies.

Monday morning at Harrison & Associates, Public Relations Consultants. Beside me my friend Marcus Everett, political specialist, former Olympic runner, graduate of Howard University and Wharton, who had managed over the past five and a half years to make Harrison & Associates bearable. Across from us, in the power position in his large corner office overlooking perpetual construction on Massachusetts Avenue, sat Harrison, a once attractive but now rather dissipated middle-aged man, with the soft gloss that often settles on older movie stars, which I suspect comes from their taking too much care of themselves. Harrison never faced us squarely but mumbled toward us over his shoulder as he swiveled his chair and clenched his exercise balls. He was a moving object most of the time. Short, stocky, with chemical brown hair slicked back in a stylish VIP cut, he wore the current power dress—suspenders and colored shirts with white tab collars that were de rigueur for a certain type of trend-setter in Washington. Sometimes he made me wish we all wore navy-blue pajamas.

To his right, a tank of piranhas swam and showed their teeth. Harrison bought the kind of piranhas that have their lips cut off so their teeth show. I thought it was barbaric to do that even to fish, but since he was my ultimate boss I kept that opinion to myself. I had, over the course of my five and a half years there, since I left journalism to support myself and my child better, discovered things about Harrison more offensive than his lipless fish.

Business had not been wonderful of late, but that morning Harrison was excited because we'd just been awarded a new account, by Sainte-Marie, a small island somewhere out there among the Lesser Antilles, populated by battling factions and headed by one in a series of ruthless dictators. It was a government so inept it had managed to miss receiving foreign aid from the United States. Now the newest ascendant to power wanted multinational corporate investors. He was willing to make the entire island a giveaway free-market zone, preferably to an electronics industry, but anything would do. He wanted us to demonstrate to the world that an investor would be secure going to Sainte-Marie. We were to place advocacy ads in major business publications emphasizing the cheap labor, the stable government, the attractive working environment, and the climate—all of which, except for the cheap labor, were untrue. Nevertheless, we were to assemble a kit, film, and videos to promote that idea. Meanwhile, even before Sainte-Marie became a player among multinational corporate giants, tourists were wanted. The government was desperate for tourists. This was not the way Harrison put it, of course, but it was all there between the lines. People who live within breathing distance of the government learn at age three to read between the lines.

Nearly all foreign governments have public relations agencies in Washington representing them now. It's cheaper to tell people you're running a government well than actually to do it. Marcus and I predict that before long there will be only caretaker governments, with all the action coming from PR firms. As in *Catch-22*, they'll just say they won the war. Think of our postal service, for instance: It says it serves the public and delivers the mail, while really it sells nightshirts and runs contests about Elvis stamps. My closest post office was recently open only from ten a.m. till twelve noon five days a week.

Harrison's politics shifted like the windsock atop the White House. And he was not above tossing out to us that by bringing tourism and industry to this godforsaken flea-swept island (populated also by thousands of hungry cats), we would in some way be making the world safer for democracy. So the mission was to entice investors to invest and vacationers to vacation in Sainte-Marie, despite the fact that presently the airport in Sainte-Marie could accommodate not even a corporate jet. But there were plans for a new airport, and supposedly a luxury hotel complex was rising over the hot, soggy harbor, and it was rumored that the deal involved, for Harrison, personal investment opportunities.

As we sat there soberly, I considered whether we should warn tourists to bring flea collars. I scribbled that on my white pad—we'd shifted from yellow because white could be recycled—and pushed it over for Marcus to read. He folded his lips just as Harrison swiveled. Harrison reviewed the presentation he'd pitched to the prime minister and assorted members of his military junta, and announced that in the absence of the second-in-command at Harrison & Associates, who was rumored to be "vacationing" in a well-appointed whiskey farm, he would go after corporate accounts. Marcus was to spearhead relations with Congress and the State Department. The immediate challenge of promoting tourism was mine. Marcus and I would share responsibility for promotional materials. Harrison would of course oversee. He oversaw all accounts, and that meant that he made the trips. Harrison had about a jillion preferred-flyer miles from various, and many defunct, airlines.

Marcus and I exchanged phony smiles. Only the two of us knew they were phony. The good thing was that at least I'd be working with Marcus. If I had to do something immoral, I didn't so much mind doing it if I could do it with him. Indeed, I loved Marcus, loved his good-natured humor, the smell of his Paco Rabanne after-shave, and the daily sight of his smart wardrobe. He was married to Michelle, a gorgeous AT&T executive, and they had an adorable two-and-a-half-year-old who'd already been enrolled at St. Albans Episcopal school, and they were also bringing up Marcus's twelve-year-old niece. They lived in a stylish modern house with a pool and a Jacuzzi in a Washington suburb. Marcus drove a navy BMW. If he had been white I'd probably have denounced him as a yuppie. But despite his tendency to live on the cusp of affluence, what I considered maybe too well, we were friends. And one of my life goals—after seeing Shelly adult, upright, and safe—was to remain friends with Marcus. He was seven years younger than I but didn't know it. No one but my mother and I knew my age. Even Tom wasn't sure. Once at a Christmas party Marcus and I even said we loved each other. At least that's what I said, crying and hugging him, and he answered, "Right, Rosemary, we're loving friends." I'd had a hot alcoholic drink, and hot alcohol rushes right to my bloodstream, lightens my head, loosens my tongue, and makes my knees weak. On that occasion our relationship might very well have veered in another direction. "Can I give you a ride home?" he'd asked me.

"Of course," I'd said, emboldened by yet another drink. But inside his car, away from hot alcohol and the festive atmosphere and looking at his serious, responsible profile, I realized what I needed from Marcus more than anything else in the world was friendship. I count that the first moment of true maturity, way before the first invitation to join the AARP: the moment when you realize that friends are as important as lovers.

So we sat there in Harrison's office while the fish chewed, and discussed our plans to bring tourism and economic well-being to this island no one had ever heard of, except somebody in the bowels of *The New York Times* or the Library of Congress, until a recent scandal when Sainte-Marie was mentioned as a rendezvous point for indicted drug cartel members.

I was thinking about whether I wanted it on my conscience that I encouraged tourists to go there and maybe get whacked by a machete as they got off the boat—not to mention that I would be bolstering the power of the latest dictator. Instead of bringing up any of this, however, I assumed my mashed-potato business voice and inquired about the politics of this place.

"They call themselves Christian Democrats," Marcus said, and rolled his eyes. We both knew that political parties using the word "Christian" in their names nowadays were fascist.

Harrison replied succinctly: "Fuck the politics of the place, Rosemary!"

I glanced away, toward the wall with the portrait of Harrison in a tuxedo, which hung above his taupe tweed couch, which sat upon his taupe tweed carpeting. Harrison's mother, an interior designer, regularly redecorated our offices. The current style was Santa Fe, with a lot of half-painted wooden furniture strewn around.

Part of the presentation Harrison had made to the powers that be in Sainte-Marie concerned Marcus's lobbying the Congressional Black Caucus about the strategic and developmental possibilities of the island for the U.S. military. "Could we not train amphibious assault teams in Sainte-Marie?" was the way Harrison put it. My job, he added, would be to seal the account, by committing us to bring film crews to the island. "If they can make movies in the Philippines, why not Sainte-Marie? It's closer."

Harrison set his exerciser balls down and lifted his gold putter. "And Rosemary"—Harrison looked at me as if he were about to ask me to take off my dog costume—"I want you to think: romanticism."

"What do you mean, romanticism? From what I hear, there's nothing on that island to be romantic about. There are sand fleas and cat fleas. You can't even use the beaches."

Harrison glanced at his watch. You can judge your importance in his scheme of things by how often he glances at his watch in your presence. Though it is true that he arranges his day around racquetball at his health club.

Harrison faced me head-on: "Rosemary, think about Casablanca."

"A city in North Africa," I ventured.

"The movie," he corrected.

I suppose I looked puzzled.

"Do you think Casablanca was really glamorous like that? Do you think Sydney Greenstreet was really sitting there smoking hashish under a ceiling fan and wearing a Turkish hat? Or that Humphrey Bogart and Ingrid Bergman were there fighting the Nazis?"

I stared at him. Harrison had grown up in California and actually been in a western when he was twenty. He played an outlaw's sidekick, and his only line was, "Let's ride, partner!"

"See what you can do, Rosemary," he told me. "And no negative thinking." He looked away before completing the command.

I forced myself to nod slightly and turned to go, careful not to exchange looks with Marcus. Harrison's mother entered as we left. She had had several facelifts, so that she and Harrison might have been twins, right down to their hair color. I longed to ask her whether it was true as I'd heard that once you have a facelift you have to do it again every five years. But her face was so taut it probably would have hurt her to talk.

Finally Marcus and I were free to saunter down the terracotta hallway back to our adobe-shadow–painted cubicles. "Am I crazy?" I said. "Sydney Greenstreet wasn't smoking hashish, was he?"

"Who knows what he was smoking," Marcus said.

"And was Harrison saying Sydney Greenstreet was *supposed* to be smoking hashish or *was* smoking hashish?" Harrison could get you confused.

Above my desk hung that Gilbert Stuart portrait of George Washington in the clouds that used to hang in all Texas schoolrooms. It was counter to Harrison's mother's Santa Fe decorating, but it was my way of maintaining some pride.

"Rosemary," Harrison had said once, staring at the picture, "hanging that portrait of George Washington is an act of cynicism."

I pretended to be shocked at the accusation. I told him it had belonged to my grandmother, who'd been a schoolteacher, which was true. I come from a long line of schoolteachers. Actually, I think we should hang George Washington's portrait in public relations firms throughout the nation.

"With this account I may have to turn George there to the wall," I said to Marcus.

"Hey, that place probably isn't as bad as it sounds." Marcus opened a file of photos to one of a waterfall. We'd just discovered they weren't really of Sainte-Marie, but of another, more comfortable island nearby. Even *National Geographic* avoided Sainte-Marie.

Marcus shrugged and turned toward the double window we shared, his elbows resting on our common file cabinet. He still had the lean and sinewy body of a long-distance runner. It was a pleasure just to look at him. I picked up my watering can and watered my lacy china doll plant beside him.

"Let's face it," he said quietly, "that government could be overthrown any minute. Or the whole island wiped out. Hurricane season is soon upon us."

"That's a good thought," I said.

We both laughed and I stopped watering.

Marcus was eminently practical and willing to think in terms of microeconomy, while I tend to more sweeping negatives. The arts groups that I had established as my specialty over the years, which I could work for with some enthusiasm, had hunkered down for the duration of the recession. My very raison d'être at our friendly firm was tenuous, we both realized. Marcus had led me to understand that being cynical was not always an advantage, a fact easily forgotten with the inside-the-Beltway mentality around us. So I was trying hard to hope for the best.

There then arrived the familiar morning smell of boiled coffee, wafting down the hall from where the office manager, whom we called the sergeant, brewed burned coffee each day. Today it was burned vanilla-flavored.

"This really goes against my principles, Marcus. We've managed damage control for some flaky outfits in the past, but we've never hyped something that was going to get people killed," I said. "Why don't we just take over a homeless shelter and persuade people to vacation there? Raise some money for the homeless."

Marcus looked at me with his warm smile, which always made me feel better. He was wearing his round gold-rimmed glasses instead of contacts that day, and the glasses gave him an added air of authority. He might have been a college professor, except that he was dressed better.

"Oh, Rosemary, surely nobody is dumb enough to go to

Sainte-Marie." Marcus turned toward his cubicle. I looked at George Washington in the clouds, then at a small framed photo of Shelly prior to her nose-ring stage, and thought of the island of Sainte-Marie. Beaches. Water. Sun.

"I don't know, Marcus. They have a beach. I'm probably dumb enough to go there if it's cheap enough."

ON THE BUS going home that day I ran into Hadley Owens, one of Shelly's recent boyfriends. Not only did I suspect Hadley of stealing seventeen dollars from my purse, I also feared he had developed skinhead tendencies. He nodded sullenly in my direction and then turned away, maybe embarrassed that I'd found him on public transportation or afraid someone would see him talking to an adult and therefore uncool person. He wore a white "Fuck the Authorities" T-shirt with a striped cotton vest. One of the civilized things about Shelly and her friends is that they learned early on how to get around on public transportation, though, of course, many of them find it an indignity since they all think they should own their own wheels. After Tom went native Shelly spent a summer marooned in Texas, and that made her appreciate public transportation in D.C.; especially the Metrorail, which in some parts of the city is aboveground and presents a delightful stealth view of the city. I sometimes wish riding public transportation was mandatory nationwide, so that we might improve the hostile climate of our population. It's one of the few ways for people of different social and economic strata to mix. In areas of the country with scarcely any public transportation, like Texas, the only time people of different circumstances interact seems to be during the perpetration of a crime.

"What's going on with you, Hadley Owens?" I asked. We were both standing in the crowded aisle of a Metro bus. It was air-conditioned, but some disagreeable lunatic who railed senselessly every few minutes had opened a window, and no one had the temerity to protest. The rancid summer smell of sweat and weariness merged with the palpable tension of bodies in unwilling proximity. I had already surveyed the reading habits of my neighboring riders: there was one Bible, one romance, and a self-help guerrilla management book. Hadley, the tall narrow white body beside me, said he was waiting for his trial for possession to begin. I didn't know what to say in response. "Sorry you didn't listen to Mrs. Reagan and say no to drugs"? Or "Sorry you got caught"?

"How's Shelly?" Hadley asked.

"She's good. She'll finish high school this year, God willing. She's working on her college applications," I fantasized hopefully.

"Tell her hi," Hadley Owens said.

Once kids start fooling with their hair they can't stop. He'd done something more, and awful, to the beautiful brown hair he used to wear long on his shoulders. The last time I'd seen him he'd shaved it off, but today it looked like he'd burned a reddish-green cross into the back of his head. For some reason too, all skinheads look anemic—probably because they all live on diet sodas. My neighbor Doreen claims there's one diet soda that kills rats.

I had told Hadley one day as he was lounging around our house that when I was a kid, having your head shaved was one of the worst things that could happen to you. When you had ringworm they'd shave your head and wipe something horrible like motor oil on it. If you were a girl you wore a little bonnet. Hadley hadn't laughed. I had told him I was just trying to pass on a bit of history.

Of course for kids the concept that the past could have any pertinence to the present is just not there. All life is in present tense, and what's happening at the moment is on the screen before them. My claim is they've watched TV so long they can't even turn their heads as far as previous generations.

At my stop I wished Hadley luck and pulled myself through a group of Asian tourists with cameras and teenagers with backpacks. The bus door folded, and I inhaled quickly and held my breath until the bus had pulled away, emitting its foul dark cloud of exhaust.

Outside the bus, the heat hung over the small park near my stop, a rectangle with an assortment of plantings that included two Japanese pagoda trees. As always, the sidewalks were busy, with homeless men milling around waiting for a soup kitchen van while an assortment of citizens lounged on benches or crossed the park toward the commercial section of Columbia Road. On weekends a Hispanic minister sometimes preached on the corner in Spanish. His intonations sounded just like those of an East Texas evangelist, only the language was different. The park faced three churches, including a former Christian church, now a citadel of Reverend Moon followers. Salsa music blared from a radio in the window of an apartment house across from the park, and beyond that the Muslim call to prayers rang out from a mosque not far away. I often think that somebody skydiving into the middle of that little park could mistake the area to be any number of exotic foreign lands. It is an international patchwork quilt of people—some of them a bit down at the heels—but full of life uttered in various languages.

I headed west toward the zoo and Rock Creek Park, which cuts through the middle of the District. The park historically has been something of a demarcation line between the affluent great white ghetto to the northwest and the great black ghetto to the east. The strip of neighborhood I was traversing was one of the most diverse and integrated areas of the city. Tom hadn't wanted to move there because of the plethora of rooming houses in the area; he claimed dangerous people populated rooming houses. I thought all kinds of folks, not just dangerous ones, lived in rooming houses, and I'd fallen in love with the vitality of the neighborhood as well as with an old row house with a double parlor and ceiling beams in the dining room, so Tom had finally given in.

Beyond the park the western sky was streaked with brilliant pastels. Since Mount Pinatubo erupted in the Philippines, the sunsets had been magnificent. Every evening I marveled as I left the bus and walked toward my house as if I were in some old Hollywood western. Actually, I knew that my own life was framed by Hollywood films as much as Shelly's was by television. But my sphere of reference, though somewhat larger, wasn't so omnipresent. In addition, the men in it were not only better actors but also better-looking, even if they were usually too old for the parts they played. I hadn't noticed that until I started getting too old for the part I was playing in my mind. As I walked toward my strip of row houses, I felt good to think that the world was small enough that some natural event in the Philippines could affect the sunset seen from Sixteenth Street thousands of miles away in the District of Columbia, thus reinforcing no man is an island, etc.

Hadley's mention of his waiting for his trial reminded me that a lot of my friends happened to settle in Washington because they had come for the anti–Vietnam war marches, had been arrested, and had to hang around for their trials because they didn't have the money to return to wherever they were from and then come back. So a lot of people are in the D.C. environs under protest of a certain type for perpetuity. Also, many citizens who work for the government harbor truly altruistic motives. In this cynical day and age, there are still people working for the public good here and there in Washington, even on Capitol Hill.

Before I reached home I ran into my neighbor Mrs. Moore,

walking her Bouvier, Pal, the dog who alerts us to approaching sirens. Pal wore a summer haircut, a flea collar, a regular collar, and a rubber tie. Mrs. Moore, a dedicated career civil servant, was a tall dark woman, who dressed stylishly and was always perfectly groomed. At the end of her day she still looked neat and unruffled, even carrying a pooper-scooper, as she and Pal promenaded the neighborhood.

Pal sniffed at me while Mrs. Moore reported that her husband was in the hospital and asked me to pray for him. I didn't tell her that I didn't pray, because I'm sure the last thing she wanted to hear were my religious speculations. So I just said I hoped he'd improve soon. As I walked away I wondered at what point in my life I would look Mrs. Moore and her Bouvier in the face and say what I really thought.

That Monday night I approached the door to my own house with some trepidation. I had managed in my dismay at work to forget temporarily the new chapter in life with Shelly. I had, however, asked Marcus whether he thought a young black male in a red sweatsuit was necessarily a part of a nationwide drug ring.

" 'Ring' is an outmoded term, Rosemary," he replied.

"Well, 'gang,' 'crew'—whatever," I said. Marcus's language is usually on the urban cutting edge.

I had explained about Shelly's bringing Dee home. Marcus thought I was too lax with her, though he'd never said that flat-out. Of course, I thought I was too. I just didn't know how to exert control anymore. In fact, I never had known. I wasn't a disciplinarian. I didn't know of anyone, including the sad but rich Queen of England, who was anymore, except maybe the Communist Chinese.

"Where did she meet him?" Marcus asked.

"I don't know. Georgetown maybe. You know, she just meets people."

"Yeah, she's friendly. Like her mama." Marcus glanced at

me. He didn't think I handled my life right either. He had at various times implied that I should move to the suburbs like him, drive a Honda and take Shelly to church and use more hairspray. Though all those things he hadn't exactly said.

"What would you do?" I said.

"Does he work? Is he in school? Is he on the street?"

"I don't know."

"Well, hey, why don't you find out something about the dude?"

"She doesn't like me to ask questions." That sounded ridiculous, even to me. I hid my face, and when I looked back Marcus gave his Rolodex a 360-degree twirl.

"Rosemary . . ." He shook his head.

"He's wonderful-looking," I added.

"Oh, well, that says it all."

Sometimes I just hope I'll be around when Marcus's son and niece hit teendom and start pumping anxiety into him.

"If he carries a beeper, I'd discourage it," Marcus said.

"I already discourage everything. She thinks I want her to be a nun. Sometimes I wish I had that option."

Marcus, who bears my daily anxiety over Shelly, keeps telling me that if she can survive to twenty she'll be all right. Or if she can make it to college.

"Maybe he just likes red," I said. "It's my mother's favorite color."

Marcus was checking his list of appointments. Not only was he tight with the Congressional Black Caucus, but he seemed to know everyone else in town. You couldn't walk down the street with him without having to stop for him to talk to at least fourteen friends or acquaintances.

"Can you tell by looking at someone if he's using drugs?" I asked.

"Sure," Marcus said.

"How?"

"If his nose drips and he breathes through his mouth and he looks like he's nodding and kind of shuffles along."

I had to laugh.

"Rosemary, you're the only person I know who jives their own self."

Although it was not quite dark, my house looked like a slot-machine win, with every window blazing, even in the attic and basement. Two air conditioners, one upstairs, one down, each gagging a window, droned faithfully to allay the August heat. Once inside, I could smell the cigarettes I begged Shelly not to smoke. The TV screen was in action but muted, and the heavy bass sound of rap boomed from upstairs. I could see the kitchen in process, with canister lids lying about, water boiling, and the door to the patio wide open. There was enough kilowatt drain to light Mexico City. Of course it didn't necessarily mean anyone was home, but it so happened they were. After I closed and locked the patio door, I went to where Shelly and Dee sat in front of the TV set, playing cards on the coffee table. Dee still wore a red sweatsuit. Had he changed, I wondered. Did he have a whole wardrobe of red sweatsuits, or had he been here since the day before? Had he been hiding in a closet that morning while I was getting ready for work? Was I becoming as mean-minded and suspicious as Mama's city council?

Arlo was asleep on his back in my black leather chair, the one comfortable seat in the house. Shelly wore white shorts and my white T-shirt that read: "A Woman's Place Is in the House and in the Senate." Our cordless phone sat, as usual, at the ready beside her on the loveseat. Around them partially filled glasses of soda were sweating and creating new circles on my teak coffee table. A torn package of Doritos and a crumpled cookie box were scattered on the floor.

I had, up until that summer, tried hard to enforce the rule that Shelly was not allowed to have males inside the house when I wasn't there, which not only seemed reasonable but was recommended by Dear Abby. That meant she could talk to young men on the front stoop or on the back patio. But they had to trail through the house to get to the patio and then someone always wanted a glass of water or needed to use the phone or the bathroom, and it all became more complicated than the Treaty of Versailles, and since I didn't happen to have a platoon at my disposal to enforce the rule, I eventually surrendered.

Shelly held her cards in front of her tanned face. A large pile of poker chips was strewn before her, and a lesser, neatly stacked pile sat before Dee. He wore a chunky ring on his left hand, a heavy-looking bracelet on his left wrist, and a neck chain that I knew were not necessarily real gold. The refinery smell of New Jersey and nail polish adhesive lingered in the air. Shelly's nails were flame-red, with black spiders in the middle.

"Hey, woman. You're cheating!" Dee shouted suddenly. Arlo rolled over on his side, then jumped to the floor, and I started at the sound of Dee's anger just as Shelly collapsed in delightful giggles. They turned and greeted me, and pale though I probably was, I felt a surge of relief at finding this innocent though energy-wasteful scene.

"I am not cheating!" Shelly shouted back at Dee, jabbing her right fist toward his shoulder for emphasis. He leaned back casually to evade her blow and picked up the cards scattered between them.

I paused to study them. It appeared to me that Dee was the darkly tanned color everyone but a geisha would want to be. His pale brown eyes slanted upward slightly. He had a dimpled chin. "He with a cleft chin has the devil within," went an old Texas saying. Another said, "Once you've gone black you'll never come back." Looking across to Shelly, with her tawny tall good looks, I thought how smashing these two were together, especially at that moment, with Shelly minus her nose ring and her often excessive makeup. And how much attention they must draw, not to mention hostility. It was not exactly popular, even in this city of diversity, for a white girl to appropriate the attentions of a young black man. Desirable young black men were in great demand among young black women. Whatever my concerns here, there could be more serious ramifications to consider. Indeed, as I began sorting through the mail, the thought of the possible dangers involved in such a relationship boggled my mind.

Dee sat up very straight. Shelly was hunched over, leaning on her elbows.

"Okay, this time I'm dealing," he announced grimly.

"Fine." Shelly struggled and only pretended to hide her mirth at Dee's awkward card-shuffling. It was all a part of the mating ritual, first showing off your strengths and eventually testing tolerance for your weaknesses.

I sorted through a Potomac Electric bill, an L. L. Bean catalogue, a neighborhood newsletter, and solicitations from a homeless shelter, an AIDS clinic, Planned Parenthood.

Shelly was humming in a display of nonchalance. Like my mother, she loved playing games. One of my favorite photos was of Shelly and Mama playing checkers when Shelly was about five. They were outside on Mama's deck, both wearing straw hats. Their games were often loud and filled with drama and kidding. Like this one.

"Cut," Dee said.

Shelly cut the deck quietly, and Dee proceeded to deal each card with mock authority, trying to make up for his lack of finesse at shuffling. Shelly glanced at her cards, rearranged them, humming again, then gave him a bright smile. I admit I was drawn by the sight of her lighting up every time she looked at him. What a pleasure to see so many smiles.

"Your daughter cheats!" Dee exclaimed to me. He wasn't smiling, and I wasn't sure his words were all in humor.

"I certainly hope not," I said, and looked to see if Shelly had caught the edge.

"I do not cheat," she answered. "I'm just lucky."

"God, I hope so," I muttered.

"Well, you're the luckiest damn person I ever saw. You oughta play Lotto." Dee rearranged his cards and held them tight to his chest.

"Oh, that's just throwing money away." I dropped the L. L. Bean catalogue on the side table. I sounded just like Mama.

"My cousin won four hundred dollars playing Lotto," Dee said. "He took it to Atlantic City and made over two thousand dollars." He said this as if the two thousand dollars might have been two million.

"Good for him." I hadn't intended the sarcasm that crept into my voice, and I tried to cover it with a smile. I found them both looking at me, assessing my tone.

"I'll take one card." Shelly returned to the game, and I went to the hallway to switch off some lights. Still, I was pulled back by the tension in the room.

"Uh-oh." Dee dealt with a flourish, his arm circling in the air before setting a card before Shelly.

"You dealt that off the bottom!"

"I did not." Dee remained calm.

"You most certainly did!"

"I did not." Dee's voice was louder, and he rose to his knees.

"I saw you! You most certainly did!"

I couldn't stand it any longer. "Why play if y'all are going to cheat?" I tried to sound relaxed.

"I didn't cheat," Dee said firmly to Shelly, ignoring me. "Did you look at it?"

"No," Shelly said.

"Okay, here." He pulled a card from the top of the deck and buried the first card in the middle.

I opened the neighborhood newsletter. It announced auditions for a youth orchestra and the opening of a new Latino restaurant. The neighborhood association was organizing to buy security alarms; a meeting was scheduled for the following week. Volunteers were needed for the orange-hat patrol. Volunteers were always needed for the orange-hat patrol.

"Did you go to work today?" I tossed the question casually to Shelly.

She responded with a sound somewhere between "uh-huh" and "I heard you, don't bother me."

"What you bettin'?" Dee held his cards in front of his face.

"You didn't ante," Shelly said.

"I did so. *You* didn't ante."

"I most certainly did! Mama, didn't I just ante?"

"Now *you're* cheatin'!"

Shelly counted her chips. "Oh, I forgot!"

She shoved a blue chip onto the table. Sometimes, watching her, I would remember that freedom from time concerns, the endless talk, the hours spent riding around in a car in East Texas, listening to music, just fooling around. Sometimes, thinking of that timeless limbo, I hated to break the spell.

"Your play . . ." Dee said.

I moved closer to them and caught the faint smell of chlorine on Shelly's hair.

She laid down a straight, eight high.

Dee stared at it, then tossed his cards into the air. "Well, damn!" he said as cards rained around him.

Shelly laughed and threw her arms around him in a fast, friendly hug. Dee pulled away smiling.

"Hell, I'm watching TV," he said, and reached for the remote. The TV was loud now, and Shelly began picking up the cards, saying, "Can I help it if I'm lucky?"

As I left to change my clothes, relieved that the game was

over and the tension eased, Shelly called out, "Hey, Moms, we're cooking supper."

"Really?" I didn't hide my surprise.

"Dee wants to."

"Terrific," I called, but thinking I wasn't ready to be involved in domestic life with this edgy stranger. I headed upstairs wearily, past the faded wallpaper, stained from years of Shelly's and her friends' hands, up the worn brick-colored carpeting, which needed vacuuming. Here was a single-headed household in need of care.

I went in Shelly's bedroom and punched the power button on her sound system. The music died. There was the faint smell of cigarettes again. Her bed was unmade, the blue comforter hanging off to the side. Clothes were strewn over the floor. Tampax spilled out of an opened box onto the dresser. Shelly's favorite stuffed bear, which she slept with, lay on the bed with his remaining brown eye staring at the ceiling. For Valentine's she'd wanted a rap record by Big Daddy Kane and a new teddy bear for her collection. Teddy bears in assorted dress and manner were propped around the room, their button eyes watching from shelves and the dresser and a doll bed. Her room would be an archaeologist's dream in the year 3000. Besides the shelves of bears and other stuffed animals, there were posters of Hammer and rap groups and Madonna in her wedding getup, and photographs of friends wearing shades and dressed in the desired criminal attire.

I wondered who would win out in Shelly's life, the teddy bears or the lineup of fugitive-from-justice-style entertainers. I had tried over the years to keep up with the music she listened to, but the lyrics always sounded ominous, with as many expletives as a Nixon White House tape. Though whenever I asked Shelly to translate, she'd recite something about peace in the ghetto and loving your brothers.

When I went back downstairs to the kitchen, Dee, wearing my apron, was at the stove stirring some concoction in a skillet with the heat too high. Shelly was tearing open a package of frozen vegetables, and on a back burner a pound of macaroni boiled in half enough water.

I poured myself a glass of wine and went into the next room and switched on the news on TV. It occurred to me there were some nice things about having Dee there. He was something of a buffer between me and Shelly. And he made her laugh!—maybe my favorite sound, my daughter's laughter, better than Beethoven.

After a while Shelly called me to dinner. She was serving buffet style so we could watch TV as we ate. Avoid face-to-face talk, always. I'm convinced her entire life will be lived with the TV running like Muzak.

The meal was awful, some kind of macaroni and corn and ground beef with a spicy MSG seasoning that Shelly used on the rare occasions when she cooked. I consoled myself by thinking that if Dee hung around awhile and they kept on cooking, at least I'd lose weight.

During our supper the phone rang, and Shelly answered and passed it to Dee. He spoke quietly in a street lingo I couldn't understand. Was it my imagination, or did the phone call change his mood? After he hung up, he suddenly seemed brooding and hostile. Shelly glanced at him nervously. A few minutes later, without finishing his meal, he took his plate into the kitchen. Shelly followed him, holding on to the back of his shirt. Their whispering disappeared amid the sound of dishes being put in the dishwasher. All the dishes in the house seemed to be dirty.

"I'll clean up," I called, trying to set a precedent. There was no response. The water ran at full blast. Then Shelly walked Dee to the front door.

"Good night, Ms. Kenny," he said politely.

Shelly opened the front door and followed him onto the porch, leaving the door ajar. I could see them standing under the yellow overhead light, her arms wrapped around his waist as she spoke earnestly into his face. I wished she would be more discreet, standoffish, let's face it, chaste. I heard the metal gate in the front of the house push open and waited to hear it latch, but it didn't. Shelly came back inside, her smile gone, her vitality replaced by a sullen, dark mood.

So the two of us were left alone and uncomfortable, all my concerns hanging in the air above our heads like cartoon clouds. It was the first opportunity I'd had to mention her staying out on Saturday night, and I knew she was braced for the assault. She sat back to watch a sitcom, and for a while we were in a neutral corner of comedy. I felt like someone poised on a high dive, ready to leap into the abyss that was the simple act of questioning my own beloved daughter. I longed to warn her, to urge caution, ultimately to call attention to her own mortality. Where was the golden mean between my concern and her freedom? I began by suggesting she try to complete her essays for her college applications, which she claimed she'd been working on since July, but which had not materialized in any form as far as I could discern.

"You really should finish them before school starts," I pointed out for the umpteenth time. "You'll be so busy when school starts." I repeated myself a lot. I hated hearing my repetitions, but I couldn't avoid them, since so much was said without response or even acknowledgment on her part. There were miraculous times when she'd surprise me with what she'd spill forth, and I would lap it up gratefully, any news of her hidden, complicated, threatening world.

If only there were daily reports, basic forms for children to fill out, with questions such as: *What is on your mind today? What is your major concern? What do you plan to do today, if anything?*

Shelly dipped her head to examine her nails. She had put

her half-empty plate on a pile of books on the table beside her, which also held a shoe box full of nail polishes and remover and other paraphernalia I'd told her over and over not to use downstairs. But now, being the supplicant, I said nothing.

A commercial on TV showed a car turning into a tiger before our eyes; this new computer technique would have great influence in advertising, we'd been told at the office. I imagined my sullen daughter morphing into a warm, affectionate girl, no nose ring in sight.

I told her that Marcus and I had a new account, an island.

"Um . . ." She twisted a strand of hair, but as an expert interpreter, I knew she was listening. I gave her a few more details and suggested that this could mean an island vacation for us at some time. Sheer fantasy probably, but we hadn't been able to afford a vacation for a while and the idea was appealing. I imagined glistening beaches and aquamarine water, Sainte-Marie morphing into a lovely Caribbean island. Shelly had gone to a modest summer camp for three years but had outgrown it. We'd visited my mother in Texas for a week earlier in the summer. This vacation idea was a bribe, a carrot dangled before her with not even a likely payoff. After the attempt at a tantalizing introduction, I finally dove in.

"I was so worried when you didn't come home Saturday night, or even call. Put yourself in my place, Shelly. You should always call, no matter what time it is or where you are. You could have found a phone somewhere."

Her response was a shrug. Not a word of apology. Her body tensed before me, and I knew that no matter how righteous my anger, I had to let go of it in order to deal with the present and the future. There was never any form of closure or fair redress. I couldn't indulge myself in past recriminations.

"Tell me about Dee," I asked. It didn't work. Shelly reached for the remote and punched the sound on. My question was too general. She only shrugged. But I'd been brave enough to start;

it was too soon to give up. I tried again, a more oblique approach.

"That was nice of him to cook. He likes to cook?"

She shrugged again. "I guess. He has to take care of himself." She glanced at me to see if I'd received the message of neediness, the plea for sympathy.

"You seem to have a good time with him."

"He's darling," she said lightly.

I felt a cold fear sweep over me. You're overreacting, I told myself. Shelly raised her left arm with the lineup of silver bracelets and adjusted several of them. I'd never heard her use the word "darling." It was a strong statement. Her usual comment was, "He's okay."

I was disconcerted and paused to regroup. She kept watching an annoying sitcom with too bright colors and a laugh track. I let a moment pass, let the air that I'd stirred with a question settle slightly.

"Where did you meet him?"

I watched her, watched her watching the TV, studied her the way I always did. The great research project of my life. I sometimes wondered whether it was worth it, whether anyone was worth this daily fear and trembling.

She sighed heavily and looked at me, as if trying to decide whether she should flee or whether the program was worth her tolerating my questions. I could tell by her tense demeanor that she'd decided to get it over with. She was anticipating my questions, bracing herself just as I had before asking.

"At a party," she mumbled. "He's a rapper."

"A rapper?"

"He has a group. They're *really* good."

I contemplated the ready young dream of money, easy sex, adoration, and drugs. It added a powerful weight to Dee's influence.

"Really," I said. "He seems nice. How old is he?"

"I don't know. Nineteen or something." Her mouth turned down in disapproval at my question.

"A little old for you, isn't he?" I couldn't help myself, this overflow of protection and fear.

"I don't think so," she said with a touch of defensiveness. She stared at the paste-on nails on her thin and delicate hands. Under the long paste-ons, her own nails were bitten to the quick.

Arlo entered the room and looked around. He stretched his legs in preparation for his nightly prowl.

"Why this third degree?" Shelly asked sharply. She leaned forward to pet Arlo, who arched his back in encouragement.

We were at the crossroads here. I could respond in kind and the whole conversation would collapse into hostility, or I could try to appease her and hope for cooperation. It wasn't fair, but I took a deep breath and tried to repair. I tell you it's single parents who should work for the State Department. Ninety percent of male diplomats would pale in comparison with most single mothers on any Sunday morning.

"No third degree. I just wondered about him. What he does. Where he lives . . . No third degree."

I picked up the newspaper for some distance. Hid my face to let the tension ebb, backed away so she might take one step forward, as she sometimes does if I am careful enough. We dance a subtle and complicated minuet.

She kept watching the TV, another buffer between us, but finally, slowly, the story came out.

"He was going to community college. But he had to drop out. His mother wouldn't pay for it, so he's looking for a job . . . just till he starts making it with his group." She petted Arlo, whose summer fur floated from her hands with each stroke. "He finished high school." She looked to see if that impressed me. Her brownish-green eyes were sober and sad, too old and knowing in her young face. Often when I considered the contours of her face, the rounded chin, I feared the loss of that childish fullness; I knew when it went she would be too beautiful to be safe.

"He might go into the army. Except he has a knee injury and doesn't think they'll take him. He used to play football."

I wondered how much of this was true. Had he lied to her? Surely his life couldn't be so tenuous, so unfounded.

Outside, Pal began to howl. Shelly looked toward the window, and both of us waited for the sound of sirens, which rose after only a second. This shared experience altered the mood, and I saw her relax.

"Where's his father?" I asked.

She paused, yawned, stretched, her long red fingernails raking the air above her. "He and his mother and little sister live with his grandmother. They used to live with his stepfather, until he and Dee's mother broke up."

The sound of multiple sirens rose through the night, over the hum of the air conditioner.

"What does his mother do?"

"She's a nurse. So is his grandmother."

Shelly had once said she wanted to be a nurse, and I had to warn her of the difficulties of dedicating your life to caring for the sick and dying. I didn't even go into AIDS. "Then why not a doctor?" I'd asked. "Why a nurse?" She'd only shrugged.

"His mother drinks." Shelly looked at me, perhaps seeking sympathy.

"That's too bad."

I saw that her white shorts had food stains on them. Her long tan legs were perfect except for a line of tiny brown scabs where she'd cut her shin shaving. There was the slight smell of chlorine and shampoo about her, from her summer lifeguard job. She was easy with her lovely body, entirely comfortable in a swimsuit as I had never been in my life.

"She's real mean to him."

I picked up the remote and lowered the volume, grateful for this torrent of information.

"His mother doesn't like him 'cause she doesn't like his father. She gets mad because he goes to see his father sometimes. He doesn't get along with his sister either."

"Where's his father?" I asked.

She shrugged.

"In jail?"

She hesitated. "I think so. He wants me to go meet him."

"In jail?" I couldn't help the note of panic in my voice. My alarm cut Shelly off. I waited for her to expand, but she didn't. She shook her hair and leaned forward, pulling it in front of her face.

I tried to sound matter-of-fact. "What's he in jail for?"

She was examining the ends of her hair. They were always split, she claimed. Always in need of expensive conditioning, when actually, I argued, her hair would be fine and beautiful if she just wouldn't be forever bleaching or dyeing it. Yet I knew she was only trying to control what small part of her world she could.

"Oh, he was an accountant or something like that." She pretended to take it all in stride.

I didn't answer that it wasn't necessarily a crime to be an accountant. A white-collar criminal? I wondered. An accountant for a drug lord, as they're commonly referred to, a nearly religious term? But I knew from past experience that if I ever found out the whole or even the partial truth it would be more complicated than I could guess.

"How old is his sister?"

"Fifteen," Shelly said impatiently. I was asking too many questions, my time was up.

"Have you met them?"

She only shrugged again, and I sighed at more evidence of

how Shelly prowled the city. I never knew for certain where she was. She met guys on buses, in the subway, at the drugstore. She was open to experience, she said. Again and again I had pointed out the danger. But at sixteen she felt invulnerable. The goal was excitement, that heady elixir of romance and passion.

"That's sad," I said. "To have such a screwed-up family."

"Ours is too," she said without hesitation. Her two-tone hair was now standing out around her head like Zeus's. She became stone still, preparing for my response but not looking at me. I felt the familiar heat of anger surge through my body. I stood up and carried our dishes into the kitchen, biding my time in an attempt at calm, but I couldn't leave it alone.

I returned. "Your father isn't in jail!" I was demanding fairness from her.

"Yeah, but you're divorced."

I tried to swallow my outrage, sat down and lifted the newspaper again. Read one paragraph twice. Arlo meowed, his voice surprisingly soprano for such a macho-looking cat. I rose and went to the door, and leaned to pet him, but he was impatient with my touch and eager to take up his nocturnal prowl.

"Be careful out there, kid," I called to him. I stood with the door open and watched him trot down the steps. The night city air seemed to me too to have an appealing freedom. But I returned to Shelly, my joy and my burden.

"Your father may be in the woods a lot, but he's not in jail. My goodness! Your father is an honorable man." Sometimes I wondered whether Shelly was just waiting for the very sound of my slightly contained rage.

"Dee's father could be too," she said. "He's black. Who knows if he should really be in jail?"

I had to admire her strategy. It was as if she'd planned the whole discussion for this climactic moment. It was brilliant how she played me. She'd heard me rail about the poor schools for blacks, about their lack of jobs and opportunities, about the practice of incarcerating so many young black men rather than dealing with the social problems that led to crime and drug use and incarceration.

"Most people are in jail for a good reason," I said emphatically. But Shelly upped it again.

"Daddy could have gone to jail. . . ."

I slapped the paper closed and stared at her. She was looking at the TV, a clenched fist before her lips. She'd never gone that far, never before addressed, much less attributed blame to, her father's professional problems. I let the charge hang painfully in the air, too emotionally swamped to react.

Knowing she'd gone too far, Shelly backed off. "He has my dogs." Like a child. Sad. Sorry for herself. Outrageous.

I turned away and felt my anger subside.

"Yeah, he does have your dogs. I'm sorry about that," I managed, and wondered if there would ever be a time when we could be friends, when we wouldn't be pulling against each other in some endless daily tug-of-war.

Shelly stood up.

"Well, Shelly, love, I hope you'll be careful." I tried to say this lightly, but the words fell ominously, even to my ears. "Use your head," I added. I knew this was in part a way of getting back at her for her unfair charge. I was raising a threatening flag and once more demonstrating my position of authority.

"If you say something about AIDS, I'm gonna scream!" She was suddenly furious. "We're just friends."

She gathered the shoe box with her nail accessories, leaving cotton balls and a pile of used tissues on the table, preparing for retreat. Before she'd wanted to be a nurse, she'd considered being a veterinarian, then a lawyer. Once she talked of joining the Peace Corps. Now she wanted to manage a nail salon. What had happened?

I cut off the TV and carried her discarded cotton balls and tissues to the kitchen, where I finished loading the dishwasher. Her music went on, too loud, and then I heard her move back and forth between her bedroom and the bathroom, and the rattle of the water pipes as she prepared for a typically long splashy shower.

I read the paper while I waited to run the dishwasher; I didn't want the water pressure to vary during her shower. The president had nominated a black judge of no great distinction for the Supreme Court the month before. Criticism was rising. The Soviet Union was dissolving. A teenager had been shot in D.C. and both his brother and his father were furloughed from prison to attend the funeral.

When I went upstairs to bed, totally spent, I saw that, instead of being in her nightclothes, Shelly was dressed to go out, her clean flowing hair still damp as she talked on her phone. She wore a tight black miniskirt with black hose, a white overblouse that hung off one shoulder and revealed a lacy white vest underneath. I paused in the doorway of her cluttered room, the room with what seemed a thousand teddy bear eyes.

"Don't you think it's a little late to go out? It's nearly eleven."

"Hold on," she said into the phone. And to me, "I'm spending the night with Miranda," she announced. Annoyed that I'd interrupted her conversation, she went back to the phone.

The air soured between us, and I was too weary to repair it.

"It's too late to go out, Shelly, it's not safe," I stated emphatically. Miranda lived only two blocks away.

Shelly put her hand over the mouthpiece and spoke impatiently. "Oh, she's going to meet me halfway. And it's not that late. And I've got school next week." She said "school" as if she were saying "prison."

She turned her back to me. I didn't believe her. She was far too dressed up for going to Miranda's. She wore her nose ring and long clangy-looking earrings, green iridescent eye shadow and dark mascara. She was probably planning on a late night in a go-go bar where kids were forever being shot. Could there be anything in the world more dangerous than falling for a black rapper? I let myself admit that fact for the first time.

She sprayed cologne on her hair, her neck, her arms as she continued on the phone. I moved to my own room to muster my resources. It was only two days ago that she'd been gone all night. Should I phone Miranda's mother, and thereby demonstrate that I didn't trust Shelly? Should I risk a fight? Should I simply resign myself to tolerating her careless endangerment?

I looked out my window onto the dark empty street below. Then I went back to Shelly's room and told her I was going to call Miranda's mother as soon as she was off the phone.

"I have to go," she said into the phone. She slammed the receiver down and followed me to my bedroom, then stopped in the doorway. To step inside, it seemed, would somehow compromise her. She was wearing clunky black shoes I'd never seen before, with gold buckles and high heels. She stood with her hands on her waist, the way I did when I was angry.

"I just went through this on Saturday," I said calmly. "Worrying about you all night."

She turned away with an angry hoot, then turned back. "You treat me like a child!" Her voice was shrill and hysterical. She fluffed her damp hair.

"Shelly, you know it's not safe going out this time of night."

"Miranda's waiting for me!"

"Well, I'm sorry, you'll have to call her and tell her you're not coming."

"You're not being fair!" she shouted.

"I'm trying to keep you safe," I said uneasily.

Then the tears came, followed by more accusations, always right there at her fingertips. I was so old-fashioned. So unreasonable, so old, out of touch, unsophisticated. Why did she have to be an only child! What a fate! She wished her father were here. She wished she lived with him. Why in the world didn't she live with her father—he wouldn't be so mean! She wished everything in the world weren't so screwed up! She wished I'd let her live in peace! She displayed her angry young face, the splotched makeup, the contorted, shattering sobs.

"I am *not* staying here! I hate you!" She ran to her bedroom.

"If you leave this house you'll be punished," I called after her, my voice tight. She came out of her room with a packed pink duffel bag and fled crying down the stairs. The slam of the front door was like a slap, followed by silence; then came the familiar settling of remorse, of wanting to rewind the evening and try again for a happy ending.

I sat on the side of my bed. Surely there was some way to avoid such a scene, such enmity. After a minute I went downstairs to make sure the front door was locked. I left a light on in the living room and the chain unlatched in case she returned; Marcus claimed the chain was useless if someone really wanted to get inside. I moved from room to room, as though looking to see whether the explosion upstairs had shifted things below. In the kitchen I discovered I had forgotten to run the dishwasher. I turned the knob, and the sound of water, of something responding properly, was comforting. What kind of woman, I asked myself, is empowered by her dishwasher working?

I carried the newspaper upstairs with me, knowing that now it would take me a while to get to sleep; I might even have to resort to a crossword puzzle. I stopped in Shelly's room and pushed some of her dirty clothes into her hamper. The smell of her spray cologne hung in the air. I picked up the small, nearly empty bottle of Charlie, what she called her trademark fragrance. Standing there holding that small bottle, I felt torn between wanting to punish her for the distress she caused me and feeling overcome with sadness for her unhappiness. If we weren't enemies I could buy her a new bottle, a present for starting her last year of high school. Then we might live happily ever after. I stared at her favorite bear resting on her pillow and was tempted to carry it to my own bed.

In my room I turned on my old TV to one of the late-night talk shows, which I usually avoided. I would have to consider punishment—a word, a concept, I hated.

Undressing for bed, I contemplated the TV-mogul parents who'd no doubt come up with the idea of late-night talk shows, thinking of all the viewers like themselves waiting at home for their beloved teens to reappear. They'd realized, in some moment of misery, how many millions of us needed a laugh, even just one laugh, to help us make it through the night.

Evenings on the orange-hat patrol I make a point of studying the sky. When there are trees all around, as there are in the District—a city famed for its corridors of elms and its breathtaking cherry blossoms like mounds of pink snow in spring—you forget to look up: not like Texas, where the sky makes its presence known whenever you exit a building. Evidence of eternity, Mama says. And it is true that in Texas you are often reminded of being merely a speck in a vast, mysterious universe—which is maybe the reason people there are so into religion. That vast sweep of the heavens inspires questions. The perpetual presence of the horizon has a lot to do with the Texas personality: the never-ending juxtaposition of person against sky leads to great striving, spiritual quest, and insecurity. Even in cities in Texas that sky is the constant backdrop, and often the highways are elevated above the land, so you move like a child's toy beneath the heavens.

In the beginning, I must admit, I had mixed feelings about this whole orange-hat business. I mean we pay mucho taxes for cops and security, and they know better than we do that the Jamaican nightclub on the corner, the Bluebird Bar & Grill, named for those lovely and disappearing birds, distributes drugs. Nowadays it's easier to find drugs than bluebirds. So why don't the police do something about it, since they're getting paid to? Why on earth do we largely innocent civilians have to be out there strolling around on hot and cold nights when we could be alone and peacefully nervous in our individual domiciles? But I go for the fellowship, as Mama would say. I enjoy being with my neighbors, especially Doreen, a straight-talking woman with a sense of humor who's become a real friend. And that's the way we urban nonchurchgoing folk communicate and look after one another and form a community. Otherwise we'd never talk, except in times of crisis, when police cars or fire trucks or ambulances appear on our blocks and we undo our deadbolts and safety chains and venture outdoors to identify the trouble. Some people even say our stroll is effective. Criminals, or those people tempted by illegal activity, are not fond of an assortment of ordinary citizens wearing orange hats, staring and sometimes pointing cameras at them in the middle of illicit deals. Also, I've learned over the past months that many citizens are grateful there are people showing concern for the quality of life in our neighborhood.

Typically we orange-hats walked the commercial blocks—past the Jamaican grocery, the Jamaican nightclub, the Korean mom-and-pop grocery, the hamburger franchise that provided the neighborhood with perpetual litter, the Chinese carry-out, the Korean dry cleaner's, and the Korean gas station—from eight until ten on weekend nights. We observed and sometimes took photos, acted friendly to the street people, and now and then suggested to an obviously overamped citizen that he or she seek treatment. For the drug dealers our patrol was basically a process of unwelcome attention.

On this last Saturday in August, this Saturday that would change my life, I was looking up as I often did, thinking I might see a UFO or a falling star. Doreen laughed at my heavenly search, and Reverend Ezra Thompson predicted I'd eventually break into prayer, as he often does when we encounter drug activity on the street. So there we were, five of us that night, strolling along the central commercial street of our neighborhood, Doreen with a two-way radio, wearing an African-print caftan, me in jeans and a loose T-shirt, and Reverend Thompson in an open-necked dress shirt and slacks. There were two other men: a white lawyer I'd known casually in my earlier life with Tom, who didn't seem to recognize me in my orange hat, and a short stocky black man with a camera around his neck, who worked for the city's social services.

The city had been eerily empty that week, as it often is in late August. Mrs. Moore, Pal's benefactor, had a bed of snow-on-the-mountains growing beside her front steps; those cool, refreshing green-and-white flowers were one of the consolations of spending August in the District of Columbia.

There was a full moon that hot and muggy night, or what looked like a full moon. I wasn't sure the orange-hats should be out on such a night, when those so inclined go crazier, but there we were. The moon hung over the neon sign of Thrifty Liquor, visible through the branches of an aging sycamore, and shone on young oaks in their tree boxes struggling through their first summer on the streets. The stars were mostly obscured by the city lights; again, not like Texas, where the stars are so many and so close and you sometimes feel you can reach out and pull one toward you. But there were a few stars, and a few jets to boot, zooming south toward National Airport. While on patrol I always thought of my grandmother, sitting on her front porch in Paris, Texas, rocking in the swing and telling stories, calling out to passing neighbors. How safe the night had seemed, how quiet and peaceful.

Reverend Thompson, pastor of the New Southern Rock Church of God, had been to the hearing about the Bluebird Bar & Grill that past week. The neighborhood had generated a petition to prevent the nightclub from obtaining a renewal of its liquor license. The Bluebird was the site not only of drug dealing now, but also of three murders the year before. Rumor had it that the bar was controlled by a Jamaican "posse," which in the hierarchy of urban gangs was considered a particularly ruthless type. Doreen was brave enough on occasion to confront customers entering or leaving the Bluebird to warn them that the establishment was suspected as a site for drug dealing and could be raided at any moment. Needless to say, the proprietor was not happy with her asides or pleased about her periodic phone calls to the local police precinct updating our suspicions and offering license tag numbers.

"The hearing was a bad scene," Reverend Thompson reported as we strolled. "We waited two hours for it to start. Then the Bluebird's lawyer arrived and called me an Oreo, accusing me of trying to clear the neighborhood of black businesses. Then, on top of that, they postponed the hearing."

"Um, um, um . . ." Doreen sympathized. We'd made one dawdling trip up and down our five-block stretch, seeing the usual street-corner loiterers, to whom we were curiosities to enliven their boring nights. Occasionally we passed people heading for the Chinese carry-out or the Korean grocery for cigarettes, beer, or a Lotto ticket. There were four pay phones along those blocks. All of them were being used as we walked past, usually by young men with beepers on their belts who watched our perambulations with hostile eyes.

"Brown Bear, this is Hot Honey. We're heading up number twenty-five. Five of us. We'll call in later," Doreen radioed to our member at home, who was usually watching TV as he monitored our mission.

"Ten four," Brown Bear responded. If there was trouble he could instantly alert the police.

We turned into an alley where a number of homeless men were drinking and playing cards by candlelight. We greeted them and they called to us; by now they were accustomed to this odd assortment of strollers in orange hats. In front of an apartment house a young dealer sat by his window awaiting customers. His runners, teenagers wearing droopy pants—a style Shelly referred to as "the sag"—lounged about on the steps, talking and laughing. A car roared through a red light at an intersection, leaving the bomp-bomp-bomp of rap music behind as it sped away.

As we passed the Bluebird, a departing patron held the door ajar long enough to give us a quick rush of cold air from inside, a glimpse of the yellow lights over the bar, and a whiff of the stale odor of alcohol and cigarettes and too many bodies pent up too long without sunshine or fresh air. A large shiny white Lincoln with Maryland tags came gliding up the street slowly and stopped in front of the Bluebird. It sat low to the ground like a boat, with the lights pulsing. A nice-looking young man, whom I'd seen driving a baby-blue sports car often parked in the Bluebird's alley, emerged from the bar and grill and sidled up to the car window.

"How you folks doing tonight?" Reverend Thompson greeted him. The young man's name was Arnold, his street name Sugar T. He was one of the dealers who ignored us. But then he probably didn't do much business till after ten, and he knew that our perambulations were only a gesture, a minor annoyance.

"Here we go," Doreen said.

"Nice car," one of our men noted to no one in particular.

"Looks like a big slippery fish," Reverend Thompson said in his resonant preacher's voice. The Lincoln paused only long enough for the driver to speak to Sugar T, then slid up the block slowly, as if on oil, and turned right without stopping at the red light.

"He'll be back," Reverend Thompson said. We stood at the corner watching. Across the street, the glowing shelves of bottles inside Thrifty Liquor went dark as the manager locked the door behind the last customer. It was nine o'clock.

A moment later, the Lincoln turned onto the avenue again and pulled up slowly to double-park in front of the bar. The driver turned on his flashing emergency lights, and soon Sugar T came out of the bar and sauntered over to the driver's window; he braced himself casually as the window was lowered. Sugar T wore black pants, a black shirt, and a wide brown leather belt. He was trim and attractive; in a suit he might have been mistaken for a corporate lawyer.

"Uh-uh, something's going down," Doreen said.

The short man with the camera stepped to the curb and took a picture of the Lincoln's tags. The driver punched the horn angrily and sped off, and Sugar T retreated into the bar.

"He won't be back anytime soon," Reverend Thompson said.

"At least not between eight and ten." Doreen laughed. We moved down the block, past the gas station on the corner, where the owner had planted the edges of his property with flowers and shrubs and trained pyracantha to encircle the streetlight. We walked past the beauty shop and the record store, boarded up since a drug bust earlier in the month. The police had pulled all the fixtures and merchandise from the shops onto the sidewalk and strung yellow plastic tape around the area after arresting the shop owners for selling drugs.

Across the street a young woman in tight jeans and high-heeled boots called to us in angry, indistinguishable words.

"Stoned," Doreen announced. The woman sat down on the curb and held her head. Doreen and Reverend Thompson crossed the street and spoke to her, probably suggesting a shelter or counseling. The woman listened, then walked unsteadily up the block.

We resumed our stroll and encountered two girls carrying sacks from a fast-food restaurant. Their movement was like a challenge, slow and arrogant: Don't mess with me, they seemed to be saying. One of them, heavyset, wore tight yellow spandex shorts. Her companion, in black shorts, was reed thin. They both wore oversized cheap gold earrings like those Shelly wears sometimes, with names of rap groups carved on them. Their hair was cut in the style of the moment: asymmetrical, one side a neck-length swath half covering an eye and the other side short, nearly shaved, mannish. They were maybe Shelly's age, or as old as Doreen's youngest daughter, Martha, who was studying at Morehouse. Martha planned to pursue law at Yale. She dreamed of becoming the first black woman Supreme Court justice. She said things to Doreen like, "Okay, Mama, don't you get into trouble with that orange-hat business and ruin my chances for a Supreme Court appointment." As the two girls moved past, ignoring us, I wondered whether they knew Dee. Whether he'd ever be successful enough to have earrings to represent him.

"Sweethearts," Doreen called out to the girls, "you know you all gonna have to have plastic surgery you keep wearing those heavy earrings?"

The girls shrugged and walked on, leaving the heavy odor of fried food behind them.

"They can't think of the future," Reverend Thompson said. "They're just prisoners of their momentary appetites. I know them well." Then in a louder, yet still mellifluous voice he told them, "You young women have a good evening, you hear?" The thin girl glanced over her shoulder and smiled.

Reverend Thompson remarked at how quiet a night it was. Later I looked at my horoscope in the newspaper: "Lunar position emphasizes major domestic adjustment, highlights romance, intrigue, mystery, physical attraction," it said. I had just noticed the moon passing beyond Thrifty Liquor; it hung westward over Rock Creek Park and the zoo. Would a full moon wake the pandas in their air-conditioned glass rooms and the lesser pandas sleeping in trees outside with their lush tails hanging earthward, I wondered. Were the white tigers sleeping, or did they pace under that moon with some blood memory of freedom still coursing through their veins?

Across the street, in front of the corner grocery store, a small foreign car with its emergency lights flashing was parked heading the wrong direction in a bus zone. Now came the second convergence in the evening's lunar alignment: A small man with long dark hair, wearing a loose flower-print shirt, entered the grocery store. There was a nervousness about him that caught my attention, that and his momentary pause at the door.

As I later found out from Jeri, the store owner, Rodrigo Rodriguez moved straight to the cash register, where he spit out a few words of heavily accented English. Jeri, standing behind the counter, weary and eager to end his working day, didn't understand the man's flawed English; but sensing danger in the young man's intensity, he replied in Korean rather than his customary unreliable English. In this moment of total failure of communication inside this small, close store crammed with the cheap detritus of convenience, the two men must each have recognized the other as a fellow stranger in a foreign land, disappointed and maybe disillusioned by his unfulfilled dreams. Then, Jeri reported later, Rodrigo Rodriguez shoved his right hand into his shirt and pulled out a Smith & Wesson .38 and pointed it at Jeri.

Meanwhile, in the back of the store, Viktor Hajek, a forty-two-year-old journalist from Prague, who had parked the wrong way on the street, was selecting a suitable broom for his new townhouse. As he inspected the two styles of brooms, he was unaware of the confrontation at the other end of the store, until he heard the sharp whomp of the .38. Though he was so close, Rodrigo Rodriguez had managed to miss Jeri: he had shut his eyes and nervously tilted the gun to the right, thus blasting through a shelf of cigarettes and the window behind them. Jeri, despite a bad back, ducked under the counter while Rodrigo Rodriguez tried but failed to force open the cash register. Then, suddenly, in true journalist style, Viktor Hajek rushed to the front of the store.

Had Rodrigo Rodriguez been a true killer, one of those whose self-esteem hangs by such a thin filament that death is an option at the slightest hint of a pejorative tone, he might have shot both Jeri and Viktor Hajek. Had we orange-hats been slower up the block, the bullet might have struck one of us instead of the innocent curb across the street. But since it was the first time Rodrigo Rodriguez had carried a gun, one he had only borrowed for the evening from a neighbor who was to receive a portion of the take, he simply panicked and instead of shooting again bolted. He fled with Viktor Hajek right behind him, carrying a broom. Our patrol had paused in front of the door of the grocery, with its "Play D.C. Lotto Here" sign, when the bullet passed through the front window, leaving a star-shaped crack before disappearing across the street. Then Rodrigo Rodriguez burst forth from the store, waving the gun and running into our midst. I was struck first full-bodied by Rodrigo

Rodriguez and then, while still spinning but upright, by a larger body carrying a wooden broom. The second blow sent me down to the sidewalk, headfirst and hard, my orange hat falling into a tree box, my cheek scraping then settling against the rough dirty concrete, a cigarette butt nearby at eye level. I heard the whining advance of the camera, and Doreen's shrill command to Brown Bear to phone the police, and Reverend Thompson's voice raised in either a prayer or a curse—strange how they could sound the same. It was a lot like the first time I'd ice-skated, our first winter in D.C. I'd quickly grown overconfident, and soon I fell on my face. I saw stars now, as I had then, not the awe-inspiring stars of the vast Texas skies, but rather the sad, distant ones of D.C. And I heard Pal's howl, and shortly afterward, a siren.

"Congratulations to you," Doreen said the next morning when she phoned. "The first orange-hat casualty in the city, at least that we know of." You'd think I'd won the lottery.

"You know, right now I don't feel like it's so wonderful."

"Oh, honey, how you feeling?"

"Spacy. Kind of like Willie Nelson the time he got drunk one time too many and his wife sewed him up in a sheet and beat him with a broom."

"I didn't know about that," Doreen said. "But I get your drift."

"Like I've been hit hard on the head with a broom, and a lot of other places too."

A mild concussion, they had said at the emergency room. And the confusion was enough to leave you mentally impaired—the police, Rodrigo Rodriguez, the ambulance, the orange-hats, and Jeri bent double with his pained back.

"The newspaper may do a story on you," Doreen said. "They don't often find crime and humor in the same story."

"It's not humor, Doreen—the proper word is 'assault.' And I don't want any publicity about it. I don't feel very humorous, and besides that I'm embarrassed. How many people fall inner-city victim to a broom?"

"Well, you were victim of more than a broom. Is there anything I can do for you?"

"No, thanks." Then I reconsidered. "Unless you could come over here and inspire Shelly to write her college application essays."

Doreen laughed. Martha, the scholastic wonder woman, had probably started working on her college essays as soon as she finished grade school. Doreen's two older daughters were also success stories. One taught music in high school, and the other, a social worker with a five-year-old son, whom Doreen adored, had just presented Doreen with twin grandbabies.

I looked out the window near my bed and saw the large Reverend Thompson jogging circles in his backyard. "Thompson is running," I said to Doreen, and we chuckled; only the laughter hurt my sore stomach. Actually, we worried that he might have a heart attack some morning on his daily circles and felt obliged to watch him even though we knew he'd be humiliated if he found out we were onto his secret jogging.

Later in the morning I phoned Marcus. The sound of his voice was reassuring. After I told him what had happened, Marcus laughed, and so for the first time I managed to see a little humor in the evening's bizarre events.

"But are you okay?" Marcus asked.

"Yeah, I'm okay. Course I could have been killed." I wanted him to know that the incident might have been serious. "It was pretty scary, and I'm sore everywhere I have a nerve. I look like I've been in the ring with Sugar Ray."

"I've been telling you patrolling like that is dangerous. You ought to leave law enforcement up to the police." Even Marcus pronounced it "*po*-lice."

"Oh, it's not usually dangerous."

"It doesn't take but once to cash in."

I moaned.

Talking to Marcus made me almost want to be at work. That job would be unbearable if it weren't for him.

"Just turn your mind to those Caribbean breezes. Rum drinks with flowers. Cats. Fleas. Blue skies and cholera."

"Cholera!" I said.

"That's what I heard last night at some embassy do. I gotta run now, Rosemary."

"Oh my God," I said.

"You got it."

LATER THAT MORNING Mama phoned. Shelly had called her the night before around midnight to tell her about my orange-hat incident—exactly what I would *not* want Shelly to do, worry Mama about my involvement with urban crime. The only way I know Shelly might have concern for my welfare is that she does take it upon herself to phone Mama now and then when I've committed some indiscretion she thinks her grandmother should know about.

Mama talked for several minutes about how irresponsible it was for me as a mother to take a chance like that, doing that ridiculous orange-hat business when I had a child I was supposed to be looking after. I let Mama go on for a while, and then appealed to her political nature by reminding her that I was, like her, only trying to be a useful citizen by doing what I could to make our streets safe.

"Well, I'm glad we haven't had to do that kind of thing," Mama said. "Even though we do seem to be in the midst of a crime wave. Lloyd McKitchen shot his brother-in-law last Monday night." I told her I was sorry to hear that, and asked about the mayors' conference in Dallas.

She reported that the trip had been a big success. Aunt Lucille hadn't snored but once, and then only briefly, and they'd had delicious meals, and Art Moser had been pleasant company. Mama had gone to four and a half workshops and shaken hands with both gubernatorial candidates.

I told her I thought it was extraordinarily Christian of her to shake hands with a Republican, she being a yellow-dog Democrat, but she said she didn't want to be rude or get her town into trouble. Would that all our public servants were so conscientious, I told her.

That afternoon I received a floral display, as they're called, beyond the twenty-two-dollar secretary-basic, with roses and daisies and lavender and baby's breath.

Apologies, the card read. *Hope you feel better. Viktor Hajek.*

At about five o'clock Viktor Hajek appeared at my door. Although we'd not met formally, I knew he was the man who'd leaned over me as I lay on the sidewalk the previous night, holding my hand and asking if I could hear him. For a few moments in all that confusion, I thought I'd died and gone to a heaven where people spoke in East European accents.

Standing there looking at him now, I felt a rush of gratitude and a connection, like the sensation a good song gives you, when all at once the lights turn on in your soul. I wished I weren't barefoot and wearing my knockabout Redskin shorts and T-shirt, with assorted bruises, no makeup, and my hair au naturel, which in my case means frizzy and out of control.

"You're the man with the broom?"

"Yes, yes, the man with the broom," he repeated. "Unfortunately," he added with his weighty accent. Then he smiled warmly, reminding me of Viktor Laszlo in *Casablanca* lighting cigarettes for himself and Ingrid somewhere in Hollywood's idea of Casablanca, which I was supposed to replicate in Sainte-Marie. Viktor Hajek was tall, with a rather square jaw, curly grayish-brown hair, and dark brown eyes that smiled at me through horn-rimmed glasses. He had a friendly, honest face with a healthy glow; he looked like someone you'd trust to help you if your car broke down one dark and stormy night.

I unlatched the safety chain and opened the door. He probably couldn't appreciate my sacrifice, my letting the air-conditioning run outside onto the humid sidewalk. Violence or this man or the position of the stars had led me to break with my normally energy-cautious habits and fling a few kilowatts into the air like confetti. "Thank you for sending the flowers. They're absolutely lovely, but you didn't have to do that." I was surprised to hear myself sounding breathless.

"But it gives me the opportunity to see you again," he said, in such an utterly and convincingly concerned manner that I was light-headed. "How are you feeling?"

"Better," I said. "But I also feel kind of crazed. Being terrorized like that tears you away from real life. I feel like I should go white-water rafting. Or travel to Tibet. Or Vladivostok. I've always wanted to go to Vladivostok." *What am I saying!* I wondered to myself. *He'll think you're a lunatic!* Though it was true I'd always wanted to go to Vladivostok.

"I understand what you mean. Though actually Vladivostok is a very dull and ugly city."

"Oh, I'm sorry." I was truly disappointed. "But maybe I wouldn't find it dull and ugly."

"You would, I believe." There was humor in his eyes, and I smiled, immediately convinced.

Then I saw that he'd parked his car across the street, again heading in the wrong direction. I suggested he might be ticketed for that.

He glanced at his car, then turned back and studied me with his sincere brown eyes. "You know, I was unaware of that. I have been living in Mexico. There it is so casual."

There was an intimate whisper to his voice. He shrugged and smiled. "Please excuse me." He strode comfortably down the sidewalk, opened and closed the gate. I looked after him: Why in the world did I care whether Viktor Hajek was parked the wrong way? In my heart of hearts I didn't want the whole world parking in the right direction. But maybe, since I couldn't alter Shelly's direction, I was trying to set the rest of the world straight around her.

Viktor Hajek waved from inside his car. And feeling a bit deflated that I'd more or less chased him away, I went inside and closed the door. In a few minutes Viktor Hajek was back ringing the doorbell; he had parked, I could see, in accordance with District principles. This time I was embarrassed not to invite him in. Where I grew up we were taught it was rude to make people stand at the door, and even worse to shout through it, as I sometimes did after dark. Soothed by the intriguing face and the warmth just the sight of him created in my lonely heart, I invited him in. He was a foreigner, and after all, we now believed foreigners were safer than we were.

I poured us both wine—which perhaps I shouldn't have done, given my trembly, nervous state—and we settled across from each other in the living room, separated by three feet of supercharged air. I asked him if he'd ever played Shakespeare.

"Shakespeare?" he asked me.

"You look like an actor. And your voice suggests an actor." I thought this was a compliment, but he wasn't sure how to take it.

"No, I am a journalist," he said. "Only a journalist. There are many journalists here, right?"

"Millions." I exaggerated somewhat.

Viktor Hajek smiled at that. "Too many, I understand. But I do have a friend who is a playwright. Does that matter?"

"That's close."

Viktor Hajek wore what I called a Budapest suit—double-breasted, dark, and too heavy for Washington in August—with a conservative maroon tie and soft, narrow foreign shoes. On his left hand was a handsome gold ring with a recessed garnet in the center. I felt less wounded just looking at him.

"Ah, Poulenc," he said. It took me a moment to realize he was referring to the music playing on the radio. I could count on probably one finger the number of men I knew who could identify Poulenc right off the bat.

He surveyed the living room carefully. "What a nice room."

I thanked him and looked around. It was nice but, as I explained to him, in a state of perpetual disorder despite my diligent straightening and picking up. It was painted orangish terra-cotta, which was popular at the time; nearly all my neighbors had one room painted a similar color. The more affluent neighbors had orange rooms that had been sponge-painted or textured in some way. Since our row houses were laid out basically the same, we struggled to personalize the decor. Why we all decided to paint one room orange I couldn't understand, I told Viktor Hajek.

From the authority of my black leather chair he explained that he had just moved to Washington. "It is a magnificent city. Quite sophisticated." Perhaps he'd expected us to be running around in overalls or cowboy outfits.

I agreed it was beautiful and lively. "For all its ill repute, it's fascinating, though it helps to have a strong sense of humor."

"I believe that is true of every city. Have you lived here long?" he asked me in his breathy voice. Half a century, I thought to myself, but I said, "Since the seventies," and imagined myself aging before his eyes like the portrait of Dorian Gray.

He was from Prague, he told me.

"Prague, the new dream capital, where all the young are going these days because it is beautiful like Paris, but cheap unlike Paris, and fairly friendly to Americans, unlike most places in the world."

"I bought a townhouse up the street," he said. "Once before I lived in the United States. North Americans are so competent."

"Compared to what?"

"India. Mexico. Where I have been living. Where it takes something like an attitude of Zen to go about one's life."

He leaned forward as he talked, and that gesture of intimacy was extremely appealing, vulnerable as I was after the previous night's experience.

"We're not so competent anymore," I responded.

He smiled, apparently surprised by my criticism. He told me he was a correspondent for a European news service. I told him I'd been a journalist in an earlier life and had hated to leave the job. He followed me sympathetically as I spoke, and met my eyes easily. When he turned to examine the stack of books sitting on the coffee table between us, I looked hard at him. Except for Marcus, I'd not let myself focus on a man in a while. He could be younger than Tom and I. And obviously of a different category. He didn't spring from the good ole boys I knew so well. I had no idea how it would feel to be in the arms of a man in a Budapest suit.

My mind snagged on that thought, but Viktor Hajek was now giving me the details on Rodrigo Rodriguez, whom he'd obviously investigated thoroughly. Rodriguez did not seem a criminal type, Viktor Hajek said. And in fact this was his first offense.

"Oh yes, I know the reaction," I said. "You're absolutely terrorized by the guy, then he's arrested and you find out he's a sixteen-year-old who never learned to read."

"But it does not explain . . ." Viktor Hajek paused, searching for a word.

"The viciousness," I interjected for him, and wished I hadn't. The filling-in-the-blanks habit, the result of desperate attempts to communicate with a teenager.

"Exactly," Viktor Hajek said, but as if he were too genteel to say the word "vicious."

"We have become very cold-blooded." I realized he might not be sure what I was referring to—Rodrigo Rodriguez's willingness to stick a gun in a store owner's face or the condition of having sixteen-year-olds on the street who carry guns but can't read. I supposed it applied in both instances.

"I wondered," Viktor Hajek said after a moment, hesitantly, "would you mind . . . would you mind if I wrote about the incident last night?" I wondered if this was simply a ploy for more friendly association, but then told myself not to fantasize. He's a newsman. He describes the world as it happens to him. "Could I interview you?" he said gently, as if making some intrusive or lewd request. "Not right now, of course," he added. Certainly a different type of journalist, I thought, with this consideration of the victim.

"I wouldn't mind," I told him, thinking, Especially since it will be published in a language I am unlikely to know in my current life. But I was disappointed that his interest might be only the Washington crime story, and not some feeling of personal responsibility for my accident or the memory of my being so fetching lying there on the sidewalk beside my orange hat. Nevertheless, I smiled and agreed to be interviewed, willing to provide some guidance in this urban mystery. After all, he'd gone into a store and become involved in American crime soon after arriving here. How easy it was to become a statistic. Now, if ever called for jury duty, when asked if we'd been the recent victim of a crime, we could both raise our hands, along with most everybody else.

Then I set out the good-neighbor policy. I told Viktor Hajek about the nearest hardware store, the best place to order pizza, the only dry cleaner's that didn't just press the spots in, the best nearby bookstore, and the place to pick up the Sunday *New York Times* and buy a bagel or croissant at the same time. He nodded politely. I told him about the Neighborhood Watch group. I told him about Mrs. Anita Nance and how we live with a lot of ghosts and how some nights when she's lying in bed she hears Duke Ellington music drifting in her windows.

"Fascinating," Viktor Hajek said. Then he announced in a rather courtly manner that he had to leave. "It was very good to see you again. I hope you will feel fine soon. I hope you reach Vladivostok one day."

"Maybe I will," I said. And suddenly it came back to me: "You know, I dreamed about you last night!"

"Really. I am flattered," Viktor Hajek said.

"I don't remember it well, but we were somewhere I'd never been."

"Vladivostok?"

"I don't think so. It was foreign and beautiful."

"Prague," he said with confidence. "That was it."

We smiled at each other a moment. Then I stood too quickly, so that walking Viktor Hajek to the door I felt dizzy again. How odd, I thought, this man invading my dreams before I'd really met him.

At the door, looking at Viktor Hajek, I thought how I'd been married long enough to give off "not interested" signals except when I drank warm alcohol. Even if I did find this man attractive, I wasn't sure how to switch signals to Go. The mating game, the ritual of fluffing feathers and prancing about, I'd ceased many moons before. Besides that, I had enough vicarious romance from maternal fear and surveillance to make the very notion seem wearying. God, no, I told myself.

He paused in the doorway and looked at me with curiosity. I couldn't help but feel warmed and pleased.

"Thank you again for the flowers," I told him, meeting his eyes. I turned away, reminding myself that he was probably just another of those Washington transients who so often in this city of dreams make fleeting and insubstantial relationships. Washington, so unlike Mama's stick-in-the-mud town, which people rarely leave. And if and when they do, they're likely to return, lonesome and blue for that dinky hole-in-the-wall the interstate missed, where the telephone poles are taller than the trees.

And so Viktor Hajek walked away, a man who seemed easy with himself, whose attention seemed of value. I stood at the door confronting the heavy air of that late summer day. In the brief time we'd spent together, it had felt highly desirable to be the focus of his smile.

He paused at the gate and looked back. And once again I felt a glow of hope shine through the cobwebs of my romantic heart, and maybe even a small sputter of that long-dormant organ.

JUST AS VIKTOR HAJEK reached his correctly parked car, Shelly and Dee drove up in my gray Escort. It was packed to the gills with boxes and stereo equipment and various types of athletic paraphernalia, including, as I later found out, a collection of weights that no doubt did horrible things to my modest shock absorbers. The radio was blasting loud enough to be heard at the top of the Washington Monument. Shelly had started driving only that year, and she still terrified me with her amateur skills. I watched them get out of the car and walk to the house, Dee's arm around Shelly's shoulders signaling possession. This time he wore jeans and a white T-shirt, not the red sweatsuit. Shelly wore extremely short cutoffs with holes here and there and a loose lifeguard T-shirt over her red Speedo.

After our most recent set-to, she had been denied driving privileges for two weeks, but since Doreen had phoned her from the hospital the night before, she obviously had assumed that my crime emergency and her rescue operation had invalidated the prior restriction. How could I attack her when I myself had just been a victim and they'd come to the rescue?

"I need to talk to you," she said to me after admiring my floral arrangement. We went upstairs, leaving Dee sitting anxiously before the TV. Shelly now as supplicant: I marveled at how our roles shifted back and forth. But at that moment, the recent real-life crime had superseded my mental all-points bulletin for her arrest and I could confront her only with something like weary resignation. My anger was now layered with relief at her safety, and perhaps the simple limitations of my mental capacity to harbor just so much anger or fear. The world goes 'round, and somehow, in some miracle way, the heart and soul are restored.

"Moms," she began, then hesitated.

I made it easy. I turned off the squeaky ceiling fan and asked, "What's all that stuff in the car?" I had a pretty good idea what all that stuff in the car was.

"It's Dee's belongings." She shook her head. She didn't even have to say what she was thinking: How pitiful that he owned so little that it fit into our subcompact car. She began to build her case in the dramatic style I was accustomed to, and as always, I did not fail to marvel at the success of her manner and affect. I began folding laundry in order to anchor myself with the real world.

Shelly's hair was pulled back in a ponytail, with romantic tendrils loose around her face; she wore a gold ring in her nose. Her expression was haggard and desperate, that of one who'd just been released after months of torture and starvation in prison. Or rescued from a coal mine cave-in. Even her fingernails were down to her own basic bitten ones. She sighed heavily before proceeding.

"Dee has to move. His grandmother is breaking up the apartment. His mother and sister have to move too." She seemed near tears. She walked over and made four steady pulls for tissues out of the box beside my bed. She always pulled at least four. I tried to see if they were really tears, but she dabbed at her face with the wad of tissues before I could be sure.

"His grandmother is going to work as a live-in and his mother and sister have to move and he doesn't have anyplace to go." She sat on the side of my bed and watched as I folded a stack of towels. I knew it would never occur to her to help.

"He's really looking hard for a job. He knows that's more important than his music now." She glanced at herself in my dresser mirror and lifted her ponytail, then pulled off the red elastic with small plastic balls that held it, and her two-tone hair fell limply around her face. She fluffed her hair with her right hand as I picked up a towel lumpy with little globs of nail polish and adhesive—obviously used for one of her manicures.

"If he could just stay here a few nights, till he finds someplace else to go . . ." I paused mid-towel to see whether she could possibly be serious. She was. I lifted the towel and folded it again. I felt pleasure at this rare and lucky moment in which she wanted something from me, but at the same time I was angry that she would even ask something so inappropriate.

"Shelly, would you look at this towel?" I held it up for her to see the wanton misuse.

She stared at me as if I were trying to distract her from her suffering. "Mother . . ." she said weightily, pleading for my attention to the significant matter at hand, and raised her left arm to adjust the row of silver bracelets.

It was the oldest story. The orphan-into-the-snowy-night routine.

"Dee has relatives all over the place," I said, inspecting a pot holder with an unfamiliar burn in it. "Even I have heard at least thirty relatives mentioned."

She began to explain in what I called her Greenpeace mode, that supersincere concern-for-the world tone. Her voice was lower, slower, more controlled. It gave me hope that someday it would replace the shrill one I heard so often, the one with a note of hysteria and that rude, contemptuous inner-city rhythm she could assume so well and so quickly.

"He could go stay with his cousin, but his cousin sells drugs and Dee hates to get mixed up with him. Mario could get busted and Dee would be there. . . ." She was encouraging me to imagine the worst.

I lifted a sheet. Obviously, if I didn't let Dee camp on our sofa it would be my fault if he got into trouble and went to jail and ruined his life. I'd heard that kind of argument before. It was a remarkable paradox how helpless I could feel while she could in an instant insinuate that it was within my power to right her tumultuous landscape.

I set the sheet on the bed, trying to maintain my calm in the face of her siege. Behind her hung photographs of her at various ages—the smiling baby, the charming preschooler, the schoolgirl with a little less glow in her eyes. Now, here before me, were the same sculptured face and wide lovely eyes, but with little glow in them at all. Would it ever come back? Did life necessarily have to diminish the hopeful human spirit that shone in the eyes of a happy child?

"You know, Shelly, what you're asking is really inappropriate. Besides being too much to ask. I like Dee. I feel sorry about his situation. I don't doubt he's having a hard time, but . . ."

"Well, Mother, he'll be on the street, and how will he ever get a job then?" She stood, extended her hands, leaned toward me. I could see the fine, smooth texture of her skin, which I feared she was damaging with cheap makeup and too much sun, the small eruptions on either temple that she smeared with a lotion that in turn smeared her pillow cases, those intimate details that only a mother knew.

I turned away from her and toward the window. The crepe myrtles beside Doreen's back porch were a beautifully ripe crimson. Mrs. Thompson's white laundry, composed of underwear, swayed on a clothesline in her backyard. Another neighbor, a retired civil servant, a man I teased Doreen about as having a crush on her, was working in his vegetable garden. I could feel Shelly's plea gathering more and more strength against my reasonable defense. Then she burst forth with both barrels.

"Please, Mother." Suddenly the room seemed airless. Here was the ultimate power play, that word "please." Hearing Shelly say it was like plastic explosives blowing an open sesame to my heart.

I began to fold underwear, and then, in an unprecedented move, Shelly came beside me, took my cotton nightgown from the laundry basket, and folded it, joining me, for once without my having to ask her, in my constant war against chaos and disorder in our single-headed-household lives. For a few moments we stood there in silence, until all of the laundry was neatly folded and stacked in piles across my bed. I felt my inner turmoil being smoothed with each item. This new, groundbreaking cooperation seemed to offer promise of future cooperation, a tantalizing sample of possible order and harmony. Was this worth the outrageous idea of housing Dee?

I began pushing piles of laundry into my drawers, and Shelly lifted her own and ferried them down the hall to her room. She returned to stand in the doorway, facing me hopefully as if I had the power once again to offer her life.

"Shelly," I reasoned, "every sane person on earth would say

that it was a mistake for me to let Dee sleep on our sofa." Off the top of my head I named everyone I could think of who would disapprove: my mother, my ex-husband and her father, Dear Abby, Miss Manners, probably Gandhi and Martin Luther King, Jr., and all the saints who'd ever walked the earth. "Every white and black middle-class person in the world," I added. "And Marcus." God, I thought, what Marcus would say! "There is the weight of the world against this proposition!" Whereupon she began her escalation. Her body tensed and she leaned toward me.

"Why do you have to be like everybody else? You know, Mother, you're always saying people should try to be heroes."

Had I said that? How stupid of me. I felt overwhelmed. Her forces had rushed forward until I was lost, torn, and trampled by her passionate desire for my approval of this outrageous scheme.

"You're always talking about being sensitive to the black world and what problems there are. . . ." She didn't say, "And now you won't even offer your sofa to a needy young black man, a friend," but that was clearly the subtext.

Just then Arlo came marching into the room, and after pausing momentarily to measure the tension, he hightailed it over to Shelly. She lifted his taut body and cradled him in her arms, kissing him on his alley mouth as I had told her a thousand times not to do. Then she shifted him to her shoulder like a baby, and turned her back to me so that Arlo, with his common gray face and wide whiskers, stared at me out of contented yellow-gray eyes. And of course I was moved, won over, and even a little jealous of her passion for this plain and simple creature purring before me.

All at once she turned again and stood the cat on his feet. Just as I was recognizing the emotional blackmail and attempting to harden my melted heart, I had a brainstorm. Does the end justify the means? I asked myself that timeless question.

Could my agreeing lead to a future of hope and possibility—exactly what I had been praying for these past months?

I took a deep breath and faced her. The fact that she was taller than I made me happy for her and sad for me; it usually put me at a disadvantage. I reached up, and in my moment of power touched her hair, paying myself off with this unexpected physical gesture.

"All right, Shelly. You start on the college essays today and finish a decent first draft for them by next weekend," I said. "Then complete them to both our satisfactions." The edges of her mouth began to break into a smile. I paused for emphasis.

"But the minute the essays aren't in progress, he's out. And he's here only for a week, at the most. The very most."

She tossed her hair, and a radiance shone around her. Oh, the joy of making your child happy. How defenseless we are with such power over us. Denying our own best instincts, and the blood memory of decades of schooling and religious training, for this brief moment of sighted joy.

Shelly came to me and hugged me briefly, a rare display.

"And I want you to know, if I have any reason to feel uncomfortable about this, if you take advantage of me . . ." My voice shifted into that awful adult authority mode that rings throughout the world over loudspeakers inside schools and prisons, a sound I hated and hoped was inauthentic to my basic self. Shelly looked hurt, but then her face cleared to open and innocent. "If anything happens, anything suspicious or tacky, he'll be out in a flash." God, I sounded like Mama.

I watched her summon all her delicate strength to challenge me. "Moms, we're just friends," she said, shaking her head at the insult. Then on to the next subject: she was surely world-class in these segues. She wrinkled up her forehead and searched my face, and I realized how seldom she really looked at me.

"Boy, you sure are bunged up, aren't you," she said.

And so, before my threats were properly appreciated in the

humid air of my bedroom, she was on to the next chapter of our lives, and I was left limp with exhaustion. And that was how Dee Taylor was delivered onto our couch in that late summer of the Year of our Lord and the Republicans 1991.

Marcus and I stood in the middle of an abandoned warehouse turned artist's studio off Rhode Island Avenue in northeast D.C., surrounded by a group of huge paintings, great swaths of jungle greens and purples, ocean azures and aquamarines, palmettos and swamp cabbages, mangroves and hanging Spanish moss. It took me a few minutes to realize that within the tropical world of these vivid canvases and in the huge space open to the August heat there lay a sinister atmosphere.

The studio space was in dramatic disrepair. There were large gaps in the floor, the walls in some places exposed the underlying brick, and the skylights were partially broken. The vastness of the area allowed for mounds of rags and mops, and coffee cans of paints and brushes, and ladders and the huge canvases themselves. In the center of this, surrounded by a cloud of cigarette smoke, was a short, wiry man with a scarred face and hostile black eyes. He half sat on a stool near the center of the room, his arms folded across his chest, smoking cigarette after cigarette, then crushing them on the floor at his feet. His sister Cecilia, our interpreter, sat in a sagging chair by the door. As Marcus and I moved from one painting to the next, the painter would occasionally point and grunt at us to watch out for holes in the floor.

Marcus and I believed our first task was to develop name recognition for the island of Sainte-Marie, and what better way to do that than to find some genius from the area. We weren't sure that the painter André Bontemps was a genius, but it seemed a good idea to explore the possibility. It was not unusual in our business to proclaim genius, true or not, if tangible benefits might ensue. We had found André through Cecilia, who worked in our payroll department. When I discovered her, a Sainte-Marie resource right there under our Santa Fe noses, I asked her to lunch, in my ongoing search for all I could learn about the unfortunate isle.

We had sat at a Formica table next to a window where tanned K Street lawyers in silk summer suits passed by. Cecilia had carefully curled dark hair and a wonderful rugged brown face that made me feel as if I were looking into an ancient past. She wore a navy-blue suit made of an inexpensive linenlike material and a polyester print blouse. Her perfect red nails matched her lipstick. When she talked, the gold tooth in the front of her mouth gave the impression she was being photographed through a sunny filter. But despite that, even when she smiled there was a wistfulness about her, which suggested to me that life on Sainte-Marie had not been easy.

She had been in this country for eight years, she told me in her low and halting voice. Her family had come in relays of seniority: her oldest brother arrived first, by boat via Santo Domingo and then Miami, and during the amnesty period applied for citizenship; he then sent for the next brother, and eventually for her. After Cecilia arrived she worked three years as a nanny, studying English and saving money. For those three years she lived in a two-bedroom apartment with her brothers and their families. Later she went on to attend business school, and now she had her own apartment, which she shared with a younger sister and another brother, who had arrived a few months before. And she, like her brothers, worked two jobs. When she finished punching numbers into the computer at Harrison & Associates, she drove to a Virginia suburb, where she worked as a security guard at a mall until ten o'clock weeknights and all day on weekends. It was no surprise her eyes were darkly ringed.

The goal was to bring the entire family to the United States. But earlier in the year Cecilia and her two older brothers had lost all their money when an uninsured savings company suddenly closed its doors. Everything they'd saved to bring the rest of the family from Sainte-Marie was lost—or more precisely, it had been squandered by a flashy Latin American entrepreneur who had made some bad investments. Meanwhile Cecilia's mother had become too sick to leave Sainte-Marie, and Cecilia's sisters remained to care for her.

But despite their problems, Cecilia said, she and her brothers had a network here of fellow islanders and friends. Some holidays there would be more than fifty of them having an all-day cookout in Rock Creek Park. And nearly every week she received a call from some newly arrived Sainte-Marian, whom she would help as best she could. When this person eventually learned English and had a decent job, Cecilia would have a new link in her network.

I asked her if, with all these contacts, she'd thought of going into politics. She smiled her sunny smile, then proceeded to tell me about Sainte-Marie. I had the feeling most people weren't interested in her native island, and she was pleased to talk about it.

"Ah, very poor," she said. "People don't have enough to eat. All try to come to America." She picked up half of her tuna melt and shook her head. "Very sad. Beautiful country, but too much killing." Her father, she said, was killed by the guerrillas. Her cousin was killed by the army. Sainte-Marie had been in political turmoil all her life. Her mother and father had told her that when they were young it was better. They were very poor, but they were safe from soldiers.

Cecilia took a bite of her sandwich. I filled in the silence by telling her I'd never been to the Caribbean but was hoping to go sometime soon. Did it really have that beautiful water?

"Oh, yes." She smiled. "Beautiful." She said she went back at Christmas every year to see her mother. But the year before, her mother didn't know her. We were distracted by a cab driver on Nineteenth Street, who'd left his cab to scream at a bicycle messenger. Then, as if to lighten the mood, Cecilia said her younger brother, the latest to arrive, was a painter.

"A housepainter?" I asked.

"No, a fine painter. Go to art school. Painted murals in Sainte-Marie. Paints big. Big!" She opened her arms. "He had some success but was put in prison. Terrible—now his hands shake. He was finally released after we paid a minister to intervene." She took a sip of tea. "Then we smuggled him out of the country. Now he works nights repairing vending machines, and paints in the daytime. He's too upset"—she pointed to her head—"to learn English."

"How awful!" The more I was learning about Sainte-Marie the worse it sounded.

"Ah, you have so much here." She looked around the modest luncheonette with the devil's ivy hanging in the window. I wished I'd taken her to a fancy expense-account restaurant instead of the plain luncheonette around the corner.

For a moment I felt overwhelmed by the hopelessness of my task. We would be exploiting this pitiful island, supporting a dictator. Here the islanders were, all caught up in some ultimate struggle for liberty and a decent livelihood, and we were talking tourism and Hollywood. Of course I could always hear Harrison in the back of my mind saying we were going to help the economy, bring jobs to the common people of Sainte-Marie—those who weren't in jail. Even Marcus had pointed out that our support of dictators in South American countries had sometimes improved the economies. But I became so involved with Cecilia's story that I nearly forgot why we were there.

"Do you think you'll ever go back for good?" I asked her.

She gave me a sad, indulgent smile and shook her head. "Oh, no. I'm going to be citizen here next year."

Then I braced myself and came on with the necessary question that would pay the mortgage and keep me and Shelly provided with basic consumer products.

"Can you imagine anyone wanting to go to Sainte-Marie . . . you know, for a vacation? To a nice hotel? Away from politics? They're saying now it wasn't cholera, you know."

She observed me to see if I was serious. The light from the window made for a cruel close-up of her face, the wide nose, the heavy eyelids with traces of green eye shadow.

"The Sainte-Marie government is trying to improve the local economy, and one of the things they want to do is develop tourism. They've hired us to promote it as a vacation spot."

"Vacation spot?" she repeated. A strange look came over her, as though she was awed by the thought. Maybe for the first time I had her full attention. She paused, holding the last portion of her tuna sandwich in midair.

I went on. "We're contacting travel writers and travel agents, planning press junkets . . ."

She settled the tuna melt back on her plate, patted her mouth with her napkin, and sipped some tea. Then she glanced out the window and sighed. "Ah, Americans," she said.

Immediately I felt like the enemy, the ugly American at noon on Eighteenth and L; but I wasn't sure what she was implying. That Americans were gullible beyond imagination, or corrupt beyond belief? Rather than seek clarification, I proceeded rather desperately with my original mission. Another idea arose in my troubled mind. My overtures to the film world were going nowhere—I couldn't get even an associate producer or part-time grip to return my calls; no one had ever heard of Sainte-Marie.

"Do you think I could see your brother's work sometime?" I

asked Cecilia. I explained we were exploring the cultural life of Sainte-Marie. Possibly we could help him too, if he was trying to establish a reputation for his work here in the United States. I embraced the idea so thoroughly I was even convincing myself that's what I was about.

"We might help a struggling artist," I told Marcus later in the office. "Something decent might come from investing our energies in this flea island, after all." Marcus was heading out the door for an appointment at the State Department. Because of the political conditions in Sainte-Marie, Marcus too had been having trouble finding an interested ear.

"Okay, we'll explore it," he answered, but he sounded skeptical. He wasn't as easily excited as I was. I was always looking for a quick fix to our immediate challenges, while he tended to examine possibilities from a longer range. But Harrison liked the idea; he thought an art show was prestigious. He didn't know the art world, like almost everything else, was all long knives. He thought an art show would sound great, not only to the Sainte-Marie prime minister but around his health club as well.

So here we were on this hot day in André's studio. First off, he didn't speak English—or wouldn't. And Cecilia was so pleasant it had never occurred to me that her brother might snarl and nip at us like a fox terrier.

After we admired his work and saw that his notebook listed shows on Saint-Martin and Antigua and in Mexico City, he made a long speech in French, with large, over-the-mountain gestures. Cecilia interpreted: "He says his lifework is trying to capture Sainte-Marie."

"Your work is very strong," I said to him. Cecilia translated. He didn't look at me or acknowledge my praise but kept rolling a cigarette with his paint- and nicotine-stained hands.

"He is suspicious," Cecilia explained. "He doesn't know why you would be interested in his work."

"Imagine! He doesn't trust us!" I muttered to Marcus under my breath.

Marcus shot me a warning look and asked Cecilia how much one of the big paintings would cost.

André answered immediately and Cecilia translated: "In America he thinks maybe twenty thousand dollars."

"Whoa!" Marcus exclaimed, and exchanged smiles with me. With the annual per capita income in Sainte-Marie about three hundred dollars, we could hardly believe this. Had we really stumbled upon a true artist from Sainte-Marie?

I asked Cecilia to ask her brother whether he'd be interested in our organizing a show for him. He listened but kept smoking. He glanced at me and then Marcus suspiciously before releasing a torrent of French.

"He says he's a patriot," Cecilia said.

"This isn't politics," I said. "Tell him."

Cecilia spoke to him. He shrugged and looked away; how could I be so naive, he appeared to be asking. Of course he was right, but I didn't have the patience to stand there in the heat and play whatever games would persuade André Bontemps we might be able to help him. It seemed so obvious and simple—which goes to show how wrong you can be for thinking anything in the world is obvious and simple.

"Well, Marcus, I give up," I said, offended at André's rudeness and eager to leave that steamy colander of a room. I felt foolish that I had expected him to be grateful to us.

André turned his back to us and moved to a window, where he blew his dark smoke toward the afternoon sky, which hung hot and plum-colored hazy. No doubt by then he was perfectly willing to let us fall through the holes in the floor.

"Because of prison he doesn't trust anyone," Cecilia reminded me.

Later I would wonder why I didn't pause over that. Despite

my years in our nation's capital, I was still an American optimist. I thought that, person to person, everything would end with us all becoming lifelong friends and driving to the beach for frozen margaritas. When in actual fact of recent history, everything around us ended just as often in a shootout at the Taco Stop.

Cecilia went to her brother's side, put her hand on his shoulder, and spoke to him quietly. When he didn't respond she turned away, threw her hands up, and said, "Ah, mens are so silly!"

Then out of the blue, Marcus started speaking to André in French. He paused now and then, but managed what sounded like a complete paragraph.

"I didn't know you could do that," I told him.

"I had to brush up," he replied.

This was one of those times when I marveled at how Marcus and I worked in concert. We could shift from bad cop to good cop at the drop of a hat. André turned to Marcus and responded in French.

"He wants to know who we're dealing with from Sainte-Marie." Marcus looked questioningly to Cecilia, who nodded.

Marcus told him the prime minister, who, we'd noticed, seemed to spend more time in the States than in Sainte-Marie.

André stomped on his latest cigarette butt and rattled off a few words, which Cecilia translated, having to do with the fact that he had only a temporary visa, so if anything went wrong he could be deported. Could we guarantee that his visa would be extended?

Marcus said he had good contacts at State and we would do everything we could to protect him. After all, the government of Sainte-Marie had reason to want this to happen.

"We have to make sure nothing will go wrong," Cecilia said, translating for André.

"If he gets favorable reviews and recognition, it would show he could support himself and be a good citizen. That should help." I fanned myself with my hand and thought of how hard it must be to work in that hot space all day with the smell of paints heavy in the air.

It was then I noticed how André's hand trembled as he brought another cigarette to his mouth. I had spotted a cot in the corner of the room, and I wondered whether the poor man slept there. But just as I was feeling a pang of sympathy for him he burst out with what sounded like a rattlingly hostile speech. Cecilia announced as if she were embarrassed: "He says he'll let you know."

Marcus said something more in French and André nodded. So Harrison & Associates, which claimed to be international, might actually be, I thought.

"Well, Cecilia," I said, "tell him if he's interested to let us know. Soon." I took her hand to thank her. I realized her life must be even more difficult than I'd assumed.

Outside, Marcus's BMW was parked in the sun beside a dented old black pickup, which we learned was André's. A large fly trapped inside the BMW buzzed frantically from window to window. We opened the doors and let it fly to freedom. I told Marcus that I'd been so annoyed by André that for a while I'd forgotten the whole proposition was bogus—though who knows, I said, maybe it was no more bogus than any other art show. It's possible he might sell some paintings and be reviewed. Like most things in Washington, this art show just would have some other motives behind it besides fine art and the furthering of civilization.

I asked Marcus what he'd said to André in French.

"I told him he should think that he's representing his country here—not the government but the people."

Of course, that idealistic thought would be something of a

white lie, since Marcus and I were representing the government. When I was a kid I used to keep count of my lies and try to do a good deed to make up for each one. To make up for this boondoggle I'd have to orange-hat Friday and Saturday nights for decades.

"I don't feel terrific about this," I muttered.

"Don't sweat it," Marcus reassured me. "He's a good painter. This could be a breakthrough for him. And it would be nice to talk to someone who's heard of the place for a change."

Marcus remained dignified even when he sweated. I patted his arm, grateful for his attempt to soothe my conscience.

"The truth is I'm more guilty than you are," I said. "Because we're coming from different cultural perspectives . . ."

"That's one way to put it."

"I'm lumbered with a history of poll taxes and eons of prejudice and suffering. Though all I've suffered personally is disdain from eastern intellectuals. So you shouldn't feel any guilt, Marcus. Just let me."

He laughed.

Cecilia emerged from the studio and climbed into Marcus's car. On the way back to the Republican side of town she spotted one of her compatriots trudging down Seventh Street carrying a shopping bag and pushing a child in a stroller, and asked Marcus to blow the horn.

I had some qualms about the reliability of Cecilia's brother, but we have all been taught the myth that the brilliant are inevitably difficult. So I pushed those qualms to the back of my mind and felt the pleasure of driving down the streets of our city with a good-looking man in his BMW. I even wished we'd run into Viktor Hajek, so I could wave, casually, looking a bit more sophisticated than I had lying on the sidewalk in front of the grocery store or surprised at home in my Redskin shorts and bunged-up face.

"Was this your first experience of crime?" Viktor Hajek asked me in his deep but intimate voice. He said the last word softly and watched me closely, perhaps afraid of offending me with the question.

We were in my patio, where the impatiens were in their lavish late-blooming stage, if that adjective can be applied to such modest and hearty flowers. Viktor Hajek was sitting across from me at the rusting round table with the yellow mound of citronella wax in the center, as we drank hot tea together. Autumn was in the air; the dogwood in Dan and Don's backyard already had some vivid red branches. The blossoms of the confederate jasmine were mostly gone, leaving only thin tentacles on the green vines. On arrival Viktor had strolled around inquiring about the plants. "It is cozy," he'd said of the patio. The way he said "cozy" was incredibly sexy.

I told Viktor that one of my previous experiences of crime involved some mashers on Capitol Hill. Then I realized that someone who no doubt wrote about revolutions and gulags probably wasn't interested in the fact I'd had my skirt lifted by two guys on the sidewalk.

"Masher?" He smiled at the word. "What does that mean exactly?"

"Mashing is an act of sexual harassment, the kind of thing that drives women nuts even though it doesn't endanger life or limb," I said vaguely. Viktor Hajek was so civilized he didn't pursue the matter further.

I told him how Tom and I had been burgled the day we moved to Capitol Hill. We soon learned burglary was the contemporary version of the welcome wagon.

When he asked me a lot of basic questions, I hoped he

wanted more than just journalistic background. I told him that I'd begun my career in Texas in the great tradition of writing obits and that sometimes I'd phone families for information and discover no one knew the family member had passed on.

I told him about the deputy sheriff I'd reported on who set fires in order to watch the fire trucks arrive. And another deputy who shot out his TV practicing the quick draw. Deputy sheriffs in general didn't have a very good reputation.

Viktor gave me his story too, which made my entry into journalism through the obit page seem extremely dull. He'd become a journalist after fleeing Czechoslovakia in the late sixties. In 1977, after he went back, he and other dissidents provoked a revolution when they protested the trial of a rock group called the Plastic People of the Universe.

Then the sixty-four-billion-dollar question: "Why, do you think," he asked solemnly, looking into my eyes, "there is so much crime in America?"

"Well," I said, "first it has to do with the fact every other person has a gun. And it also has something to do with the incredible success of television advertising, which so whets the appetite for consumer goods as tokens of success that it overwhelms all the forces of moral teaching, religious training, and social intercourse." I had a few more, minor theories, but I thought I'd offer just the major ones and not muddy the waters.

"Interesting." Viktor Hajek made a note, as if he'd never heard these theories before.

I told him I had a friend who'd thrown her TV into Boston Harbor as a kind of updated Tea Party, only she didn't achieve the same press attention as the first.

Of course it was an ego trip to be interviewed, especially by Viktor Hajek, who listened well and warmly, as if my words were sheer wisdom.

"Well, I've probably told you more about crime and Rosemary Kenny than you wanted to know," I said.

"No, no," he replied. "I am interested in how you explain . . . how you tolerate the violence."

"We *don't* tolerate it. That's exactly why we were out there in those silly orange hats. We were trying to do something about it." I couldn't hide the annoyance in my voice, and Viktor politely shifted the conversation.

"Perhaps I am fortunate to have been involved in an all-American crime so early on."

I blanched at that. Someone could have been seriously hurt. Indeed, I still had an itchy scab on my elbow that prevented me from wearing certain delicate blouses. And Jeri was still so traumatized he was installing bulletproof glass.

"I did not mean to offend you," Viktor said. "It is what everyone predicts to someone coming to the United States. It is ironic, and I am glad to have had the opportunity to meet you." He said it diplomatically, yet so sincerely it nearly erased every particle of annoyance from my emotional blackboard.

As I showed him to the door, we passed Shelly and Dee leaning against each other on the loveseat. I thought to myself, I should write to Dear Abby and warn the world that people with teenage daughters shouldn't buy loveseats.

At the door Viktor said he was liking the neighborhood but there were signs that his basement leaked. Looking into his nice face I considered asking him over for dinner. We could talk home maintenance, but I knew as sure as I did Shelly and Dee would cook some awful goop. Also, I'd have to explain why Dee was sojourning in my living room. How could I focus on a friendship for myself when I had to stand around with a fire extinguisher in my own living room?

"Thank you so much." Viktor Hajek took my hand to shake it, then held it a moment. Maybe the interview was, after all, more than just Journalism 101. "I find Americans fascinating," he said. "I admire you orange-hat people, and you have given me some insights."

As he walked away, I thought that maybe when Shelly reached forty I'd be able to muster enough emotional energy for a romance of my own. Even so, it nestled in my mind how Viktor Hajek had watched me closely, with something like a gleam of delight in his brown eyes.

So it was with a full house that I entered the striving month of September, when the ginkgo trees dropped their smelly berries on the warm sidewalks and bright chrysanthemums made their cheerful appearance on front stoops. On the Hill, Congress reassembled, rested, and with venom peaked for the approaching election year. Dee was still looking for work and Shelly was piling out the door mornings with her bookbag and without enthusiasm but at least giving more order to our days. With Dee around, the perpetual tug-of-war between Shelly and me moved into a new phase. While her wanting Dee to stay there gave me additional bargaining power, I found myself using the leverage to fight battles I'd already fought. Even her singing in the school chorus, which would have been a given years before, now had to be renegotiated.

"But you've always loved that!" I insisted. "This year you'd be a soloist!"

"I don't love it anymore," she said. "I don't like that kind of music!"

I didn't even have to explore that; I knew what she was talking about, since the pounding of rap music was omnipresent when she was around. So perhaps I overresponded, only later realizing it was because I sensed her taking another step away from me and further into a new and ominous world I didn't understand and feared.

I confided this to Marcus, who sometimes could put a consoling cultural spin on what Shelly was up to.

"What's wrong with rap?" he asked me. "Its roots are in black poetry. Frankly, I don't hear a lot of white music that sounds like poetry."

"It's not the music," I confessed. "She'd be into snake-handling if Dee was." I immediately felt guilty at my putdown of her basic intelligence. "She's just in love."

"Maybe she'll get over it. That make you happy?" Marcus adjusted his gold glasses.

"That's a trick question," I said.

Before Dee moved in, I'd asked Shelly if his red sweatsuits meant he was a member of an L.A. gang, and she took that as so ridiculous she'd only laughed. But I'd noticed he hadn't found it so funny or far-fetched when she made me sound like the Ancient Mariner by repeating my question in front of him. "Of course that was before I knew you," I'd explained to Dee quickly.

The Saturday following the beginning of school, after they'd helped clean the house, I offered to treat Shelly and Dee to a movie and pizza. We sat in a booth at Maggie's, the two of them across from me, discussing recent reports that in a suburban church, statues of the Virgin Mary were crying whenever a particular priest passed by. Dee said his grandmother had experienced several miracles, like the one of the bedridden woman she'd been nursing who rose up in the middle of the night and lifted her arms and her face lighted up. There was a glow all around her; then she let out a death rattle and fell back dead.

"Really!" Shelly said.

Dee raised his hand. "Swear to God. My grandmother wouldn't tell a lie if it killed her."

Shelly said she believed in reincarnation. I said I hadn't given it a lot of thought. Shelly said that was a real cop-out. Dee said he'd considered becoming a preacher. Shelly bent over the table in giggles at this revelation.

"Hey, girl, I don't think that's so funny. Shows I was an imaginative child."

I could never tell when Dee was really angry and when he was just pretending.

"I might still be a preacher." He proceeded to entertain us with some religious rap, beating time on the table. "Jesus come down from the mountain . . . said I got a idea . . . Jesus said things lookin' bad 'round here . . . gotta get me some bodies . . . gotta get me a gang . . ."

I'd never thought of the apostles as a gang, but I guess it was one point of view. Dee's performance attracted smiles from diners at nearby tables, which he acknowledged with a rather arrogant shrug.

"I think that was 'Moses come down from the mountain,' " I murmured quietly.

"Whatever," Shelly said.

After dinner they dropped me at home and were off to a club where Dee's rap group was performing around midnight. I was left to watch *Saturday Night Live* by myself, and experience had already taught me that *Saturday Night Live* was not much fun alone. But I felt some consolation because on the dining table was a rough but definite draft of Shelly's basic college application essay, to reassure me that maybe I'd made a reasonable deal.

Having Dee as a live-in guest had been an interesting tradeoff. He sang loud rap in the shower and played louder rap on the radio; the TV was always tuned to the black shows, and he rented nearly every black movie video in existence. At the same time, he tried to help me by insisting Shelly make her bed and conduct her daily life in a more civil manner. He even made her study without television. He folded his bedding neatly every morning and hid it behind the couch. He carried trash to the alley for me and brought the air conditioners to the attic when it turned cool. He kept a yellow legal pad beside the downstairs phone with a list of jobs from the employment ads, and annotated it neatly, with "Phone" or "Write letter" and the dates and responses. Most days he'd put on his one pair of dress pants with a shirt he'd pressed the night before and his one tie to go for an interview. Dee seemed the best possible example of earnest and steady striving for employment, a living example to Shelly and even me. When I was tempted to skip the September Neighborhood Watch meeting in order to avoid embarrassing inquiries about my recent orange-hat incident, I reconsidered and felt obliged to do my duty and attend. Doreen too had insisted that my absence could undermine the morale of the whole organization. So on the appointed Monday night I set forth to pretend at least that I was a good sport. It seemed there was no end to the ramifications of my encounter with crime.

The meeting was held on a surprisingly cool night at the home of Reverend Thompson, who had a multitude of folding church chairs. His house was furnished in traditional minister mode, with heavy gold drapes, overstuffed chairs, and over the mantel, a huge close-up painting of Jesus—the kind in which the eyes seem to follow you across the room. Several people asked how I was feeling, and I just nodded and said, "Fine," noncommittally, the way Shelly did when I asked how her school day had gone. As usual, Mrs. Nance contributed store-bought cookies and passed out Avon catalogues to all the women. Dan and Don arrived late with the scrumptious brownies Don makes, one of the main attractions of these meetings. Then, lo and behold, Viktor Hajek appeared. For this new member we introduced ourselves around the room. When we reached "Rosemary Kenny, 1769," Viktor Hajek, 1804, looked at me with such interest that I wondered whether there was some East European sexy secret about my house number.

Reverend Thompson, lean from his backyard jogging, opened the meeting with an enumeration of recent break-ins, followed by a report on the status of the liquor license for the Bluebird. Dan, a slim, attractive lawyer with one gold earring, passed around a copy of a letter he'd written to the mayor concerning the bar. Doreen, impeccable in a fashionable three-color lavender-dominated athletic suit, told us she had once again phoned the police about the drug activity in front of the bar and had of late been receiving obscene phone calls, which, she believed, were attempts to thwart her crime-stopper role.

Mrs. Nance, 1823, seventy-something, wearing her usual raincoat and knit cloche hat, suggested that Doreen buy a whistle to blow into the receiver, which is what she did with telephone solicitors.

I announced that the detective heading the investigation of our orange-hat crime incident had told me Rodrigo Rodriguez had been allowed to plea-bargain because it was a first offense. The detective said we'd probably all be brain-dead by the time the case would have come up on the crowded court docket anyway.

The next items on the agenda were the possibility of another halfway house in the neighborhood, a complaint about dogs crapping in the tree boxes, and one from a woman who complained her patio smelled like cat pee although she didn't have a single animal. Mrs. Nance explained that there were herds of wild cats living in the alleys, traveling in packs. I said I'd never in my life seen cats traveling in packs. Mrs. Nance thought it was only during a full moon. We paused for a moment of silence while everyone shoved that whole idea into the Mrs. Nance wacko file.

The headliner of the evening was the appearance of two

policepersons to talk about home security—a chunky white male who was about to retire, and a young Afro-American female who'd been on the force for only two years. She wore a short Afro and dangling turquoise earrings, and had a friendly smile. Their basic message was: Cut down all trees and shrubs close to the house; light and bar all windows; buy security doors; and don't go out after dark. Mrs. Moore recommended a large dog, although she admitted that Pal hadn't prevented her third car radio from being stolen. The male cop said, "Just be glad they didn't steal the car."

Reverend Thompson graciously asked the cops if there was anything we could do for them, whereupon we heard a lengthy heartfelt plea for new police cars. Theirs were so old, the policeman claimed, sometimes the radios don't even work, a fact we, needless to say, were all alarmed to hear.

Afterward, we adjourned to the dining room, where Mrs. Thompson had set out punch and tea, Mrs. Nance's store-bought cookies and Don's brownies, which were gone by the time I passed the Jesus eyes and reached the table.

All during the meeting I was trying not to focus on Viktor Hajek. Now he moved to my side, as people around us chatted about summer vacations and discussed who'd been sick or on jury duty. Reverend Thompson told Viktor Hajek he'd visited Prague while he was stationed in the Army in Germany, and he'd thought it was as beautiful as Paris. Reverend Thompson was always surprising me with his life experiences. Doreen once told me he suffered some permanent injury as the result of being beaten while he was jailed in Alabama during the civil rights struggle. Thompson asked Doreen about her twin grandbabies, and she passed around a photo of them on their mother's lap.

As I was leaving, Viktor Hajek fell in step beside me and remarked on the diversity of our neighborhood. It's true that within our four-block area there were a cab driver, a doctor, two nurses, two lawyers, and Anita Nance, a retired school crossing guard who sells Avon products, plus assorted overtaxed white-collar sellouts like me.

"Nice of you to come," I told Viktor Hajek. He said it was all in the line of duty, since he was considering doing an article about our neighborhood and the experience of living in Washington in general.

Realizing Viktor was strolling toward my house instead of his own, I asked how his home furnishing was coming along; he admitted he was not much of a decorator. We reached my gate just as Dan and Don were arriving next door. Dan began the ritual of unlocking their deadbolt as Don picked dead leaves off their geranium windowbox. They both called good night as they entered their well-decorated orange-sponged hallway.

Across the street Mrs. Moore arrived at her own doorway just as Pal began to howl, and a moment later sirens rose in the distance.

After being with the group at the meeting, Viktor seemed lonesome and reluctant to leave. He was standing on the sidewalk and I was on my stoop, so I had the heady experience of looking down at him. He said it amazed him that in our neighborhood we'd developed such a community since in most American cities, he'd heard, neighbors didn't know one another. I explained that when I'd left my nosy Texas town I'd hoped to be an anonymous city-dweller. But after a while I realized that wasn't a humane way to live, and especially with a child, who needed a diverse community of different people and ages. Then with Viktor Hajek's apparent interest in what I was saying, I proceeded to confide what I'd had no intention of confiding, that I was divorced and had actually rather lowered my flag, which was indeed true. There just seemed to be no reason for me to say it at that moment. "The idea of romance about tires me out thinking of it." I kind of fanned myself with my hand, although I wasn't warm at all, and then brushed his arm.

"You are certainly honest," Viktor Hajek said. I didn't know what he meant by that, since I didn't know what I'd meant to begin with. I suppose I'd meant that at my age, with my responsibilities and past history, I didn't take up with someone without having a lot of yellow caution lights flashing in my mind and soul. In the tension of the moment, I resorted to an inane comment that it was a nice night, which it was. You could still hear the sound of cicadas, as if the summer was trying to hold on. Some nights I'd lie in bed just listening to the chorus, I told Viktor. And some nights I could hear the lions roaring in the zoo, and I'd think of them all caged up and lonely and maybe remembering when they were free.

That's when Viktor told me that he had spent a total of eight years in prison, and that to survive prison you learn to think not of the future but only of the present. "It is not a bad thing to learn," he said quietly. I understood this was also his own declaration concerning romance. For him it was a matter of present tense only.

Suddenly I once again had that feeling I'd had with Cecilia Bontemps of being an unworldly American; my categories of relationship were narrow and maybe out-of-date. I should admit to myself that the attraction I felt for this man was something beyond being partners in crime victimhood. There was some substance about him that I found attractive and interesting. I could learn something of the world from this man, I told myself. And God knew I needed to look beyond my own living room traumas and put everything into perspective.

Before he left, Viktor said, "I keep listening for Duke Ellington music."

"You know Ellington?"

"Oh, yes." He smiled. " 'Mood Indigo,' 'I Got It Bad and

That Ain't Good.' " In his heavy accent the words sounded funny, and we both laughed. Then he proceeded, against the background of cicadas, in the soft glow of light from my bay window, to whistle soulfully in a low melodic tone several bars of "Mood Indigo," that haunting song about loneliness. I tried to imagine what it must have been like to spend eight years in prison, but it was beyond my comprehension. However, he had probably experienced as much mood indigo as anyone I knew. And standing there before him, I felt it as a sweetly moving serenade just for me, a sharing of his own melancholy past. Then he said good night and walked away. At the gate, Viktor Hajek, the gentleman, waited until I opened the door and slipped inside.

Twice during those early weeks of September, Dee seemed to have found a job, but each later fell through. The first was as assistant manager of an athletic store in a Maryland mall. We'd celebrated with Paradiso pizza and fresh apple cider on the day he was told he'd gotten the job, only to learn otherwise when he reported for work the next Monday. A senior manager decided he was too young. Later, after being hired by a chain shoe store, he was told that the position required him to have his own car for travel to suburban stores. After these two disappointments Dee picked himself up and attacked the want ads again. I cautiously offered suggestions, which he seemed to consider. But as the weeks passed I wondered how many rebuffs he could tolerate. The strain grew in our daily lives. He withdrew more and more into his bomping music, pulling Shelly along with him, away from me and what I knew and understood.

"Just remember, as soon as he gets a job he's out," I told

Shelly after she'd skipped school to console Dee when he'd lost the shoe store job. I was perhaps more eager for him to find a job than he was. Sometimes I wondered if I was jealous of Shelly's steady devotion to him. When I asked her if she wasn't missing something of her senior year by limiting her social life to Dee, she said high school guys were immature and boring. I had to admit, Dee was not boring. His life was filled with the ups and downs of a soap opera or even real life; with him I felt we were riding a roller coaster and likely to sail off track any instant. Yet by being with Dee, Shelly was missing things she had looked forward to experiencing that last year of high school; she might eventually regret that. Meanwhile, I prayed for patience, thinking that if I could be cool, they might break up on their own, since Shelly's romances were, as a rule, of brief duration. Still, I knew I was kidding myself that this was like the young high school romances of her recent years. This, I would say to myself, admiring the handsome and charged presence of them together, is another thing. Dee was the attractive underdog I'd taught her to respect and make alliance with, a striving person in a mysterious world to decipher, closer than I ever allowed myself.

"Why are you so taken with him?" I asked her one rare day when we were alone.

She paused only a moment. "He's different. He looks at things in a different way. He's funny, he's smart. And he turns me on." She smiled and squinted slightly, reminding me of her father.

Finally I read the draft for her college application essays. "Let me tell you about my friend Dee," it began, and went on to discuss problems of public school education and racism, and why the nation's capital should be a state. She wanted my criticism—as long as it was positive.

As I returned the draft to her, I pointed out that the District of Columbia already had an oversized bureaucracy compared with other cities. She was wearing my treasured bluebonnet T-shirt. She lay on her bed, where she had been alternately studying and painting her nails, while drinking a cherry Slurpee. Wads of cotton separated her crimson-tipped toes. Dee was doing laundry. I could hear the bomp-bomp of his boom box from the basement.

I continued: "If Washington, D.C., were a state, think how expensive it would be to have an added state bureaucracy."

"You said you were for statehood," she said impatiently.

"I am for some kind of autonomy. But it's complicated."

I picked up jeans, panties, and a sweatshirt from the floor and stuffed them into her laundry hamper, then sat two teddy bears upright on a shelf. It annoyed her that I was always straightening up. But it had become a compulsion with me. It was either that or fuss at her. I couldn't witness the perpetual disorder without doing something.

Although we hadn't had a major argument in at least a week, the atmosphere was still uneasy. I kept careful count in my mind, dreaming of the day when our fights would be fewer and further between, until they were eventually no more.

"You're just trying to make this difficult," she charged. "According to you, everything in the world is impossible. If everybody thought like you, nothing would ever get any better."

Be calm, I told myself, and took a deep breath before answering. "I'm just saying it's a complicated thing all around, Shelly, and if you're going to tackle a difficult subject in your essay you must explore all factors. It's not fair to blame all the problems on racism. That's how fascists operate." That was the kind of giant oversimplification to which I sometimes retreated, and I realized the irony of my doing exactly what I was accusing her of. At what age, I wondered, would she be willing to accept the variables and complexities of the world?

Shelly had just started plucking her brown eyebrows. They were narrow enough that she looked like a thirties movie star, and her greenish-brown eyes seemed even larger and more startling.

Now she had moved on to more pressing things. "Well, are you coming or not?" Shelly asked before I could exit her room. What she wanted was for me to drive out to Bladensburg Road to a rap club where Dee and his group were performing Saturday night.

"Please," she added. I was so surprised at her urgency I couldn't deal with her request immediately. Many more "pleases" and I didn't know what I'd do. So I retreated into my bedroom, where I was trying to find some transitional September clothes for work. Shelly followed me, walking like Frankenstein with the cotton between her toes.

"That's asking a lot," I said. "I'll have to think about it." I confess I was flattered that she and Dee wanted me to come. This was the first gig where his group would be the main attraction, she claimed.

"He really wants you to hear him. It'll hurt his feelings if you don't come."

"I imagine he can stand that," I said in a tone I myself didn't like, then escaped momentarily into my closet.

I was thinking that Dee didn't really give a fig whether I heard him perform or not. There must be something more to it. He claimed to be moving into a whole new hip-hop phase, and there I was just learning what hip-hop was supposed to be, by reading his magazines, and already it was changing.

I realized I'd forgotten what I was looking for, so I exited the closet, to find Shelly, with her abused eyebrows, waiting for my response. "I'm not driving out Bladensburg Road by myself, Shelly," I said, leaving the rest unsaid. Not without an armored-car escort or the Texas Rangers. Not that I'd feel safe with the Texas Rangers. "And anyway, I told Doreen I'd orange-hat." I turned away, knowing she was watching me closely for signs of cave-in.

"Moms, orange-hats are over at ten," she said in her speak-to-a-simpleton voice. "Come then. You only have to stay an hour. Don't you have some friend who could go with you?" She said it as if I were the only person in the world without a friend eager to go along to a hip-hop club on Bladensburg Road. "Or get the orange-hats to go. They owe you one."

"That's true. But most orange-hats go to church on Sunday, they don't go honky-tonkin' the night before."

Shelly shifted to make sure I caught her smirk. Since beginning her relationship with Dee, she was an expert on the social mores of the African-American community. Obviously she was skeptical of my knowledge of their churchgoing and honky-tonkin'.

The truth was that Shelly didn't think much of the orange-hats. To her they were fascist brownshirts, instead of the peace-loving Guardian Angels I imagined them to be. But I was feeling a lot of pressure since I couldn't remember her ever being so insistent I go somewhere.

"You need to get out, Moms," she said, implying that I was getting old before my time, dreary and moss-backed and out of it, and that driving out Bladensburg Road was just the thing to revive me. As well as help me understand her and Dee.

"Get Marcus to go with you," she said, finally pulling the cotton out and admiring her toes. She tossed the cotton balls toward my trash basket, and missed.

Though she hadn't admitted it outright, and though once she had said that he had betrayed his people by driving a BMW, I knew Shelly thought Marcus was cool. I could tell our friendship gave her some hope for me.

"Marcus," I told her, "probably wouldn't be caught dead in a club on Bladensburg Road."

I retreated again into my closet and pulled out a long-sleeved silk blouse with a stain on the collar. Could I hide it with a scarf, I wondered. I could feel Shelly staring at my neck nerves as she waited for my next move. I turned back just in time to see her take a drink of Slurpee, and watched as a trickle of cherry drink ran down the front of my bluebonnet T-shirt.

"Are there ever any white people at this club besides you?" I asked finally.

"I don't know," she said. "I've never been there."

"You've never been there!"

She shook her head. I stared at the probably indelible stain on the T-shirt, and wondered if Doreen would think I was crazy asking her to go to a hip-hop club out on Bladensburg Road.

Shelly kept nudging, until she finally hit the right nerve. She placed her hands on her hips, her narrow tormented eyebrows lifted, and challenged, "Well, it sounds like you won't go because it's out in Northeast." As opposed to safer, whiter Northwest, she implied. It was a racial thing.

So that settled it. She'd won. It was a matter of honor.

I pulled a skirt out of a storage bag that reeked of mothballs, and then capitulated.

"The problem with you, Shelly, is that you're always trying to make me live up to my principles."

She folded her lips, and despite herself broke into a smile before retreating in triumph.

So I picked up the phone. "Marcus? Rosemary. I know on Saturdays we usually have some relief from Harrison et cetera, but I have a superduper favor to ask."

I told him about Dee's playing at a club and asked him if he and Michelle would join me. "I know this might sound ridiculous, but Shelly's acting like it's the most important thing since the polio vaccine."

Marcus's voice sounded scratchy. "Rosemary, you been out Bladensburg Road lately?"

"Sure, it's lovely, all gentrified. Full of fern bars . . ."

"Yeah, sure."

"Are you sick?" I asked.

"No, just sleepy," he said. Why would Marcus be falling asleep at nine o'clock?

"Oh, come on. You like rap music. You say it's like poetry. Live dangerously for a change."

"I happen to live dangerously every day of my life. I may not take as many chances as you. . . ."

"I wasn't criticizing you," I told him. "Honestly."

So that's how I happened to be in a hip-hop club on Bladensburg Road with Marcus and Doreen on a Saturday night in September. Michelle couldn't make it; Marcus didn't offer any further explanation. We managed to park nearby and enter without a shot being fired.

Inside, the club brought back memories of my own past, the strained, electric atmosphere generated by people focused on fun, on excitement, overlaid with the obviousness of sex and alcohol. That tension of possibilities beyond the immediate imagination. The club had a nice selection of neon beer signs and a few oldies like Ray Charles on the jukebox, which played between sets. I'd been to clubs in Texas a million times crummier. Sometimes fights broke out in these clubs and people got beer bottles broken on their heads in parking lots, but generally they weren't too scary. For the first half-hour here, we sat sipping beer and making estimates of how many guns must be in the room despite the security guard at the door, who occasionally frisked new arrivals.

After a while Shelly entered with some of Dee's friends. So now there were two obviously white people in the place.

Shelly was made up like a starlet, and cheaply bejeweled, her hair extravagantly gelled. She hugged Marcus and Doreen and joined our table, smiling, joking, even casting a warm glance my way now and then as if I weren't her daily tormentor. What joy to fall within the radiance of her smile, bear witness to her young Saturday-night charm, slip for a few moments through the perpetual barrier of hostility. So that when she finally left our table, Marcus looked at me quizzically: Could this lovely young woman be the dragon I talked about? I was torn between gratitude and disgust that she would deliver such an act, the very opposite of the norm. But I had to laugh.

"Maybe I should start going to nightclubs every weekend," I told Marcus and Doreen.

Doreen patted my hand. "At least it gives you some hope, doesn't it?"

"Yeah, but it makes me want to kill her too. Just to see how she could be, can be!"

Dee's performance with his group overwhelmed me. No wonder Shelly was so enamored. There was something magic and raw and risky in what he did. It seemed less a performance, as with many white rockers, than something nearly natural. Energetic. Athletic. Very angry. A lot of clenched fists. Dee played with three other guys—on keyboard, electric guitar, and drums—who joined him in loud rap. But Dee was the lead, with the most patter—only it was more stomp than patter. He stomped around the small stage, shouting with the bomp-bomp I heard so often from my basement. As musicians, they could use some work. But as communicators of a hunger and a frustration with life, they were scary and almost compelling.

Until that evening I hadn't known the name of Dee's group: Ladykillers. I gasped when I saw the poster. "Oh, it's like an old-fashioned ladykiller, somebody who's good with women," Shelly explained. She shrugged, as if weary of interpreting the world for me.

"Don't jive me." I raised my voice above the racket. "And even if that's true, he's exploiting the idea."

Marcus gave me a dubious look that said surely I wasn't choosing this time and place to fight with my daughter.

"It's a tough world out there, Moms. You have to do anything you can to call attention to yourself."

I sighed and assumed a friendlier tone. "Shelly, I'd hoped you'd have a few idealistic years before you fell in with media hype."

"You're asking a lot, Mother."

"You're right. But somebody has to."

I could pick out only a word or two of Dee's songs. "Passing On" had to do with guns and dying. Another one was about a sweet-talkin' gal; it had that bomp-bomp beat, but something of a tune too, unlike most of the songs.

The group wore L.A. Raider caps and black leather, even in that overheated room. Doreen claimed the getup had an outlaw panache. The sweat ran down Dee's face and through the gold chains on his chest, and I remembered the first time I'd seen him, how good-looking but also frightening he'd appeared to me. And now I'd come to think of him as a basically sweet kid with an uncertain future. But in that charged atmosphere, his abrasive rapping made me once again fear what he might mean for Shelly's life.

When the Ladykillers finished their set, a powerful keening sound from a rear table gave me a shiver. Shelly had gone there to sit with some of Dee's friends, and I couldn't help wondering whether one of them was his cousin Mario, the drug dealer. Dee raised his hands over his head like a prizefighter, turning slowly, soaking in the applause. Did I know this angry man? But when he came into the audience, he shook hands with Marcus and gave him and Doreen a warm smile and thanked us for coming. When he moved away, his hand rested on my shoulder for just a moment, a gesture of familiarity that you would make only toward someone you were comfortable with. Marcus saw it and caught my eye knowingly.

When Marcus and Doreen and I left, we agreed Dee

seemed truly pleased we'd come. "He's fond of you, Rosemary," Marcus said. "He wanted you to see him as a star, not just as an unemployed kid."

"He certainly needs all the support he can get, don't you think?" I asked. Neither of them responded. But that was okay, I thought. It had been worth the effort to make it through all the mean streets to get there.

After we dropped Doreen at her house, I asked Marcus what he really thought about Dee.

"I think you're letting yourself in for trouble. That guy is like a bomb waiting to go off."

"I know that," I said. By then I'd had two Samuel Adamses, so my speech came straight from the uncensored heart. Marcus had pulled over in front of a fire hydrant near my house. In the headlights appeared Arlo, on one of his furtive night missions, his taut gray body trotting steadily across the street. Down the block, the lights still shone on the second floor of Viktor's house, in what I assumed was the master bedroom.

"I know you think Shelly should be one of those preppy whites who carries an organizer, Marcus, but she's just not. It's not my fault. Kids seem to be born programmed, you know. I mean, if she'd been raised by Dr. Spock she'd be the same. She was always independent. And I have to try the best I can to stay her friend through this. Believe me, I'd rather not have Dee sleeping in my living room and all this boom-boom-boom rocking my house every day. No telling the damage that music has done to the foundations."

Marcus's silence was curious. "Are you okay?" I asked him. "You seem kind of down tonight."

"What makes you think that?" His voice still sounded like he was getting a cold.

"I dunno. You just seem sad."

"Yeah . . . well . . ."

"What?"

"Oh, lots of things, Rosemary. Being married. Making a living. Just living. Sometimes it all piles up, leans on you. Know what I mean?" There was impatience in his voice. In the pale glow of the streetlight I could see how grave his face was. I was accustomed to his laughter, his kidding, his generous interest in me and my welfare. This sad focus on himself was new.

"Yeah. I know what you mean." I said it, but I didn't know—and we both were aware of that. Whatever Marcus went through was different and, I assumed, harder. Once he'd told me that he had to live the rest of his life knowing the best was behind him—when he was young and ran like the wind and had bands playing and flags waving. On one level he felt himself lucky, American lucky. That was ironic.

"You wanna talk about it? I tell you my problems. . . ."

"I just got something on my mind." He sighed and leaned back and hammered the steering wheel lightly. "You know, sometimes I get real low. I go home and go to bed and pull the covers over my head."

"Sometimes I soak in the bathtub." I touched his arm. "Is there anything I can do? I owe you about five hundred hours of kind consultation."

Marcus shook his head.

"Sorry Michelle couldn't come," I remarked.

"Michelle wouldn't do Bladensburg Road. And . . ." Marcus let his head fall back. "Michelle and I haven't been keeping too much company of late."

"I'm sorry," I said. "You want to talk about it?"

"Not really."

"Could I fix you some coffee or hot chocolate or something? You know what I have that's really special? Some Dr Peppers from around Waco. The ones from Waco are still made with regular sugar. They're better than any other Dr Peppers in the world."

"Thanks . . ." He leaned forward on the steering wheel. A

mellow Thelonious Monk tape was playing. We watched as Mrs. Moore's nephew came out of the house to take Pal on his final stroll of the night.

"That the dog that howls?"

"Yeah," I said. "I wish you could hear him. See, he wears a tie too."

I was startled by Marcus's down mood and didn't know what to say or do. Finally I realized maybe the best thing was to let him go home to bed.

"Thanks so much for going with me," I told him. "I really appreciate it. And I owe you one. At least one."

"It was a blast," Marcus said with a note of rather weary sarcasm.

In the middle of the night the phone rang. I grabbed it even before I fumbled around and turned on the light. I had been sound asleep. Sometimes I think I should have been a firefighter. When the phone rings I wake in an instant.

"Mother," Shelly said with the formality of fear in her voice. "Dee has been arrested. I'm at the police station. Fourth Precinct. Georgia Avenue. Can you come?"

For a second or two the word "arrested" didn't make sense. I'd always expected a phone call in the night to mean an accident, even death.

"Arrested! For what?" I asked her.

"They say he shot someone. But he didn't."

I could hear a phone ringing in the background. People talking, someone shouting.

"Shot someone? Where?"

"At a party. He had this argument with this guy and we left. The police came after us and said Dee'd gone back and shot someone. But he was with me."

Suddenly everything seemed too real and magnified. I was aware of my heart thumping.

"How badly shot?" I asked.

"Oh, dead," she said, her voice breathless, as if she'd run a long way.

SHELLY SLEPT most of the next day. When she finally rose from bed, she moved like a zombie into the kitchen, without speaking. I followed her and offered orange juice. She ignored me, but I poured some anyway and set it before her.

"What's gonna happen to him?" she asked. The same question she'd asked the night before. "They hit him," she'd said. "They handcuffed him. . . . It was so awful! They treated him like an animal!" Her descriptions made me shiver. I'd heard them over and over in my sleep all night.

"I suppose he'll be arraigned tomorrow. They'll probably set bail. If he's innocent, I imagine he'll eventually get off."

"Of course he's innocent!" she said angrily.

"I didn't mean he's not innocent." I defended myself, wanting to be her ally in this latest crisis.

Outside it was cool, gray and cloudy. Shelly had slept in her clothes. She hadn't washed her face, and she smelled of smoke and sweat. I remembered how I'd always loved the gentle scent of her as a child, how I'd hold her in my arms, her warm churning little-girl body and soft golden-brown hair.

She started making a jelly sandwich and I turned to the Sunday papers.

"I don't know if I can stand to go back to school!" she shouted suddenly. I stopped. I had been preparing myself for that one. At the slightest excuse she could self-destruct. And this seemed a big excuse. Stay calm, I directed myself.

It had begun to rain and I hurried to the patio, where I had draped some fall clothes to air out the odor of mothballs. The air smelled fresh and lonely. I looked at the old gutter sagging along the back of the house and wished I had the money needed to have it repaired. On the fence the leaves and tendrils of the confederate jasmine were the only green remaining. A brown leaf drifted down from the elm tree. I looked at the sky and thought of Dee, of how only last night he had been so vital and proud, of how much sadder the rain must seem from whatever jail he was in.

I carried the weighty clothes of autumn inside and slung them over the back of a chair. The sight of them was depressing and they still smelled of mothballs, but what difference did it make if I smelled like mothballs, if Shelly was going to quit school and ruin her life.

She'd settled in front of the TV to eat her jelly sandwich, and was flicking through channels with the remote. "They'll have to raise a lot of money for his bail. Mario said five thousand dollars probably. Dee's family doesn't have money like that." A pause, and then: "Can I borrow five thousand dollars?"

I was patting the rain from my arms with a kitchen towel. "I don't have five thousand dollars, Shelly," I said quietly.

I retreated to the kitchen and leaned my head against the refrigerator, wishing the day to be over, so I could avoid what all I knew was coming. The radio was playing "Fly Me to the Moon," and I hummed along with real feeling before I turned it off. I took a pill for the headache I suddenly realized I had, and poured myself some lukewarm coffee.

"You could come up with five thousand dollars," she went on when I'd returned. "Couldn't you mortgage the house?"

I nearly smiled at her predictability in arguing, but caught myself and tried to sound calm. "I might be able to get a second mortgage. And I'd do that in an instant for you."

"But not for Dee. Why?" She turned to confront me.

I thought for a moment, watching the rain fall against the three windows in the bay. Be honest, I told myself. I looked at her, the silly eyebrows, the pained furrows of her forehead, the wide eyes which belied what she knew she was doing.

"Because he's not my child. Because I have to hoard all my financial options for you and me. Because there are limits to my generosity."

She was crying now, tears running down her cheeks, mixing with her leftover makeup. I handed her a tissue from the pocket of my sweater. I wanted to put my arms around her to comfort her, but I knew better.

She had been steely when I picked her up at the Fourth Precinct, a modern building with a towering antenna in back and dirty glass doors in front. Riding home, she had matter-of-factly recited the events: They left after the second set. They went to a party with Mario. There was an argument. They left the party, went to Mario's home, where the police showed up. Dee's innocence, his surprise, his helplessness, her fury. Going to the precinct with Mario. Then phoning me. Only then did she begin to cry. Once home, she'd made a phone call and gone to bed. I knew all I could do in this particular crisis besides listen was to endure, survive her anger, let her vent her fury. And to try to enlist as much rationality in the discussion as possible. Maybe for once she wouldn't direct her anger at me, and I would remain calm, remember some wonderful happy time, some peaceful day on a warm beach, take deep breaths and not notice how my stomach was knotting up until it felt like a drum, not notice how I'd grit my teeth until my jaws ached. Rise above it, as Mama used to admonish.

"You're always saying people won't put themselves out for others anymore," Shelly said.

"That's true. But Dee has some family, it's their responsibility. They wouldn't have to pay the full amount. You can borrow bail if you have collateral."

"You know his father's in jail," she cried. "His mother is a drunk. His grandmother is only a nurse. She doesn't have money! They don't have anything. They play the Lotto!"

She'd set her sandwich down after only a few small bites.

There was always the danger that she would starve herself to death or ruin her health with junk food or, in her misery, turn to drugs and alcohol, flee to Texas to live with her father, or run away, becoming one of those faces above the "Have you seen this girl?" posters. The tears were dripping off her chin onto her soiled white blouse, leaving damp gray circles on her breasts.

"Well, Shelly, I really don't have money like that."

"That's not true."

"Let me try to explain to you. I regret what has happened to Dee, and I believe you that he's innocent. I can't imagine him killing someone. I regret his entire life situation, that his cousin sells drugs, that he's probably had a poor education, that he can't find a job and his possibilities in this day and age and in this city may be limited. There are a lot of problems. But I can't solve them. And I can't change them. All I can do is try to take care of you and me the best I can."

Her mind was heading down the same path as usual, like a bowling ball that always veered into the alley. It seemed as if anger was the only emotion she could draw up.

"Why can't you admit that you could help, if you just would?"

To some extent she was right. I didn't have money like that in the bank, but I had resources in property and there were others I could turn to, resources that Dee's grandmother and mother maybe didn't have. And the reason for the difference in our resources had nothing to do with us as individuals but was the result of a complicated trail of history, I had no doubt of that. But I knew that my recognition of that fact would do nothing to soothe my hostile daughter.

Shelly turned back to the TV. For a minute I thought she was involved with the program. Then she kicked the footstool between us, and the Sunday papers toppled over and fanned out across the floor. Neither of us moved. I felt a seething fury: once again I was the necessary enemy.

"I know this is terrible for you, Shelly," I said, "but there's no excuse for you to act like King Kong. Pick up the papers."

But she didn't. I lifted the Outlook section and glanced at her glowering, tear-stained face.

"You're not a child. And I'm not the enemy." It was important, and only fair, that I clarify our positions. "Jesus Christ, I hope you grow up someday."

I waited a moment, then took the offensive. "You know, Dee could be released anytime. The police could find out they'd made a mistake. Find the right person. Being innocent is the most powerful defense."

She kept staring at the TV screen. I held my breath, hoping I had diverted what had seemed the inexorable explosion.

"I'm going to call Daddy," she announced. "And Grandmother. And if I can't raise the money any other way, I'll quit school and get a job." She gave me a pained look, wiped away her tears, stood up. "It stinks in here," she said, and walked out of the room, leaving her partial jelly sandwich on the loveseat and the newspapers on the floor.

I had learned a while back that it was enormously important to her to have the last word, and very often the last word involved insults blown my way like poison darts. I rubbed my temples, feeling the ache still there beneath the stuffy haze of the medicine. I sat back and let myself suffer the afternoon movie, which seemed to be ending. The hero was holding an automatic rifle and making his way past multiple explosions when I punched the power off.

Shelly spent the next couple of hours on the telephone, and for the next few weeks I found little notes scattered about the house: phone numbers, beeper numbers, names, and strange addresses in parts of town I was not familiar with.

Dee was arraigned and charged with second-degree murder. His bail was set at twenty-five thousand dollars.

I prepared speeches and presented them periodically. As far

as I knew, Shelly hadn't solicited Tom or Mama. She probably realized they'd turn her down too, and understood in her heart of hearts it was too much to ask, though whenever I thought of Dee in D.C. jail I wasn't even sure it was.

I wrote her a note reminding her to finish her school application essays. There had been a contract between us, I said, and she must honor it. That was the adult thing to do. But she missed the first deadline. The next was November. She never mentioned my note.

In my fear and disappointment I began to prepare myself for what seemed inevitable. What, indeed, was I wanting for her so desperately? A path to the great white upward mobility, a marble stairway to charge cards, a decent salary, and safety? Was that happiness for her? Could she be happy managing a nail salon with a man who'd just gotten out of jail for not killing someone?

When I later talked to Mama on the phone, I told her what had happened to Dee. It wasn't easy to explain.

"Is that an Afro-American person?" she asked.

"Yes, ma'am. He's a very nice young man. I'm very fond of him."

"Rosemary. Sometimes I just don't understand you."

"Mama, the world is complicated."

"I know the world is complicated, but if the world up there is that complicated, maybe you should move back down here, where things are a little clearer."

Mama wasn't a racist. She'd fought to integrate the city council, and she'd managed to keep it integrated for about two months, until the poor man couldn't stand to deal with either the fundamentalists or the beer drinkers any longer. She'd fought to integrate the schools before the courts ordered it. She'd always been fair-minded, brave, in an area where it wasn't easy. But she also always made a point of mentioning if someone was black. "A nice black woman," she'd say.

"Believe me," I told her, when she found out I had let Dee move in, "if you were here you would have done the same thing."

"Let a young man that my daughter was involved with—whatever color he was—move into my house! No, Rosemary. I don't think I would have."

"Well, I don't know, Mama. I was only trying to do the right thing."

We didn't have too much to say after that. She told me a tornado had ripped through north of town and pulled a roof off a house, and a horse had completely disappeared. That was a typical East Texas story. In the red clay and piney woods and swamps there, nature was still wild and random and sometimes miraculous.

For a minute I wished I hadn't told Mama about Dee. But I needed to tell someone. I couldn't always make this lonely, single-headed journey by myself.

After I hung up with her I looked out my bay windows into the rain and thought of Viktor's lonely serenade. He wanted to know about America; maybe I should phone him. Let him share this latest disaster. But I was suspicious of my motives. And afraid to turn to anyone else when I needed to direct all my energy toward Shelly, should she want it or accept it.

"What do I do?" I asked Marcus the day after Dee's bail was set. "Sell my house? Rob a bank? Just sit by and let her join the Mafia? I'm not sure I'm going to survive this kid. She's driving me crazy. Do people ever die of childbirth after sixteen years?"

Marcus was dressed wonderfully as usual, with a dark olive shirt and a print tie, but he looked tired, beset by his own troubles. "You were out of your mind, Rosemary, getting mixed up with somebody like that in the first place." He seemed disgusted with me. I was shocked.

"Well, I'm afraid this time Shelly is really crazy about this guy. And I couldn't stop her from getting mixed up with him.

Believe me. Besides, I like him. He's funny. And I feel sorry for him. And Shelly says he's innocent. And Marcus, he would not kill someone. You should see his Stevie Wonder act."

Marcus was watching me glumly. It was the first time I'd felt genuine and complete disapproval from him. "What do you expect?" he asked. "You do careless things to make yourself feel good, and then when there's trouble, you're surprised. There are reasons for rules, you know. It's the way people protect themselves from disaster. And there are places to help people like that guy. He's not so bad off. He can obviously pull a good con."

There was, I knew, some element of truth in what Marcus said. It stung me, but I was too upset to figure it all out. "Well, thanks a lot," I told him. "And why won't you even say his name? Can't you give me a little credit here? Can I or people like me never do anything right because we happen to have been born the wrong color? Can I do nothing but give to the United Way? Come on, Marcus, that's not fair."

He just kept staring hard at me. Then, fortunately, his phone rang, and I had a minute to regroup. I sat down and drew a peace symbol on my "From the desk of Rosemary Kenny" pad and put it in front of his face. I could see his expression relax as he spoke. When he hung up I was ready.

"Remember 'Let me live in a house by the side of the road and be a friend to man'? Remember that poem?"

Marcus shook his head and turned to his desk. Once, when Shelly had disappeared for a weekend, he'd asked me why I didn't send her to a boarding school.

"Because I want to be with her," I'd replied. "Even if she does drive me crazy. Why would I not want to be with my daughter? She'll be gone soon enough, if I'm lucky. Of course she's difficult! Of course it isn't easy dealing with her alone! But boarding school?"

"Sometimes it's the only way," he'd said.

Now, for the first time I could remember, the atmosphere in our adjoining cubicles was uneasy. I walked into mine, and if I'd had a door I might have slammed it. I looked up at George Washington in his white cloud and it occurred to me what the problem might be. So I took two steps back.

"Marcus, maybe I should explain. I'm not talking to you about this because you're black and Dee's black." I felt as if I was going to cry. I'd had hardly any sleep the past few nights, for fear Shelly would drop out of school and go to work at a People's drugstore or take up waitressing or become a drug runner. "I'm talking to you about this because you're my friend. My best friend. And I don't know what to do."

That nice, honest, taut face looked at me squarely, trying to understand. Marcus was one of the few people in my life who cared enough to face me. But right now it was too much—too much eye contact, too much morning light in our adobe-shadow cubicles. We both were feeling too much, and we needed to look away.

Marcus sighed and glanced at his Rolex. "Harrison wants to see us." He pulled out his leather binder.

As we started down the hall I moved in front of him, still feeling I might cry, totally unready to face Harrison. Then I felt Marcus's hand on my shoulder.

"Hey," he said, "lighten up." But for the first time I realized I had an emotional dependence that was burdensome for him, more than he wanted me to have, that maybe wasn't fair or right for either of us. I wondered if I imposed on him because he was black and I could get away with it because I felt he was safe, the way some women do with gay men. It was a horrible thought and I was nearly glad when we confronted Harrison and I had to think of other problems.

When we entered his office, Harrison was a symphony in

banker's pin-striped gray. He held a golf club and was putting across his mauve carpet into what looked like a dustpan. Harrison, like all the beautiful people he identified with, was still tan from summer. He would somehow remain tan through the winter, would soon be a golden tan from skiing.

I began. "I think we've worked out a nice show for this young artist. It should generate some good publicity and word of mouth and name recognition. . . ." I embellished as I went along, painting the image from what had come of several conversations with the sad Cecilia and her hostile but talented brother. I made it sound as if the name André Bontemps was the newest on the Rolodex at the Museum of Modern Art. I realized as I spoke that this job, and /or Harrison, had inspired me with my own Hollywood style of commercial fantasy. I glanced at Marcus. No wonder he thought I was a flake. We were in a flake business. I rattled off how much media attention we might get with this show and updated Harrison on the one production company that had demonstrated some interest in filming in Sainte-Marie.

Harrison approved of the gallery show idea. It sounded glitzy, and Harrison, like so much of official Washington, adored glitz.

I told him I was in touch with the Sainte-Marie embassy and we were discussing the possibility of a reception for the VIPs after the opening of the show. Of course, since the artist was an enemy of the government, that seemed unlikely, but I didn't feel the need to go into political details at that point. After all, it was Harrison himself who'd said, "Fuck the politics, Rosemary!" I finished with the possibility of some celebrities' attending the opening.

"Names," Harrison demanded, practicing his wrist motion with his golf club.

"Well," I began, and he interrupted.

"Not those Democratic homeless activists. We don't want

any down-at-the-heel context here." He tapped the ball, and we watched it head straight for the dustpan, only to veer off at the last minute. "Republican celebrities is what we need," Harrison said.

I didn't know any Republican celebrities.

"I'll look into that," I told him, "but I can't see Arnold Schwarzenegger at an art show."

It was a joke, but Harrison had no sense of humor. He shook his golf club and addressed the ball. "Rosemary, he's not the only Republican celebrity."

"Pat Boone, then." I realized I was screwing it up after my brilliant but loathsome initial pitch.

But Marcus came to my rescue with mention of some people from the Hill who might appear. Harrison seemed satisfied, and we finished with a vaudeville flourish, mentally cakewalking out the door just as Harrison's golf ball veered once again.

"That's got to be a trick ball," I told Marcus.

Back in our adobe shadows I said, "Marcus, I don't mean to lean on you too much."

I was thinking that maybe I was going crazy. Maybe after the divorce and living with this teenager with a hole in her nose I'd lost it without even realizing.

Then Marcus lobbed his grenade.

"I'm kind of . . ." He shrugged. "Well, Michelle and I are . . ." He signaled a time-out. Marcus had a more sophisticated communication level than I did. I always wanted everything spoken plainly and obviously.

"Separated?"

He nodded.

"Oh, no." I was truly horrified for him. I had suspected once or twice there might be problems, maybe other women. But even so, I knew that the last thing in the world he wanted was to have his marriage break up.

"Oh, Marcus!" I said. "How long?"

"About two weeks." He removed his glasses and rubbed the bridge of his nose. There was such pain in his eyes when he looked up at me, and I turned away, but my gaze fell on the photos on his desk: Michelle and their son smiling on some beautiful tropical beach.

"Is it permanent?"

"I don't know."

"What happened?"

He put his glasses back on. "You know, Rosemary, I don't have to tell you everything." He nervously tapped his desk with his right hand. He wore a silver ring inset with turquoise that I'd always considered extremely sexy.

"I tell you everything."

"No you don't."

"That's true. But I tell you most things, everything but things about you and other men." His face softened. I loved the way that happened, as if he really trusted me. He walked over and stared out a window that overlooked an air-conditioner exhaust duct for the next building. The way that fat duct protruded always made me think of the *Titanic* going down.

I felt so bad for Marcus I came up behind him and put my arms around his chest and hugged his back. I could feel his heart beating.

"Oh, Marcus. I am sorry." I laid my head against his back. It felt cool and strong, and his olive shirt smelled like cologne and high-class dry cleaning.

"Thanks." He clasped his hands over mine. I think he was kind of choked up. We had both intended to marry someone we'd love forever, and have a good life. All that in-and-out marriage business was for egotistical politicians and insecure people in Hollywood; neither of us could afford it, and it hurt too much. It screwed up your life and lowered your living standard and made your children crazy.

I had always told myself I would never lie to Marcus. I had to be honest with him. And usually I was. But at that moment, I knew from how he clasped my hands that I'd sent a wrong signal, when he was especially vulnerable. And he realized it too. So I awkwardly pulled away, toward my desk. I could feel myself blush. "You wanna have lunch?" I said.

"I can't," he replied. His phone rang.

I saw from his eyes that I had gone too far. Despite thinking I would run over coals to be honest, I'd been too eager to give comfort. It was a profound mistake and I hated myself for it. Men and women were different. Men could be crude, but women could be careless.

As I was traversing the bulk-bargain aisles at the supermarket that weekend, I ran into Viktor Hajek. I had not spoken to him, only waved down the street, since the Neighborhood Watch meeting. I was so glad to see him I ran my grocery cart right into his, which I noticed was stacked with a lot of Lean Cuisine. He seemed cheerful; he was wearing American clothes—jeans and cowboy boots and a blue denim shirt.

"Oh, you look like a good ole boy," I said.

"Is that a compliment?"

"Not always," I said. "But this time I meant it as one."

He explained in his heavy, exotic *Casablanca* accent that the boots were Mexican. "How is your daughter?" he asked kindly.

"My daughter is still sixteen. Need I say more?" I had to make light of it so as not to break down and sob on his denim shirt.

"No, no." Viktor laughed. "I understand."

Then he leaned toward me and asked in such a way that I expected a more intimate topic: "Do you ever make chili?"

I said, "Are you kidding? Do I make chili? I'm from Texas, I'm from the neck of the woods where men are elected to Congress on the basis of their chili."

"Really!" He looked extremely interested.

"Some women even make tamales from scratch," I continued. Viktor Hajek didn't appear to understand the full import of that fact.

We were heading in different directions with our grocery carts, completely blocking traffic. Again Viktor Hajek seemed to be going in the wrong traffic direction. We pushed to a wider aisle to let people pass.

"To tell the truth," I said, "when I make chili I use a mix. My ex-husband used to make fabulous chili I couldn't possibly duplicate, so I'm intimidated for life."

Viktor Hajek said he'd had no idea making chili was a ritual of such significance.

"Oh, yes," I told him, wondering why, once again, in knee-jerk fashion, I had had to bring up my ex-husband.

"Complicated," he said.

"Isn't everything?" As I led Viktor to the chili-mix section, I added that I did make cornbread to go with my chili, thinking that might make up somewhat for my domestic failure.

Then, out of the blue, struck by my southwestern over-friendliness, no doubt, he asked if I'd like to join him Friday night for a reception at the Canadian embassy and dinner afterward. I was so unaccustomed to being asked out I reacted with total surprise.

"Sure," I said, my heart going thump. I realized I should have pulled out a Filofax and checked my calendar before saying yes as if I never had another engagement for the rest of my life, which was largely true. Then we pushed on in our separate ways, though we kept running into each other embarrassingly up and down the aisles. I wanted to tell him that his Lean

Cuisine was going to be defrosted before he reached checkout. But I managed to keep my mouth shut and just smile or nod each time we passed.

What am I getting myself into, I wondered. My first un-American infatuation. The idea shook up a lot of thoughts I'd been avoiding, and I felt like a figure in one of those glass balls where it snows. By the time I got to a checkout counter and Viktor Hajek pushed his cart behind mine, I was considering backing out, saying I had just remembered another engagement. How about giving me a call sometime in the twenty-fifth century, when I'll have rested up from my daughter and ex-husband? But I didn't. I pushed my cart out the door with the thought of Tom's body in my mind.

That Thursday there was a shooting at Shelly's high school. According to the television news, an argument that had started in the cafeteria spilled over into the schoolyard when one of the parties left and came back with a gun. No one was killed, but two were wounded and the whole student body was terrorized. The evening news showed two stretchers being pushed into ambulances, and students standing around in groups, crying and trying to comfort one another.

Shelly wasn't there, because she'd taken off that afternoon to visit Dee. As I was coming home from work, I'd seen her leaving a red Nissan Pathfinder that I knew belonged to Mario.

"I don't like the idea of your visiting jail in the first place," I told her later, "even to see Dee, but especially going with Mario!" She was on Dee's list of five people permitted to see him, though according to her, Dee didn't have five people who wanted to visit him. She claimed Mario was like Dee's brother, they'd grown up together, both of them brought up by Dee's grandmother. And Shelly liked Mario. He was the only other person who really cared about Dee, she claimed. The only person she could talk to about Dee.

She was still trying to raise bail and threatening to leave school and take a job. Over the weekend I'd heard her making mysterious phone calls to people with names like "Iron Man." In the middle of the night I would ask myself if I shouldn't put up my own house as collateral for Dee's bail. At three a.m. that could seem reasonable. Though I could also envision a made-for-TV movie in which both Mama and Tom would bring charges against me as an unfit mother.

Shelly said that half the boys at school carried guns, and metal detectors were being installed in the main entrance. Sometimes I'd offer to drive her to school just to make sure she reached the premises safely. She was sick a lot. I reminded her that this was her senior year, it should be fun. I reminded her of her college application essays, of the approach of the next deadline. I suggested she see a therapist. If I couldn't persuade her to move on with her life, maybe a professional could.

The night of the shooting she was sitting in front of the TV, painting her nails and watching the news.

"Why can't Mario put up his Nissan for collateral?" I asked her.

"He hasn't made enough payments."

Aren't drug dealers supposed to be rich? I thought. But I didn't say it. Scenes of the day's shooting at the high school came on the screen. Shelly pointed out the various people she knew.

I was sitting near her, already in shock from the image of my daughter being frisked to go into a jail. What would that experience do to a girl's psyche? I'd read about young women bringing drugs hidden in sanitary napkins into jails, women who once a week, sometimes for years, rode a bus to a prison in suburban Virginia to visit their loved ones.

I asked Shelly whether she'd finished her homework. She nodded without speaking and studied her nails. With Dee gone, she was back to doing her homework in front of the television.

"How in the world did we get mixed up in all this?" I asked myself as much as her.

Shelly stared at me to see if this was an attack on her. "Where have you been, Mother? It's my world!" she said.

That was one of the moments when I asked myself if East Texas would have been a wiser decision.

"Look at the choices you're making, Shelly. You could be ruining your life!"

"What about Dee's life?"

"I'm not responsible for Dee's life."

"Is that all it is? A matter of your responsibility?" Her face was hard.

I tried to speak calmly, to defuse the atmosphere. "Of course not," I said. "I love you. I want you to have the pleasures of an education and a stimulating career. Not to be bored. To be self-supporting and independent. To travel. To fall in love and have a good and happy life. To have your own family if you want that."

She glanced at me. "Maybe I don't," she said.

Maybe. At least she was equivocal. Was my idea of a happy life for her as outmoded as dates and proms, chrysanthemum corsages and *Father Knows Best*? Maybe possibilities had changed while I was focusing elsewhere. Maybe I didn't really know what my daughter wanted or what would be best for her.

I knew I had failed again in urging caution about Mario. But certainly, I tried to reassure myself, it was important to register a complaint, even simply to present a point of view that involved safety and common civility. With that in mind, I changed the subject. I told her I was going out the next night, and in an effort to communicate further asked if she could get her own supper.

"I'll manage," she responded.

"There's some chicken in the refrigerator," I told her. But I knew she'd probably use the opportunity to buy some greasy carry-out.

"Where you going?" she asked, reminding me how rare it was, this social outing. I felt soothed somewhat by her show of interest. I told her I was going to the Canadian embassy with Viktor Hajek.

She thought that over, squinting at the TV. "Oh, he's the man that ran into you with the broom?"

"That's right." Her anger seemed to have dissipated.

"He gave you flowers?"

"Um . . ."

"He was here that other time? Sounds serious." She looked up to see my reaction. Then she smiled for the first time since Dee's arrest. I was glad to see those rich teeth even if the humor was at my expense, but I was embarrassed and a little annoyed, and I countered without really intending to.

"That nail junk smells like a petroleum plant. It's bound to cause brain damage," I told her. "Please don't use it."

Later, while getting ready for bed, I looked in the mirror as I pulled on my cotton sleep shirt with the image of Martin Luther King, Jr., on the front. It certainly wouldn't get me far in the personal search for romance. But the thought of Viktor Hajek was inching toward the front of my brain, settling there, building like a hornets' nest 'round and 'round, offering a daily reprieve from the world of disputes and violence.

Marcus had, of course, already been to the new Canadian embassy. He was on the short list of blacks who were on both black and white social lists. He joked he could make a killing renting black stand-up cutouts for white parties. But of the Canadian embassy he said, "Clean white. Very stainless-steel-and-marble. Your George Washington would feel comfortable there."

It was morning and we were on the elevator with a few others. The cologne quotient at this time of day was about four thousand decibels, or whatever it is that measures fragrance.

"Who's the lucky escort?" he asked me.

"A man, a neighbor." I felt myself blushing—what had happened to me?

And just as I was thinking that, Marcus said, "What is it with this blushing, Rosemary?"

I wondered whether I should tell him it was the hornet's nest of possible romance building in my mind, or whether there in the close phony-mahogany-and-brass confines of the elevator it was clear to him.

"I met a man. I can't help it."

"Well, how about that. But I never expected love to turn you into a nineteenth-century female."

"I didn't say anything about love," I said quickly. "I said 'a man.' "

The elevator stopped on seven and we passed through the corridor of scent and into the hallway to our suite.

"Oh," Marcus said, "just sex."

"There's a long, long road a-winding between man, sex, and love," I said. The hallway was so still and airless and without character that it always made me think of purgatory, the souls of former associates floating ghostlike about the gray textured space. Inside the pretentious double doors of Harrison & Associates and beyond the sun-bleached Santa Fe console we said good morning to the receptionist and passed to our cubicles.

I admit, if I'm not faint from an overdose of cologne, I like offices first thing in the morning. I like the freshly made-up, hopeful faces prepared for a new day of possibilities, a newly dealt hand to play in the form of mail, the quiet, efficient hum of an incoming fax, the silent stack of pink while-you-were-out slips awaiting attention.

Marcus dropped his beautiful Italian leather briefcase beside his desk and said, "Well, congratulations. I knew life wouldn't pass you by."

"That sounds absolutely sarcastic," I said. "Sarcasm doesn't become you. And there's much more to life than love or sex. They're not so important. Right?"

He paused, then ignored my question. "I think that's terrific. And he's Canadian?"

"No, East European."

I guess I'd made a face, because then Marcus asked, "What's wrong with that?"

"Nothing." In a moment of illumination, I understood why I was making a face, why there always had been something disquieting about Viktor Hajek.

"Until lately I just never thought of the possibility of having un-American sex," I said.

This caught Marcus's undivided attention. He scrutinized me seriously. "East European. What kind of East European?"

"Czech. He's the man who ran into me with the broom." I had pulled out my hairbrush and was trying to restructure.

"How romantic," Marcus said matter-of-factly.

"It is kind of Fred-Astaire-and-Ginger-Rogers, isn't it? Without music. Only sirens." Marcus laughed, and I felt relief that we had passed our previous awkwardness and were back to an easy, friendly relationship.

"This is just a casual thing. Extremely casual. We're just neighbors. But he's interesting," I said. "The only thing I know about Eastern Europe is the movie *The Third Man.* Is Austria Eastern Europe?" I dropped my brush into my bag and went to water my china doll plant.

"I don't think so," Marcus said.

"You know how I'm only used to good ole boys? Is that provincial?"

"Yeah, I'd say." Marcus was opening his briefcase.

"But look at it this way. If he's from Prague, is he going to be interested in D.C. statehood? I figure we won't have anything to talk about after going over our common-crime story."

"Come on, Rosemary. Is your disc filled?" Marcus tapped his head.

"I hope not." Water suddenly poured over the side of the china doll's saucer and I had to pull out a sheaf of tissues to mop it up before it ran into a file drawer.

When I'd recovered, Marcus said, "It's about time."

"Don't be a male chauvinist. I don't have to have a man. It's not so important." Just as I said that, an assortment of pigeons came flying up outside the window and settled on the next roof. "Pigeons don't always pair up," I added.

Marcus stopped all motion and looked at me. "You believe it's not important?"

I wiped the wet tissues across the dusty top of the file cabinet. The leaves of the china doll were delicate and feminine. Who names plants, I wondered.

"No," I said. "Not really. It's what everyone wants, isn't it. Just not *all* everyone wants. Love and equal pay. But it's the real bottom line, isn't it? Even Einstein fell in love."

In a staff meeting that morning, Harrison outlined the upcoming art show to our colleagues. He made it sound like one of those blockbuster exhibits, something like *Thirty Centuries of Mexican Art,* that toured the world and inspired reshaping of historical perspectives. The hyperbole, as inflated as a Pentagon budget, was a warm-up for speaking to the client, I knew. But even so, it made me wince. I reported the final details of the art show and Marcus told about a pitch he was making to public television about Sainte-Marie. We both knew that if PBS really looked hard at Sainte-Marie we'd probably be dead in the water, but this sounded good and slightly plausible in the overdry air of the conference room. Harrison moved on to the next account, a new airline for VIPs that would probably go belly-up before we could bill it.

That afternoon, while I was wandering through a bookstore, I found a comic book that gave tips about safe sex, in English and Spanish. There were explicit lists of sexual acts, what was safe and what was not, oral and anal, the whole bit. Some things I'd never even heard of. On one page was a cartoon drawing of a couple in bed. The curly-haired woman was gaily blowing up a condom. *Play, make jokes about it,* was the message. Somehow I had a hard time imagining myself in my Martin Luther King, Jr., sleep shirt playing with a condom. But I bought the comic book anyway, thinking that I was buying it for Shelly and thinking too that when I got really lovelorn, instead of reading John Updike I could turn to the list of safe and unsafe sex acts.

I MET VIKTOR HAJEK at the Canadian embassy after work that evening. The exterior was surrounded by high steps that gave the feeling of a fortress, but a mid-level ledge was planted with welcoming small trees. Viktor Hajek looked attractive and at ease in a navy suit, striped tie, and white shirt, like a 1950s diplomat from some small country with an unpronounceable name. After he gave me one of those kiss-each-cheek European greetings, which was a first, we took the elevator upstairs to a white-and-stainless-steel reception room full of tables laden with delicacies.

Viktor knew a lot of people and introduced me around, but some of the foreign names went in one ear and out the other—always a problem for someone in public relations. I wore a suit that I saved for special occasions because it had to be dry-cleaned every time you looked at it. I had bought it on sale, like everything else I bought, but it was too tight in the waist and I couldn't eat when I wore it. So I put food on a junior-sized plate and just shifted it around, feeling guilty as I thought of all the nearby homeless.

Later, inside Viktor Hajek's small German car, I struggled to fasten my seat belt, until he turned to help. The touch of his warm, aiding hand created a small electrical shock between us, and he pulled back.

"Sorry," he said, and we both laughed as he touched my hand again and pressed it for a moment. When the headlights flashed on and the motor started, it was like an ignition of future possibilities. That moment the world seemed a more welcoming place, and we both smiled through a dark but stately block of Pennsylvania Avenue.

Since Viktor was still new to the area, I directed him to a Latin restaurant on Eighteenth Street, where the maître d' was short, and attractive enough to be a movie star. There, at a small table by the window, we laid out our personal résumés. I told him about Tom's moving back to Texas, making it all seem as unemotional as a board game where the dice allowed me to move from here to there and back. It was curious how, sipping Spanish red wine in the bustling middle of a restaurant with lively smells of Latin herbs wafting about, we could present a skeletal outline of our lives so dispassionately. At this stage of life, kindly referred to as prime, one must abridge the résumé. Starting a relationship is like attending a series of meetings, making a presentation for an account: you unfurl more and more facts, summarize your life through different stages until you reach a satisfactory understanding and acceptance—or disapproval, and go your separate ways. It is a study in risk perception, with yourself as the product on sale, and if you make that sale you enter the blue-chip happily-ever-after phase, if there is indeed such a thing.

Even before I'd seen the photograph of Viktor Hajek on a

liberated Russian tank, there was a reassuring quality about him. Maybe it was the simple fact that he was comfortable with himself. Then, not far into the conversation, Viktor confided that he was a widower. Only he didn't say it like that, using that unattractive, ornithological-sounding word. He said his wife had died of hepatitis in Delhi. They'd been married thirteen years.

"How tragic," I said, looking at his sad brown eyes through his slightly smudged glasses. "When did this happen?"

"Six years ago," he said. I wondered if he could possibly have been alone all that time. Twice three lonely years. Or, as the song says, six years is a lot of nights sleeping single in a double bed.

Viktor told me he had a son who had just finished high school and was traveling in Australia before going on to college, and a daughter who was in school in Spain. So right before my eyes, he had magnified into a complicated web of relationships and tragedies. How silly of me to think an evening with him might lead to anything more than a glimpse of the Canadian embassy and a friendly chat. This new information took the wind right out of my sails.

In Mama's little town, if you fell in love you didn't have to learn everything about the other person, since everyone already knew everyone else's business. You probably knew about the other person's most embarrassing moments, and with whom he had his first sex and where.

When the waiter came, we ordered romantic salads with hearts of palm and decided to share a paella.

I asked Viktor what it was like to work in India. He said he'd found the country fascinating but it was frustrating to work there. Mexico was easier. I asked where he'd most like to be in the world if he had his choice.

"Oh, Prague. Maybe the most interesting place to be now is Europe. But it is interesting to see what is happening in this country. Any other country that has gone through what America has . . ." He did not finish, but politely sliced one heart of palm.

"Would be what?" I asked. "Washed up . . . ?"

"Washed up," he repeated, looking at me. The "up" had an "oop" to it. Whenever he repeated something I'd said, it sounded much more emphatic with that *Casablanca* accent.

"I suppose you're speaking of the twelve brief years in which we moved from the most economically sound nation to the world's greatest debtor nation?"

He smiled. "Something like that."

"The decline of the great world power is the subtext of everything now," I said. "Probably every stitch of clothing in this restaurant was made in another country."

Of course I had talked about the economic predicament of our country before, to Marcus and others. But I hadn't heard it discussed from the point of view of a foreigner in a Budapest suit. Hearing it was disturbing, even if the particular foreigner was appealing. To my sincere surprise it brought forth combativeness I would never have expected from me.

"I was reading just the other day how there's still more energy and new ideas like medical technologies coming out of the U.S. than any other place," I said.

"The economy is certainly changing. . . ." He ran his right hand through his hair, clearly disconcerted. I was sorry I'd put him on the defensive, and wished we'd started out discussing movies.

He went on to talk about the vitality of those hot developing nations in Asia where everyone works for seven cents an hour, and of course about Japan's workforce and how the unions have screwed this country. ". . . and the racial strife, the hostility, the polarization, so appalling, like South Africa," he said earnestly.

"And the joblessness and homelessness," I added. I could have thrown in a few more problems, but it upset me that a non-American was listing them, in an accent. After all, it was okay for me to say we were going down the tubes, but not someone who parked his German car headed the wrong way! Maybe hearing our problems from some fairly neutral outsider hurt my feelings. I couldn't pinpoint the emotion, but whatever it was, it was painful.

"But you don't understand," I told Viktor. "A hundred years ago Texas was still a frontier. Women weren't safe alone." It occurred to me that women were hardly safe alone today. "So don't count us out yet," I said, not even trying to smile.

"That's what I was saying," he insisted. "You're a remarkable country." He was leaning forward, hands extended, aware that he'd offended me.

Suddenly I felt choked up. I looked out the window, where two girls in the kind of provocatively short skirts Shelly often wore were walking a large black poodle. When I turned back, I saw Viktor Hajek was horrified. I was horrified. I moved my napkin to my eyes.

"I didn't mean to offend you," he said.

I smiled, and for an instant thought Viktor Hajek was going to leap from his chair and mop away my tears with his napkin.

"I promise I don't usually cry in restaurants," I said. He put his hand over mine, and despite my hurt I felt some internal warmth that made me want to hold on to him.

"I don't know what's wrong with me." I sniffed. "That embassy was so white. Of course, you're absolutely right. We're just going down the drain, every day we're sinking more and more into third-world status. There's so much violence. We don't vaccinate all our babies. We've laid off so many workers. Our president runs around wearing little whales on his pants. A fourth of our young black men are in jail or have been or are about to be. Everything you said is absolutely right. I say the same things and worse, all the time. But it's just that I'd never heard it from a non-American. It was something of a shock." A tear rolled down my left cheek and I dabbed it away by pretending to give my mouth a generous wipe.

The waiter came to ask if we wanted more wine.

"God, no," I answered.

"How about dessert?" he said.

"Dessert?" Victor Hajek repeated hopefully, like a parent trying to cheer up a child who's performed badly in a piano recital. I pretended to consider it, knowing he would feel better, but I remembered my tight suit and declined.

"No, thanks," Viktor told the waiter, "just the check."

There was a moment of embarrassed silence. Then Viktor said, "What a pleasant restaurant."

"I understand that people in Europe are delighted at our decline. You know, I once tried for thirty minutes to order orange juice in a café in Paris, and for thirty minutes the waiter refused to understand '*orange pressé.*' Can you imagine how many ways you can say that in thirty minutes? I just know that waiter could have understood one of them. I thought that was really tacky."

"Really tacky," he said, nodding. "Tacky" came out "tocky."

"I'm perfectly open to the success of Eastern Europe. Despite how awful Romania is to Gypsies. I would feel bad if France was going down the tubes. As it is, I feel bad that some of the sidewalk cafés are being replaced by fast-food joints. I even feel bad about Euro Disney. I agree it's a cultural Chernobyl."

Viktor looked at me with his concerned Eastern European face. "You shouldn't take it so personally," he said, and smiled fondly. Then he poured off the remains of the red wine between us and took my hand, as if indicating that in an often painful world, touching another person can help. After all, I thought, he should know, losing a wife like that and coming from a tormented land. I suppose Americans can often seem both naive and dangerous.

"This is a very beautiful city," Viktor said, trying desperately to get on more stable ground.

"This city is too close to the government. Government is such a compromise."

When the bill came, I offered to split it with Viktor; that seemed to embarrass him. As we were leaving, I reminded myself to check my horoscope. It was bound to say, "Not a good day to start a relationship."

As we walked to the car, I wished I'd told him about my stupid job: we could have had a laugh or two about that. But maybe that wasn't such a good idea, since he already was obviously presenting the American world to Eastern Europe as only a breath away from the situation in Chad. And there was the question of professional ethics, which I was far too strung-out to deal with. I vowed that henceforth, instead of storing up facts and figures to criticize the nation with, to exclaim how we were going to hell, I would collect facts and figures about something we did right, besides export hamburgers.

In the night air, leaves sailed down from the oaks on R Street, and against the streetlights they looked like great gold coins. Viktor's car wore a pink ticket for having been parked too close to a fire hydrant.

"You'd think the police would be busy with more serious crime-stopping," I said.

Inside the car, I managed my seat belt without help. On the way home we passed the grocery store where crime had brought us together. There certainly was nothing romantic about the setting. It was not at all like a Fred Astaire–Ginger Rogers movie set. Indeed, with the lights out and the door barred, the place seemed seedier than it had before. On the way home I wondered how Viktor Hajek could drive a German car when Germany had been invading and slapping around Eastern Europe throughout history. But I kept my mouth shut about that. When he got to my house and looked for a place to park, I said, "That's okay, really, don't bother." It would mean another traffic ticket, I thought. "I'll just get out here. It's really late, and I have to work tomorrow," I said nervously, realizing as I said so that it was Friday and I didn't have to work tomorrow.

He put his arm around me, his hand securely clasping my shoulder, and I leaned forward and kissed him softly on the mouth. "Thank you," I said, and left him there waiting graciously to make sure that I got inside my door without being tomahawked.

I came in to find Shelly and her friend Miranda, who had a dark, vampire look about her, watching a trashy video. If I hadn't been so depressed at my behavior with Viktor, I would have protested.

"How was your date?" Shelly asked, saying the word "date" mockingly.

"Fine." I ignored her tone. "The Canadian embassy is attractive." I heard her and Miranda laugh as I went to the kitchen for a glass of water.

While I undressed for bed, I thought over the evening, trying to decide whether to proclaim it a complete or only a partial disaster. Settled in bed full of wine and regret, I wondered why I'd sabotaged things. And the word came to me—fear. Fear of reentering the world of men and possible rejection. It had been a long time since I'd put myself in such jeopardy. I had been perfectly willing to excuse myself by saying exactly what Mama would have said: *My duty is to my child,* that spoken in my mother's voice. And after so many lonely nights, the idea of feeling attraction to a man was more than a challenge; with my overburdened emotional energies, it might even be a threat. Yet turning out the light I recalled the confident touch of Viktor Hajek's hand on mine, his clasping my shoulder as we kissed, and wondered if that was the end of that.

Although I admired Shelly's loyalty and conviction in refusing to celebrate her birthday without Dee, I was alarmed that she wasn't giving an inch, much less finishing her essays. Each time I passed her bedroom, I saw the drafts lying there on the edge of her dresser, abandoned and stained with more and more drink rings. Some days I was tempted to complete them myself.

"Dee wouldn't want you to miss going to college, Shelly, you know that," I pleaded with her one night. She now claimed that Dee's grandmother and an aunt would each contribute to his bail. All she needed was a thousand dollars, plus her own savings from her summer job and gifts from Mama over the years.

"A thousand dollars, a mere pittance to most middle-class white people!" She gestured to me Italian style with her hands extended.

I wondered where she'd come up with the word "pittance."

As if she were in mourning, which I suppose she was, she'd taken to wearing black, like her friend Miranda. There was a disturbing disorder about her. All that week she'd worn the same jeans with the knees torn out, and something that looked like a rock in her nose, and her black sweater with holes in it over a black leotard. Her multihued hair hung drearily about her face, and her silver bracelets had fallen down her arm to form a thick cuff around her wrist.

"A thousand dollars is a lot of money to everybody I know," I told her.

She was supposed to be writing a book report. Instead she'd been thumbing through a lingerie catalogue not far removed from pornography. I was concerned about her grades, her graduating, her mental health. She'd spent her birthday money from Mama to go to a Mother Angelica, who claimed to solve current problems and provide safety for the future. Then she'd set up a grotto in the corner of her bedroom, where she burned candles and incense and dripped oil on the floor, which made the whole house smell like a cheap carnival.

"I do not have a thousand dollars in the bank, anywhere," I said. "We live on the edge, Shelly. I thought you knew that."

She smirked. "On the edge," she echoed, pulling her mouth into a broad grimace and rolling her eyes.

"Relatively speaking," I said. "I realize this isn't Somalia. But neither do we have two healthy incomes coming in, like Marcus and Michelle, for instance."

She shrugged. She looked thinner, her face nearly gaunt. She needed a good meal, a birthday meal with cake and candles and happiness and surprise packages. Images flashed through my mind of past birthdays, the snapshots I'd carefully saved each year and stored in a photo album for annual review. Looking at those early years was like falling in love again with this beautiful miracle of a person.

Outside, Pal began a loud low howl that rose with multiple sirens.

"It seems to me that to celebrate your seventeenth birthday, we could at least go out to eat," I pleaded.

"Why is that ritual so important to you? You just want to play like nothing is wrong. And that's not true!"

Shelly studied me then, all my failures being read through her head like a bar code. "If you had the money, would you do it?" she now asked calmly, pulling back from total disdain.

"I don't know, Shelly. I'd have to give it some thought."

"I know you wouldn't," she said and burst into tears. I watched the ratty back of her black sweater as she rushed from the room.

"It's a test," Marcus said the next day. "Don't you see, Rosemary, she thinks you don't have any respect for her or her opinions and desires. It's not just the money."

Suddenly the curtain opened. Of course. Why hadn't I understood? Her wanting the money from me had become a test of my commitment to her, or my rejection of her and Dee, of the very direction of her life. Exactly how far would I go to back her up, to believe in Dee's innocence, to respect her wishes? It had become a test of all my principles, and I was failing without ever having realized how much was at stake.

"Marcus, maybe you should be a therapist."

"I am to some people," he said smiling, "just unpaid. And don't mention fruitcakes."

The truth was that sometimes Marcus could say only a few words that would provide the key to my internal mechanism. He could somehow restore my damaged discs, mend the synapses between heart and mind, which were so often hung with Out of Order signs.

I could hardly wait to get home and present Shelly with my new understanding. On the bus I rehearsed scenes wherein I spoke wisely and she smothered me with gratitude and said of course we'd have a wonderful birthday dinner, aglow with familial love.

I walked into the house, and before I could live my fantasy, I saw—sitting at the kitchen table—Dee. Shelly, radiant, stood over the stove frying bacon, which we never have. If Dee had wanted elephant obviously she'd have snatched one from the zoo.

They seemed so happy to be together it made me nearly

cry. I gave him a big hug. "Bless your heart," I said, like Mama. I could see the tension in his face, the weariness: there was a dullness to his skin tone, a studied slowness in his movements, and extra pounds had settled unbecomingly in his face. But with the resilience of youth—along with several bacon sandwiches and a quart of milk—he began to relax.

Later Shelly explained to me that the police had arrested the person who actually shot the young man at the party. "Oh, please, please," she added, "just let him stay here till he finds something. He doesn't have anyplace to go, he'll be out on the street. It was a hideous experience, and he needs some peace and quiet."

What savage could doubt that Dee needed peace and quiet? It might even mean another period of civility within our household. I was overwhelmed with gratitude that fate had once more delivered my daughter from what had seemed total estrangement and disaster, even if I had missed the opportunity to demonstrate my new sensitivity.

On Shelly's birthday, I took them both to a nice restaurant for dinner, and afterward, since it was part of her birthday wish, we built a fire in the fireplace with those phony colored logs. Shelly turned out all the lamps and lighted some candles, and Dee, drinking a beer, told us about his stay in jail.

"One time I was waiting in line to use the phone. Supposed to have only three minutes. And there's this long line and the dude been talking and won't get off the phone and people getting real upset. Ever'body's fuse is short in that place, 'cause it's so crowded, one thing. And on the phone there's just so long a time, and this dude just keeps on talking. Finally this other dude walks up, a short, kinda wide, thick guy nobody messes with, and he takes this shiv and stabs him in the back. The guy drops like a load of bricks, and the other guy just as cool picks up that phone, hangs up, and dials a number. . . .

Don't nobody say a word. That line of guys just fades away, man."

"Oh my God," I exclaimed.

Shelly rose to poke the logs in the fireplace. Then she sat back on the loveseat and propped her feet on the stool she was sharing with Dee.

"Another night, they catch this guy they think's a snitch. They start beating on him and after a while they pour oil on him and set him on fire. There was some weird dudes in there. Some of 'em crazy."

It was almost peaceful to be sitting there in front of the fire while Dee talked. I wondered how it could feel so comfortable with what he had just described. Maybe it was because I lived with fearful images running through my mind all the time.

"Ain't no way I'm going back there," Dee said. "Ain't no way."

Shelly and I looked at each other, and I knew we were thinking the same thing: There was no way Dee could be certain of that.

And Dee seemed different after being in prison. He was never again quite as cool, confident, and easy as before. He moved slower, hesitated. Had this vulnerability been there previously, and I just hadn't seen it?

So the Monday after his release, Dee was out looking for a job as if his life depended on it. And maybe it did. For a couple of weeks he didn't mention his rap group, and I began to wonder what his safety, his being off the streets and out of jail, had to do with that part of his life. But soon the Ladykillers reappeared on the scene and the bomp-bomp-bomp in my basement began again.

So that's how it came to be that Dee Taylor and his meager assortment of possessions, along with his trunkful of hopes and dreams, once again took up residence on my living room couch.

With Dee's prison crisis passed and Shelly restored to her semi-good humor, I returned to replaying my disastrous evening with Viktor Hajek, editing it in my mind to what I should have said or would say if I ever had the chance again.

That next Sunday, Mama reported that, inspired by a workshop she'd attended at the mayors' conference in Dallas, she'd suggested the city council organize a bowling tournament to break down the factions on the council.

"But you can imagine what happened, Rosemary. There are two teams, and one is the beer drinkers and the other is the fundamentalists."

"So why don't you have them draw straws or something to break them up?"

"I did! But they exchanged straws."

I told her she should give up on the idea. "Oh, Dee is out of prison," I said, offhandedly.

Her response was a rather hesitant, "Oh, that's nice. . . ."

"He was innocent all along. They found the right man."

"I hope you're not letting him live there," Mama said. When I didn't answer she said she had to go, no doubt to avoid facing my continuing moral failure.

A two-inch article in *The New York Times* that same Sunday had reported on terrorism in Sainte-Marie. Guerrillas wearing black masks stormed into a popular oceanfront restaurant and shot eight people with the latest in automatic weapons, killing five of them.

"Too bad we couldn't buy up all the Sunday *Times*," I said to Marcus the next morning. "I doubt that's going to help Sainte-Marie as a tourist draw."

"It will help with name recognition," Marcus joked.

We were in Harrison's office waiting for him to return from the Eastern Shore, where he and his wife owned a house. A truck had jackknifed on the Beltway and he was sitting in traffic, his Mercedes heating up, he complained from his car phone. Through the sounds of helicopters and fire engines and cars honking, he shouted at us to sit tight; he'd be there momentarily.

"I don't know how he can be here momentarily unless he hitches a ride with a helicopter," I said. But in fifteen miracle minutes, Harrison swept in, uncharacteristically rattled by being late and caught in the madness of the morning's rush hour. Still wearing his raincoat, he proceeded to sneer at my choice of restaurant for the post–gallery opening dinner. The restaurant had been reviewed well by the *Post*'s food critic, I said, and was mentioned occasionally in the social whirl as a place where local VIPs and even out-of-town celebrities often gathered. I knew for a fact—actually, the fact that it was mentioned in a newspaper—that Elizabeth Taylor had had lunch with Al Pacino there once. Furthermore, the restaurant was near the gallery. But none of this impressed Harrison.

"That restaurant is just not the right place now," he said, his tanned neck nestled in the collar of his Burberry. Wrong administration, was what he was implying. Democrats went there, not Republicans.

"We are following a motif. After all, the central emphasis is the island of Sainte-Marie, and this restaurant's owner grew up there, or his mother did, and they serve jerk and avocados, spiced fish and mangoes, and other island fare," I said.

I glanced at Marcus and could see the muscles in his jaw flex. The truth was that if that truck hadn't jackknifed on the Beltway and Harrison hadn't been caught in traffic and eight people hadn't been shot on the shores of Sainte-Marie, Harrison might have been delighted with the choice, even if he considered it a Democratic restaurant. Such random events are the stuff that careers are made or broken over.

Marcus and I sallied back to our cubicles.

"Let's go out for a drink," I said.

"It's only ten-fifteen, Rosemary."

"I know. Now I understand why so many people start with Bloody Marys at ten in the morning. They work for people like Harrison."

"Oh, don't take it so hard," Marcus said. "He's having a no-good, nasty day." But I could tell Marcus was discouraged too.

I sat down in my swivel chair, and slipped off my shoes and wiggled my toes, half hoping to tear my panty hose so some particle of my feet and legs could breathe.

"I'd like to see Harrison try to deal with that little painter. They'd be a good pair. We'll probably get fired and be sleeping in our cars by Christmas."

"Jesus, Rosemary." Marcus disappeared into his cubicle, and I realized my tendency to testify to the worst possible scenario could sometimes be a burden to the witness at hand. I rose from my chair and followed him.

"I'd hoped something decent might come out of this show. That it might really help that painter."

Marcus turned and faced me. He had that clean and fresh, early-morning browned-biscuit color that I loved. His eyes had a speck of humor that his voice didn't convey. "Really?" His question was a jolt back to reality.

Of course, I didn't mean that. I was lying to myself. What we were ultimately trying to do was survive. To hell with the little painter. In this business it was hard to be honest, even with yourself.

Marcus set off toward the men's room. Before he disappeared I gritted my teeth and said, "My mother always says, 'When in pain grit your teeth.' "

He looked back. "Hey," he said. "So did my grandmother."

To my grave disappointment, Viktor Hajek did not attend the October Neighborhood Watch meeting, at which we discussed two break-ins, the disappearance of trees from tree boxes, and the noise from car alarms going off in the middle of the night. Doreen reported that a notice of application for renewal of a liquor license had been posted in the window of the Bluebird Bar & Grill. Which meant our time had come to appear at the liquor board hearing, if only we could find out the actual date of the board's meetings.

"It's like living in a banana republic," Doreen said with disgust.

I sat near Mrs. Nance, who had developed an autumn cold and smelled of Vicks VapoRub. At the end of the meeting I passed around invitations to the approaching art show. Though I doubted many of my neighbors would attend, Marcus and I were hoping for throngs and I personally was hoping that amid the throngs might be Viktor Hajek. Since our Canadian embassy evening a few weeks earlier, Viktor had only waved warmly from a distance. I could hardly blame him. And when I ran into him at the supermarket the previous Saturday he'd asked my advice about what color to paint the front of his house. I didn't like any of the pastels on the chart he had, and said that. I could tell he thought I was just being contrary.

"Come by and let me show you my paint charts," I told him. I had forgotten what a nice height he was. Most of our jousting had been done sitting down.

"Oh, thank you so much," he said, looking into my eyes, "but I'm going out of town for a few days."

"Can I do anything for you?" I asked him.

He seemed surprised, and I guess I must have blushed.

"I mean any neighborly thing. Feed your fish or bring in your newspapers. Anything like that?"

He paused. "How kind of you," he said. "But thanks."

"Thanks, yes? Thanks, no?"

"Thank you, no. Not this time. Perhaps I'll see your paint charts when I return."

"Have a good trip," I called as we pushed our separate ways. Well, I thought, at least I let him know I was still interested. I did everything but jump into his grocery cart. When I turned to watch him head toward the frozen food, I wished I'd invited him to the art show. Now I would have to impersonally drop an invitation through his mail slot.

In desperation, after two weeks of searching, Dee finally accepted a job at a fast-food restaurant near the University of Maryland. The manager told him he could start at forty hours a week and work up to a manager's position; in three months he'd receive benefits. I was sorry that Dee had to settle for a greasy-spoon franchise, but I didn't say it. I could tell Shelly felt bad about it too, but we toasted and celebrated anyway. Dee had to take two buses to reach the restaurant, and the first week he worked only twenty-one hours. The second Monday he spent an hour getting there, only to be told there were too many people working that day so he could leave. It turned out that no one, even managers, worked a forty-hour week or received benefits: typical of employment for the young or for people willing to take anything to survive.

So the next day Dee began looking around for something else. One morning he went to Beltsville for an interview to be a clerk in a large discount store. He waited two hours to be interviewed by the regional manager, who then told him there weren't any openings.

"How did he get to Beltsville?" I asked Shelly.

"His cousin took him." My heart sank. I knew she meant Mario, the drug dealer.

"Oh, dear," I said.

"Well, what else could he do? I could've taken off school but you would've had a fit." Shelly was heading out the door for school, eating a Snickers bar because she didn't have time for breakfast.

"Please drink some orange juice." I followed after her.

"Don't have time." She settled her weighty backpack over her shoulder. I watched her move slowly down the sidewalk toward the bus stop. She'd adopted what I called the inner-city plod, in which the body seems to be pulling itself through heavy air. She never hurried. But at least with Dee around she was more pleasant. And now that he had a job I had dreams that he might even find someplace to live besides my couch.

At a computer software company Dee failed the typing test. He took the government civil service exam and failed that.

"He should take it again," I told Shelly.

"That's easy for you to say." She lifted her skinny brown eyebrows.

At the end of the second week he was let go by the fast-food restaurant. They'd overhired, the manager said. He'd never liked Dee, Shelly claimed, from the very beginning. When Mario had come around, the manager said he was bringing in trouble.

"Mario must really be a winner," I said to Shelly as I was emptying the dishwasher. "I want you to stay away from him. I'm very serious about this."

"He's Dee's best friend. How can I stay away from him? They're like brothers."

"You can stay away from him. I warn you. And Dee should

stay away from him too. Jesus, I wish this saga would end," I said, half under my breath, forgetting that I had previously reached a more sensitive understanding of what Shelly's relationship to Dee meant to her.

"Let me tell you, Moms, this saga won't end," she said definitively, and made her exit.

That evening, however, the night before the art show, I first noticed Shelly correcting Dee's grammar.

"We're going," she said, after he'd said, "We gon." And then "with" for his "wif."

The second time it happened, Dee muttered, "Shut your mouth, bitch," and jumped up from the loveseat and left the house.

"Well, fuck you," Shelly called after him. "Did you hear that? Fuck you!" Out the front door, ringing through the clear night air for all the world to hear.

She slammed the door and walked back toward me, her face contorted. She pulled the elastic band out of her hair and shook her hair loose.

"I was just trying to help him!" she shouted, and ran upstairs in a cloud of furious tears. I followed after her, then stood in her bedroom doorway and watched her sort through a box of tapes looking for the right sound for the moment's crisis.

"I'm always trying to help you, and sometimes you get mad," I pointed out. "Sometimes people don't want to be helped."

She didn't respond, just slid a tape into her boom box, and Tina Turner began to sing "What's Love Got to Do with It" at high volume. I walked to a window and opened it a crack, thinking maybe Tina could bring us together. She was someone we both admired.

"You have to be patient with him," I told Shelly. "He's awfully sensitive right now."

She sat on the side of her bed, peeling off a phony fingernail. "I know that," she said in a calmer voice as she closed the window I'd just opened.

Just then the phone rang. It was Harrison, telling me there'd been a coup in Sainte-Marie.

"A coup?"

"A coup," he repeated. "They have a tank."

"Who has a tank? And only one tank?"

"Russian-made," he said, without answering my question. I didn't know whether this was his resorting to cold-war domino theory or whether he was indicating something else. "What this means, Rosemary, is that we may not get paid!" He repeated a Nixon-tape expletive.

"Well, I'm sorry." Harrison was acting as if I were personally responsible for the coup. If we'd had a movie in production there this never would have happened, he seemed to be implying. Or maybe he thought I, as a Democrat, was responsible for the one tank emerging from the forests of Sainte-Marie. "What do you propose we do?" I asked.

"We'll proceed and hope they crush it."

"But from what I've been told, *they*'re corrupt," I said. "We probably should support the coup. The painter we're presenting has even been in prison."

"Jesus, Rosemary!" Harrison said. "You think the others aren't corrupt?"

"Well, the painter was tortured." I realized immediately I should not have shared that with Harrison.

"Oh, that's just your leftover sixties commie pinko opinion. I can't believe you'd fall for that line. All those little indigenous peoples have stories like that. Politics in places like Sainte-Marie are very complicated."

I considered resigning that very moment, but I heard Pal howl and was reminded of the mortgage, panty hose, and hair products of necessity.

Harrison asked me to phone Marcus. We would be meeting with the prime minister the following day. For some reason Marcus one-on-one made Harrison nervous. Sometimes I fantasized to Marcus that Harrison and his mother were both in love with him.

I phoned Marcus. "Brace yourself," I warned him.

"I'm always braced, Rosemary. I thought you knew that," he replied.

THE DAY of the art show dawned crisp and clear. What we called in Texas a "blue norther" had blown in. After Shelly left for school, I went into the living room, where Dee was on the couch with the quilt wrapped around him, watching TV. He turned the set off with the remote.

"It got cold," I said to him.

"Yeah," he answered.

I sat down on the chair across from him. His face, fresh from sleep, had a childlike softness. He was hunched over, his arms hugging himself, his spirits obviously sagging. After Shelly's corrections the night before, he'd stayed out until after we'd gone to bed. She'd left for school without speaking to him. Things were rocky in the true-love department.

"Dee, honey," I said, "you're doing all the right things. Just don't get discouraged. What happened with the job is outrageous and you have reason to be angry, but you'll get a decent job eventually. You just have to hang in there."

He nodded as if he were embarrassed at my mouthing such worn words of encouragement. And all the while I was talking, I knew that I was simply playing the old game. I didn't have the courage not to. I could say otherwise in generalized political outpourings to Marcus or Doreen. But when it came down to flesh and blood I cared about, sweet Dee sitting there facing yet another discouraging day, I couldn't bring myself to utter my cynicism. I couldn't face what was maybe his truth, because I wanted so much for him to succeed, for us all to continue to some kind of happy ending. So I just motor-mouthed on.

"I know you've heard this before. But really, don't give up. I know you'll make it. You know, 'If at first you don't succeed, try, try again,' and 'Look for the silver lining whenever clouds appear in the blue.' "

He gave me a grim smile and dropped his head.

I stood up. The sun shone brightly into the bay windows. Outside, the hydraulic grind of a garbage truck with young men about Dee's age riding on its side sounded loudly from the alley. I hoped he would have a better future than that.

"Hey, there are blueberry bagels," I said as I left the room.

"No, thanks," he answered. He liked to eat breakfast at McDonald's. He and Shelly both, whenever they had a dollar or two. Before I left for work he was waiting for me.

"Hey, I hate to ask," he said, not meeting my eyes. "I've got a paycheck due from my job but . . . Could I borrow some . . . just till it comes? I've got a gig Friday night."

Usually Shelly intervened. *Can you loan Dee some money?*

"Sure," I told him. I took twenty dollars from my purse and tucked it under the sugar bowl. He entered the kitchen then, wearing the loose clothes he slept in and carrying a red sweatsuit under his arm. Did this mean he wasn't looking for a job today?

He gave me a nod that was part grimace. Settled about him now was the lethargy of depression. He'd been so lively before. I sighed—my cheerleading wasn't the answer—and patted his arm as I passed.

"Thanks," he said. "I'll make it up to you."

"I know you will." What I really knew was that he hoped he could make it up to me.

I told him I'd see him and Shelly at the art show that night.

I had intended to take a cab to work on this special day, but without the twenty dollars that option was gone. What the hell. I headed for the bus stop hoping I'd run into a neighbor driving to town. But I didn't see any neighbors, so I walked on in the crisp wind among the blowing leaves, all the green of summer now turned to auburn except for the stubborn tendrils of confederate jasmine that clung to green life through the bitter months. The walk gave me an opportunity to review my pep talk with Dee and wonder what his options were. I realized I truly didn't know.

That afternoon the ambassador of Sainte-Marie appeared at the office accompanied by two bulldog bodyguards in shiny gray suits and dark glasses. The narrower bodyguard wore a gold ring in his ear and chewed gum—the only movement as the two stood on either side of the front office doors with their arms crossed. The ambassador spent fifteen or twenty minutes in Harrison's office. He'd already told Harrison that because of the attempted coup, the prime minister had flown to Sainte-Marie, but was hoping to return for the evening's festivities.

"No doubt anything to get away from Sainte-Marie," I said to Marcus. "How can we inspire people to visit the place when even the prime minister doesn't like to be there?"

We were looking out a window to see if the ambassador had come in a camouflaged tank, but all we saw was the usual black Cadillac, which Sainte-Marie could ill afford. Finally Harrison's secretary buzzed us in, and Marcus and I filed into his office, where he introduced us to the Honorable Ambassador Desan, a short, plump man in a shiny black suit with a head too large for his body. Heretofore, I had dealt with a series of attachés, never the mysterious man before us. I looked into his dark watery eyes as he spoke a few heavily accented words about how he appreciated our brilliant work. It took only a second for me to be convinced that Sainte-Marie was indeed filled with secrets and intrigue. The ambassador told us he looked forward to the evening ahead, then swept out of the office along with his silent protectors.

"He's rather attractive, in a scary way," I said to Marcus. "He should wear a cape."

"Maybe in midlife you're getting boy-crazy."

Before I could retort, Harrison was back from escorting Desan to the outer doors. He began pacing in front of his windows.

"Desan says the situation in Sainte-Marie is stable. Things seem to have quieted down," Harrison reported. "He says terrorism is something they've learned to live with." He shrugged. "They know how to handle it."

I shivered when he said that.

"How's it looking?" He glanced toward us.

We repeated the same reassurances we'd given him first thing that morning and the day before and the day before that. He could never be too reassured.

"There should be a good turnout," Marcus said. I reported on media play, and said that the Style section had more or less committed. They're looking for upbeat stories on people of color, Marcus interjected. The *Times* was less committal, I added. He mentioned some of Washington's semi-celebrities and some influential Black Caucus names, and closed saying it should be a splendid evening.

It seems that you have to play PR with everyone, even your employer—or especially your employer. And Marcus knew to throw in a memorable word like "splendid," which would register in Harrison's subconscious even if he seemed too harried to be listening at the moment. It was another instance of having to fluff your feathers all the damn time.

By evening, the norther had turned more wild and blustery. The wind blows all the time in parts of Texas, especially around Fort Worth, where the west begins, as they say, and there's nothing to stop a steady wind blowing across the western plains. That's why women such as Ann Richards wear their hair sprayed stiff as wrought iron. The wind in D.C. is disturbing because there are too many objects at hand. On the way to the opening, Marcus and I passed a loose stop sign rocking in the wind so hard I was afraid it might pull free and fly off like a missile.

Inside the gallery, André Bontemps's paintings were bold and exuberant against the stark white walls, and to my great satisfaction they created the same aura of exotic and distant life that we'd experienced in that hot studio off Rhode Island Avenue when Marcus and I first saw them. The cold air outside contrasted sharply with the magical Caribbean world created by the flamboyant paintings. Before we positioned ourselves near the entrance to welcome the hoped-for throngs, the proprietor, a friend of Marcus's, ushered us around the gallery and through an installation in the back. She reported that André had been perfectly cooperative, even in hanging the paintings. She'd been concerned because of their linguistic differences, but with Cecilia translating, everything had gone smoothly.

The artist showed up, only a little late, wearing dress pants, a limp mustard-colored jacket, and a buttoned-up shirt without a tie, which I supposed was standard dress for a dissident painter. I had feared he would appear in jungle camouflage fatigues. Marcus and I congratulated him; I'd expected him to thank us for making it happen. But then I come from a part of the world where people go out of their way to say the right thing whether they mean it or not, and I have to try here in the harsher East to overcome my knee-jerk expectations of politesse.

André looked attractive standing at the back of the gallery. He was flanked by a large corps of relatives and friends: women in bright outfits, men and little boys in their Sunday suits, little girls in ruffled dresses, their hair tied back with ribbons and barrettes. Seeing the children dart about like merry, glittering birds made me happy; I was pleased to have given them this festive occasion.

I'd urged Shelly and Dee to make a drop-in—inside-the-Beltway language for a quick "Hello, I'm so busy, good-bye." And they did arrive, Dee in his work-seeking slacks and tie and Shelly in a vintage thrift-store black crepe dress. They looked so young, and I was ashamed that in my daily battles with Shelly I sometimes forgot that she was just a kid, not my equal in age and experience and maturity. Why couldn't I just rise above our conflicts and be the quiet, strong, loving mother of *Little Women,* who never raises her voice or gets angry or makes petty, sarcastic remarks? I would have to remember that the next time we locked horns.

I saw Marcus looking at Shelly and Dee. Then he glanced at me and grinned. Perhaps their being so refreshingly attractive and young and visibly in love would lead him to agree that offering Dee a roof wasn't so foolish after all.

Shelly and Dee stayed for approximately fourteen minutes, long enough for her to show her rich smile a couple of times, which made me feel even better. I introduced them to Cecilia, in a smart gray suit with bugle beads on the shoulder, who'd come over to say how excited her family was about the show; then I left them to be introduced to a flurry of large and small Bontemps brothers, sisters, and children. By then the room was filled comfortably with the quiet hum of people talking and laughing. Many of the regular art crowd showed up, people sporting wearable art who typically drank the sparkling water and cheap white wine served at these occasions and stood back and made comments about the paintings and talked about artists by only one name. They all read *Art in America,* bought paintings by name-brand artists, usually from New York, and knew what art everyone else had bought.

Cecilia excused herself and moved beside André, who was listening to a gallery regular speaking loudly to him in English. I felt an added tension in the room, but just then the gallery owner posted a tiny red dot, indicating a sale, on one of the paintings. Things were going so well, I thought: Harrison was bound to be pleased, despite the restaurant I'd chosen for afterward. And the ambassador and prime minister of Sainte-Marie would be pleased, and ultimately I would be pleased with the preservation of my job and livelihood.

As I was congratulating myself, Harrison entered the gallery with his mother—the twin team, we called them. Marcus came to my side and I complimented him on what a nice job he'd done. But he didn't smile, and I noticed something tight about his mouth.

"Have you noticed that painting over there?" he whispered. "And the little one on the side wall?"

I turned to each of the paintings, with all their vivid, wild colors.

"Yeah, that big one's really wonderful, isn't it? We saw it at the studio. It was my favorite."

Suddenly the nice face of Viktor Hajek appeared in the room, and I smiled and lifted my hand. I was beginning to feel as warm and glowing as a TV ad, when Marcus muttered, "You better take a closer look at that painting, Rosemary. Or maybe a more distant view of it. Look at it from here."

Viktor began to move my way, and I looked again at the painting across the room. It was maybe ten feet by eight, an impressionistic painting of marsh grasses and coconut palms and mangroves. But now, amid the vegetation, I could see figures—bodies hanging in the trees, washed up among the marsh grasses, impressionistic maybe, but still bodies. The little painter André Bontemps had altered his canvas.

"Oh my God," I said. I felt as if the Russian-made tank had

just rolled into the room, crushing every iota of warm glow. "Oh my God," I repeated. "Maybe only you and I will notice it." Marcus's eyes were steely behind his gold-rimmed glasses. Of course he wouldn't expect me to make sense at that moment.

I saw the ambassador enter in his shiny black suit, accompanied by his bulldog bodyguards. And then the prime minister appeared, tall and straight and handsome in an elegant white suit. He stood in the doorway as if waiting for trumpets to announce him. All heads turned and conversation lapsed as his presence was noted. Viktor Hajek made it to my side, and I introduced him to Marcus. But Marcus was so upset it didn't even register that this was my East European mental romance. I looked around to see whether Harrison realized the paintings were a revolutionary manifesto. But he and his mother were calmly drinking wine and talking to a congressman. Harrison would push himself back on his heels now and then to look for other important people. When he saw the ambassador and prime minister, he made his way toward them. I excused myself to Viktor and whispered to Marcus.

"André went into the back room. What should we do?"

Marcus didn't respond. Actually, I was speaking on automatic hysteria.

Harrison was shaking hands with the prime minister, who was smiling, his bronze face looking a bit condescendingly, I thought, at Harrison. Harrison lifted his shoulders slightly, as I had seen him do before when he was with taller men or men with greater authority. Then, with Harrison and the ambassador at his elbows, the prime minister began to tour the exhibit. He paused before each painting as if reviewing troops, tilting his head in considered judgment.

When the ambassador saw me and Marcus, he ushered the prime minister in our direction.

"Is there something wrong?" Viktor asked me breathily.

"I'm afraid so. See the bodies in that painting? They weren't there when we saw it initially."

Viktor looked around just as the ambassador and prime minister reached us. The ambassador introduced us to the prime minister, remembering both our names. I introduced Viktor, who, to my amazement, knew the prime minister.

"Lovely occasion," the ambassador said smoothly. The prime minister was already moving toward another group.

"You know him?" I asked Viktor.

"I interviewed him a while back."

That made me feel better. Not only was I impressed with Viktor Hajek, but this was a connection, like finding some East Texas relative to put you at your ease and make the world seem a smaller, more hospitable place. Also the prime minister seemed more interested in the people than the paintings, as I quickly pointed out to Marcus.

"He'll notice," Marcus muttered.

But the prime minister was heading toward *Midnight Ritual,* the most intriguing piece in the exhibit, an installation set up in a small room at the back of the gallery. There you passed through a doorway hung with crude burlap and into a dark cavelike space lighted with a few candles and cordoned off so that only one or two people could enter at a time. In the low glow of the light, it took a little while to make out the midnight ritual. In the center of the floor lay a shallow grave, so shallow the outline of a spread-eagle body was visible. There was the taped sound of a female voice speaking in a whispered language that I took to be native to Sainte-Marie. Around the grave, which was cordoned off with barbed wire, were symbols of the voodoo conjurer, models of dismembered chickens, lighted candles, chains, and manacles, and on the wall was a sculpture of a pained and bleeding Christ with red votive candles underneath. But what most created the atmosphere of horror was the sound of laborious breathing over the woman's whispering voice, and the fact that the chest of the buried body heaved up and sank down, as if the body had been buried alive. It was a shocking scene, even to someone like myself, uninvolved, I thought, in the politics of Sainte-Marie. At first glance it might seem a presentation of some native religious ritual, but in conjunction with the bodies in the painting, the installation took on a more sinister quality.

As the prime minister approached the doorway to *Midnight Ritual,* Marcus moved toward him, hoping to shepherd him in another direction. But a tall and beautifully exotic woman in black came up to give the prime minister a warm kiss on each cheek. They spoke for a moment, and then he took in the big painting with the bodies. He stood motionless. He seemed stunned. From across the room, he found me watching him and met my eyes. For a moment I believed I knew the feeling of standing before a firing squad.

The prime minister turned and started toward the front doors, and the entire room grew cold and nervous. As he reached the entrance, his face solemn, he spat out an order and the sentries on either side of the doors were in motion, pulling out guns from inside their coats. Thank God Shelly and Dee are gone, I thought. A swish of air stirred the room, as if someone had held the doors open and let the wild wind inside. The prime minister pushed through the doors, and I could hear the pop-pop-pop of gunfire, the sound of crashing glass, the shouts of men, and a shrill scream from the woman in black. Cries and screams filled the crowded room, and waiters dropped their trays of empanadas and Sainte-Marie wine and pulled out more guns from under their white jackets. There ensued what the newspaper later called a "melee," with people falling to the floor, stacking themselves inside the tiny bathroom, and hiding under the gallery owner's desk.

At some point I heard Cecilia shouting her brother's name, but I suppose he was already gone, through a secret tunnel or on a magic carpet, because as far as the United States Immigration Service and every other official national agency was concerned, André Bontemps disappeared from U.S. territory in the twinkling of an eye.

Later, when the sirens had ceased and the gallerygoers, who would not soon forget this opening, had fled outside to the blustery street and the ambulance had come to carry the prime minister to the nearest hospital, Cecilia tearfully told the police and officials from the embassy and the State Department that the disappeared André Bontemps would never, ever be involved in such a thing with children from his own family present. Of the original group, there remained only a few of us: Marcus, who was talking with the police; the gallery owner, who was hysterical; and Viktor Hajek, who stood by my heart-thumping side to the bitter end. He had pushed me around a corner and out of danger during the shooting and held his arms around my body until the gunfire was over. And when it was over, we realized to our astonishment that inside the mysterious *Midnight Ritual* chamber, the buried, spread-eagle body had ceased to breathe.

WHEN I WAS a child, a Gypsy king lay mortally ill in a hospital in the small city of Texarkana, best known for a string of beer joints that lined Arkansas Highway 67 into town and for its main street, State Line Avenue, where you could stand with one foot in Texas and the other in Arkansas. To the astonishment of the local population, there appeared from throughout the country hundreds of Gypsies—or Romanies, as they prefer—on pilgrimage to the bedside of the Romany king. Scores of somber, dark people in a variety of beat-up Cadillacs and other old cars and tilting trucks camped out on the lawn surrounding the hospital waiting for news about their king. This was a glimpse of a world we didn't even know existed, and I was reminded of that when natives of Sainte-Marie—not in tatters and rags and accompanied by flea-bitten cats, but in fine clothing and elegant automobiles, including shiny black Mercedeses—descended upon a D.C. hospital to attend the prime minister of their country. They jammed the corridors and the reception area, and beautifully and colorfully dressed as they were, they reminded me of André Bontemps's paintings.

We stayed, Viktor Hajek and Marcus and I, amid the angry stares of the vigilant countrymen and women, long enough to hear the announcement from a doctor that the prime minister would survive. Of the three bullets that had struck him, the only one that had caused serious injury was in the chest, lodged centimeters below the heart; it had chipped a rib and collapsed a lung. Another bullet had torn through his right side and exited his gluteus maximus, and the third penetrated the lower lobe of his right ear. There were shrieks of joy at the doctor's announcement. In relief I sagged against Viktor's arm and immediately phoned Harrison, leaving a message with his answering service.

In Viktor Hajek's car, we discussed how the evening's events and the sight of those elegant natives of Sainte-Marie had completely altered our mental images of the island.

"Maybe the elegant natives live here," Marcus said, "and the people in Sainte-Marie are more what we'd expected."

"Probably so," Viktor said. "It is a very poor island, with most of the arable lands owned by a few wealthy people."

We agreed that things are always more complicated than you first expect them to be. And I remembered that Viktor Hajek had said the same thing to me earlier as we walked down windy K Street, with the sound of sirens behind us and his arm around me.

We dropped Marcus at his parking lot. He'd made a call

from the hospital earlier, asking to speak to someone named Elena. So I wasn't surprised that he said no to joining us for a meal. I caught his hand as he left the car. It felt cold and dry, and his face was drawn with exhaustion.

"Are you okay?"

"Sure," he said. "Just fine," he added with a note of sarcasm.

"Marcus, look at it this way. It was nearly a terrific show. And truly an unforgettable night."

He gave me a half-smile for my effort.

The headlights illuminated the deserted parking lot where he had left his car. We watched him move gracefully across the lot to his BMW, unlock it, and climb inside. I was glad Marcus wouldn't be alone tonight.

Viktor put in a tape of Gregorian chant and headed up Connecticut Avenue toward our neighborhood along dark gusty streets. People were still parading around Columbia Road and Eighteenth. The clubs, like Chief Ike's Mambo Room, were just closing, and on Sixteenth a few homeless were settling for a long night on the benches of glass bus shelters.

I don't remember Viktor's asking me if I wanted to go to his house. I was so shaken by the night's events that maybe he did and I just forgot. But sometime later I was sitting on his comfortable leather couch in front of a fire of colorful burning logs, drinking wine, listening to soothing music while Viktor Hajek was cheerfully whisking together food in the adjoining kitchen.

Don't people often fall in love with their rescuers? In perverse modern times, sometimes even with their kidnappers? Is there a specific moment that one falls in love, or is it a cumulative process over time? Certainly, sitting there listening to glorious chamber music and realizing how Viktor Hajek had stood by my side through the long and painful night of warfare and unrest, I knew I would be grateful for his warm support for the rest of my life.

The next remarkable thing was that Viktor Hajek had fresh

basil. I could never get basil to grow in my kitchen, though I tried every fall; it always browned mid-stem, leaned over, and died. But there it was, the purple Italian variety, sprinkled in the omelette. He also made a green salad with walnuts and balsamic vinegar. And it was so peaceful sitting there it seemed a million miles from K Street and the fire trucks and ambulance and the voodoo and André Bontemps and all the problems of Sainte-Marie. Maybe the voodoo ritual, scary as it seemed, had cast a spell over the city, maybe everyone would encounter some rare delight on this night of a full moon and voodoo.

After we ate we listened to a Beethoven symphony that Viktor recalled hearing at a concert in Berlin years before. He remembered concerts the way I remember Fred Astaire movies. Meanwhile I kept removing clothes—shoes, jacket—and unbuttoned my tight skirt, trying to be more comfortable. Viktor brought out a blanket for warmth, and we sat under it together, looking at the fire and drinking wine. And I ask you, What else can a man and a woman do under a blanket in front of a fire after a recent demonstration of how tenuous life can be?

I leaned back and closed my eyes and said, "Let's play like we're in a wonderful, safe place. Is there any safe place?"

"Yes," Viktor said, "definitely."

I was so grateful for his certitude that I believed him.

"There are many safe places." He put his arm around me and I was even more grateful.

"Maybe Australia?" I said. "New Zealand has all those insects. Have you been to Australia?"

"Yes. I lived in Sydney for a while. I very much liked Sydney. It's quite a civilized city."

"Unlike Washington?" I said mournfully. "It's become like old western movies, only real. But still beautiful." I asked him what his favorite place was.

"In Prague," he said, "even the pavement stones are laid

artfully. It's full of beautiful old churches, and the Vltava flowing through the city gives it a peaceful serenity. History is there. And there is much gorgeous music."

"But don't you think the only safe places are in the past?" I told him about the old Dallas Starlight Operettas I had attended as a child, where you would sit in the peaceful night under the stars. And how once a brave soprano had finished "Indian Love Call" despite the fact that a moth had flown into her mouth.

This struck Viktor Hajek as very funny, and he said that indeed sounded like an innocent and safe place. Of course, I admitted that it wasn't anymore, since everyone in Dallas had a gun. I lifted my glass then and toasted Viktor for standing by me through the entire evening, for being so polite after our orange-hat collision, and for forgiving my semi-hysteria about the American economy when last we dined. "I not only appreciate it, I feel like you saved my life."

"I didn't save your life," he answered. "But you're welcome anyway."

"Well, your being there tonight made it less scary." Any fear I'd had was exorcised by the magic of our laughter, and suddenly my mind could move forward. Beside this man and in the warm glow of the fire, new possibilities seemed to stretch before me, even another way to live, which included a long-lost emotion. I had forgotten that I could feel safe and happy and possess future possibilities for myself apart from Shelly.

At some point in our conversation he whispered, "You're very sweet"—a trigger word for me, like in *The Manchurian Candidate.* Or like in the old Groucho Marx quiz show when you'd say the magic word and a bell would go off and a stuffed chicken would fall from the ceiling. Because I had been programmed by my mother. When I was a child she would say, as I left the house, "Be sweet." Not, Be smart, Be kind, Be firm and take care of yourself, Be right, or Be honest, though she certainly intended all those things. What she said was just, "Be sweet." And Viktor's saying I was sweet, that still innocent word, was the first nice or loving thing anyone had said to me in years. The closest anyone had come to saying a kind thing to me was when Shelly had commented, "Boy, you sure are bunged up, aren't you."

I suppose it was a case of needing someone, some decent act of love with a decent man, but it was more than that. This was like finally, after oh-so-many tries, coming up with the proper numbers and winning the lottery. It was a release from some deep well of feelings that had been buried by pain and loneliness and the complicated remnants of failure in love.

Ah, sex. What one learns about a person from sex, even from a hug, much less the whole, entire goopy thing. The pressure of the body and what is held back, the feel of the skin, the clasp of the arms, the whole smelly, mushy, sweet, hungry, wonderful agony of sex. Since I had last had real sex we had all learned from the science pages of *The New York Times* that the reason we are attracted to one person and not another has to do with some simple and distinct olfactory product of our individual bodies. Just like bugs, I suppose. But oh, the wildly thrilling comfort of a foreign bed, the wonderful presence of a kind and comforting and sexy man lying beside you, the generous, marvelous, ultimate design perfection of two bodies together.

Sometime later I realized that it was also the natural consequence of fear and loneliness and Beethoven and the omelette with fresh basil and the inevitable poignancy a woman feels at the austerity of a place where a man lives alone. There were also the tantalizing photographs of an unknown life, including one of a young Viktor Hajek atop a liberated Russian tank in 1968.

Lying there in that half-dark room on the blue sheets beside Viktor Hajek, whom, I told myself, I should now call Viktor, I sensed the fragrance of Marcus's cologne. And I was stunned. Could it be that, in my lonely state, I had been mistaking a generic male scent for a wonderful fragrance?

After we had gone to bed, the phone rang. The answering machine picked up a woman's message in a rich and lusty voice, speaking in a foreign tongue.

"*Ciao*," she said at the end. It was a rude awakening. It took me a moment to remember where I was and what had happened, and it all came back to me with the thud of a falling brick. I closed my eyes tighter and tried to go back to sleep, until I thought of Shelly. *Shelly! My God!* She'd think I'd been shot or kidnapped! She could be wandering up and down K Street or making desperate phone calls to area hospitals—or worse, to Mama.

So I kind of rolled myself off the bed, and when Viktor stirred, I muttered that I had to go home.

He raised up on an elbow and looked at the clock beside the bed. Tilting his head toward me and squinting, he asked, "Can't you stay?" It was after four a.m. The idea of rising was agony, I knew. I felt like one of the twelve dancing princesses when the story was over and the book closed.

"No, sorry," I said, and began to dress.

When I came out of the bathroom Viktor was dressing. "Oh no, you don't need to get up," I told him, "it's just down the street. But Shelly won't know where I am. She'll have the Texas Rangers out looking for me, or maybe the orange-hats. You see, I've never done this." I let this fact sink in. Never, not once, in the seventeen years of my daughter's life had I failed to perform the conventional mother-in-her-proper-bed role. How dull, I thought.

Viktor ran his hand through his curly hair as though he weren't quite awake. "I don't mind," he lied. I could have loved him for that old-world lie alone. "I can't let you go out alone this time of night." He smiled kindly, his face warm and youthful, and for a moment I felt that through the miracle of sex we were both revived and younger. And what I wanted to do was fall once more onto that warm, safe place his bed seemed to be.

I asked to borrow some socks so I wouldn't have to wear my shoes, swollen as I was by wine and self-indulgence.

Viktor fumbled around for some socks. After I put them on, he wrapped a blanket around my shoulders and we walked down the dark street arm in arm, my hand in his coat pocket.

"If Anita Nance sees us, she'll think we're ghosts." The wind had died down, and my words carried sharply through the cold, crisp air. For once the street seemed innocent and friendly with its sturdy old houses and inviting stoops. At the corner there appeared the listing van of the secret and solitary soul who delivered the world according to *The New York Times* while most of our city slept.

Inside my hallway I hugged Viktor. "Thank you for everything, and good night," I said against his ear. "The dinner was wonderful. I haven't felt like this in years and years. I may be a new person." I kissed him with all my heart, and removed the blanket and wrapped it around his shoulders. We kissed again. I could hardly bear to pull away.

"Good night," Viktor said. He ran his hand through his hair and stared at me as if just waking up to consider where he was.

From inside I watched him walk back down the street like an Indian chief. I could really love that man, I thought. But did I dare? Did I have any control over that? I honestly didn't know. It had been a long time.

Shelly had fallen asleep in front of the television set. I turned it off, woke her and told her to go to bed. She sat up and collected herself, then stared at my disarray.

Before she could say anything, I offered, "Oh, you just won't believe the disasters of this evening."

"Yeah, I would." She pushed her hair out of her eyes and yawned. "What happened?"

"Someone shot the prime minister of Sainte-Marie. I'll tell you about it tomorrow."

Despite the lingering horror, I was pleased to have news that would wake her up. Then I noticed that Dee's body wasn't wrapped in the quilt on the sofa.

"Where's Dee?"

Shelly shrugged. "We had a fight."

Lots of fights, I thought to myself.

She struggled upright. I waited for her to lumber up the stairs and followed her wearily.

"Good night," I said at her bedroom door.

"Um . . ." she answered. How nice it was to go to our separate beds without tears or rancor.

I considered for a brief instant showering, but before I knew it, I'd thrown off my clothes and climbed into bed, which felt cold and empty and sterile. Before I fell asleep it occurred to me that I had failed to concern myself with birth control or even blow up a condom and make a joke about safe sex. But before I could worry about that I realized too that I might very well begin the new year of 1992 as one of the many ungainfully unemployed. The thought didn't settle, because I switched to Viktor and his bed, and if I hadn't been so tired I'd have smiled.

Over the weekend I considered phoning Marcus and suggesting that we plan a joint strategy to defend ourselves, but I wasn't sure how receptive he would be. And furthermore, I didn't even know where he was hiding out. If I was right that he was involved with another woman, I would have to rethink our whole relationship. Why hadn't he told me earlier? Wasn't I his best friend? Was that a false assumption? And could I be in love with Viktor Hajek without changing my relationship with Marcus? Is it possible to share romantic secrets with another man?

I considered phoning the hospital to see how the prime minister was doing. I considered phoning Cecilia, but I was hesitant to bother her at home after all the trauma. So I just followed my heart and fears and did nothing except clean the bathrooms and more or less hide from the Harrison & Associates part of my world.

I had awakened that Saturday morning—nearly noon—with happy ruminations about the latter part of the previous evening. I had tried not to think about the art show massacre and melee, and concentrated on the nice happy glow of aftersex. It was the first time I'd smiled to myself in bed in years. Bed had been of late a place of worry and waiting for Shelly. And I was glad I had been wise—or wary—enough not to get involved with the assortment of hungry guys who'd come on to me in the past three years. Yet I had to consider the possibility that the previous evening might be of little consequence to Viktor Hajek. Before I was completely carried away by daydreams I had to think about his early-warning signal. In prison he had learned to live only for the present, he'd said: one had to. This was bound to affect any relationship he had. I argued with myself that maybe he didn't feel that way any longer, perhaps he'd returned to a life of romantic myth. But I couldn't convince myself of that. And there was also the matter of the phone call in the night from the foreign woman. I could tell a green light when I heard it, no matter what the language. Still, simply that I was lying in bed thinking of my own love life and not Shelly's was in itself an overnight miracle. If I could get my emotional life more together, then I could pull my whole self into a more confident, single-headed person who would be a stronger example to the seventeen-year-old I most wanted to impress. And at the same time maybe I'd be less dependent and burdensome on my friend Marcus.

So, having fallen in love, I told myself, and having forgotten the precipices of that condition, I went about the house cleaning and singing. Now and then I would be struck by a glow of happiness not unlike a flash of lightning. About four hundred times I looked out the window toward Viktor's house for a sign of love. A flag maybe, smoke billowing from his chimney, something to show the startling and life-enhancing experience of the previous night.

Shelly eventually dragged herself downstairs, barefoot in leggings and a camouflage T-shirt with only one sleeve. I gave her a quick rundown on the previous night of violence after she and Dee had departed the art show. I had just fed the good gray Arlo, returned from his night on the town and ready for food and rest and discombobulated by our change in time pattern. Shelly waited until he finished his tuna buffet, then swooped him up and rocked his big gray body like a baby. Her two-tone hair hung over both their faces. When she set him down she pushed hers back in order for me to read the numbed misery on her face.

"Where were you?" she asked.

"We went to the hospital. Then I went home with Viktor Hajek to get something to eat." I was drinking coffee from my radio mug. My favorite radio host was signing off by playing Bobby "Blue" Bland's "I Got a Woman."

"You like that guy?" she asked.

"The disc jockey?" I teased her.

"No." She gave me a disgusted smirk.

"Yeah, I do," I said.

"That's nice," she said matter-of-factly.

I followed her into the sitting room, grateful she didn't ask anything further about Viktor, and relieved she was reacting so maturely. We were in a wartime holiday respite, both of us agreeing to a temporary truce.

See, she *will* grow up, I told myself. I was fantasizing that maybe even one night of love might improve my relationship with her.

"Tell me about Dee," I said.

Shelly paused, stretched her arms, and groaned loudly. Her movements were so like my own that I felt like I was looking at myself, only a thin, taut-bodied blond version of myself.

"Well, he wanted to go to some club in Southeast to talk to his cousin. . . ." She turned on the TV and flipped channels until she found cartoons. Then she settled back on the sofa and pulled Dee's pillow from behind the couch and lay down facing the screen.

"That cousin who sells drugs?"

She put the side of her hand to her mouth, just as she used to suck her hand when she was little. "Yeah, Mario. And Dee's daddy told him to stay away from him too."

"The cousin?"

She gave a minuscule nod, her eyes fixed on the cartoons. She'll watch cartoons on her honeymoon, I'm convinced, and when she's in the nursing home, God forbid.

"I told him I wasn't going to Southeast." She rose on her elbow and socked the pillow. "I don't like to go over there. Some of the people who hang out with Mario make me nervous. When Dee leaves the room, one of them always . . ." She made a face and lay back down.

"Flirts with you?" I finished for her.

She glanced at me and snickered.

"Comes on to you?" I rephrased.

"Yeah." Her nose was ringless; it made her seem more young and vulnerable. Her toenails were painted a reddish brown, and the soles of her feet were dirty. She had bedroom slippers, of course—her grandmother gave them to her regu-

looked to see whether there was any sign of life at Viktor's newly painted house. It was ivory, not a color I would have chosen. Total ivory, without even a contrasting window trim. The color seemed sweet, tentative, an attempt to be inoffensive or nonaggressive.

As I poured my cereal and skim milk, thoughts of Harrison & Associates kept intruding in my mind. Wasn't it just my luck that when something good happened in my personal life after all this time, it was preceded by a seven-point-two-on-the-Richter-scale at work.

Doreen phoned later to say someone had been turning over her dumpsters in the alley, and somebody had started a fire in one of them the week before. She had two dumpsters—a sign of real power and influence in D.C.—because her brother-in-law worked for the city. Furthermore, someone had scribbled a threat on the outside of an envelope in her mail one day telling her to lay off the Bluebird. I told her maybe she should do just that; this sounded pretty serious. She asked if I would join the orange-hats that night so everyone would know I'd gotten over the broom incident.

"I'm getting tired of this guilt trip," I told her. "I was the one injured, and I'm the one who keeps having to buck everyone else up. That's not fair."

"Well, Rosemary, people feel real bad about it."

"I feel bad about it too. But will I have to be reacting to the aftermath of the broom incident for the rest of my community life?"

Doreen laughed, in her wonderful, sexy gravel voice that she was going to ruin if she didn't quit smoking. "Be a sport. We need you. And you owe me one." Which was true. She had ventured out Bladensburg Road, where normally she wouldn't have been caught dead.

So that night, feeling vulnerable after the art show debacle and secretly disappointed not to have heard from my new love,

larly—but they were lost somewhere in the pile of shoes and socks and discarded clothes and teddy bear limbs in the bottom of her closet.

"Well, we know people get shot for less." It scared me that I'd said that. And it must have scared her too, because she turned to me with a surly glance. She didn't want to move this any closer to real-life possibilities and experiences than it had to be or already was, and I couldn't blame her.

I patted her cold foot. "Why don't you wear your slippers," I interjected, then resumed the central subject as I tried to cover her feet with throw pillows. "I'm sure you were right not to go to Southeast. And hanging out with those people isn't going to help Dee find a job." I was always grateful for a chance to reassure Shelly that she'd done something I considered sensible and safe.

"It's not his fault he can't find a job!" Her temper could explode in a millisecond.

"I didn't say it was his fault. I just said those people aren't going to help." We were on the brink of that familiar downward spiral of disagreement.

"I don't know how *you* could know that. Or what that has to do with anything!"

I gave up. There was no use in talking to her in the morning, and no use talking to her at night either.

"How 'bout some waffles?"

She shook her head. The TV went to a commercial for a toy automatic rifle that looked to me like the real thing. I found the quilt Dee usually wrapped himself in at night and tucked it around Shelly. She reached under the sofa and pulled out a bag of chips I most certainly hadn't bought, and began eating them steadily as she watched the cartoon.

"Oh, come on," I said. "I can't make waffles for one."

She shrugged, and I told myself I didn't need waffles anyway. I went to the bay window for the forty-ninth time and

I trudged along with the orange-hats. I figured if I was shot and died, at least I wouldn't have to face Harrison on Monday morning. And it would be healthy to turn my attention to problems like local crime and urban decay—and then there was the sheer delight of being outside during the advent of winter, which is wonderful wherever you are but especially in our city, which sits under the Atlantic flyway, one of the nation's four great north–south migratory bird routes.

That night we were so assaulted by acorns that we joked our orange hats should be hard hats. Here and there Japanese maples had turned a brilliant scarlet, and a few scattered maples were now golden. Nearby were dogwoods and spicebushes and wild grape. Pyracanthas were brightly adorned with red berries, and swamp roses offered hips for the deer that inhabited Rock Creek Park. We'd just emerged from a dark and desolate alley and were heading toward the Bluebird Bar & Grill. Reverend Thompson mentioned the vandalism in Doreen's alleyway.

"They think that will intimidate me, they got another think coming," Doreen said.

"Well, I hope you told the precinct about what's going on," Reverend Thompson said.

"I don't see any use in wasting my time phoning the police, when they don't do a thing about the drug activity outside the Bluebird."

"You still oughta do it, though," he told her, and I agreed.

We continued strolling along, discussing a recent scandal wherein a government employee claimed her boss had made her a love slave—a term that garnered plenty of media mileage. Cars were zipping up and down the street, passersby were sneering at us as usual, and occasional acorns were pelting us, when I saw a young man in a red sweatsuit, perfect for this weather, at a pay phone near the Exxon station. From a distance he looked like Dee.

I kept telling myself this surely could not be Dee; there

were lots and lots of young men wearing red sweatsuits. But as we drew closer it began to look more and more like him: he turned nervously as he spoke, and shifted just as I'd so often seen him do in the doorway of my kitchen, talking on the phone to possible employers. Don't jump to any conclusions, I reminded myself. Still, I was more suspicious and upset than I thought I should be. He could be phoning his dad—or even Shelly.

I took my orange hat off before walking up to him, as if I wanted to be friends. I was about eight feet from him, and he still had the receiver to his ear, when he saw me.

"What's happening, Dee?"

His face turned immediately hostile, as if he had not recognized me.

"Dee?"

"Hey." He smiled and pushed the disconnect button.

"What's going on?"

"Oh, a cousin in Southeast got into some trouble, and I've been staying out there with my aunt. I'm trying to reach some other relatives right now. . . . Shelly home?"

"What kind of trouble?"

"He got hit by a car. He's just a kid."

I thought it odd he would refer to that as getting into trouble. "I'm sorry," I said, and told him Shelly was at home.

"I'll give her a call."

I said good-bye and hurried to catch up with the orange-hats, waiting for me at the corner.

Doreen pointed over her shoulder. "That your rapper?"

"Yeah, it is. He and Shelly had a fight." I spoke with an obvious note of defensiveness.

She had pinned her orange hat high on her head with the visor up. Her wide, pretty face was full of concern. She raised her eyebrows skeptically at me, and I felt embarrassed and then mad at myself for feeling that way. Could I help what was happening to that young man's life? Had I risked Doreen's life by dragging her out Northeast to a hip-hop club for somebody maybe in the drug trade?

We crossed the street, and the orange-hat with the radio told our contact the direction we were heading.

"You know that guy?" Reverend Thompson asked me then. There was a clear tone of disapproval in his voice.

"Yeah, I do. Why?"

We passed the third liquor store in a three-block area and paused there for a few minutes. Two cars from Maryland were double-parked in front.

"He used to hang out with my nephew. He's been in trouble before, and it looks like he's heading in the same direction again." He pronounced it "*di*-rection."

My heart sank—a reaction I was accustomed to as a mother. But I resented feeling that about someone besides Shelly. "Are you sure it's the same person?"

"Dee Taylor?" he asked. "Nice-looking kid?"

"Yeah. Dee Taylor. He raps," I said.

"Yeah, they all do," the preacher said, dismissively.

When we headed back, Dee was gone. We didn't mention him again, but the previous conversation had thrown a pall over things and dampened the love-and-honeymoon feeling I'd been basking in since the night before. I felt yet another concern settle itself in the nervous pit of my stomach. I feared I'd end up like my crazy Aunt Lucille, who claimed that because of DDT her heart had dropped into her stomach. Maybe if you get enough heartaches that really happens.

The gnawing concern stayed with me, and that night, instead of shrugging off a ride home and walking the two blocks from where we assemble, as I usually do, I took the offered ride. When I got out of Doreen's car she patted my hand sympathetically. All the lights were on in the house; normally that would have made me mad. Shelly never in her life turned off a light. But now each lighted window was like a search for life and happiness, and the sight made me sad. What would I say to her? And what in the world was I going to do if Dee came back? I paused to pet Arlo, who sat on the front stoop surveying the night like a watch cat.

Shelly was on the phone when I walked in. "Dee," she mouthed to me. She talked for a long time, in that low murmur I could never make out. When she finally hung up, I waited, hoping for some communication.

"Look, Shelly," I told her when it seemed as if none was forthcoming. "I deserve some truth here. Would you tell me what's going on?"

She ran her mandarin fingernails through hair she still hadn't washed. A whole day without washing her hair was a sign of grave depression. She studied her nails, then looked at me in a way I believed sincere. Sometimes she could surprise me by being so calm and frank and intelligent it gave me hope.

"I don't know what's going on. You have to ask Dee. He's been acting weird. He's real discouraged about not getting a job." She chewed on a fingernail, thereby ingesting some of that chemical adhesive which would probably lead to intestinal cancer.

"I can understand that. But you have to know, if he's into drug stuff he can't stay here. That's out of the question."

She sighed. Her shoulders sagged. "I know. But if we don't help him, nobody will." She looked up at me and laughed, hiding her pretty teeth with those grotesque fingernails. "Would you take off that hideous hat!"

"Oh, I forgot." I put the orange hat on the coat tree, thinking I should wear it more often: we'd had a conversation that hadn't ended in verbal fisticuffs. Maybe I should wear it to the office on Monday. It might generate sympathy, make Harrison think I'd had a nervous breakdown and not be too rough. Or I could tell him that because of a genetic defect that runs in my family, my heart had fallen into my stomach.

All the Sunday papers carried stories about the shooting of the prime minister of Sainte-Marie. Not a good way to start off a PR campaign. Despite that, and the fact I hadn't heard from Viktor Hajek, I still had some energy and hopefulness. Taking advantage of it, I made one grand and final stand for authority and future order. I did the white-middle-class thing and, having carefully rehearsed my lines, at eleven thirty-four a.m. Eastern Standard Time, when she first appeared, announced: "Okay, Shelly. I haven't said anything in weeks. But you've got to sit down and write your essays today or you're going to miss the next deadlines. You may think this isn't important now, but you'll feel different later on, believe me."

Granted, my speech wasn't revised much from what I'd said before. And too, the problem with saying such things is that as I say them I hear the thundering of Mama's voice. I put my arm around Shelly's shoulder in case she was still half asleep. She was wearing my Martin Luther King, Jr., sleep shirt, and I suddenly remembered how when I was pregnant I'd prayed for a boy. If I had a girl, I thought, it would be too painful knowing what she could go through, knowing the feeling of female heartbreak. It was such a simple thing to fall in love with the wrong person. How can you protect yourself from love, when the hormones are ablaze and the whole world, especially the U.S. advertising business, is saying what the world needs now is love, sweet love?

"Please," I added as a last, desperate tack. But I knew better than to insist on a response. If I'd had a grotto in my bedroom I'd have gone up and lighted candles—or lighted more candles, since I'd already have some burning over a future for me and Viktor.

Shelly watched TV awhile, then went upstairs and showered. I pretended to concentrate on the newspapers. Then, miracle of miracles, midafternoon she sat down at the dining table and began chewing her pencil. I held my breath and said one of those desperation prayers.

Soon after, the phone rang. "Hello," I answered, and then repeated it breathlessly when I realized who was calling.

After our how-are-you, how-are-you, Viktor asked if I'd like to have dinner and see a Czech movie at the American Film Institute that night. He was sorry to be calling so late; he'd had a deadline and he hadn't been sure when he'd be finished. I was thrilled, but I thought of Shelly: Dee might appear, or she'd turn on the TV and stop working on her essays as soon as I left. I couldn't wander off into a world of my own. So I said no, thanks, I had to get to bed early on Sunday, which was a stupid thing to say and made me sound like Grandma Moses. But, I told him, I appreciated the invitation and would love to see him. He said he was going away on Tuesday for a few weeks and he'd like to see me before he left. Could I possibly have dinner or a drink with him after work tomorrow? Oh, wasn't that just like a man, to draw you into the sticky wicket of sex and romance and then disappear, into Eastern Europe no doubt.

After work tomorrow, I thought to myself, I might not even be alive, and if I was I would probably be on a torture rack in Harrison's office. But maybe I could pull my body through the office gauntlet. I said okay and invited Viktor to come by the house after work for a drink. Ten minutes discussing his approaching trip, ten minutes of inquiry about the Czech movie, and maybe a brief conversation about some item on the front page of the *Post,* which I would study on my way from work. I'd say nothing about love or romance. I'd be businesslike and keep my shoes on. I'd wear my new aqua washable-silk blouse that I was afraid to wash and my manner would be, "So we had foreign sex and I seemed to have been struck by the lightning of love, so what?"

In the euphoria of speaking to Viktor and seeing Shelly work on her essays, I decided to be generous and phone Mama before she made her usual call.

"What's the matter with you, Rosemary?" she asked. "You sound strange."

"Everything, Mama. I may lose my job and I got involved with a man without intending to and I really like him."

" 'Involved'—what do you mean by 'involved'?"

"Just what you're thinking, Mama."

"Oh, Rosemary!" she said. "You're supposed to be an example." Mama thinks the world would be a lot better off without sex. She should have been a Shaker.

"What's wrong with your job?"

I told her about the art show and the shooting.

"Oh, Rosemary, that city!"

"Mama, that was international crime, not local."

"Well, I don't know what's going to happen to this country." She switched to the immediate crisis: "Oh, if only the Democrats could win the next election."

"Mama, dream on. Many lines like that and you'll be carted off to Terrell." That's the home of the East Texas state loony bin we were taught to contemplate with fear and loathing. "How is everything there?"

"Well, Roger Nichols pulled a gun at the city council meeting Thursday night."

"You might as well move to Washington."

"Then all the Baptists tackled him. It was a horrible scene. Ralph Freely dislocated his shoulder."

"And I thought I had problems. How's Art?"

Mama told me she wasn't seeing Art. She said he had some bad habits.

"What kind?"

"Oh, honey, you know."

"No, Mama, I don't know. Be specific."

"Oh, you know. I can't go into it. He's a male, a man."

"A mailman?" I teased her.

"A male!" she underlined the word.

I got the drift. "You aren't going to see him again?"

"Oh, I have to see him all the time. That's the problem with this place. He's even talking about running for city council. Or mayor." Her voice broke.

"Mayor! He'd challenge you?"

"That's what he's saying."

"How romantic! That's sixty-something for pulling your pigtail, isn't it? He must be in love!"

"I don't find that at all comforting," Mama said. "How's Shelly?"

"Okay. A little heartbroken, I think."

"Why is that?"

"Oh, you know, boyfriend, just like me and you."

Mama groaned disapprovingly. She didn't care for being lumped in the general mess of peoplekind and their love crises. "I hope not," she said. "Well, I better go."

"Mama, this is my nickel."

"I know, Rosemary, and you may lose your job! You better be saving your nickels." Mama is ever practical.

"Well, I know it would be a disaster to be unemployed, but really, my conscience hurts me over a lot of things that stupid firm does—beginning with having fish with their lips cut off, on down to plugging some god-awful, flea-ridden island that is a political hell."

"Lips cut off? What are you talking about, Rosemary?"

"Oh, Mama, it's too hard to explain. Just cross your fingers it won't happen. Then again, maybe it should. I just wish I could get through Monday without being there."

Miraculously, over the course of the afternoon, Shelly all but finished her essays, even did her homework, so for a celebration I went out to get pizza and a video. Over dinner I wondered whether my refusing to go to the Czech movie with Viktor had something to do with cowardice. Is this the way I want my life to be, I asked myself as I picked pepperoni off my pizza. In less than a year Shelly would be leaving for college, God willing, for her own life. What if Viktor thought I wasn't interested? I gave myself a pep talk about how we have to be brave with whatever the world confronts us with, and not be afraid to take chances and fall in love—even with foreigners. And in some respects, wasn't Dee like a foreigner, wasn't Southeast as foreign as Prague in some ways?

Shelly hardly said a word during dinner and she went upstairs in the middle of the movie. I don't know how she does that. I never walked out of but one movie in my life, and that was when I was twelve and the movie about scared me to death.

Dee returned that night. Around ten, when I was already face-creamed for bed and working on my heels. I heard the gate open and the bell ring. He didn't use his key. In a few minutes Shelly came upstairs and, as if she were announcing an autopsy in the living room, said he wanted to talk to us. He was nervous, and he didn't look good. I figured he was living on fast food instead of the healthy vegetables and fruit and cartons of milk he'd had at our house. I started to put my hand on his shoulder as I passed, but when I saw how wound-up he was—tapping his right hand and jiggling his left knee—I knew that was a mistake. So I sat down and said a few words about how cold it was and how I was dreading winter, when it wasn't winter I was dreading. I suddenly realized how much I'd come to care about this kid and his struggles. Only he wasn't a kid. He was a young man, a young black man, with all the problems that entailed. And I cared about him not just for Shelly's sake, but because he'd tried so hard for a better life, had tried so diligently and with such good spirit.

"You know," Dee began, "it's like impossible to get a job. You know?" He lifted his hands and spoke in a singsong voice that reminded me of his rap performance, as if this had all been rehearsed, heartfelt but nevertheless rehearsed. "And I was hanging around and ran into Richard, this guy I know through my cousin."

"Your cousin Mario, the drug dealer on Alabama Avenue?"

Dee looked at me as if my clarification was not appreciated.

He continued. "And Richard said, 'How you been?' And we start hanging out, and he says he could use some help. You know . . ." He opened his hands again as if he were trying to explain a miracle that had fallen into them.

"There was nothing wrong with it. All I had to do was go to some different stores in Virginia and make a purchase. Handguns. Wasn't illegal. It was so . . ."

"Simple?" I said for him. He nodded but without meeting my eyes.

"Yeah. You know, he gives me some money and I just go over there and pick something up and bring it back. He says, 'No sweat, and you go home with something.' "

Dee sat up and felt in the pocket of his pants. He pulled out a wad of bills and counted out the approximate dollars he owed me and pushed them across the table between us.

"I want to thank you for lettin' me stay here," he said quietly. "For everything."

We let that money sit there, all of us watching it as if it were a scorpion, its tail poised to sting.

"Where do you think this is heading?" I asked. It was as

close as I could come to what should be said. I had only one card to play.

Dee shrugged, and still he wouldn't meet my eyes.

"I'm truly fond of you, Dee, and I admire how hard you've looked for a job," I told him. "I sympathize with your problem, but you can't stay here anymore. I was willing to let you stay as long as you were looking for a job, but this isn't a job. I appreciate your honesty. But you'll have to leave." I wanted to take hold of him and physically pull him back from the direction he was going. "And I have to say I hope Shelly doesn't see you anymore."

She was slouched over, holding her face.

"No problem," Dee said, and ducked to stare at his snow-white Reeboks, which he kept patting on the floor nervously. He was shifting into an automatic emotional-cooling system.

I made a move to go.

"If he leaves, I'm leaving," Shelly said. I should have anticipated that. She lifted her chin in a cold challenge and then turned away. I shivered, wishing I'd gone to the Czech movie. I could have missed this. I looked at Shelly, who was turned to Dee, who was still staring at his sneakers. She folded her fingers together, here's the church, here's the steeple.

I felt the face cream on my forehead; it seemed so foolish. It made me feel more helpless. How silly of me to think we might get through one weekend without a conflagration.

I knew I had to gamble now. I stood up, as tall as I could be in bare feet, wishing I had some magic slippers to lift me above the fray.

"If you leave . . . when you leave, leave your keys on the table, both of you." Maybe the hardest sentence I'd ever spoken. "I'm going to bed."

Shelly collapsed her fingers into two fists and stared hard at me. Was I serious? Was I really for once not begging or threatening, but leaving it up to her?

"Soon as my music gets going . . ." Dee said as I crossed the room.

"Where's he going to find a place to stay this time of night?" Shelly challenged me.

"Where's he been staying, Shelly?"

"You can't just turn him out like that!" she shouted. "You think I won't go! You think I won't go, don't you! You are such a bitch! This is my house too, you know!"

Here the road branches, I thought. I couldn't look at her. I hated her, hated her for all the hurt and agony and aloneness and helplessness she made me feel.

I started toward the stairs. "Take care of yourself, Dee."

"Ms. Kenny," he answered, "I'm still trying to find a job."

I turned and nodded, not wanting wholeheartedly to take part in this last-minute charade.

"Keep the money, Dee," I said, and left.

I lay in bed a long time listening to the quiet downstairs, my heart pounding with fear now that I was alone, that this was it. She would leave. It would be the disaster I'd been afraid of. I heard her come up the stairs, to pack her things, I guessed. Dee called her back. I lay in bed and wished for the loud buzz of cicadas to fill the night.

Later I heard her shouting at him. I listened to the intonation of anger I'd heard so often directed at me. Even when I couldn't make out the words, I could hear the repetition, the rise and fall of her fury. What a sad girl, I thought, and suddenly felt my own tears at her pain and anger.

Then I heard the front door open, heard her cry out after him with the assault of a curse before she slammed the door.

Shortly I heard her come up the stairs crying. I waited for her to get in bed and then went and sat by her in the dark and rubbed her back, the way I used to do when she was a little girl, trying to knead the pain away so she could sleep.

Before long she ceased crying and I could feel her body relax under my hands. And finally, when I had kneaded away my own anger, I said good night and left the room. I thanked whatever God there might be that she was there, safe for another few hours.

Many Monday mornings I've had trouble climbing out of bed, especially those right after Tom dropped out of my life and drove to Texas with the dogs. And this was one of those Monday mornings. I put on my aqua silk blouse and considered wearing sunshades and saying I had pinkeye. I wasn't brave enough to wear my orange hat, though with the aqua blouse it would have been a weapon. Just as I was struggling to place one foot in front of the other to walk out the door, the phone rang.

"How're you doing, Rosemary?" It was Marcus's warm voice.

"Frankly, I'd as soon break bread with the National Rifle Association as face Harrison this morning. You're going to be there, aren't you?" I asked him in a near panic.

"Hey, would I miss it? That kind of real-life drama? I just phoned to say, Never fear, Marcus is here." It wasn't like him to use a cliché. He was nervous too.

"I appreciate that. I can't tell you how much."

"Have a good weekend?"

"Okay," I said, wishing for a tunnel back to Viktor's warm bed, where I could hide from the world.

"Good. Just thought we should reconnoiter before we faced the major suit."

I noticed that under the vivid fall sun beaming into my kitchen window, my aged African violet, dormant since Tom left, had produced three tiny buds.

"Marcus, my African violet has buds!"

"Now don't be racist, Rosemary," Marcus said. "And keep in mind it wasn't our fault. If asshole Harrison wants to make it our fault, put it in perspective. Remember, as you yourself often say, how often the Yangtze floods."

"I think the Chinese are working on that now. But thanks for the thought."

"And look around us, Rosemary. We got it good, you know?" He said this with the conviction of someone who'd been trying to convince himself.

"I know. Remember that scene in *The Third Man* when Orson Welles shows Joseph Cotten how tiny other people look from the top of the Ferris wheel to explain his immorality?"

"Um . . ."

"Let's think of Harrison that way."

"You're right. From the top of a Ferris wheel."

But Marcus was late to the office. I was pacing in our cubicles when he arrived, not looking well, despite his brave words. He'd been caught in traffic, he muttered.

"That's what happens when you live in the 'burbs," I chided—not a helpful comment.

He poured himself a glass of water and we went into Harrison's office, where three other account executives were already assembled.

"Well," Harrison said, without his usual preliminaries, "would you like to report on the art show, Rosemary?"

I felt the Yangtze rising. He looked right at me but fortunately he wasn't holding his golf club weapon.

"Dying to," I said. Harrison's aide, standing by the fish tank, tittered.

Marcus cracked me an encouraging grin. I had no idea what I was going to say. I thought of Orson Welles looking down at the top of Harrison's chemical-brown hair and took a deep breath.

"Attendance at Friday night's reception was outstanding," I began. "There was a lively, diverse crowd. The paintings provoked real excitement, and several were sold. Some of the real movers and shakers of our city who were in attendance will not soon forget the island of Sainte-Marie, its possibilities, or that particular art show. The prime minister appeared, creating a sensation. The event was reported in all the major targeted newspapers—certainly more than we know at this point, which the clipping service will no doubt reveal. I think the evening could be called an unforgettable event for all involved."

Harrison stared at me, and there was a long silence. He tapped his teeth. Someone harrumphed. I held my head high and silently prayed for the lingering voodoo spirits to lend me strength. Then I added that the prime minister, who was out of the hospital, would no doubt agree that we'd gotten more publicity for his island than he could have dreamed of.

"Quite a spin, Rosemary," Harrison said.

Marcus laughed out loud.

Back in our cubicles, Marcus told me, "Rosemary, every now and then you do something that keeps me going."

For a moment I basked in the glow of his approval. Then I felt I should be honest. A little chutzpah goes only so far.

"You know, sometimes desperation inspires me. But I doubt that will save our necks if they are indeed in danger."

"Yeah, I know." Marcus sat down in his swivel chair and leaned on his desk.

"How about lunch?" I asked while he was still awed by my audacity.

Lunch usually means we go to a carry-out for salads, and back to our cubicles or to the park in Dupont Circle if the weather's nice. That day was cool but sunny, so we went to the park. The only empty bench we could find was across from a homeless man wrapped in plastic.

"There we are," I told Marcus.

"Please, don't joke like that."

"Maybe we should start our own firm. We'd be great."

"Yeah. We'd be great. Except you'd want to represent people like that guy."

The man wrapped in plastic hadn't stirred. Assorted clothes of various colors—and no telling what else—were visible through the plastic bags around him. It all looked like the bottom of Shelly's closet. Only his face protruded from his plastic sheet, but it was turned the other way.

"Reckon he's alive?" I asked.

"Maybe not, lucky guy."

"Marcus, come on. You're kidding."

"Yep, I'm kidding," Marcus said. But I remembered him describing himself climbing in bed and covering his head, and a chill passed over me.

"Dee is working as a courier for guns," I said.

"How do you know?"

"He told me. I said he had to move out. Of course Shelly said she was going too. But she didn't. I don't think he let her. She did finish her college essays. And went to school this morning. Though I had to about shove her out the door."

"Well, you did what you could. You can't right someone else's life. Everyone has to do that for himself. Individually. One lone runner at a time."

"There are also relays, Marcus. We don't always have to run alone. That's part of Dee's problem. No family team. I can't tell you how hard he tried to find a job."

"I don't doubt that. But when you run, when you're competing, there's a moment when you think you can't go on, but you can. When someone else drops back, that can pull you on too. I know about Dee. And there but for the grace of God . . . I think that every damn day. We're all about two steps from the street."

I removed the lid of my coffee cup and watched the steam rise in the sunlight. A tiny oil spill floated on top. Of course Marcus was right that Dee should have kept trying, taken the civil service exam again, applied to more sporting goods stores, spent more Sundays marking the classifieds. But how long can a young man practice such patience and endurance?

"He should keep trying," I told him. "My mother has a saying: 'Lean on your own beans.' I'm trying to lean on my own beans, too." I thought of Viktor Hajek. I wanted to tell Marcus about him and me and this new excitement in my life. But after my declaration of independence I held back.

"You want half my cookie?"

"Not really," Marcus said.

"I shouldn't have bought it. It was just an impulse, a treat for getting through the morning. You think he'd want it?" I gestured toward the man in plastic.

Marcus only grimaced.

We drank our coffee in silence. A steady stream of people passed through the circle. The sun felt warm on the backs of my hands and I began to nibble on the cookie, then resigned myself to eating it after all.

"I gather you're with somebody else," I said. My voice sounded breathless.

Marcus didn't answer right away. He sipped his coffee with two creams and three sugars and stared at the empty fountain in the middle of the circle. "Being married is the hardest damn thing. After a while there're too many mean moments, and nothing good happening, and you think, Who needs this? Course I know who needs it. But a man kind of needs somebody who looks up to him, and when that stops it's hard. You start feeling bad about yourself, and that takes over everything and the feeling dies. You're just hangin' in there for the sake of hangin'. Which ain't no good way to live."

Like me and Tom, I thought. I'd tried to be helpful to Tom

by saying how unfairly he'd been treated. A little less pity might have been in order.

"I wish to hell it wasn't like that, but it is. And I don't know how to get back."

"Maybe you keep on trying," I said.

"Backatcha." Marcus smiled at me. He changed the subject, and his voice sounded strained. "One of the cops wanted to take me in for questioning Friday night."

I nearly spilled my coffee. "You're kidding! Why?" I sat up and looked at him.

"Why?" Marcus echoed. " 'Cause I was there. It was 'round up the usual suspects' time. That's why." He closed his eyes and tilted his head to face the sun. I studied the sharp outline of his chin. Everything was so neat but his life.

"Oh, God." I spoke so loudly the man across from us stirred on his bench and opened one eye briefly.

"I tell you, it was real hard for me to go into that office this morning," Marcus said.

At that moment one of the suicide bicycle messengers the city was riddled with, in black leather with streaks of glow tape on his helmet and jumpsuit, came wheeling past us so fast we both had to jerk our feet back from where they were stretched out. We watched him defying traffic by wheeling steadily across two lanes.

I didn't know how to respond to Marcus. And for once I told myself, Just don't say anything, Rosemary. I wished I could hold Marcus's hand. Instead I took the white sack from between us and stuffed our trash inside.

"Okay, Marcus. When I say 'three' we'll grit our teeth. One, two, three." He turned toward me, gritting his teeth. A smile flickered across his face as we rose and headed back to the office.

After I got home from work, Viktor Hajek appeared with a mixed bouquet, including a bird-of-paradise, which I adore. I wondered whether he always appeared bearing gifts, like the Wise Men. He was gift enough.

We exchanged how-are-yous.

He gave me the usual two-cheek European kiss, when what I wanted was to press up against him, body to body. We went into the living room and I held his warm and dreamy hand. Can hands be dreamy?

"So how was the movie last night?" I asked. "And how about a glass of wine?"

"A beer, perhaps?" he said.

"Sorry, no beer."

"Oh, okay. Wine would be fine, wonderful."

I made a mental note to buy beer and went into the kitchen, Viktor behind me. I asked him where he was going. He said he was traveling to the Texas–Mexico border to write about environmental pollution, and then to Mexico City and Cuba. From Cuba he was going on to Europe to see his children for the holidays.

"You must miss your children," I said.

"Yes. But I talk to them a lot. Terrible phone bills."

"As long as you're in Cuba, maybe you should stop by Sainte-Marie and spend a few days on the beach." To my surprise I laughed, and Viktor joined me. "But I forgot, you've been there."

"Very briefly." He explained that he'd been roughed up by some local Tonton Macoute types and held for several hours when he'd first arrived. Later he found out that a Scandinavian journalist had been shot the previous week.

I handed Viktor a glass of wine, and we went into the living room. One of the best things about living in this city is that you never know when you might meet someone so involved with the world that he'd been roughed up by something like the Tontons Macoutes.

We speculated about the disappearance of André Bontemps.

I asked about the Czech movie and said I was sorry I'd missed it. He said he would be sorry to miss the next Neighborhood Watch meeting.

Then he smiled warmly and leaned toward me, and in a sincere whisper said, "Rosemary, I hope everything is all right about the other night."

"I tell my daughter to practice safe sex," I said.

"Oh." He looked at me so warmly it took my breath away. "I didn't think."

"I know. I didn't either."

He started that wonderful chuckle which delighted my soul and spoke with mock seriousness: "But in considering the earlier part of the evening, it does seem that you have a proclivity for violent encounters. I don't exactly understand that. Have you always lived such an exciting life?"

"Not really," I replied. "Most of the excitement in my life, until lately, came from the teenager in my household."

"Well, I thank you for introducing me to such excitement. Here I am, for only a brief time in this city, and already I have been witness to two crimes. I would be such an innocent if I had not met you." He smiled.

"I'm afraid you may think my life is a lot more exciting than it really is. And a word more on the latter part of the evening—it was a big thing for me. I know that in a lot of places people seem to hop in and out of bed like frogs, but I don't meet people like that. I was happily married during most of the sexual revolution. I can count on one hand the people I've had sex with. I take it pretty seriously, and whatever you've read about American women, I'm probably not one of them. And nowhere close to French."

"I'm not sure I understand what you're saying," Viktor said. "I didn't take it so lightly either. But sex, a man . . . it's also not a Sicilian commitment." He was watching me closely.

"I don't mean commitment or anything like that. I just wanted you to know I don't go hog-wild like that casually."

"Hog-wild?" Viktor laughed.

"What I'm saying is, maybe the mores of sex vary from region to region, like the climate and flora and fauna."

"Not so much," he replied. "Pretty similar. Flora and fauna are similar most places also."

He put his arms around me, and my heart started doing strange things. It had been a long time since my heart had done strange things in daylight. But since I'd met Viktor Hajek, on that night of orange-hat violence, my heart had been involved in several episodes of athletic activity.

Suddenly I knew what I wanted, and it wasn't a Sicilian commitment. I wanted a relationship, a nice friendly relationship, with sex and caring. That was all. I hadn't realized it before. Mama might feel the need to marry Art Moser one day, but I wasn't so sure I wanted that kind of thing ever again.

When Shelly came home, looking fairly normal except for the nose ring, I introduced Viktor to her once more. She stared at him hard, dropped her bookbag on the coffee table between us, and went upstairs.

Soon afterward Viktor left. He held my hand as I walked him to the door, then kissed me on each cheek with the door open. Mrs. Moore stood near the tree box across the street as Pal took a leak. I waved at her. Now the whole neighborhood would know that Viktor and I had a relationship.

Well, what the hell! I thought. It's been a while since we've had a romance in these few blocks.

"This trip has been planned for some time. But I'm sorry to be away so long," Viktor said. Then he paused and held my eyes, like a promise. "I'm so glad I've met you. I will look forward to the next time. Bye-bye." And he left it like that.

I watched him walk to the gate. He looked back at me and

smiled before striding gracefully up our street. *Our street.* What a nice phrase.

The next week I took Cecilia Bontemps to lunch at a Caribbean restaurant in Adams-Morgan—a duty I'd been putting off since the Friday-night Sainte-Marie melee. We sat beside a window and watched people pass by all bundled up. I listened to Cecilia rattle off in her thick accent a series of disastrous repercussions from the art show. One of her brothers was being threatened with deportation. He was terribly depressed and threatening suicide. She was concerned it would jeopardize her own possibilities for U.S. citizenship, which she'd thought was imminent. She'd heard indirectly that André had escaped to Mexico. His family had yet to receive money from the sale of his paintings. The gallery owner would pay only André directly, and there was the matter of the cost of replacing the gallery's plate-glass window.

Meanwhile, back in Sainte-Marie, Cecilia's mother was on her deathbed. Cecilia and her brothers and sisters in the United States were afraid to leave the country for fear they wouldn't be allowed to return. Cecilia related all this with a sad matter-of-factness.

I tried to soothe her by saying, "Cecilia, try this avocado appetizer. It's delicious."

She saved the worst news for the end. Her nephew back in Sainte-Marie, André's son, had joined the army. "André would die if he knew. Maybe kill him."

My God, I thought, but I said, "Try the biscuits, Cecilia, they have chili peppers in them."

Then she said she thought she was going to lose her job.

I told her I would speak to the gallery owner and see if we couldn't work out a way for the family to receive the money.

"What's wrong with your mother?"

"Heart failure," Cecilia said.

Well, I thought, there's not much even Jesus could do about that. I turned to watch a pair of teenagers skateboarding along the sidewalk, recklessly dodging pedestrians.

"Why do you think you're going to lose your job?"

Cecilia gave me another of those looks that said, How could you be so naive? She said she expected that Harrison would have her fired.

"Actually, Marcus and I are worried about the same thing. But you have no responsibility for that fiasco," I said. "Surely Harrison wouldn't do that."

"Those things happens," she said.

"I know."

Cecilia shook her head. "Troubles, get away from my door."

"Mine too," I added.

Nobody, not even Scrooge Harrison, would fire us right before Christmas, I told Marcus. I'd just reported to him on my lunch with Cecilia. I predicted that Harrison would wait until the end of the year to give us the axe if indeed he was going to.

"Maybe I should write a note of apology to the prime minister," I said.

"I don't think that will do it," Marcus said.

So Marcus and I attempted to tread softly through the bustling pre-Christmas season. We smiled properly, we avoided making waves. Harrison claimed to have a line on a new account that had to do with a sheik from Bahrain. I suggested we stick to all-American accounts. These foreign accounts caused only trouble. It was foreigners who had money, Harrison reminded me. And we were an international company.

At home, Shelly moped about. Her energy level plummeted

without Dee's presence, and she returned to her gloomy old self. Occasionally she would get a phone call from him, and he and I would exchange a stiff hello. I overheard her arranging to meet him on several occasions. I asked her to have him return our house key. I'd heard her tell Miranda she was saving to buy him a leather jacket for Christmas, which she could ill afford. But I was loath to complain: we'd Fed-Exed her college applications to make the December 15 deadlines.

"How is Dee?" I asked her one night.

She shrugged and scowled. "Okay," she answered, then after a pause decided to add more. "He's working with his music. He may make a recording. Somebody's interested."

"Good for him. Where's he staying?"

"With his cousin."

"On Alabama Avenue?"

"Um . . ."

On the twentieth I received a large poinsettia plant with a card saying, "Thinking of you. Have a Merry Christmas. Viktor." It was the same day the axe fell at the office, the Friday before Christmas.

When I reached my desk that morning I had a message that Harrison wanted to see me ASAP. A similar message lay on Marcus's desk. I watered my china doll plant, and then Marcus appeared.

"Harrison will see you now," he announced. His face was yellowish and taut. He looked older, a man with grief and worries and maybe an uncertain future.

As I approached Harrison's office, I wondered whether this was worse for Marcus or for me. I'd been wondering that ever since the uncertain future became more likely, and wondering whether I hated it for him more than for me. I realized I wouldn't really know till it happened. Actually, I had thought Marcus's being black would save him. How could Harrison fire his token? I told myself to say as little as possible to Harrison, not to wise off. Why not, I asked myself. I knew the answer: Now it wouldn't matter. Dignity, Rosemary, I ordered myself.

Harrison, in a charcoal Wall Street suit, gave me a spiel that was not gender-specific, so I figured he'd cheaply composed the same dismissal for both me and Marcus. It wasn't because the prime minister had been shot, it wasn't the fact the account had been lost, it was the general recession; in this economy, everyone was downsizing.

Harrison went on with his finishing flourishes, offering a fairly decent severance, recommendations, plus hope for my future. When he came to the end, he looked at me and awaited my response.

"Well," I said, "Merry Christmas to you too." And I walked out, along the edge of the carpeting with one foot on the bare parquet floor so it sounded like one foot walking. When I left his office, Harrison's assistant spun from her computer to watch after me. The phone rang and I heard her answer, "Mr. Harrison's office," in that false cheerfulness of people who answer phones the world over.

The office manager was there when I got back to my cubicle, so I knew the whole thing had been coordinated like a battle plan. Only Marcus wasn't packing up. He was standing with his arms crossed, looking out the window. The office manager stood sentry to make sure I took only my simple personal belongings, not my files and Rolodex.

"Marcus?" I paused.

He turned to me. "I only got a warning, Rosemary."

I was stunned. Suddenly I felt worse, and then I felt horrible and guilty and confused. Of course I didn't want Marcus to lose his job.

"Oh. Good." My voice wavered. I climbed onto my desk to

retrieve George Washington. From that height, I considered diving straight through the window and into the bright morning sun. Instead I detached George from the wall and handed him to the office manager, hoping to dust up her red blazer as I crawled back down.

"Don't forget your plant," she said.

"I'm leaving that plant here to die," I said, looking at my lacy china doll, the only thing in that office besides Marcus I cared about. I was sacrificing it to punish my coworkers. Not that they really cared whether it died or not. But at that moment I just couldn't face lugging it downstairs.

"It's hard times," the office manager had the nerve to say as she brushed at her jacket.

"Tell me about it."

For a minute I had to hold on to the file cabinet. I couldn't breathe. I'm having a panic attack, I thought. Then I wrapped my arms around George Washington and turned. Marcus was standing watching me. He looked dreadful, stricken. I told myself, If I cry I'll shoot myself. I tried not to look at Marcus. I'd talk to him later, I mumbled.

"Let me drive you home," he offered.

"Oh, no. I'm fine," I said. "I'll be okay." If I could just make it to the elevator without tears. I couldn't believe how bad I felt, how spongy my legs seemed.

"I'll miss the Christmas party," I said. That wasn't even important: I hated Christmas parties. At the last one a husband and wife chased each other around till Harrison had to call security. What was wrong with me? Why could I not look Marcus in the face? Of course, I didn't want Marcus to lose his job. I just didn't want to lose Marcus.

"Oh, your key . . ." The office manager had apparently just remembered. I set George Washington down and fumbled around, my hands shaking. I broke a fingernail. It seemed to take forever to remove the key from the ring. Finally I dropped it on my desk. I took a deep breath and walked to the front doors. The entire office was silent as death, not even a phone ringing. It was the first time I'd ever been grateful to get inside that gloomy gray hallway.

I took a cab home, viewing the world with a whole new perspective, seeing what looked like gainfully employed people moving busily along the sunny holiday-decorated streets, and trying to ignore the glimpses of panhandlers in MacPherson Square. It occurred to me that this development, yet another insecurity, would no doubt push Shelly off the edge into the irrational depths she was continually skirting.

But I was soon distracted by the cabby, who seemed to speak little English and have no idea where he was going, so that I had to hand-direct his every turn, which takes all the joy out of a cab ride. When I reached the safe and lonely interior of my house, I sat old George on the kitchen table and made myself a cup of coffee. As I was drinking it I decided that I didn't even like George Washington all that much. Besides his wooden teeth, he was too white—white skin, white wig, white collar, white cloud. Entirely too white.

Usually Shelly and I went to Texas for Christmas. Mama felt it was her obligation to prepare Christmas dinner for assorted lonely or castoff relatives like my jerk optometrist cousin and his mother, Aunt Lucille, whose heart still beat in her stomach. That way too, Shelly could spend a few days with her father. But this year Mama, along with others in her church, was cooking at the dank church basement for the homeless and shut-ins, and the day after was flying to yet another mayors' conference, right here in Washington, D.C. Shelly was scheduled to return to Texas with her after that for a few days' visit with her father.

"I just want you to know," Mama said on the phone a couple of days before her arrival, "that several people have warned me about the danger of coming to the District of Columbia. Art has given me a gold-plated whistle to wear while I'm there."

"I thought Art might be coming with you." I teased her in order to change the subject from the danger of D.C. There must come a time when even a Redskins lineman becomes weary of defense.

"No, indeed." Mama was not flustered by my comment. "This is business. Though I am looking forward to seeing you and Shelly and the national Christmas tree," she said.

For the first time in several years, I proceeded to extract from the basement the collection of Christmas ornaments I'd started collecting so happily when Tom and I married. There were little armadillos and boots from the early years, and multicultural angels and stars from later. I had decided to wait until after Christmas to tell Shelly about my job loss. It made sense for me to be off a little over the holidays, and it wouldn't throw such a damper on the occasion, which was always hard anyway. Holidays, as we all know, are difficult for depressed people and children of divorce. So I tried to be jolly and maintain a cheerful countenance for Shelly. I brought a Christmas tree home on the back of my old Escort and tried to maintain my cool when Shelly spurned it for being lopsided. I went right ahead and pulled out a recipe for oyster dressing and sweet potato casserole to contribute to Christmas dinner at Doreen's. Doreen, like Mama, felt obliged to take in unattached neighbors for Christmas. Her sons-in-law watched football while the women cooked, just like in East Texas, so it was as disgusting to Shelly as Mama's vast and overcooked meal would have been.

When we got back from Doreen's, Shelly told me that Dee

was coming over that night. She became angry when I didn't welcome this news with a big ho-ho-ho of holiday cheer.

"I'm not happy about your still seeing him, you know that."

"You think I'm gonna dump Dee because of your whitey hangups!"

"I really hate to argue on Christmas," I said.

"What difference does that make? You're not religious!"

"Don't you think it's a nice idea to have one day when people are nice to each other?" I said.

"I hate holidays when everybody becomes a hypocrite," she replied. "It's all just commercialism."

"What I hate, Shelly, is the idea of your going around with someone who sells guns to people to commit crimes. I don't find that very admirable, let me tell you."

"He doesn't sell the guns. He just buys them."

"What's the difference? It's the same thing in the end."

"The guns are for protection."

"Shelly. There is no such thing as being a little involved in crime. Either you are or you aren't. And Dee is. And it probably means that if something doesn't happen to wake him up, he'll become more and more involved in crime. He may not understand that, though I imagine he does. But I'm telling you—and believe me, you could find out really fast one of these days or nights."

If the doorbell hadn't rung at that moment I guess we'd have fallen into another stranglehold argument on Christmas Day, when, I had promised myself, I wouldn't fight with her, for fear I'd lose control and tell her about being fired and then have her go berserk and run off right when Mama was coming to visit. I admit my motives for keeping the peace weren't all pure and simple.

And it was Dee at the door, with a shopping bag of presents, including two for me: a box of Godiva chocolates, the very sight of which would make me agree to being a right-wing spy for all seasons, and a box of gardenia-scented soap. I was touched, and even felt somewhat better about Shelly's having spent three hundred dollars of her hard-earned lifeguarding money on a leather jacket for him. It was better than throwing it away on bail, I told myself.

Shelly made Dee open his present immediately. She'd wrapped the box with silver paper and pasted cutouts of singers and rappers across the top. When he pulled out the jacket he seemed truly awed.

"Hey, wo-man!" he exclaimed, holding the jacket up, smiling, pressing it against his chest. They both beamed. I was sorry I couldn't join them in their pleasure. Dee slipped the jacket on and admired it before the hall mirror. His present to Shelly was an expensive new perfume I'd seen advertised on television. Even though she threw her arms around him and hugged him, it seemed anticlimactic after his leather jacket. I could see her seventeen-year-old expectations disappointed. And I could remember that sense of sadness that the excitement was over for another year, and amid all the lights and decorations you could never fully find the solace you were seeking.

Dee sat down, still wearing his jacket, and while Shelly poured him a nonalcoholic eggnog, he began to tell me his plans. He and the Ladykillers had signed a contract with a local outfit called Rap-a-Lot to do a single right after the first of the year. Once that was out, it was only a matter of time before he'd have a contract with a big company. All the Ladykillers needed was a manager; that was the only thing between them and superstardom. Furthermore, they were performing at a private club in Georgetown on New Year's Eve. It was a big break, he said, a crossover gig, since a lot of influential people would be there. Shelly glanced at me occasionally, to read my take when Dee predicted something particularly unlikely. This led me to wonder if she too was beginning to fear that his dreams were more hopeful than likely. At what point in a young life did you start to think the dreams were not just impractical but foolish?

So I compromised and kept my mouth shut as the price for having Shelly—in her black motorcycle jacket with her Walkman on her two-tone head—stand next to me the following afternoon at National Airport when Mama arrived. In a fleeting moment of holiday spirit or recognition at what we all go through to maintain a semblance of peace, I put my arm around Shelly's shoulders and gestured for her to turn off her Walkman. She pulled it from one ear, and I thanked her for coming. She took a step to the left so that my arm fell away, and said, more or less out of the corner of her mouth, painted heavily with bright red lip gloss, "It's better than being in Texas." A hint of a smile crossed her face before she restored the headset to her ear. It was not exactly an endorsement, but I was grateful she'd gone through some motions of politesse.

Mama's plane came in a half-hour late. She looked pert and lively, with a new, longer hairdo accented by a brown rinse.

"My goodness, you look wonderful," I said, hugging her. "You look younger than I do."

Mama laughed, but I could tell she was flattered and was feeling good about herself. And she did look lively and slim, but in my heart of hearts I was a bit shocked to see her after a period of months. Her pretty face was rounded below her spectacles and ever more settled to her chin, and her skin had gone a downy pink despite the religious attention with Mary Kay products. She had insisted on staying at a downtown hotel for the three-day conference so she could make the early-morning seminars and thereby return to East Texas with the good news on such subjects as the information superhighway. So we drove Mama by the national Christmas tree and then dropped her off at her hotel.

The next evening she arrived at my house via cab. As soon as she glanced around the rooms I saw my house looking a bit shabby and down at the heels. I really should have gotten slip-covers for the couch and trained Arlo not to sharpen his claws on the end of it. I was relieved at least that Dee's bedroll wasn't stashed behind the couch.

"I don't know how you live without curtains on your windows," Mama said. For her benefit I had pulled down the shades in the bay window. She asked Shelly about school and college, and Shelly managed to mumble through an answer. Her heart wasn't in higher education right now, I told Mama.

"At seventeen, hearts aren't always practical," Mama told her sweetly. "But you will be." She patted Shelly's arm over her black sweater with holes. "Maybe you'll fall in love with something like math," Mama fantasized, sounding a little like me. Shelly rolled her eyes and groaned. Mama said she'd been hoping maybe Shelly would come back to Texas to go to college, and I had to remind her that Shelly had after all never actually lived in Texas.

"All the more reason to go to college there, so she can become a full-fledged Texan." I knew I would adopt Mama's soft drawl after about two minutes of being with her.

"Oh, Mama, I wish people could love D.C. like Texans love Texas."

"Honey, that's a pitiful thought." She laughed as if she thought I was only teasing.

I inquired about her political position and her volatile love life. Of course she said she was involved in no-such-a-thing.

For dinner I cooked a much larger meal than Shelly and I usually ate, and I saw that Mama too ate lightly. "This is just delicious, Rosemary," she kept saying, but I noticed she didn't ask me for any recipes.

It was a pleasure for me to watch Mama and Shelly together. Shelly was so much more at ease basking in Mama's all-giving, nonjudgmental adoration of her only grandchild. Mama didn't even once mention the nose ring. And Shelly managed to be civil until she left to go to a movie with Miranda and some other friends. Then Mama calmly tossed the latest bombshell into the middle of my life.

"Rosemary," she began, "I have some news I think you'd want to know, though I hate to tell you. . . ."

Mama is given to such introductions. I went rigid with anticipation. She sipped her decaf and looked at me through her smart tinted glasses.

"Tom is getting married," she said simply.

I stopped in mid-bite of fat-free frozen yogurt, and the room tilted despite only one and a half glasses of wine. I set my spoon down and looked toward the Christmas tree in the next room, where my strand of red-pepper lights burned cheerily. Tom had started the tradition of red-pepper lights. He'd worn a sombrero when he played Santa and passed out presents. With him, festive occasions were truly festive. I felt like I hadn't had a truly festive occasion since he left.

I asked Mama if she wanted more decaf.

"No, thank you, honey," she said, with a note of tenderness in her voice. When we first separated and divorced, I had thought of Tom's remarrying, but I hadn't considered the possibility in a long time, so I wasn't ready for the news. This felt like a mine exploding years after the war had ended.

I went to the kitchen and poured myself some coffee. "Well, I hope he'll be happy," I said when I returned. "Who is it?"

"I haven't met her," Mama said. "I was real sorry about this trip kind of changing the routine. I knew you'd probably have come down there, and it might have been easier for Shelly if you'd been there too when she finds out. She's some woman who teaches at the college in Texarkana."

"Teaches what?"

"I don't know. She has a boy about ten. I've heard she's a widow. And I hear she's real nice," Mama said. According to Mama, everybody in Texas is "nice," and all the women she knows are "real sweet."

I had the horrible feeling I was going to burst into tears and embarrass us both, and not just because of Tom's getting married. I could live with that. It was everything else in my life that seemed to be out of sync.

Since we were baring life-changing developments, I thought I might as well contribute my own. I proceeded to tell her that I'd lost my job.

"Oh, Rosie!" Mama exclaimed. She hadn't called me that in years. Then she pulled herself together. "Well, I know everybody is downsizing."

I couldn't keep from smiling. Here Mama was, putting things into cultural context, and being so versed in the jargon of the present to use the term "downsizing."

"You were halfway expecting it, I gather?"

"I was still surprised," I admitted, and shook my head.

When she patted my hand I could smell her tea rose cologne. "But I'm sure you'll do fine," she told me. Her hand felt light and thin. "You're such a bright and talented person, Rosemary."

She'd never said that before. She sounded as if she were reviewing my résumé from a position of professional authority.

"I didn't know you thought that."

"Of course I do. But if I had known that you'd lost your job, I wouldn't have told you about Tom. At least not right off the bat." Her eyes were sad, and I didn't want her to worry.

"What does that have to do with Tom?" I asked her.

"Well . . ." she said. "Another blow. It has to be."

"I'm glad you told me. I'd rather know so I can prepare

myself. No telling what crazy thing Shelly will do when she finds out."

Then, to my relief, Mama said, "I'm glad you're here in this city, where there'll be some opportunities."

"I appreciate your not trying to say I should put my tail between my legs and run back to East Texas."

"Oh, honey, there's nothing for you in East Texas, unless you want to work in a prison." The state was building a new prison in a town near Mama's. Most people there were thrilled, thinking it might help the local economy.

I told her I'd rather panhandle in D.C. than work in a prison in East Texas. I was exaggerating, of course, but I shouldn't have said it; I could see that the vision of me begging on the streets of D.C. did not fit into Mama's current up-with-people worldview.

"How is Shelly?" Mama asked as we were clearing the table. She carefully rinsed the dishes that I always just stuck inside the dishwasher. So orderly and proper, she'd tied an apron around her smart, practical knit dress. Did I dare answer honestly when, after wiping off my stove, she watered my too dry aloe vera plant, an offshoot from her aloe vera plant? How could I tell her that between me and Shelly it was nonstop war, with hardly ever a warm moment? And that not only was I unemployed and once again losing Tom, whom she still loved, but whatever worked as a mother I didn't seem to have?

Some things Mama didn't want to know. I was certain of that. When I pointed out the beautiful poinsettia Viktor had sent, she just nodded and smiled. But this child was hers too.

"What's the matter, Rosemary?" Mama paused over the yellow dishwashing sponge and looked at me with concern.

"I'm trying to answer you about how Shelly is." I felt my throat clutch up. "She's awful. Half the time I hate her. She probably won't survive the year. She's so difficult, impossible.

Sometimes I think I could actually kill her. She keeps me crazy most of the time. I never have any control or authority. Was I difficult at seventeen?" I asked tearfully.

Mama moved closer and put her arm around my shoulders. "Rosemary, everyone's difficult at seventeen," she said. "But you were more mature. More than Shelly is, I think. You grew up early. Though you were still going up fool's hill for a while there. Course it's a lot harder now. The whole culture is so unkind, so un-Christian. Is she still seeing that young man?"

I mumbled yes and went for a tissue.

"I know it's hard," she said. "And you alone. I wish I was more help."

"You are a lot of help. How many young women have such a role model for a grandmother? It's her mother who's the failure. Me."

"It's a hard row to hoe," Mama said kindly. "I remember. I know I made mistakes with you."

"You did?" I looked at her hopefully.

"Of course."

"That makes me feel better." I was laughing and crying at the same time. "I certainly don't remember your making mistakes. Not like the ones I make."

"You just have to do the best you can, Rosemary. I'm sure you're doing that."

"I try, but it's one disaster after another. Sometimes I wonder if she'll survive to adulthood."

"I'm sure she will," Mama said confidently. "I pray for you both."

At about ten I drove Mama to the hotel. She said she had to be up early for a seminar on the costs and alternatives to incarceration. "We can't keep putting everybody and his dog in jail," she told me.

When it came time for them to leave, I drove Mama and

Shelly to the airport. Tom would meet them in Dallas. Shelly would visit with him for a few days and no doubt meet the intended. I watched Mama, in a dress-for-success casual suit and sensible shoes, carrying her ever-ready makeup kit, pass through the security check with all the panache of James Bond. She waited for Shelly to shed herself of her jewelry, then, after she got through, put her arm around Shelly and turned to wave at me. Even Shelly lifted her hand briefly. Seeing them together, and so comfortable, made me feel hope for Shelly and me. I imagined them on the plane, side by side, Shelly plugged into her hip-hop tapes, Mama reading one of her romantic novels. Maybe Mama would say a few words in my behalf.

I headed home to prepare myself—take vitamins, meditate, pray for wisdom, whatever I could do to summon strength for Shelly's return, when she'd have the new development of her father's marriage to handle, and when I'd have to reveal my sad state of unemployment. After a dinner of leftovers, I turned on the Christmas tree lights and lit some candles and let myself indulge in the fantasy of deplaning in Dallas. That was like entering another world, where suddenly all the people sounded like me. Tom would be waiting to drive us to the scrub oak area of East Texas that I still sometimes called home. What I really loved was the black bottomland along the Red River, the red clay hills and loblolly pines, the bois d'arc posts and barbed-wire fences, and the horizon that reached forever.

I put in a tape and wondered where Viktor was at that moment, and whether he ever thought of me over there among the lovely cobblestones. I wondered why Marcus hadn't called me since my painful exit from Harrison & Associates. I thought about how my life had come to yet another fork in the road. And as I listened to George Strait singing "All My Ex's Live in Texas," I concluded that if Mama could invest her energies in a more useful Christmas holiday, surely I should be able to do something more constructive than sit there feeling sorry for myself.

Shelly was waiting in the rain at National Airport to make certain she looked as bedraggled and miserable as possible. She carried a wet shopping bag full of hair products and presents from her father that she hadn't opened.

"How was your trip?" I asked when we were in the car.

She didn't answer me at first, just sat there staring damply ahead. I looked at her until someone behind me honked and I had to take off.

"You knew," she charged, glancing my way. "Why didn't you tell me!"

"That your father's getting married?"

"Yah," she answered with sarcasm.

"Mama told me when she was here. But I thought Tom should tell you in his own way. Why in the world don't they widen this road?" I asked no one in particular.

"You should have told me. I should have been prepared. It was horrible!"

Of course she would find a way to blame me. I'd expected as much.

She wiped her face with the back of her hand, but I couldn't tell whether she was crying or whether it was just the rain on her face. "He didn't even tell me before I met her. I hate surprises," she said in an even voice. "And what made you decide that he should tell me? Why didn't you think about *me* and how it would be better for me to be prepared? You're always trying to do the right thing for somebody else. You're as bad as Grandmother."

I had to admit she might be right. "I'm sorry," I said. "Maybe I should have told you."

"You need new windshield wiper blades."

"You're right." The blades were sliding across the window, leaving it only blurred.

"That woman hated me," Shelly said. "She sticks artificial flowers around everywhere and has ruffles on her furniture, and she talks baby talk to Dad. This is the worst thing that's ever happened."

She said this with such conviction I decided not to bring up other tragedies. I'd hoped to talk to her about her dating someone other than Dee while I had her captured in her seat belt beside me. I'd composed several speeches, including one about my current unemployment. But she seemed too fragile for another jolt.

"What is she like?" I asked. "What's her name?"

"Debbie. I hate that name. She's an old hippie. She sews and makes stuffed duck pillows she throws around on her crappy plaid furniture!"

"I like hippies," I said. "There were a lot of good things about them. They make bread. . . ." I grinned.

The Potomac, the sky, and the federal buildings were all as gray and dreary as Shelly. But at the same time lovely in a melancholy way. I reached over and patted her hands.

"Your hands are cold," I said. She lifted them and rubbed them together in the very same motion that I would have used.

"I'm really sorry it didn't go well," I said. "It's bound to be hard at first. But when you get to know her, you'll probably like her. I can't imagine Tom marrying some ditsy person." Which was absolutely true.

When she didn't respond, I put on a Marvin Gaye tape we both liked. Cars were backed up turning onto the Fourteenth Street Bridge, and as we sat there in the rain I hoped this might be one of those few good times when we could be together without being cross. After all, I might be easier for her to be with than Debbie.

"What all did you do?" I asked her.

"I had to take care of her stupid kid. Daddy takes him hunting. He's just ten." She said "ten" with disgust: a ready-made son for her father.

"He said they might have more kids!"

"That would be nice. You'd have more siblings."

"Ugh."

We moved onto the bridge and passed the section that I'd heard had been under repair for the last twenty-five years. Was that an urban myth or truth? I supposed it could happen. I should ask Marcus, I thought, and then remembered with a twinge of sorrow that I didn't see Marcus anymore to ask him anything.

As I parked in front of the house I told Shelly I was glad she was back. And indeed, I was glad to see her. Watching her pull her heavy duffel out of the back of the car, I felt such a rush of love for her that tears came to my eyes. Remember this moment the next time you could wring her neck, I told myself.

I carried her sack of presents inside and upstairs to her room while she dragged her duffel.

"Aren't you going to unwrap your presents?" I asked.

"Not now."

While she'd been away, I'd cleaned her room, put things away, washed her curtains—the kinds of things unemployed people have time to do. Now I brought her a towel, which she wrapped around her damp hair. Her mascara had leaked below her eyes and she smelled faintly of Mama's tea rose cologne.

"You smell good," I told her.

She removed the towel and dropped it on her bed on top of her damp jacket. I picked them both up and wiped the jacket dry with the towel. She was pondering her hair in the mirror.

"Honey, let's be happy for your dad. He must be lonely." He doesn't have you there, I was about to say, and then censored that for fear she'd think I was being sarcastic. "Nobody wants to live alone. And that may be wonderful for you too. You'll probably come to like Debbie and her son. Try not to be too upset."

She looked at me in the mirror. "I don't want some strange stepbrother from Texarkana who breathes through his mouth!" She turned and faced me, making sure I knew her position exactly. "I hate Texarkana. You said the last time it was on the national news it was for law officers shooting rats."

My God, was I going to live to regret every word I'd said to this child?

"That was a long time ago, Shelly. And you should think of your father. He's a dear person." When I said that, my voice wavered. I try never to cry in front of her. And now I felt as if I was experiencing a four-car collision. "I may as well tell you now," I said, "I've lost my job." I held my breath, watching for her response.

"I know," she said, offhandedly. "Grandmother told me."

Thank God, I thought, relieved that at least the blow was cushioned.

To my amazement she came over and put an arm around my shoulders. "I'm sorry, Moms," she said, and turned away.

I picked up her jacket. For a moment I hugged its weight against me.

"Your grandmother is something else, isn't she?"

New Year's Eve is one of the great speed bumps of my year. I gird myself weeks ahead for all the retrospectives, which necessarily lead to a review of the year's personal highlights and disasters. I always wonder if there's anyone in the world who glides smoothly through that intersection. The single encouraging note was that the just returned Viktor Hajek had asked me out for New Year's Eve. I was hoping that would help guide me down the rocky road into the unknown new year.

The day after Shelly came back, Dee appeared, presumably to return his house key and pick up some clothes he'd left in the hall closet.

"It's not that I don't trust Dee," I'd told Shelly, "but let's face it, some of his compatriots are questionable, and furthermore, I wouldn't want even Jesus out there walking around with my house key!"

Dee stayed for dinner. He helped Shelly set the table, then took his regular seat and entertained us with a summary of a new Whoopi Goldberg movie. I almost felt nostalgic about his having lived here. Dee was always good for a story, and life being short, that meant a lot. More important, when Dee was around there were many glimpses of Shelly's million-dollar teeth, the smiles that fueled my motor. His visit made it clear she was still crazy about him, but when he left I pleaded with her to at least see some other young men. But she claimed she'd spoken to him several times from Texas and he'd sworn he wasn't buying guns anymore and when he'd saved enough money, he was going to enroll at the University of the District of Columbia.

"Just where is he getting the money to save?" I asked.

Not having an answer to that, Shelly, of course, attacked, accusing me of always expecting the worst from him because he was black. Wasn't he supposed to be improving himself? That was exactly what he was trying to do.

I knew I'd been stupid to attempt to talk her out of her steady relationship with him, especially when she was still glowing from his charming presence.

For New Year's Eve, Shelly wore a pink spandex dress about the size of a dish towel, with a bare midriff. She'd piled her hair on top of her head, and I had to admit she looked stunning, if none too subtle, with long scarlet nails and matching lip polish. She was going to meet some friends and then see Dee perform at the private club. His single, she announced, as she paraded before the mirror in my fake-fur coat, would be recorded the following week.

In the middle of "The March of the Toreadors" I told Viktor I'd lost my job. We were having dinner at an Italian restaurant that had opera on the jukebox. I had chosen this eccentric but romantic place because I thought he might like its scruffy East European aura.

Viktor looked at me with great alarm. Later I wondered whether he was taking my news as a personal threat. After all, when he first got mixed up with me, literally, I was at least gainfully employed. He hadn't counted on a woman prone to violent encounters who also was out of a job.

"Don't worry," I told him.

"Oh, but I'm so sorry," he said, taking my hand. He wore a greenish heather sweater over a herringbone shirt, and a tweedy sports coat that looked American, or at least Western. I focused on Viktor's neck, where his shirt started; this always seemed to me a sexy place, where a man's neck met his shirt. And I thought too that if I stared at his neck nerves maybe I could entice him into sex on this last and first day of the year; I would meet the new year with sexual fulfillment, if nothing else. For this special occasion, I was wearing a vintage flowered crepe blouse that I pretended had belonged to Rita Hayworth when she was in love with Orson Welles.

"It was a compromising job," I admitted. "I had a lot of problems with it. My boss was unprincipled. I only took the job when I divorced and needed more money. It was just a living, I never invested my heart and soul into it. And it has totally compromised my journalistic standards."

Viktor's large brown eyes made me think of lonely moors, and spies in damp thatch-roofed cottages, and zither music.

"Of course, I guess few people have their heart and soul in what they do. I guess you do."

"Yes," Viktor said. "You might say that. I've been very lucky."

"Lucky. A curious pronouncement for someone who's spent eight years in prison."

"Yes, but it turned out right in the end," he said. "The good guys won, I think you would say."

"I'm so glad you're back," I told him.

"What do you plan to do?"

"Oh, I have an ambitious strategy to market myself, but it's too much to contemplate on New Year's Eve. I'll deal with it next week. I'm just hoping Shelly doesn't freak out and join a cult in the meantime." I smiled, letting him know I was exaggerating slightly.

Viktor shook his head soberly. "Oh no, surely not," he said. "To new beginnings." He lifted his wineglass in a toast. "A wonderful new year for us both."

We enjoyed our long Italian meal. Viktor liked the restaurant and hummed along quietly to an aria on the jukebox.

"This restaurant could be in Prague," he said, "if the food was heavier." He told me about spending Christmas with his daughter and friends in Rome. And I told him about Christmas at Doreen's and about Mama's mayoral visit from East Texas. At the end of the meal he asked if I'd like to stop by his house for coffee and brandy.

He had learned Washington already, I thought. "Stop by for coffee" being no doubt a code phrase for sex. I agreed enthusiastically, admiring his shaggy-buffalo profile. Could a serious relationship develop out of this? Could a man who'd liberated a Russian tank find happiness with a yellow-dog Democrat from East Texas?

At midnight, propped up in bed, legs entwined, we heard

car horns honking, firecrackers, a momentary blast of salsa music through the Mahler symphony Viktor had put on. We toasted the new year, along with world peace, a good year for Havel and Czechoslovakia, a job for me, a Democratic landslide, peace in the Balkans, a happy academic year for Shelly, the end of drift nets, a future for the superconductor supercollider, protection of the redwood forests, and a cure for AIDS. This was, I told Viktor, the way all years should start.

What could be better on New Year's Eve than sex, a nice man, and a good red wine? Having a job, I answered myself immediately, and tried to push that thought away. I propped my chin on Viktor's shoulder and breathed in the wonderful presence of this man's body. I could truly appreciate him now that I'd been a solitary soul for so long. I thought of myself and Viktor overlooking a Venice canal, at a café in St. Mark's Square. That was as close to Eastern Europe as I could imagine. I should go to the library and bone up on Eastern Europe, I told myself. At least I had time to do that now.

"Do you ever listen to rhythm and blues?" I asked.

"No, never. Why?"

"It's the music of my soul. Always has been."

Viktor took this information very seriously. "I will have to listen," he said.

"Yes, that would be good. At my place." It occurred to me that I'd just made love to a man who'd probably never heard the sounds I grew up with. Would it even be possible to make love to Viktor Hajek with the music of Chuck Berry or Muddy Waters or Johnny Ace or Janis Joplin or Etta James in the background? Could one ever alter the basic music of the soul?

"I would like to see East Texas sometime," he said.

"Oh, you should. Most people think it's tacky. But the landscape is beautiful. Well, not beautiful, maybe that's not the word. But at least ruggedly compelling."

"Ruggedly compelling," he repeated, and chuckled.

OUTSIDE VIKTOR'S HOUSE in the early morning, a blustery wind carried the smell of wood burning in fireplaces and the pungent odor of pine trees. We stood in front of the house while I whispered to Viktor to listen for Duke Ellington music. His ghost was bound to be out playing on New Year's. But we heard only the metallic peals of a neighbor's wind chime.

The muffled sounds of an ongoing party escaped from a house on the corner as a man and woman emerged, laughing, calling good night. "Happy New Year," the man greeted us, and Viktor returned his greeting. As we crossed the street, a red Firebird carrying four men passed us, moving slowly, the rhythmic throb of reggae blasting from inside.

At my house Arlo was waiting, trapped within past his time to roam. "Oh, you missed the New Year!" I told him as he rushed by me and down the steps, swishing his gray ringed tail in annoyance.

I closed the door and kissed Viktor, clung to him, hating to say good night. His arms were inside my coat, around my body.

"This was the nicest New Year's I've had in years and years and years," I said. "Maybe ever." His neck was rough and warm, his nose was cold, and his glasses steamed over. He laughed and took them off and kissed me before pulling away.

"Oh, I don't want you to go." I wanted to pull him upstairs to my bed.

"I know. It will be so lonely now . . ." he whispered.

But the thought of Shelly, who might appear at any moment, fresh from her Georgetown party, Dee perhaps trailing behind her, stopped me cold. So Viktor and I exchanged a final good night.

After he left, I poured myself a glass of water. I leaned against the counter, feeling weary but safe—the singular safety of my own home. The dripping faucet, the quiet buzz of the refrigerator, the electrical hum of the clock created a soothing, familiar melody.

I pushed my body up the stairs to my room, where I stripped and tossed my clothes onto the ironing board and slipped my nightgown over my newly awakened body. I can't start the new year not brushing my teeth, I lectured myself, and as I stared in the bathroom mirror, I looked for the manifest signs of satisfactory sex and communion. I was reaching for the toothpaste, imagining possible unemployed, uninsured dental disasters, when I heard a car speed up the alley and stop just beyond the house. The music from the car was too loud for past three a.m., even for New Year's. The deep bass throbbed as if it might penetrate the earth; it grew louder—I guess a door opened—and a moment later I heard a quick shout, followed by the sounds of crashing glass.

I heard running, a door slamming, and a car accelerating up the alley, tires squealing. I went to the window, toothbrush in hand. I didn't have to wait long for a follow-up: the high, rising shout of a man, the kind of sharp, intense cry that urban dwellers dread in life as well as dreams, a sound that your instincts immediately tell you is not casual.

Out the window, I saw nothing out of the ordinary—the winter skeletons of trees, the houses across the alley with their dark sleeping bedrooms, the scattered streetlights, the dark clouds racing beyond the reddish glow of the city lights. The old dying elm tree's bare branches were swaying in the wind. Then I heard another shout from the alley and saw a flicker of light. I watched, waiting. A moment later I could see flames. They seemed to come from the back of Doreen's house, from the small deck where in summer she nursed purple clematis on a trellis, where on a pleasant day she might sit and read the newspaper or talk on a cordless phone.

For a moment I closed my eyes, willing the flames to go

away, nearly overcome with the desire to crawl into bed or run back to the warmth and safety of Viktor's bed. But I pulled myself together and reached for the phone, though in my panic I forgot Doreen's number so that I had to hunt through the drawer for my neighborhood phone list. As I dialed, the room seemed remarkably still. The yellow light from the lamp beside my bed fell across the worn beige rug. I could see my festive crepe blouse tossed on the gray metallic ironing board cover, and the iron's trailing, disconnected cord.

It seemed ages before I got a busy signal. She'd taken the phone off the hook, of course. Doreen did that to avoid the harassing calls at night; and when she was keeping her grandsons, Thomas and the twin babies, and they were sleeping. And probably she was keeping them on New Year's. Doreen would have put them in what she called her grandmother's room, with the small bed and two new cribs for the babies, which she'd shown us so proudly at Christmas.

I phoned 911. My voice sounded shrill and breathless as I gave Doreen's address. Then I put on jeans and a sweatshirt and ran downstairs and grabbed my coat. Dan and Don, dressed like movie stars, wearing overcoats over tuxedos, were just parking their car. As I ran past, I yelled to them that Doreen's house was on fire. They slammed the doors and rushed after me.

"Oh no, the goddamn drug dealers!" Dan cried out.

By the time we reached the corner, we could hear the rumbling of the fire and see an orange-and-red glow at the rear of Doreen's house, though the windows were all dark. The only illumination came from the porch light, which Doreen usually left on at night.

How could it move so fast? I wondered to myself. I heard Pal begin a loud, low wail.

Other neighbors had already gathered. Several were at Doreen's front door, ringing the bell, hammering with their fists. Dan and Don and I stood in front with Mrs. Nance and others, hugging ourselves in the cold. From the front we couldn't see the fire.

"Doreen!" Mrs. Nance called out toward the darkened upper windows. "Doreen!" She cupped her hands around her mouth. "There's a light on up there somewhere in the back," she told us. "I could see it from my bedroom."

Next door, Reverend Thompson was pulling his lawn hose up the front steps and into his house to move through to the backyard. He wore an old-fashioned paisley robe with a fringed belt around the waist.

A neighbor shouted to him: "Call the fire department!"

"We did," Thompson shouted back. "Move the cars on the street!" he ordered. "Get people to move their cars before the fire trucks get here!"

I saw my own car, which Shelly had driven that night, parked down the block at an angle. Shelly and Dee were on Doreen's porch, Shelly ringing the doorbell, still in what I call my bear coat, which came only to mid-thigh, and in her black lace tights and ridiculously high heels. Dee wore the leather jacket she had given him for Christmas. He was banging his fist on the locked security door, black scrolled metal and glass, newly installed at a discount because several neighbors had ordered them together.

"Is there someone inside?" a stranger called out.

"We can't just stand here!" Don said.

"We need a ladder, let's get a ladder," Dan suggested.

"We need the fire department," Don replied.

"Where's the fire department?" someone asked. I could hear sirens wailing in the distance. "She's probably keeping the babies," I said.

"Did you phone?" Dan asked me.

"It was busy. She must have taken it off the hook."

"She's got to have a fire alarm!" Don said.

"Them things don't work half the time," Mrs. Nance said. "Mine went off every time I fried something. Finally I just give up, took the battery out."

Dee and a man on the stoop were lifting a planter, lining it up in front of the door to use as a battering ram.

"The firemen are coming," someone called to them, and the man dropped his end of the planter.

Shelly was suddenly at my side. "Mother," she said, "this is so horrible!"

Again Dee was pounding at the door. The front porch light flashed off, then went on again. The door opened and Doreen emerged in a pink terry-cloth robe, carrying a white plastic laundry basket. Her hair was covered with a bubble nightcap. Pink foam rollers protruded from the cap on either side of her face.

"Thank the Lord," said Mrs. Nance.

As Doreen struggled for breath, Shelly moved to take the laundry basket. She brought it to where I stood beside Mrs. Moore. Inside the basket, partially covered with towels and crying, were the two babies.

"Like finding the baby Moses," Mrs. Nance said.

Mrs. Moore lifted one of the babies. His mouth opened wide in a bawl. I took the other one, wrapped him in one of the towels, and opened the front of my coat to shield him the best I could.

"Thomas is inside," Doreen shouted. "Head of the stairs. And Mama's in the dining room." She pointed out the windows.

"This baby is fine, Doreen. He's fine," I reassured her.

Stairs were hard on her mother, eighty-four years old now. Bad knees. After Christmas she'd moved her mother down to the dining room so she wouldn't have to bother with the stairs. She had become forgetful, and Doreen wasn't sure how long she could leave her alone.

"Thomas is still up there," Doreen said. She had worried that he would seem her favorite. "I'm afraid I'm gonna be partial," she had once told me. "He's just so bright. First snow he said to Linda, 'Mama, who's doing that?' "

I rocked the baby in my arms. We could see smoke inside the door, but still no flames. Dee tented his coat over his head and rushed inside, disappearing from view. Shelly clutched her mouth.

"I was asleep," Doreen explained. "The TV was still on. Ezra woke me throwing rocks at my windows. Walter had called." Walter was her ex-husband. "He likes to call on holidays. In his cups. Tells me a bunch of crap. Then doesn't remember a thing he says the next day." Sweat ran down her face despite the cold. "Oh, sweet Jesus. I never thought they'd go this far. I tried to wake Thomas up."

Anita Nance, who came only to Doreen's shoulder, put an arm around her back.

"Oh, I hope Linda doesn't come driving up now," Doreen said. She patted the baby in my arms and held us both.

"I guess I dozed off in front of the TV after Walter called. I heard the fire alarm, I guess it woke me up, and I went downstairs to see why. Fire was rolling across the kitchen floor, burning the wax, tiny blue flames . . . the whole back wall was burning.

"Thomas! I tried to wake him up. He's such a heavy sleeper, always hard to wake up. I tell Linda, 'You'll never get that boy to school on time.' "

Now Dee appeared in the doorway, carrying Doreen's mother in his arms like a child. Dan and Don took her from him and supported her between them. Doreen moved forward, pointing at an upstairs window, repeating that Thomas was still there.

We could hear sirens and the honks of approaching fire

trucks. Policemen arrived in a squad car, followed by a plainclothes officer in an unmarked vehicle. The plainclothesman spoke to Doreen, took a white towel from his car, wrapped it around his head, and rushed up the stoop and into the house. He came out after only a few seconds, coughing and shaking his head. Dee tented his coat over his head again and rushed inside, as someone afraid of water or cold might go dashing into the ocean. Just then the fire trucks appeared, with their swirling lights and clanging horns, and firemen ran forward hauling hoses and moving us across the street. The lights of the trucks illuminated the area as if creating their own fires. An ambulance pulled up, and paramedics hurried to Doreen's mother on a neighbor's porch.

Mrs. Moore and I, holding the crying babies, stepped beside the beautiful old sycamore across from Doreen's house. The babies cried in the same rhythm and at the same time, as though singing together. I began walking back and forth, rocking the baby's taut, plump body until he quieted and I could feel his body relax and grow heavier in my arms. I tucked my head down to his and smelled the soft baby smell of sleep and milk.

Anita Nance touched my arm and said, "Let's take these babies inside my house, out of this cold and commotion."

We followed her to her stoop and inside to the warmth, where we settled the babies on a crocheted afghan on the floor of her living room, which was cluttered with plush furniture and velvet drapes and Austrian curtains and chandelier-style lamps and knickknacks and doilies. She'd keep an eye on the babies and watch the action outside from her bay window, she said. I paused at her front windows before going back out, wishing the scene framed there were only a nightmare.

Over the loud crackle of the emergency radios, Doreen was shouting to the firemen that someone had gone inside to try to rescue her grandson on the second floor. She pointed to the window and moved toward the house until one fireman had to restrain her.

The fire ladders rose slowly in the night air, and a hose was trained on the back of the house. I glanced at Shelly and reached for her gloveless hand, which was icy cold. Her hair was down, flowing loose and tousled around her head. There was much more noise now: the engines of the fire trucks, their loudspeakers, and more people arriving, Latinos in party clothes. We could see the fire now through the front door.

Reverend Thompson began praying. "Jesus!" he opened, as if making an angry demand.

"He'll be all right," I told Shelly. The calm in my voice surprised me. She glanced at me as if to verify that I was the one who'd spoken so optimistically.

"He'll be all right," I repeated, playing the mother's role of offering solace, if only imagined. False witness, the Bible calls it.

Suddenly a storm window on the second floor shattered, and like a miracle, Dee was there, beating at the remaining glass with a chair. Then we saw he was holding Thomas wrapped in a yellow-daisy comforter. The sight of the comforter was so startling someone laughed. Dee pushed Thomas farther out the broken window, and Thomas looked down as if he was still half asleep. Doreen called to him. The comforter fell away and caught on the broken glass; it hung behind him like a backdrop. Dee spoke to Thomas as a fireman positioned himself under the window and called for Dee to let the child go. But Thomas, wearing print pajamas with Ninja Turtles and flannel feet, wailed now; he clutched at Dee's arm and hung on, his sturdy five-year-old body turning. Doreen called to him to let go, she'd catch him, to let go. But Thomas wouldn't let go; he hung there while smoke curled out the window around Dee. Doreen called out again, and a second later Thomas fell, along with the comforter, and was caught easily by the fireman.

Around us, people applauded and cheered, and by then a

ladder was angling toward the window where Dee and Thomas had been. Dee had disappeared, and in the window where Doreen's daisy-print curtains had hung, there was only dark smoke spiraling out.

"Dee!" Shelly called. "He's got to come back to the window!" She ran forward to where a fireman was holding back the crowd. "He's afraid of heights!" Shelly said. "He's afraid of heights!" she repeated.

A fireman made it quickly up the ladder to the window. He covered his face with his gas mask and climbed through, disappearing into the gray smoke. There was nothing but smoke now, billowing out the window. Then the fireman leaned out and waved his arm and disappeared again, and another fireman started up the ladder.

Doreen moved to where we were standing, Thomas crying in her arms, his legs clamped around her body. "He'll come out the door . . ." she said. Her voice was too loud. Beads of sweat stood on her forehead.

I shifted my gaze toward the open front door and stared past the darkness to the flames inside, imagining Dee appearing framed in the doorway. Shelly and I would both dream of that same image. "Like looking into hell," Reverend Thompson said. I was suddenly aware of someone screaming and realized it was Shelly beside me, but I was so intent to will Dee through the open door that I couldn't turn away. Then I heard Viktor Hajek speaking to Shelly. I turned and looked into his eyes and clasped his arm behind her.

In that instant a fireman appeared at the window supporting Dee. The fireman at the top of the ladder reached into the window, and together they lifted Dee onto the ladder and carried him slowly, painfully slowly, down the ladder.

Wind whipped the fire until it broke through the shingled roof and the flames flew roiling into the night, lifting large particles, which rose in the wind like lighted lantern cutouts. Now there were two more hoses trained on the house.

By the time the paramedics had administered oxygen and pushed Dee into the back of the ambulance, fire was pouring from all of the windows.

We left then, Shelly and Viktor and I, Viktor's car following the ambulance to Howard Hospital. For nearly an hour we stood in the hall outside the emergency room. It was the third evening that Viktor and I had spent together in a hospital. We held hands.

"I've never been disaster-prone before," I said to him.

"If I continue to associate with you, I'm taking out American insurance," Viktor said.

After a while a young doctor came out and told us, with calm authority and in a musical accent that reminded me of Sainte-Marie, that Dee would be all right. He'd be kept on a respirator through the night.

"Can't I talk to him at all?" Shelly asked.

"Not tonight," the doctor said. "But he'll be fine."

When we returned home, the fire at Doreen's was out. We saw the blackened brick walls of the house, the empty windows like bare eye sockets, and all the officials of disaster hovering about—policemen, a newsman taking notes, a TV cameraman and a photographer, a fire chief. It was dawn, the sky lightening, the wind subsiding. The dreadful soggy odor of a burned house permeated the area.

We went our separate ways, Viktor to his house, Shelly and I to ours.

"Dee's supposed to make that recording this week," Shelly said as we went in. "What if he can't?"

"They said he'd be all right," I assured her.

She spent the early morning in front of the television, dully watching cartoons, drinking Snapple. Around nine o'clock I persuaded her to go to bed, and then took the phone off the hook and piled into my own bed. When I woke up in the early afternoon, Shelly was still asleep. I put the phone back on the hook, hoping Dee hadn't tried to call her. Around four she woke and phoned the hospital. Dee had been discharged. She phoned his grandmother but there was no answer.

"Well, he's obviously all right if he's left the hospital," I said.

Shelly took a long shower and sat sullenly watching television and waiting for him to call. Dee, the threatened hero, I thought. I recalled her hysteria of the night before, and realized once again how strongly she was involved with him.

"How was the performance in Georgetown?" I asked her, thinking I should get her to talk about it.

"Okay," she said, and shrugged.

"Were there lots of people? Was it a fancy place?"

"I guess." She picked up the television guide as an additional signal that she didn't want to talk. So I offered the only comfort I felt she would accept from me.

"He was certainly brave," I said. "He was certainly a hero."

Several neighbors phoned to ask how Dee was doing. I told them he'd left the hospital and the doctor had said he'd be fine. We discussed how horrible the fire had been. What a miracle no one had died. How remarkably courageous Dee had been. Everyone had a story about people being burned out of their homes by drug dealers. Don knew a man who had been burned out twice. After the second time the man moved to Maryland.

Shelly and I stayed home that first night of 1992. The television news reported several arrests of inebriated celebrants in Georgetown the night before. There were the usual predictions for the new year and some footage of the first baby born just after midnight. Doreen's fire didn't even rate the local news.

I made chili and cornbread and a salad for supper. Shelly

continued to phone Dee's grandmother. Finally, around ten o'clock, Dee's grandmother answered; she hadn't been home because she'd had to work that morning. Mario had picked Dee up at the hospital, and she hadn't heard from them since.

I tried to read while Shelly watched television, but finally the program was too intrusive.

"Good night," I called to her. I hated to go to bed without saying good night. I thought it was bad luck not to say it to someone you lived with and loved.

Around five a.m. the phone rang. It was one of the Lady-killers, who said he had to speak to Shelly. From the dry, sober sound of his voice I knew I had to wake her up. I stood nearby while she took the call. When she hung up she told me the news: Dee and Mario had been getting out of Mario's car, which was parked outside a fast-food restaurant on East Capitol, when they'd been attacked by a drive-by shooter. Mario was shot in the head, and he died on the spot. Miraculously, Dee was not hit.

The first week of January, instead of coping with romance and unemployment, I was coping with the aftermath of Mario's death. Shelly was shaken. She'd driven to Dee's grandmother's after she'd gotten the phone call. Dee was there, and so traumatized that Shelly felt she had to stay with him. Eat there. Sleep there for two days. The newspapers ran the story about the brave young rapper who'd rescued two people from a fire on New Year's only to have his best friend and cousin shot dead in front of him not twenty-four hours later. At first, Dee's bravery kept Mario's drug involvement out of the papers; there were innocent pictures of the cousins together. But finally a columnist wrote about the differences in their lives, Dee going straight, struggling to find work, a contrast to Mario with his drug connections. The cause of the fire at Doreen's was thought to be arson, in retaliation for her antidrug activity. The newspapers didn't have the story exactly right, but then maybe I didn't either.

Midweek I suggested that Shelly's most important responsibility was to go back to school, rather than comfort the grieving Dee. That's when she brought up my unemployment for her own uses.

"I don't know why it's so important to go to school. I mean, after all that effort to get my applications in, looks like it won't matter anyway." She was zipping herself into her black motorcycle jacket. Before she could exit, I caught up with her.

"Shelly, believe me," I replied, "I'll find a way to send you to college. You know your father intends for you to go to school. Mother will help if necessary. What's important for you now is to finish high school." I barred the door with my body. "And by the way, how come Dee's grandmother's home has suddenly become a viable sanctuary again?"

"Her live-in job is over," she said. "And things are complicated, Moms."

In her role as attendant, Shelly became involved in working out Mario's funeral. Reverend Thompson, grateful to Dee for saving Doreen's family, agreed to hold the funeral in his church. The church in Anacostia that Dee's grandmother attended was too small for the occasion. And if Reverend Thompson conducted the funeral, maybe the family could avoid embarrassment.

"What kind of embarrassment?" I asked Shelly.

"Oh, you know," she said matter-of-factly, "a gangsta-rap funeral where Mario's friends wear their sagging pants and play rap music and toss drugs into the casket and pour malt liquor on the grave."

I had never heard of such a thing and was shocked at the

idea. Shelly shrugged, indicating that there was no end to my naiveté.

In the middle of the week, Doreen and Shelly and I drove to Anacostia to see Dee and his family. Doreen wanted to express her thanks to them all. And they were all there, in Dee's grandmother's neat but crowded apartment with family photographs on the walls and tables: his grandmother, his mother, his little sister, eight months pregnant, and Mario's girlfriend, Juanita, and their six-month-old baby. Dee was with the other Ladykillers watching television in a bedroom when we arrived. He came into the hall to talk to us; he was wearing one of his red sweatsuits. I gave him a hug. Shelly gazed at him worshipfully as Doreen thanked him and told him she wanted to keep in touch, help him if she could. Would he come and talk to her when all this was over, the funeral and all?

"Yeah, sure." Dee ducked his head. He seemed embarrassed, and wouldn't look Doreen in the eye.

Later I told Shelly that he'd seemed all right to me. But in fact he didn't smile; his face wore a street-protective solemnity.

Before we left, his grandmother, a small, thin woman with a lively face, asked if we'd have something to eat. The kitchen counter and table were lined with food.

"They catch who started that fire?" she asked Doreen.

Not yet, Doreen told her.

"I sure hope they catch them," Dee's grandmother said.

I asked her when the funeral would be. She was noncommittal. Afterward Shelly told me the family still had to raise the money. It took them nearly a week.

THE MORNING of Mario's funeral was warm for January, and the sun glared through my dirty windshield. The church was one block from Georgia Avenue, on a street lined with elm trees. Shelly and I parked on a side street and walked around the corner. Across from the church and the satiny black hearse sat two cars of police officers, plainclothes and uniformed, watching the crowd assemble. Whenever I saw a cop car now, I automatically wondered if the radio worked. Jackhammers were pounding the street on Georgia Avenue, but there in the churchyard I could hear a mockingbird singing from a dogwood. It might have been spring already, and the warmth might even bring out the forsythia buds too soon in this seasonally bipolar city. In April deciduous eastern magnolias give us large pink blooms. Two months later their evergreen relatives produce the lush perfumed blossoms of the South. It is enough to make everyone dizzy.

The church was new, large, and low—tan brick with a steeple on the side, functional and austere. The framed glass sign announced the New Southern Rock Church of God, with the Reverend Ezra Thompson preaching, at eleven o'clock on Sunday, "God's Promises to You." I wondered what he would say God's promises were, and whether they were for another time and place.

I was surprised to see so many young people free on a weekday morning. Young men stood beside the church in their Sunday clothes, smoking cigarettes, glancing at the cops across the street. Then before climbing the steps and going inside, they tossed their cigarettes into the dead winter grass. There was a palpable tension in the air. Would Mario's friends storm the church, in their gangsta-rap clothes? Would they take over the service, bring in their own music, their own now familiar rituals of death?

In the vestibule, Shelly and I were handed leaflets with a dark photograph of Mario. I could have mistaken him for Dee—handsome, unsmiling. But he wasn't as handsome as Dee, Shelly said.

The church hall was slowly filling as we entered. There were sounds of babies and small children. In the front, above the baptistery, hung a large painting of a swarthy Christ praying in the garden of Gethsemane. Black curtains were draped over the baptistery. The church hall was too warm; it smelled of lemon oil and clashing colognes. Two large yellow banners proclaimed: "The Lord makes us free" and "God is love!" An organist was playing hymns, and at the front was Mario's casket, shiny metallic green like a new car, covered with a spray of red carnations. We had sent flowers; it was a necessity, Shelly had said, job or no job.

When we'd gone with Doreen to see Dee, his mother had said, "You know, the young men talk about what their casket will look like. We wanna buy Mario something real nice, something he'd be proud of." She was a beautiful woman. Her dark tired eyes suggested she was weighted with a life too difficult to handle.

"Dee has a lot of good in him," she had told me. "He's always been good to me and his grandmother. Maybe after these newspaper stories something nice will happen to him. I pray something good will happen." I had been struck by how she seemed to feel what happened to Mario was random, as random as opportunity for Dee. "It coulda happened to anyone," she had said.

I followed Shelly down the carpeted aisle to the middle of the hall, where she slipped into a pew. Her hair was pulled back into a severe knot at the neck. Behind her large sunglasses, she wore her familiar scowl.

I started reading the leaflet, which gave a brief summary of Mario's life: Graduated from Anacostia High School. Played football and basketball. Cofounder of a singing group called the Ladykillers, who were about to make their first recording. The beloved son of . . . nephew of . . . grandson of . . . father of . . . Died January 2, 1992. *The Lord giveth and the Lord taketh away*. So brief and simple, when it wasn't at all simple. And I'd had no idea Mario had been involved with the Ladykillers. "Earlier on," Shelly told me.

The organ and piano joined together suddenly, and everyone rose as the choir, in blue robes, filed into the choir loft singing "Amazing Grace." They were followed by Reverend Thompson, large and rangy in his black preacher's robe. Then everyone turned as Mario's family proceeded down the aisle to the front pews: maybe thirty people, young and old. Dee's grandmother on the arm of a woman in a white nurse's uniform. Juanita with her baby—Mario's baby—in her arms. Dee beside her walking heavily, like his mother. Weighted. His face impassive.

Shelly pointed out Dee's father to me. He was a large man, not so old, and dignified, with the slow, graceful movements of his son. Against the side wall was the marshal who'd accompanied him, standing in a heavy jacket with his hands clasped behind him, balancing on both feet like a cop.

In the aisle behind Dee's father were three young men, loose-limbed and attractive—the other Ladykillers, in their shiny suits and dark glasses. They were followed by several young men in street clothes who sauntered, one with a stocking cap, one rolling his head back to study his surroundings. When the family was seated one of the women emitted a brief pained cry, which was cut off as a nurse put an arm around her shoulders and whispered to her. The choir finished the hymn, and Reverend Thompson rose from his carved wooden chair and moved to the pulpit. He said nothing for a moment, just looked out at the people assembled under the slow stirring fans, his face so deeply lined, so dark and shadowed he seemed to have aged years in the past week.

He began to pray in his deep, resonant voice. "Oh Lord, in this time of sorrow, comfort this family and these friends. Comfort us all. . . . Amen."

Shelly opened her purse and pulled out a tiny, carefully

ironed linen handkerchief with tatting on the edges that she'd bought at a yard sale.

"If he says it's God's will, I swear I'm going to stand up and scream!" she'd told me earlier.

Reverend Thompson opened his Bible and announced he was reading from the prophet Isaiah: " 'Though thy enemy hast destroyed cities their memorial is perished with them. But the Lord shall endure forever; he hath prepared his throne for judgment. And he shall judge the world in righteousness, he shall minister judgment to the people in uprightness.' "

Shelly clutched the handkerchief as if hanging on for dear life. I had tried to warn her how emotional this could be. The funeral of a young person. The first young person she'd known to die. Half of me hoped the experience would shock her, make her more careful, more cognizant that all things were possible, even the darkest possibilities. I'd wanted to hold her hand and talk about it instead of having her drown in television or sit in her bedroom listening to angry tapes of the Ladykillers and smoking cigarettes and talking on the phone with Dee for hours even in the middle of the night. But with her wild emotions and passions, everything the world handed out fell like weights on her shoulders, and I was never allowed to help. I kept hoping there'd come a moment when she needed me and I'd be there. When she'd need more than the dull drone of the TV, her own drug, whose excesses and assaultive sounds deadened her sensibilities, like alcohol. I looked at her glum profile, shifted my crossed legs, and felt my last pair of new hose catch and pull on the edge of the pew.

The reverend continued reading: " 'Have mercy upon me, O Lord, consider my trouble which I suffer of them that hate me, thou that liftest me up from the gates of death.' "

He paused and closed his Bible.

"Amen," someone said.

Reverend Thompson looked out at the assembly, studying

the family, then the row of young men wearing dark glasses. He moved wearily back to his chair, where he leaned his head in his hands. I had to wonder at this mystery of faith in the face of what seemed so often, as Dee's mother said, random fortune. How could people remain so steadfastly committed to their churches, their God? People of faith—that strange, untrendy, and most complex word.

The piano began the introduction to a familiar hymn, and a young woman in the choir, heavyset, dark, her hair corn-rowed, stood and sang in a powerful contralto: "His eye is on the sparrow, and I know he watches me. . . ."

I remembered a night long before in East Texas, four white teenagers parked near a black church's revival tent. We'd gone there for entertainment, to see someone get the spirit, we called it, be provoked into a frenzied dance or convulsive shouting. We sat there in the dark, looking toward the orange lights under the tent, laughing cruelly. From a distance the people in the tent seemed objects of comedy and scorn. Another view from the top of a Ferris wheel.

When the young woman had finished her song and Reverend Thompson was at the pulpit, he turned to her. "Young lady," he said, "I want you to sing that at my funeral. Will you do that for me, sing that at my funeral?" The woman, embarrassed, nodded and turned to the older woman beside her and smiled shyly.

Thompson once again faced the assembly. The sun from a window shone on him like a spotlight.

"These are evil days, my friends," he began. And down front another voice replied, "Yes, Lord . . ."

"Now Isaiah was a prophet of the Lord, and he was an angry man," the reverend went on. "He lived in a time much like our own. A time of great trouble. God said to Isaiah, You tell the children of Israel to hold on. To hold on! If you can just hold on, God told Isaiah, you'll be saved. The Messiah will come, your enemies will be defeated, and you will be saved from eternal hell."

Reverend Thompson paused and pulled a handkerchief from his pocket and wiped his face. He paused for so long there was an uneasy stirring in the audience.

"But speaking of hell," Reverend Thompson resumed, "speaking of hell . . ." His voice grew stronger. "We know about hell, don't we. We who live in this city know a lot about hell. And this young man here"—he gestured toward the shiny green casket—"he knew about hell too. Because, my friends, you and I know there is a hell on earth right outside these doors. And I'm talking about those momentary survivors who have chosen the destiny of the streets, who have made our lives a living hell. And I'm talking also about the powerful behind them."

"Yes, Lord," a voice up front echoed.

The reverend stretched his long arms as if to envelop his audience. "Isaiah says that the Lord's people will always have enemies. What we have to do, my friends, is realize our enemies." There was a chorus of response as Reverend Thompson again wiped his face.

"Oh God," he shouted, "I am weary of burying young men." He held up his fist and shook it. There was a great, simultaneous intake of breath from the audience.

Shelly clasped her arms around her waist and turned to me quizzically. I had told her it would be painful, but she hadn't understood. How could she? She turned away quickly, not letting me offer even a look of solace.

"Oh, the sadness of burying another of our young men every week. To see night after night on the television the bodies shoved inside ambulances, the sneakers some will kill for protruding from the end of a stretcher! Night after night after night!"

Reverend Thompson shook his fist, and his shouts grew

even louder and stronger: "This must end, this must end! This must end!" His voice vibrated through the building, accompanied by loud "Amens" and other cries.

There was the sound of a siren outside, and for a moment I expected to hear Pal's familiar howl. This siren was joined by a second, and from the family's pews came a loud, abrupt wail. In the back of the church hall a baby cried, breathlessly, stopping to catch its breath, so you waited for the next cry.

Reverend Thompson leaned forward over the pulpit as if to confide. "You know, they don't have to lynch us anymore. We have these drugs, these guns. . . . And those fools out there on the street, they do it to one another! These young men before us, our handsome young men, hiding behind their dark glasses—they should be our future, but instead they're only momentary survivors. Only momentary survivors!"

"Yes, Lord," voices echoed.

"Isaiah was a prophet. He told the children of God that the Messiah would come. But we are still waiting, Lord, for deliverance! I tell you, we are still waiting!" Thompson looked up. "Is it only to be in heaven, Lord?" He looked at the congregation, the sweat streaming down his face. "I tell you today, my friends, my people, that I'm calling for deliverance, I'm calling for help, I'm calling for a new messiah, who will not turn his back on the black people! Who will rescue us! Who will lead us out of this vale of iniquity, out of this path of annihilation!"

There was a gasp from up front, and a woman stood and cried out, "That's blasphemy!" "That's right," Reverend Thompson answered, "that's right, that's what I said, I'm waiting for a new messiah!" He gestured with both arms toward the woman, his hands shaking.

I thought of him frantically tugging his green garden hose into his hallway, running in circles inside his back fence, leading our Neighborhood Watch group, acting as our point man on the dark streets.

Thompson looked up then and said, "Mama, forgive me," and his voice broke.

Everyone was too stunned to move. I felt a trickle of sweat down the side of my face. There wasn't enough air in the building. A wail and loud sobs were heard from the direction of the family, and in the back the baby was crying steadily. Outside the church, there were more sirens from Georgia Avenue. Four older men in suits stood in the front pews, turned to one another uneasily, then went up the steps to the platform and surrounded Reverend Thompson, who was bent over the pulpit. One of the men put his arm around the reverend, patted his shoulder, spoke to him as to a comrade-in-arms. There was something profoundly caring about his motion. Reverend Thompson lifted his head and faced the congregation, tears streaming down his face, then allowed the four men to lead him out the side door. The pianist began to play, and the organist joined in. The choir members stood raggedly, some of them crying. A group of young men including Dee, all wearing white gloves, went to the front and took their places on either side of the coffin. One of them was crying, but Dee's face was taut and strained; he seemed to be using every bit of strength he could summon to maintain control. The young men began rolling the green casket up the aisle.

By then we were all standing, and I was clutching the back of the pew in front of me. Tears rolled down Shelly's cheeks from under her sunglasses. The church was filled with cries and moans as the family filed up the aisle. The choir sang, "Further along we'll know all about it . . . Further along we'll understand why . . ."

Outside, the sun was dazzling and the cops were still there in their cars. People congregated in hushed circles and some seemed eager to leave. Shelly and I rounded the corner. She was still crying, and I put my arm around her until we reached the car. We left the doors open to let the car cool. Across the street a young man in a white undershirt was lovingly washing his blue Nissan. Shelly looked back toward the church before she slid inside the car, her chin trembling.

I had told her I wouldn't go to the cemetery. If she wanted to go she'd have to go with the family. I would feel it an intolerable intrusion on my part, I had tried to explain. The final parting. And how could I explain to her that my concern was really for myself. Seeing how Mario's family might feel, ambivalent perhaps, to be put out of their constant misery of concern. Was there an iota of relief, as I sometimes imagined it could be, to be finally and forever spared this fear and ambivalence of love? But leaving the church, I saw that in sorrow the family had closed ranks. Dee was settled inside a limousine with others of his family, his handsome head staring straight ahead, as if he were avoiding the sight of us emerging from the church.

When we pulled away I felt a hundred years old. As we turned onto Georgia Avenue, I wondered how on earth we'd get through the rest of the day.

The week after the funeral, on a rainy afternoon when Shelly and I had an appointment with a counselor at her school, Viktor arrived unexpectedly with roses, beautiful long-stemmed pink roses, too perfect to believe, in a long white box, just like in the movies. Fred Astaire with sex appeal, I thought, pulling the green tissue back.

"And it's not even Valentine's!" I gave Viktor a kiss before I waltzed to the kitchen, where I found a wine carafe tall enough for the roses.

We sat down in my living room before the gray, rainy windows. I told him the school had requested the appointment because of Shelly's ongoing absenteeism. "She seems to be flaking apart more every day, and she comes home late from visiting Dee in Anacostia, which makes me incredibly nervous. She's even more incommunicado than usual. How many days can she go without saying anything to me unless I ask a direct question?"

"It is her own war," Viktor said. "Under siege a people can hold out for a long time, until they understand it is costing them more than they can bear."

"But why should she war against me?" I said.

"Because she can. Because you are here and convenient, because you'll still love her."

"Do you think we'll become homeless?" she'd asked me that morning over a doughnut, which was the only thing I could get her to eat for breakfast. "Wouldn't that be a joke? Dee's grandmother could take us in."

With little preamble, Viktor announced he was moving.

"Oh, really," I said, thinking he meant to another neighborhood, maybe another block. After all, he didn't need that big house. I'd always wondered why he'd bought a place that was so large. Maybe it was a prelude to his asking me to move in with him. "Where to?" I asked.

"Prague." The word fell like a stone. I actually looked down, thinking something had fallen to the floor. Then I looked beyond his tortoiseshell glasses into his sincere eyes.

"Prague!"

"Prague," he repeated, taking my hand.

"Prague."

I focused on the laugh lines around his mouth, wanting to touch them, waiting for him to smile. But he didn't. His eyes were East European sad and serious.

"Perhaps I am coming at this hindside forward, or however you say that. Let me explain."

I looked around the room. The Help Wanted pages were

on the coffee table with red circles up and down the columns. In a vase were some flowers he'd brought us the day of Mario's funeral, now faded. I just couldn't believe there was yet another crisis right here before my weary eyes.

"I have been offered a position . . . really, asked to return." He clasped my hand in both of his as he explained. "The editor of a newspaper in Prague died very suddenly. They have asked me to take over for now. It was a great shock, his death. And this newspaper is somewhat"—he paused to find the right word—"somewhat important. What I mean . . . it is important that it go on, you see, the same way. There are people who would like to change its editorial policies."

I held on to him then as if he were slipping away. I touched his attractive gold ring with the unraised garnet in the center. I'd always wanted to ask him about it. Now it won't matter, I thought.

"It is not just a job. If it were just a job, just an opportunity . . ." He shrugged, and looked at me so attentively I wondered how he could say that he was leaving. "But this is political too. You know how there is such upheaval right now, with talk of the country dividing."

"I see." I was trying to.

I didn't doubt what Viktor said. I knew everything was changing in Czechoslovakia. Surely everyone in the world, besides a few people in Borneo, knew that.

"There has been pressure. People in the government have phoned and . . . some friends I feel a duty to . . ." He meant Havel. "They have urged me . . ." He lifted my hands and kissed them with what I still considered old-world sincerity.

"I see," I said again. "That's nice." The East Texas girl minding her manners. Isn't that sweet! I told myself. Don't cry!

"There are so many problems there, you see. I feel a part of that. I must be honest with you. I have tried to be honest. I care for you very much. And it is fascinating here, but . . ."

He rose and started walking around the room. He needed to get away from me, not look at me, not hold my hands, to explain more.

"It's not that we don't have some of the same problems you do." He gestured as he spoke. "But for an outsider, the problems here are impersonal. I don't feel that way about my own country." He'd always planned to go back, he went on to say, he'd expected he would at some point.

Viktor turned, wanting me to say that I understood. And I did. He was right.

"For how long?" I asked.

"I don't know," he said.

Slowly it dawned on me what this meant. Forever. I leaned back against the inoffensive beige of my couch. I could feel my face changing hues, probably becoming deathly white and clammy, as it did after I suffered a fender bender or a crisis with Shelly.

Viktor had stopped pacing and was watching me.

"I'm so sorry," I said.

He came across the room and knelt down beside me, then put his arms around my waist and hugged me to him. I knew he cared for me. I knew this was painful for him. But I knew also that he could get over it pretty readily. Probably neither of us had a lot of romantic illusions. Could it be that we were of an age when life was more important than love? He pulled away and looked at me. I smiled, letting him know I was okay.

"I am so sorry too," he said.

Of course, I believed him. Why did I believe everything this man said? Why did I believe he had an old-fashioned Superman-style honesty, as if he'd escaped the cynicism I associated with most men and women in America nowadays? Why was I acting like he was Heathcliff, the later Heathcliff, gainfully employed, romantic, and goodhearted, truthful and well dressed?

"When?" I asked.

"As soon as possible. I have to go to New York for a few days, then finish up some things here."

"Oh," I said. I would be left with the cruelest winter months to pass alone. "And you just got your mini-blinds installed!"

"I know," he said sadly.

Don't cry, I told myself again.

"Please don't cry," Viktor Hajek said.

"I can't help it," I said, crying. "It's this funeral and losing my job and now you and everything. This has not been one of my better"—I looked for the word—"intervals. In fact, this year is not starting out very well!"

"I understand." Viktor was always saying that he understood, and the truth is I always had the feeling Viktor Hajek *did* understand, or tried to.

"And you bought all those bulbs you were going to plant this spring!"

"You can have them," he said. "I was too late anyway."

"I don't want your bulbs," I said, crying and laughing together.

"I know," he told me. "I'm very sad to be leaving. I considered not going because of you. But it would be irresponsible not to do this." He was smiling and looking sad at the same time.

"Prague . . ." I said. "What a rich word."

"Yes, I look forward to being back there. And I'll probably see my children more often. My son may join me. But I'll miss here. I'll miss you." He wiped the tears off my face and took my hand and kissed it. That moment I looked into his eyes and couldn't imagine any American on earth kissing my hand.

"Seems like I'm always crying around you," I said, "and I don't normally cry at all. Hardly ever. I hate to cry." His arms felt so comforting. People who are wrapped in somebody else's arms every day just forget how to appreciate it.

He pulled back and looked at my face, red and swollen and probably hideous-looking. Then he kissed me tenderly on either damp cheek.

"We really don't know each other very well," I said.

"No, we don't."

"But it's been so nice." I sniffed.

"Very nice." He let me go but looked at me as if he enjoyed doing so.

"What an irony that after suffering politics here all these years I'd be done in by a whole other set of politics." I sighed.

"Yes, ironic."

"I guess I'm kind of a romantic." I laughed. "I try not to be."

"Yes," he said. "Me too. How would you like to come to Prague?"

"I don't know a word of Czech."

"I mean for a visit, soon."

"That's what I meant," I said, blushing. "Maybe sometime." Then I came to my senses. "Oh no, I forgot. I can't afford it for the rest of my life. I don't even have a job."

"You would not have to worry about that. Besides, I'm sure you'll find a job." The way he said it I could nearly believe it. He didn't even glance at the newspaper spread out on the coffee table, the way Tom used to, sometimes reading things when he talked to me. Viktor Hajek always gave me his complete, undivided attention, which I appreciated.

"I guess we could be pen pals," I said. "I had a German pen pal once, when I was little. You know, they were trying to let us know they weren't all Nazis. She sent me her photo. She was chunky. I can just see her. She wore a short pleated skirt and had blond hair with bangs. Her name was Edith."

"Let's go to my house," Viktor suggested.

"Of course." I felt a torrent of passion. But as soon as I stood and my head cleared, I looked at my watch and remembered the appointment with Shelly's counselor. I explained this to Viktor, and he seemed to understand. The reason he was moving to Prague was the same reason I couldn't rush down the block to his bed and drown myself in love and sex in the afternoon.

We talked about which realtor he should use to sell his house. There was a painful undercurrent to every word. At the door he said, "I will phone you later."

"Yes, good. That would be nice. And let me know if I can do anything to help you." I was ever the good neighbor. "You know, like dust your mini-blinds."

He opened the front door, extended his big black umbrella, punched a button, and it opened, whomp.

"Like magic," I said, smiling at him. For a minute I thought he might sail off into the heavens like Mary Poppins. But he remained there looking back at me as if he could hardly bear to leave.

"Washington is just an extremely transient city," I said finally. "That's one of its major problems."

SHELLY ABSOLUTELY AND TOTALLY forgot about our appointment with the counselor, she claimed when she appeared at home four hours later.

"Dee was upset," she said, angrily defensive. "I had to go talk to him." She marched upstairs to her room, dropping her bookbag and purse on the way. I followed, picking up her possessions and making what she denounced as "speech one million forty-nine" about responsibility and consideration. She kept her back to me, then turned to play an imaginary fiddle as I spoke, which was like dropping a match into a gasoline tank.

"After all the money we spent on those college applications, and you may not even graduate if you keep missing school!" Even if she had no sympathy for my feelings, I thought, she might at least understand the economic hardship.

"All you think about is money." She tossed her head and aligned her bracelets.

As if the hardwood floor had fallen away beneath me, I felt myself caught in the downward spiral of unbridled fury. "I have to think about money for your sake. Do you think I like having to fight to make a living when you could care less? Why can you never think of anyone but yourself and Dee? Do you ever think how I feel? Do you ever stop to consider how I have problems and feelings? My life is pretty screwed up now too. Why can't you for once think of someone besides yourself? I try so hard to do everything I can for you. And what do I get? Meanness, never a kind word. You are such a little bitch!"

As soon as the words left my mouth I felt like a monster, and Shelly nearly smiled in triumph at my loss of control. And then it was as if I'd struck her. Her face grew fierce and she screamed, "You are the bitch! You are the fucking bitch, and I hate you! And I'm getting out of here, and when I go I hope I'll never have to set eyes on you again!"

I wished I could die on the spot for being such a fool and letting her get the better of me. Victimizing my own child, I thought as I stomped downstairs to the kitchen, where I put away the meal I'd left out for her while I'd worried about her not showing up, out after dark, and who knows what horror might have happened to her. I switched on the garbage disposal and listened an extra minute to the terrible grinding sound; it matched the sound of my soul.

I sat down, still mentally sizzling, and turned on the TV to some high-minded public affairs programming that I thought might make me feel better about myself and the disaster that had just occurred. But instead I sat there numb before the talking heads, hardly hearing a word, the bitter aftertaste of failure seeping through my veins like a slow poison. I thought about Viktor's leaving, and knew that development had provoked the breakdown of my primary mission, which was to protect my child and maintain some sense of peace, dignity, and decorum.

I considered putting a Fred Astaire movie in the VCR but realized I didn't deserve a mental tap with Fred and Ginger. I decided to go to bed. I stopped before the closed door of Shelly's room and knocked.

"Yeah?" she responded calmly.

"I'm sorry, Shelly. I didn't mean that. I was upset about something else. Forgive me."

There was a moment's pause as, I knew, she was sorting through her possible responses.

"No problem," she called through the door. But her voice was tentative, soft, wounded. I wanted to go in and hug her, yet I knew that was out of the question, so I went on to my room with the newspaper. In bed I read about the mistreatment of the Kurds by the Turks and Iraqis. Before falling asleep, I told myself that if our basic problems had been simpler, had Shelly and I lived back in the hunter-gatherer era and my duties been merely obtaining food and shelter, I'd surely have done better.

THE NEXT DAY, after a still silent and now overtly wounded Shelly went to school, I pulled out a yellow legal pad and sat down to try to deal with the problems in my life. I had so many that I couldn't even think of them all at once. I made myself a cup of tea; being truly in love with a non-American might lead me to liking hot tea more than I used to. Viktor had labored in a uranium mine when he was in prison. To protect themselves from the uranium, he told me, the workers drank gallons of green tea. I wondered if green tea would do anything to protect the heart.

But I was so rattled I couldn't organize my thoughts. I

needed to talk to someone. This was all too much to deal with alone. I considered phoning Marcus, but I couldn't bear to dial the number of Harrison & Associates, no matter how much I missed him. I picked up the legal pad and found Dee's list of jobs with his neat notations beside each on a few turned-back pages. I remembered how he had repaired the screen on the kitchen window and the latch on a kitchen cabinet and how he sang when he vacuumed. There were still some of his things scattered around the house, his rap music magazines, mail, job ads he'd clipped out of the newspaper, even the grape jelly and regular mustard he'd bought. Maybe since he was a genuine hero, to whom the city was going to award a medal, according to Shelly, someone would offer him a job. Why not phone Dee, I thought. Reestablish our relationship. It might help Shelly forgive my verbal abuse. I went to her room, rummaged through the pile of papers around her dresser, and found a list of phone numbers that seemed associated with Dee.

After two failures, including a curt "He ain't here" from a young woman, I reached him.

"Yeah?" he answered. He sounded sleepy.

"Did I wake you?" I asked.

"I was up. I been up." His tone changed, grew energetic.

"Well, I wanted to see how you were. I didn't get to talk to you at the funeral."

"I 'preciate you coming," he said. In the background I could hear a fuzzy TV sound, a woman speaking to a child. There was an awkward silence.

"You doing okay?"

"Yeah. I'm making it." But a hollow, hopeless tone had returned to his voice. He called to someone to turn the TV down.

"You still recording this month?"

The volume on the television set went up with a commercial, and Dee again told someone to turn it down. The volume was suddenly low.

"Not yet," Dee answered me. "The people ran out of money. Later, maybe."

"Oh, I'm sorry," I muttered, wishing I hadn't asked. Will I never learn not to ask questions? "They think you're always quizzing them!" Shelly would tell me. "Well, I wish you the best, Dee, I just wanted to say that. I'm sorry about Mario."

"Yeah . . ." His voice trailed off.

What was I expecting? Gratitude for my still thinking of him, wanting the best for him?

"I'll let you go," I said. "Take care."

I felt worse after the call. I went to the living room to smell the roses Viktor had brought, even more beautiful the second day. I was surprised they hadn't wilted under the barrage of my previous evening's quarrel with Shelly. It still made me soul sick to think of it.

Do not get depressed, Rosemary, I lectured myself. You'll get through this. But I had the feeling that something like a volcano, something I had absolutely no control over, was building up inside the house. I could imagine it slowly expanding, the walls swelling dangerously, as in the tale of the Mexican cactus that swells and swells until it explodes with living scorpions. Two days later, it happened.

I had been to a headhunter in Georgetown and thought I'd be home before Shelly. But when I got there, I found her sitting at the dining table writing on that same nonrecyclable yellow pad. Our largest suitcase stood packed in the hall, its brown leatherish sides swollen to their full extension. After wearing none for a week, Shelly now had on a lot of makeup; she was also wearing some cheap go-go earrings I hadn't seen her wear in a long time. A small braid of her long two-tone hair hung oddly from one side of her forehead. It looked like a long scar running the length of her face.

"What's happening?" I asked, dropping my purse on the hall floor, beside the umbrella stand forever empty because Shelly never returned the umbrellas she used.

"I'm moving out," she announced calmly.

I was motionless. I stared at her, summoning my internal elite forces, as if those play soldiers could bar her way.

"You were just going to leave me a note?" I asked her, realizing that was what she must have been writing on the yellow pad. I could not believe this, even though I had tried to prepare myself a million times for just such a scenario.

She looked up then, more like her old self—since of late I seemed to have been lost from her emotional radar—and sneered at my dress-for-success suit. When she looked at me like that I no longer thought she was pretty, and that always shocked me. But I couldn't completely blame the sneer. I was even wearing high heels, which are against my basic principles.

"I know," I said, "but I've got to get a job."

"Compromise, compromise."

"Such is life, Shelly." I sat down opposite her, and steadied myself with my elbows on the table.

She dropped her chewed-on pencil, which she held too far down, and it rolled off the side of the table. Why did all kids hold their pencils wrong nowadays?

I stirred myself to pick it up off the red Oriental rug, which needed vacuuming, and returned it to her as if that might repair something.

She ignored the pencil and said, "I'm moving in with one of Dee's aunts out in Virginia. I'm going to work in her store. She needs help. Dee's going to work there too. He needs to get out of the city." She ripped the top sheet of paper off the pad and for emphasis wadded it up.

"You're dropping out of school with only five months to go before graduating?"

She shrugged and raised her thin eyebrows, which she'd darkened with brown pencil. She'd made a mole on her chin with the same brown; she called it a beauty mark. I stepped out of my shoes, knowing that this was the type of crisis in which I needed two full feet on the floor. I stood up and walked around the table; maybe it would help to get closer, to touch her.

I broached the therapeutic approach first. "Look, you've been through a really traumatic experience, Shelly. First the fire, then Mario getting killed. Why don't you talk to a therapist?"

She lifted her eyes as if she couldn't believe my words. "We've been through this, Moms," she said. Her voice sounded lower than usual. She was smoking too much, and she was nervous. That gave me hope I might change her mind.

"You know, they say that after you've been through a traumatic experience, like that fire and all, you shouldn't make life-changing decisions immediately. That's a rule of thumb." I used a term I hated.

Shelly shook her head. As I moved closer, she turned her back to me, kicked out her feet, and studied her red cowboy boots, expensive antique boots her father had bought her for Christmas.

"What's important now is to be with Dee. He's had a hard time. He needs me." She glanced over her shoulder toward me. "Then you won't have to support me." That was like a kick in the shin with the red boots.

"Maybe we should go to a therapist together," I said. "Maybe that would work."

Shelly had always ranked the psychiatric profession with witch doctors. She made fun of the whole idea, though she believed in tarot cards and the I Ching and horoscopes and ghosts. Indeed, if I'd made her an appointment with a witch doctor, she might have gone.

I folded my arms, trying to gather some authority. She leaned forward, still sitting in the chair, allowing her hair to obscure her sad young face with the gold ring in her nose. Why, I wondered, did the young have to be so self-destructive? Was it fate, was it some grand Darwinian design to winnow the species?

Shelly didn't even respond to my suggestion. She glanced toward me and said to my right shoulder, "You're such a control freak."

"Now stop and think, Shelly. You're too smart to throw yourself away like this. It's no tribute to Dee to ruin your life." My heart was running in place. I was speaking too broadly, I told myself. Be more specific.

"You won't let him stay here, so this is what we have to do." She squinted at me with this reminder that whatever self-destructive act she proposed was the result of my failure to observe her rights, her own commandments, those standards I was judged by that seemed forever unobtainable.

Then she changed tone, shrugged as though it was no big deal, but something she could put into perspective. "I'm not ruining my life. This is the thing I want to do. We don't all have to be college graduates and taxpayers. Besides, you can't afford my school anyway."

My throat was all of a sudden so dry I didn't think I could utter another word. I picked up her near-empty glass sweating on the dining table and swallowed the few drops of the too sweet diet cola she'd been drinking, feeling the wax of her bright red lipstick left on the rim. And she rose, standing taller than I did.

"Believe me, I'll work it out," I said. "Your father will borrow money if necessary." My voice was shaky. I had to be calm.

"My father is getting married," she said. She said "married" as if marriage were equivalent to death. Then her face grew hard, and everything flooded forth. After all those silent days she stood facing me, rendering me defenseless, her eyes so filled with loathing that I felt both horror and a kind of gratitude that it was finally there in the open, visible, what I had been feeling and what had been accumulating for all the years of what she saw as wrong.

Her voice rose at the end of her phrases, in that strange, nearly Irish lilt of so many young wounded women. "That just proves what I've thought for a long time. Like you're always doing everything for me. I'm so important to you, but the most important thing is you and my father being together. And you didn't even try. . . . Not once over all these years . . . years and years"—she was crying now—"have you even tried to make up with him. So don't tell me what I ought to do."

She wiped her nose with the back of her hand. I reached in my pocket for a tissue.

"Really, what you do is just what makes you happy, and that's what I'm going to do now. Dee and his friends, they all accept me for what I am, they're not always trying to make me into someone like you. That's all you want, for me to be like you!"

Someone like you . . . I extended a limp tissue, but instead of taking it she wiped her nose with her hand again.

"What do you mean, someone like me?"

She didn't pause, not even for a second. "Somebody middle-class. Privileged. Educated, segregated, secure, and white!" She used an inner-city rhythm that I could imagine in a rap song. Even her diction had a hostile intonation.

"I don't think I have to play the race game with you, Shelly. If you want to start from there, you'll never get anywhere near fairness."

"I know what you're going to say. 'It's so much more *complicated* than that.' That's what you always say. 'Everything is so *complicated*.' " She emphasized the word mockingly.

"Unfortunately, that's true," I said.

"You just want to sit here and be safe and secure and talk about everything being complicated."

"I don't see how your leaving school and moving to Virginia is going to solve any problems."

Surely there was some way to reach her. Surely if I kept digging I would reach that splinter under her skin, and then remove it and stop the pain. I thought of what Marcus had said about keeping on.

"Shelly, you and Dee have to keep trying, to think of your future. One of these days people will come up with solutions. Don't you want to be one of those people?"

For a moment she seemed to be listening to what I was saying. But then she turned away and stared out the window. The winter dark was threatening, though the streetlights weren't on yet. It seemed gray outside, and that was closer to the truth, I thought. That gray world I'd heard Marcus talk about had more meaning than perhaps he'd intended. Shelly tossed the wadded paper into the middle of the table, and went to the front door and turned on the porch light. When she returned, she had her leather jacket and the smart Coach bag she'd recently bought hot on some corner in Southeast. She put on her jacket and hung the bag over her shoulder and stood looking out the bay windows, which Mama always said needed curtains. If I were the type of person who'd draped my windows, maybe this wouldn't have happened.

So the wound of my divorce from her father had been festering all along. Of course I knew, but I hadn't realized the strength of her anger. And there was no way on earth that I could explain to a young, romantic girl that some broken things can't be repaired.

After that I pulled out all the stops I could think of, phrases from Parenting 101 and more. Even books I didn't know I remembered . . . I threw every bit of sense I could come up with at her and tried to stay calm. Responsibility, fair play, emotional investment, opportunities—the words flowed, sounding stale even to me. She would not engage. She just stood there pulling on her jacket, looking out the window, ready to spring. So young and capable and determined.

"We should have talked about your father's marriage earlier," I said. "I should have insisted you talk more about Dee. About Mario's death. And the fire."

"I wouldn't have talked," she stated. "It's too late."

I didn't know what to say. We stood there, as always, I looking at her, she looking away.

Finally she spoke. "Dee really needs to get away from some people."

I sighed, intimidated by her loyalty and determination, though recognizing the titillation of the danger around him. I loved the passion in her at the same time it terrified me.

"Tell me about this aunt. I didn't even know he had an aunt in Virginia."

"It's his father's sister."

"What's her name? And where in Virginia?"

"Questions, questions . . ." Already she'd pulled away. The worst from me was over. She was on to the next challenge, which she saw as freedom.

"Does she have children? Does she have room for you?"

"I guess."

"So you and Dee will both be staying with her?"

She shrugged.

"You know you're not eighteen yet. You can't lawfully do this," I said desperately.

She'd picked up a department store sale brochure from a table and was thumbing through it. "So call the police, have me arrested." She tossed the brochure back on the table.

"Maybe we should go to Texas. Get away for a few days."

"I am getting away," she said, and just then a car pulled up and stopped in front of the house. The streetlamps were on now, and light pooled on top of an old burgundy car with a crumpled, rusted rear fender. There was a single honk.

"Who's that?" I asked.

"A friend."

"Well, where will you be? Will you give me a phone number, somewhere to reach you, some way to hear from you?"

She lifted the overpacked suitcase and a shopping bag that clinked when she moved it. I knew it contained a hair dryer and hairspray and curling irons and mousse and multitudinous other hair products dumped loose inside. She never had the patience to finish packing, but always reached a point where she'd just toss things into a carryall.

"What if there's an emergency? What if—"

"I'll give you a call," she interrupted.

She set her bags down and opened the door. I started toward her, but she stopped me by turning and looking over her shoulder.

"Bye, Mom," she said.

With that, she was out the door. I watched her move slantwise down the walk, lugging the heavy suitcase. Arlo came loping up to greet her and she set the suitcase down to pet him.

A young black man in a long denim jacket got out of the car. He strolled in a slow, self-conscious slouch to the rear of the car and unlocked the trunk. Now I could see how old and banged up the car was, how unsafe at any speed. The young man took Shelly's suitcase and shoved some things around inside the trunk, then put her bag in and slammed the trunk closed. He gave her an encouraging pat on the shoulder and she went to the passenger side and opened the door. Dee got out then and Shelly slid inside. He turned toward the house, and must have seen me standing there in the doorway. He paused, then got in and slammed the car door, leaving part of a seat belt hanging out. When the engine turned over, the muffler rattled so loudly Arlo jumped off the stoop and hid under a shrub. The car drove off quickly, and only then did I ruin my new job-hunt hose: I rushed out to the curb just in time to see the car run through a yellow light that turned red as they were in the middle of the intersection, and speed away.

The next day I had to talk to somebody.

"I have some new problems," I told Mama on the phone.

"I do too," she said. "Five stores were broken into last night and robbed."

Five stores! That must have been about a quarter of all the stores in town. The week before, there'd been a holdup at the True Value.

"You know, I was just thinking about calling you," Mama said. "Guess what else happened last night."

"Art proposed?"

"How did you know?"

"You sounded so grim, I guess."

"Well, what do you think?"

"Mama, it's, What do *you* think?"

"I sure don't like cooking for one," she said with conviction.

"How do you feel about Art?"

"Rosemary, you know I've always liked Art. Even admired him. He's a nice man. He's handsome. And his sister is one of my best friends. But I don't know if I want to get married again."

"I'd take my time and think about it. Then again, maybe you should get married and have a baby."

"Rosemary, don't be crude. That isn't like you."

"I know, but Viktor is moving to Prague."

"Oh." Obviously Mama didn't realize the significance of that information. "I'm sorry. Are you real disappointed?"

At that, I wished I hadn't called. "I'm more than disappointed, Mama. 'Devastated' is a word that would fit."

"Well, that city . . ."

"I don't know what it has to do with this city."

"So many foreigners is what I mean. And foreigners return to foreign places."

"You're right, Mama. That's just what I said. But there are foreigners everywhere—except maybe East Texas."

Mama said there were plenty of foreigners in East Texas and then segued back to the subject of Art Moser and how if they did decide to marry they'd work out a prenuptial agreement and keep their incomes separate. Not that Mama's income was any more than enough to get by fairly comfortably. My mother might be moving more rapidly and acceptingly toward the new century than I was.

"Don't marry him if you're not sure," I told her.

"When are you sure, Rosemary? And it would be cheaper," she said. "I do get lonesome. And sometimes I can't open jars." I told her about a handy round piece of rubber that cost less than a dollar, invented, no doubt by the women's movement, to open jars.

At that point Mama seemed to have forgotten that I was the caller. I went ahead and told her Shelly had dropped out of school and gone to Virginia to work in the country store of one of Dee's relatives.

She was silent, then said, "Have you lost your mind? Why are you letting her do this?"

"What am I going to do, Mama? Tie her to a chair? I tried to talk her out of it. You know the world has changed. I can't *make* her do things."

Mama paused again. I could see her sitting there, trying to

do the right thing as always. In her case that meant battling the disorder of the city council, clipping coupons, buying Christmas wrapping paper on sale in late December, and tithing to her church. And having taken the lesson of the good Samaritan to heart, she was always helping people down on their luck. That was her real political base before she ever thought about becoming a politician.

"I'm sorry, Rosemary. What a shame. I know you must be upset."

"I'm all right," I said, sounding like Shelly.

Mama said that she would pray for us both and that I should do the same. She noted in closing that she was having her house repainted in the spring and was thinking of making the front door blue. For sixty-something and East Texas, such a notion was a sure sign of empowerment.

After I finished talking to Mama I didn't feel much better about Shelly. But I tried to comfort myself by saying that maybe the worst had happened and it could be only upward after this. What I had to do now was think of my own future. Since Harrison & Associates had broken the tether and left me to float free from the earth, I had felt not weightless but burdened, heavy and sinking. It was time for me to reattach myself to the workaday world.

That night I slept badly. I kept thinking the phone would ring and it would be Shelly. Maybe I was only dreaming, I told myself, and when I woke up in the morning she'd be sleeping in her bed. Why hadn't I jumped in my car and tailed them into Virginia, I wondered. The following day, another gray day, I phoned some of the numbers on the list I'd found in Shelly's room but found out nothing. I considered calling the police. In the afternoon, I phoned Shelly's friend Miranda, who said she hadn't heard from her and wished she'd return her black skirt. In the afternoon the sun came out and I got a call from Marcus.

"Hey, let's do lunch, Rosemary."

"Marcus, what's happened to you? You didn't use to talk like *Vanity Fair.*"

"It's a joke, Rosemary. Where's your sense of humor?"

"Gone," I said. "Replaced by despair."

"I see. I don't even have to ask how you're doing."

"I've seriously thought of running off to Sainte-Marie and just throwing myself to the fleas."

"That bad, huh?" Marcus chuckled. It made me think of the soon-to-be-departed Viktor. A good man's warm chuckle is high on the list of nice things in life.

"Just let me say it makes me feel a whole lot better to hear from you. I've now had un-American sex and he's moving back to Prague. Mama's town is having a crime wave, and she's letting someone talk her into getting married but she wants a prenuptial agreement. Dee seems to have gone berserk over his cousin's being killed, and Shelly has dropped out of school and run off with him and is working somewhere in the wilds of Virginia in a country store, selling worms, I suppose."

Marcus didn't say anything immediately. I could hear jazz playing in the background. Marcus really knew jazz. He listened to my blues program but he preferred jazz. Blues, what he called "that droopy-drawers music," made him, well, blue.

"I read about the fire and Dee and his cousin. I kept meaning to phone you. I picked up the phone once or twice. But I didn't know what to say."

"You shouldn't have felt you owed me any more explanation than anyone else," I said.

"Well . . . Harrison & Associates is sure getting me down."

As if it were orchestrated to our conversation, some loopy sax went into a mellow solo in the background.

"We need to talk, Rosemary. How about we go to Cecilia's naturalization ceremony and have lunch afterward and settle all our problems?"

With that thought my spirits rose. It was as if I'd heard

some good old down-and-brown blues, the kind that helps you shoulder your load and puts you back in tune with the world.

"Hey, that sounds terrific," I said. "I need to start a new chapter in my life, alter my karma." Which was something Shelly would say.

After I hung up I thought about Marcus's not calling, his knowing about the fire and still not calling. Maybe one reason I was so fond of Marcus was that we had a lot in common. More than most folks, we'd both go a long way to avoid heartache if we possibly could. After all, sometimes a telephone receiver can weigh a ton.

I'd never been to a naturalization ceremony before. Cecilia Bontemps's was held in a courthouse in Alexandria, and there were about a hundred other new citizens, all dressed up and jolly. The ceremony was brief, but long enough for these hundred to "renounce and abjure all allegiance and fidelity to any foreign prince, potentate, state, or sovereignty" and swear to take this obligation "freely without any mental reservation or purpose of evasion; so help me God."

It was lucky I didn't have to pledge all that, because I certainly had some mental reservations about a whole lot of government policy, not to mention about living disenfranchised in the District of Columbia.

I let myself fantasize that Viktor Hajek had fallen so in love with me he had decided to become an American citizen. He would be a stronger force in the Neighborhood Watch group and stay with me and have un-American sex forever. But I couldn't hang on to that daydream for more than half a minute.

Marcus and I took Cecilia to lunch at the Hard Times Cafe, which has the advantage of being cheap and having a great jukebox, with plenty of Hank Williams and Patsy Cline and even Jerry Jeff Walker. We toasted Cecilia's new Americanism with municipal water and listened to Patsy Cline sing "I Fall to Pieces."

"So how is life at that place, Marcus?" I couldn't bear to pronounce the name.

"Pretty awful." He proceeded to tell us some of the details of Harrison's newest client, a polygamist from the Middle East who was courting the Pentagon in hopes of becoming a middleman for outmoded weapons.

Cecilia's prediction had been right: she had lost her job at Harrison & Associates and was now working only her mall security job while she looked for something else. She filled us in on her brother. It turned out that André's set-to with the prime minister of Sainte-Marie had made him a hero among the left in Latin America. He was traveling and being revolutionary and having successful exhibitions. Right now he was in Mexico for a show of his work.

"You know," Cecilia said, "how in Mexico all the rich people say they're Marxists?"

No, I told her, I didn't know that.

"Oh yes, they will be in their mansions talking about their Marxism with their servants all around waiting on them. So André is selling lots of paintings there."

"I'm glad he survived," I said.

"And how are things in Sainte-Marie?" Marcus asked Cecilia.

She shook her head. "Still very sad. All my family coming here."

"Do you think your nieces and nephews would ever want to return to Sainte-Marie if things improved?" I asked.

"I don't know," Cecilia said thoughtfully. "I don't know."

After Cecilia had to leave for her job, Marcus and I lingered over coffee.

There was more gray in his hair, and he was starting to

grow a beard, which looked very distinguished. He had missed me, he said. "I don't know how long I can hang in at that place. I'm growing an ulcer." He patted his perfectly flat stomach. "What are your plans? You going back into journalism?"

"I've thought of that," I said. "But it's not really a viable possibility unless I relocate to someplace like Wink, Texas. Every other person in this city is a journalist. And to get started nowadays you have to be seventeen and a half, a Rhodes scholar, and have been born on the news desk at *The New York Times.* Even then, you don't get paid for a while. I think that option is out. Besides, I have to make a living. I mean, I assume at some point Shelly will come back into my life." I had to pause and drink some coffee.

The generous waitperson appeared to offer us more coffee, and Marcus pushed his mug toward her. I looked at the cowboy photos on the wall. I'd been mind-wrestling about asking him to help Dee. Don't risk your friendship by leaning on Marcus for Dee's and Shelly's sake, one side of me said. Show some control, or uncontrol. Think of your own life too. I looked around the room for a cowgirl photo. Don't lumber Marcus with Dee's problems, I told myself. Sometimes the wise thing to do is to step back. Step back, if for no other reason than out of respect for Marcus. Even out of respect for Shelly and Dee.

"Marcus, I have a proposition for you," I said. "I know I've mentioned this before, but now I'm serious. I've been thinking about our trying our own thing. Our own partnership. And I have some ideas."

"You've always got ideas." Marcus smiled. "But matter of fact, the way things are going I've been thinking about that myself."

I sat back. "Really!"

"Yeah." He took a sip of coffee, then smiled at me again. "You got a tendency to shoot yourself in the foot now and then, but when you believe in something you're terrific."

"Really!" I said again. "I didn't know you thought that."

"Now you know."

"And here I was, beginning to think another good thing would never come my way."

"Hey, maybe the best is yet to come."

We began to discuss the possibilities. I told Marcus I'd already talked to the Small Business Administration. The number of new businesses that actually made it was minuscule, but the latest employment figures indicated that the bulk of new jobs were in small businesses. I began to feel a wave of optimism sweep through the Hard Times Cafe.

So we sat there, Marcus and I, letting the staff clean around us and mop under our feet in preparation for the dinner crowd. We drank more coffee and split a piece of pecan pie and discussed our business possibilities. One prospect involved environmental groups: now that they had discovered that large corporations were hiring agencies to keep their environmental problems out of the news and away from lawmakers' attention, these environmental groups were looking for their own representatives. Some of these groups wanted the public to know how their interests were being even more subtly undermined. As Marcus said, there were battles to be fought in the gray world of lobbyists and the halls of Congress. I had talked to one nonprofit group that might be interested in hiring us, and Marcus and I now came up with a list of five possible accounts we could go after.

"I've got to think about this," he said.

"Oh, I agree. You should think about it long and hard."

"We'll talk about it more tomorrow."

"You know, we could work out of my house," I offered. "It's empty. Boy, is it empty! And maybe we can hire Cecilia eventually."

"Good." Marcus rolled his eyes at me, but he smiled.

"And I seem to have lost your new phone number. . . ."

"You have it," Marcus said as we left our booth. He took my coat and held it open for me.

"You're back home?"

He nodded. I watched him slip into his smart camel's-hair overcoat. "I am." He glanced at me a moment and started toward the door.

"I'm happy for you," I said.

He didn't look happy. "We'll see," he said.

We stepped outside the Hard Times onto King Street, Alexandria's main thoroughfare, with its old storefronts gone colorful and upscale. I waited for Marcus to explain. Were we going to be friends or just business partners?

"I'm really going to try," he said. "I didn't want to move out to begin with. I don't want a divorce. We can't afford a divorce. But after what we've been through, I don't know if we can make it or not."

We stopped for a light and he turned to me. "Stay tuned."

I GOT HOME to find that Shelly had left a number on the answering machine where I could leave a message for her. I felt a grand relief at this thin thread of connection. There was also a call from Mrs. Moore, pleading with me to come to the emergency Neighborhood Watch meeting at her house that night. She made it sound urgent. I made some hummus dip to take and swore to myself I'd keep my mouth shut and be a passive observer.

Walking to the meeting, I saw a For Sale sign in front of Viktor's house—like a stab in my heart. I wondered if he was back from New York. What if he'd fled to Prague without saying good-bye?

Mrs. Moore's living room was done in white, so her chairs and sofa had plastic slipcovers. I preferred sitting on the floor to trying to stay upright on the slick furniture. About eighteen people were at the meeting; that wasn't surprising given Mrs. Moore's insistence. Pal sat under her chair and watched me the whole time. Mrs. Nance had brought her usual paper plate of store-bought cookies, but Dan and Don had outdone themselves by making biscotti.

In the absence of Reverend Thompson, Mrs. Moore called the meeting to order. She announced that Doreen was staying with her sister. Reverend Thompson was somewhere in western Maryland resting. Without him, his church was in turmoil. Mrs. Moore sent two "Thinking of you" cards around for each of us to sign, one for Doreen and the other for the reverend.

Mrs. Moore inquired about Dee's health, and several people expressed their condolences about his cousin. There was a brief discussion of the media coverage. Dan asked about Shelly, and I told him that she'd dropped out of school and gone into the wilderness. For an awkward moment everyone seemed to be contemplating how Shelly was ruining her life.

Then Mrs. Moore mentioned the sign in front of Viktor Hajek's house and I had to tell them that he was moving to Prague. I spoke with enthusiasm about his important opportunity in that shifting landscape. By then our affair had been hot neighborhood news for weeks, so everyone scrutinized me to see how I was taking this latest tragedy. Mrs. Nance broke the silence that followed by saying that she hoped whoever set that fire got capital punishment. At that point, when I wasn't sure I could take the meeting any longer, our regular pro-capital-punishment neighbor who had relatives in the police department said that the police had received a tip; someone had been arrested and charged with arson, it would be in tomorrow's paper.

I thought that with all this grim news, if they knew I'd lost my job they might start up a collection for me on the spot.

Then Mrs. Moore brought up the immediate crisis, which

was, of course, that now that Doreen and Ezra—only Mrs. Moore had the nerve to use his given name—were out of commission, as it were, who would take over the orange-hat patrol?

"We know why the house was torched," Mrs. Moore said, "and it would be a terrible shame if we stopped our patrols now. It would be as though the forces of evil had won." She went on in this vein.

The big problem for me is that when I'm there with all my neighbors I'm inspired to volunteer to do things I don't really want to do when I'm home by myself. But taking over the Orange Hat patrol was a responsibility I so strongly didn't want that I considered rolling out the front door before anyone looked my way. But everyone was already looking my way.

I surveyed the room. It was true I was a bit younger than most of the others and had had experience with the orange-hat patrol. My very own Day-Glo orange hat hung inside my front door. And it was true also that in that room was a series of ailments that would half fill an emergency room any day. And it was true also that it seemed immensely important to lift the torch and move forward, as Mrs. Moore put it.

Mrs. Moore asked us to consider how it would look to the world if our neighborhood shrank from responsibility. Especially now that the Alcohol Control Board had told us the next step would be our petitioning for a refusal to approve the Bluebird's relicensing. With everyone chiming in, the subject became something like an international incident affecting the entire free world, whatever that is nowadays.

"Rosemary, I know it will be hard," Mrs. Moore finally said to me. My eyes fell on Dan and Don trying to stay upright on the white couch, and inspiration struck me. Dan and Don, interracial and healthy, enthusiastic and willing. It was an unspoken but imperative urban rule that each orange-hat group had to be of mixed race, to prove we were in this together, forever and always.

"How about if Dan and Don and I share it," I suggested. "If we organize it together and not let just one person be the focus, we'll all be safer too."

That made sense to everyone. Dan said that he'd already had some experience marching with the Pink Panthers, an anti–gay-bashing group. Don seemed pleased and graciously offered to take Pal along for his exercise some nights. Everyone else applauded with relief. Mrs. Moore rose to pass the cookies and biscotti around, ignoring my hummus.

"With three people, it will be not only safer but also less of a burden," I kept on, reasoning mostly to myself.

Dan and Don smiled at me, and I treated myself to two biscotti. I went home feeling that we'd managed to avert a crisis of confidence, a demoralization of our little neighborhood world.

The next night Dan, Don, and I and four others set out on our familiar rounds. We stopped momentarily before the skeleton of Doreen's house, cordoned off with yellow plastic tape, its windows boarded up.

We'd been strolling about an hour on that cold night, when Viktor Hajek appeared, running up the street looking for me. He had just that moment returned from New York, he said.

So Viktor joined us walking up and down the alleys. He walked by my side, me in my orange hat, and took my arm whenever we crossed the street or turned into an alley. Once, in a dark alley where someone had thrown eggs at us a few months before, we even held hands. An orange-hat romance.

At ten o'clock the patrol broke up. Viktor and I walked back to my house, where I offered him a beer. I poured myself some Dr Pepper with real sugar, and we sat down to talk. I kept my orange hat on as a test. If he could still want to maintain a relationship with me in this orange hat, oceans might not separate us after all.

He sat beside me with a kind of cold air hovering about

him. I told him about Shelly, and he was enormously sympathetic. I wished he would just put his arms around me and everything in our lives would move back a few weeks—like in the movie where Superman turns the earth back a few rotations to save Lois Lane.

"You know," he said, "the world is very small. We can still be together." He must really care for me, I thought, if, worldly as he was, he could be so optimistic. So I removed my orange hat. That test was over.

"Well, let's see what happens tonight," I said.

"What do you mean, what happens tonight?"

"I mean that I would like you to stay here tonight and listen to some of my music."

Viktor smiled and agreed with enthusiasm. He drank another beer while I went through my records and pulled out the old, precious favorites that I played on my old phonograph upstairs. There was "Hallelujah, I Just Love Her So" by Ray Charles, "Pledging My Love" by Johnny Ace, some Ruth Brown, Marvin Gaye, Fats Domino, Muddy Waters, Little Richard, Chuck Brown. The sounds of my soul serenaded us that night, presenting with scratchy authenticity my East Texas honky-tonk history. That night, the first full night we'd spent together.

Two weeks after we'd met for Cecilia's naturalization ceremony, Marcus gave notice at Harrison & Associates and appeared at my door with my china doll plant. It needed care, northern light, and regular misting. The leaves had browned delicately here and there, but the plant was upright and alive.

Four days later, in the afternoon, Shelly appeared. She let herself in the front door. I was in the kitchen when I heard it open.

"Shelly?" I called.

And there she was in the hallway, an exhausted miracle, pulling her heavy suitcase, a green plastic garbage bag thrown over her shoulder, Santa Claus fashion. She had dark circles under her eyes, and her face was wan and broken out. Her hair hung loose and limp, minus the usual quality-controlling beauty aids. She dropped the garbage bag and said hi, then came into the kitchen without taking her coat off. I marveled at how her presence filled the house, at how powerful she really was. It wasn't just my imagination in her absence.

She pushed her hair back from her face and turned toward me. The hole in her nose was empty, as were the three holes in her ears. She wore no makeup, and the blue sweatshirt under her leather jacket was stained. There was a pained look on her face. But not defensive, only weary maybe.

"I'm back," she announced. She had been gone twenty-three days and nights. She drank some water and then turned away, leaving her glass in the middle of the counter, as she always had. Seeing it there, I felt blessed.

"I'll tell you about it later," she said.

"Fine," I replied. The word was not big enough for what I felt. I went over and hugged her still ungiving body and told her I loved her and was glad she was home. She tolerated my hug, then pulled away to the living room, where she punched on the TV and flipped to a rerun of *I Love Lucy*. I took a seat and turned on the nearby lamp; I hated a room lighted only by television.

"How's Dee?" I asked.

"Okay. I guess." She started taking off some scuffed black leather shoes I'd never seen. Her socks were dirty. Indeed, she looked as if she needed a good soaking bath.

"It didn't work out." She shifted nervously and thumped the side of her mouth with her bitten fingernail. I was afraid that was all she was going to say.

"His aunt and all . . . It just didn't work out. Dee was hiding from these guys. He couldn't go anywhere. . . ." She glanced at me. "He started telling me what to do. Then he started hanging out with these other guys." She sighed heavily, shook her head, sat back, and shook her head again.

"Then he went to Baltimore. Just ran off . . . didn't tell me where he was going." She pulled at her hair, muted the TV ad. "He just disappeared, and finally he phoned and said he was working for somebody up in Baltimore. He's going to night school, he claims." Her skeptical tone reminded me of my own at times in the past. She punched the mute when Lucy returned.

"I thought I was pregnant." She was looking at the TV.

I waited before responding. "That was why you left?"

"Not really." She held her head as if she had a headache. "What would you have done?" She was looking at me now.

"I'd have helped you work it out, of course."

"Um . . ." She leaned forward, resting her chin on her hands. Her nails were bitten down to the quick. "I'm not, though." She sounded disappointed. "They have a lot of problems. His aunt. And her kids. But it was so quiet out there at night. It was creepy."

I moved over and put my arm around her shoulders. She leaned against me, crying. I could smell cigarettes and cheap perfume and dirty socks.

"It would have been nice to have Dee's baby. In a way. Now I don't have anything."

I held her as she cried. Maybe it is only in the perspective of the wider, painful world that the mother moves from obstacle to friend, I thought.

"I don't know how anybody lives with anybody," she mumbled through the tears.

"I know," I said, wanting to rock her in my arms until the

pain was gone. "But one day you'll look back and be glad. One day you'll be grateful for everyone you've loved."

She was quiet; then she sniffed and sat up, pulling away. "Daddy wants me to come for his wedding." Her tone was lighter, even warm.

"Oh, really? Are you going to?"

"He says he'll wait till school is out. You think I should?"

"Yeah, I think you should. You phoned your father?"

"Yeah. We needed money."

"Did you tell him I lost my job?"

"Yeah."

She got up and went to the kitchen for a tissue. On television Lucy wore some kind of costume and was clinging to the side of a tall building. I heard Shelly open the refrigerator door.

"There's not much to eat," I called. I heard the door close. "Some yogurt."

She returned with a green apple and a knife. I asked her if she'd like a cup of tea, thinking that might indicate a new adult-to-adult communication. I went to the kitchen to put the kettle on, and when I returned she was huddled on the loveseat eating the apple, which she'd cut into quarters.

"Don't you want to take your coat off?" I said. I watched her stand, remove her coat and carry it to the hall and hang it up, rather than throw it on the back of a chair. She moved differently; her angular, strong body had a rigid self-consciousness to it that I'd never seen before. She looked older, more pained and focused. Her carefree, dangerous daring seemed to have moderated. She showed some component of fear or caution that I had been trying for years to instill in her for her own protection. Now it was there and sad and not what I wanted at all. Indeed, it broke my heart. And I knew that she too had learned in her own way that no matter how hard you try, how much you love, you can't always make the world right for someone else.

"Excuse me, I've got to pee," she called from the hallway, and started up the stairs.

The next morning I drove her to school, where we met with a counselor. She had missed so much school that it was unlikely she could graduate that spring. She might have to go to summer school, the counselor said casually.

After I left her and started down the hall toward the exit, I turned back and saw her looking at me. She stood there in the dim corridor, with her hand half raised, as if to call me back. I could see how displaced she felt, how troubling and painful it was for her to turn back to the past.

"Shelly's back," I told Marcus that afternoon as we sat at my dining table examining some forms from a bank. "Dee has gone off to Baltimore to work. She'd thought she was pregnant, but she's not."

Marcus stopped cold and looked at me. "Thank God," he said with feeling.

"Yeah. Funny, what I've been worrying about is her immediate safety. Then her being accepted into a college. I hadn't thought much beyond that. Funny how what happens is always something different from what you anticipate."

"Is she all right?" Marcus asked.

I paused. "She's sobered and sad."

"Welcome to the real world," he said.

Despite the precariousness of our new venture, Marcus appeared more relaxed each day, his face less wary and taut. He was energized. It was good for us, this trying it on our own. He had a look of clear relief about his eyes, and he laughed more easily.

"You're not going to say, 'I told you so'?"

He thought for a moment, shook his head, and regarded me with sympathy through his round gold frames.

"You think we'll ever be wise?"

"Most assuredly," he answered.

The air had grown chilly, and I went to close the window I'd cracked open earlier. I stood looking at the winter landscape, the bare limbs of the trees. A couple of warm days had brought forth crocus blooms in Mrs. Moore's tree box across the street. As I returned to my chair, Marcus said, "One of these days she'll figure out just how lucky she is to have you."

He tossed that off as if he didn't know its significance. With that encouraging prospect I returned happily to our bank forms.

That weekend my public radio station was having its winter fund-raising marathon, and I had the radios in my bedroom and the kitchen turned to my favorite program host as I went about my domestic ritual. Millie Jackson began singing "If You're Not Back in Love by Monday," one of my all-time favorites, which made me feel so in love with the disappearing Viktor Hajek I had to sit down and pull myself together. I was reminded of the last fund-raiser, and that day about six months before, when Shelly appeared in her blue shorts pulling handsome Dee behind her. How can life change so quickly?

On Saturday afternoon I drove Viktor through the lovely Virginia countryside to Dulles Airport. We stopped at an overlook on the George Washington Parkway above the rushing Potomac with a vista of the spires of Georgetown and the National Cathedral, that glorious reminder of the complicated beneficence of faith. As he headed for the enchanting city of Prague, I wanted him to remember how beautiful it was here too. But Viktor was earnest about being on time, so we stayed only a moment to enjoy the view. At the airport I sat and waited with him, and gazed out the tall sloping windows of Saarinen's masterly design.

I looked at Viktor's shoes. He'd been wearing some sturdy black Reeboks lately, but for his return to his homeland he'd changed back to his European style.

"I love your shoes," I told him. He smiled, knowing I was kidding.

When the time came to leave, Viktor pulled together his laptop and his carry-on bag, and joined the people lining up, pulling out their boarding passes, heading to Amsterdam or Prague. I hadn't forgotten that woman's voice on the telephone the first night I'd been with him. I was wise enough, I kept telling myself, to be grateful for what we'd had and not to expect a lot in the future. He had, after all, served as an entrée to my new life beyond Shelly, to new possibilities. And I had to keep telling myself what I'd told Shelly: that even if it came to nothing more, I would be grateful for having loved another good man.

Viktor put his arms around me. With the rough tweed of his jacket against my cheek, I ordered myself to remember the enveloping warmth of his arms on all the cold lonely nights ahead. And for a second I felt an intimation of that place he was going to, that city he loved on the banks of the Vltava, with its churches and music and shadows of history.

He spoke into my ear with his rich whispery voice. "I have loved being with you. I will miss you." He pulled back and looked at me seriously, as if promising me a future I knew he could not deliver. "I hope to see you soon," he said.

He *is* a romantic, I thought. But he had told me we'd avail ourselves of his million frequent-flyer miles in order to continue our un-American romance.

"Remember, I'm bad at languages," I'd replied.

"You may be better now," he'd said, and we'd laughed.

We held hands over his carry-on bag and I walked along the line of passengers with him. We were lovers, I thought to myself with some satisfaction. Does that fact alter the universe, even for a brief while? Does it not put me in another demographic group?

I watched as Viktor extended his ticket to the flight attendant and turned to smile at me before boarding the mobile lounge that would shuttle the passengers to the 747 on the runway. For a moment I stood at the window wondering if I might never see him again.

Driving back to the District through the countryside, past the modern edifices of technical consulting firms, commonly referred to as Beltway bandits, I felt surprisingly peaceful. For some hours Viktor might be thinking of me; the energy of our relationship would linger with him partway over the Atlantic and maybe into the volatile air of Eastern Europe. He was gone, but I felt strong and proud that I'd managed to end upright and heading forward.

Closer to home, I pondered the postcard I'd received from Dee, a photo of Louis Armstrong. "Hi," it read. "Bet you're glad she's home. Now we're even. Tell her I'm okay. Dee."

It was just dark when I made the abrupt descent from the rolling Virginia hills onto the bridge over the Potomac and into the semi-peace of the District of Columbia. It was relaxing to leave the highways and pass onto familiar city streets. The lights of Georgetown shone invitingly as people strolled Wisconsin Avenue. On this mild winter evening, there was a festive mood of approaching spring. Soon boats would be tying up at the new waterfront development, and restaurants would be setting tables outside. Already people were speculating about when the cherry blossoms would bloom—a sign of the advent of spring and the tourist season, when buses would line the streets and visitors would wend their way up and down the Mall and gape at the marble monuments. Before long the old carousel in front of the Smithsonian Castle would crank up its charming calliope, and in the neighborhoods young girls would begin playing double jump-rope on the sidewalks—one of the true glories of spring.

When I reached my house, Hadley Owens, onetime incipient skinhead, who still probably owed me seventeen dollars, was lounging about the living room. I'd not seen him since that hot summer day on the bus when he'd told me he was awaiting his trial for possession. He had let his hair grow out and seemed past his skinhead stage, though he was still extremely white. He was accompanied by a tall, thin black guy—the keyboard player, I later learned—with dreadlocks, braces, and red suspenders.

"I just ran into them," Shelly explained to me in the kitchen, where she was assembling snacks.

I didn't bother to inquire immediately about Hadley's life of crime. He said that he and the guy with dreadlocks were starting a band, the Rainbow Raunch Hands, and Shelly had told them they could practice in our basement. I groaned to myself quietly.

From the kitchen I heard Shelly laugh as they bounded down the stairs, hauling instruments and speakers. After the lonely weeks, her laugh was like a symphony to my ears. A few minutes later I heard a horrible squeal of feedback from the Rainbow Raunch Hands' sound system. But, I thought to myself as I poured a glass of Beaujolais, courtesy of my departed neighbor, it is music that helps support the sky, that may even be the answer to it all.